Noelle had almost reached the door when Zack caught her by the waist and turned her to face him. "I've gotta give you a kiss, angel. I won't be able to sleep if I don't."

"For heaven's sake—" She tried to wriggle free, but his hands were too strong, and she might have panicked, but the kiss—so gentle and unassuming and brief—was over before she could truly react. It had been less than a brush of his lips across hers, but there had been so much love in it—or what passed for love in his absurdly sweet world—that she almost wished she'd had the presence of mind to savor it before it was finished.

"You're absolutely incorrigible," she lamented weakly. "Don't *ever* do that again."

"Do you know what I think, angel?"

"I don't care!" She bustled to the door and opened it wide, then turned and demanded with a huff, "Fine. Tell me what you think. But be quick about it."

Zack chuckled softly. "I think you're starting to fall in love with me. You sure took your sweet time about it. . . ."

Dear Romance Reader,

Last year, we launched the Ballad line with four new series, and each month we'll present both new and continuing stories set everywhere from medieval England to the American West—the kind of passionate, romantic stories you love best, written by the most gifted authors. At the back of each book, we'll tell you when you can find subsequent books in the series that have captured your heart.

This month a group of very talented authors introduces a breathtaking new series called *Hope Chest,* beginning with Pam McCutcheon's **Enchantment.** As five people unearth an abandoned hotel's century-old hope chest, each will be transported back to a bygone age—and transformed by the timeless power of true love. Kathryn Fox presents the next installment of *The Mounties.* In **The Second Vow,** a transplanted Irishman who must escort the Sioux across the U.S. border meets a woman whose loyalty to her people is as fierce as the desire that flames between them.

In the third book of the charming *Happily Ever After Co.* series, Kate Donovan offers **Meant To Be.** The free-spirited daughter of a successful matchmaker is determined to avoid matrimony—unless a rugged sharpshooter can persuade her that their union is no accident of fate . . . but a romance for all time. Finally, rising star Tammy Hilz concludes the passionate *Jewels of the Sea* trilogy with **Once an Angel,** as a woman sailing toward an uncertain future—and an arranged marriage—is taken captive by a man who will risk anything to save her from a life without the love only he can offer.

Kate Duffy
Editorial Director

Happily Ever After Company

MEANT TO BE

Kate Donovan

ZEBRA BOOKS
Kensington Publishing Corp.

http://www.zebrabooks.com

ZEBRA BOOKS are published by

Kensington Publishing Corp.
850 Third Avenue
New York, NY 10022

All Kensington titles, imprints and distributed lines are available at special quantity discounts for bulk purchases for sales promotion, premiums, fund-raising, educational or institutional use.

Special book excerpts or customized printings can also be created to fit specific needs. For details, write or phone the office of the Kensington Special Sales Manager: Kensington Publishing Corp., 850 Third Avenue, New York, NY 10022. Attn. Special Sales Department. Phone: 1-800-221-2647.

First Printing: June 2001
10 9 8 7 6 5 4 3 2 1

Printed in the United States of America

Prologue

To Lieutenant Zachary Dane:
I have received your letter requesting that I find you a bride who, in your words, is "young, sturdy, cheerful, and healthy, a good cook, and suited to a simple, hardworking life and raising sons and daughters. . . ." Ordinarily, I would make this match by mail, based upon your letter. But our mutual friend, Colonel Greer, has asked me to give special attention to your situation and, given your laudable record as a war hero, it is my pleasure to accommodate his request. Therefore, I ask that you come to my home in Chicago, as my honored guest, so that we can further determine your needs and find for you the perfect mate.

Sincerely,
Russell Braddock, Proprietor,
The Happily Ever After Company

"I'm telling you, Merc, this just beats all," Zack Dane complained to his trail-weary companion, Mercury, as they studied a stately redbrick mansion in full view of Lake Michigan. "There we were, having ourselves a fine time in New Orleans, ordering me a bride through the mail, and the next thing we know, we're within spitting distance of Canada, with a cold wind howling down our backs. And for what? What's the point in using a matchmaker if we have to do all the work ourselves?"

The horse whinnied in emphatic agreement, to which Zack replied sheepishly, "This Braddock fella's right about one thing, though. I may not have covered all my 'needs' in that letter I sent him last month. I shouldn't've asked for a sturdy female—who knows what a city fella like him thinks *that* means? I should've chose my words more careful-like. And you know how I feel about girls with long legs. I should've mentioned that straight out, too. After all, I'm gonna spend the rest of my days with this filly. Aside from choosing a good horse, a good rifle, and a good friend to watch your back in a fight, I reckon choosing a wife is the most important decision a man can make."

Brushing three days' worth of dust from his buckskin pants, he looped Mercury's reins around an iron fence railing and strode onto the porch of the Braddock residence. Maybe a man-to-man talk with this fellow wasn't such a bad idea, after all. There were probably hundreds of females in the country who would suit Zack just fine as a wife, but why not try to get himself the best of the available bunch?

Zack's commanding officer, Colonel Greer, had claimed that his friend Russell Braddock had a gift for making these sorts of matches, and the grandeur of the matchmaker's three-story edifice seemed to confirm that claim. Zack wondered if the girls were waiting inside at that very moment, breathless and eager and ready for a healthy young fellow like him to carry one of them away. It was an inspiring notion, and he refused to acknowledge one last tremor of misgiving at the thought of giving up his bachelorhood. Sure, he'd had some fun, especially lately, but this was as good a time as ever to settle down. He planned on seeking his fortune in California or Nevada, didn't he? There wouldn't be many unattached young girls out there, he imagined, so it seemed best to just bring his own.

And so, with a final sheepish grin toward Mercury, he rang the front bell of the Braddock residence, then shifted from one moccasined foot to another, wondering if one of the prospective brides might not just answer the door. That would be convenient, he decided impatiently. Unless she had two heads, he might just settle for that one on the spot, just to get the danged business over with once and for all.

But when the door swung open, it wasn't a pretty girl, but rather, a pinch-faced, portly gentleman in a dark coat and trousers who greeted Zack with a dry, inhospitable, "Can I direct you somewhere, sir?"

Zack had seen the servant's gaze shift from the dusty buckskins to the dustier horse in the distance, and didn't blame the fellow for assuming that Zack didn't belong on the premises. With a cheerful smile, he extended his hand for a reassuring shake. "Mr. Braddock's expecting me. I would've cleaned myself up some, but I was anxious to get this matchmaking business out of the way as fast as I could. Is he at home?"

The butler ignored the outstretched hand. "Whom shall I say is calling?"

"Well, unless you're the lying sort, you oughta say it's Lieutenant Zack Dane."

"Lieutenant?" Again, the servant's haughty eyes took in his backwoods attire with disdain. Still, he moved aside and gestured for Zack to step into a large marble entrance hall. "Please be so kind as to wait here, sir. I'll see if Mr. Braddock is available."

And what if he's not? Zack growled silently. *Am I supposed to make some sort of blasted appointment? Is that what they mean by "honored guest" around these parts? Can't a fella at least get a drink of water or a friendly handshake?*

Annoyed, he decided to follow the butler, to hear firsthand whether Russell Braddock was going to actually send him away after all these days of hard riding— at *his* invitation. Venturing down the hallway, he found himself alone, with a set of closed double doors on each side of him and the servant nowhere in sight. He hesitated just for a moment, before choosing the doors on his right. Pushing them wide open, he stared in open-mouthed amazement at the vision that confronted him in the Braddock dining room.

It was a bride. Or perhaps it was an angel. Either way, she was the most breathtakingly beautiful sight Zack had ever seen, from her blue-black curls to her tiny waist to the tips of her white satin shoes. Enveloped in a fog of silvery white lace skirts and a shimmering satin bodice, she seemed almost to be floating before his eyes, although in fact she was simply standing on a majestic carved oak table, while a seamstress carefully pinned the hem of her dazzling gown. Although the women had undoubtedly heard the doors open, they were too engrossed in the alterations to have yet cast a glance in Zack's direction.

He wanted to speak, but his throat was too dry. Still, he guessed that at any moment the angel would hear the thundering of his heart in his chest, and when she did, she would know what he wanted—needed!—to say to her at that moment. He only prayed she would feel the same way, so that he could pull her down from that table and into his arms for a lusty yet respectful embrace before they jumped onto Mercury's back and rode off, anxious to begin a love affair that would blaze for the rest of their lives together.

One

"The hem will drag on the ground, Winnie." Noelle Braddock flounced the layers of lace that made up the skirt of her wedding gown as she scolded her favorite dressmaker.

"It will not, miss. I've been doing this since before you were born—"

"But it has to be perfect." Whirling toward the doors that had just opened, she insisted, "Father, please tell Winifred—Oh! Goodness sakes!" She stared in dismay at the lanky, buckskin-clad stranger who had dared invade her private fitting. "Winnie, there's . . . Well, there's a hunter here."

When the young man just stared, as though mesmerized, Noelle felt her cheeks begin to burn. "May we help you, sir? If you're looking for my father—"

"I'm looking for you," he corrected reverently. "I didn't know it till just now, but I think I've been looking for you my whole life. Dang . . ."

Winifred bustled toward the newcomer, her expression stern. "You can't come in here. I don't know what business you have with Mr. Braddock, but—"

"He said he'd find me a perfect bride, and danged if he hasn't done it."

"I should have known." Noelle sighed loudly. "He's

one of Father's customers." To the prospective groom, she added briskly, "I'm not one of the brides, sir. I'm Mr. Braddock's daughter. I mean . . ." She flushed again. "Obviously I'm a bride, but—"

"She's spoken for," Winifred intervened sharply. "If you'll just step into the hall, I'm sure Edward will assist you in locating Mr. Braddock." When the newcomer didn't budge, she warned, "If you don't leave immediately, Miss Noelle will scream, and a swarm of servants will descend upon you and throw you into the street."

Noelle laughed lightly. "Let's hope it needn't come to that. I'm sure Mr. . . ."

"Dane. Zack Dane." The handsome intruder extended his hand up toward Noelle, not as a potential handshake, but as though he intended to assist her from her perch.

The gesture charmed her. "If I'm to come down there, Mr. Dane, I'll need the stepstool. Could you fetch it? It's behind the door."

"You don't need that. You have me."

Wary of his persistence, she took a step backward and called out, "Father! Edward! We have a guest." Unfortunately, her heel became entangled in the hem of her gown at that moment, and she began to topple, only to be rescued by her alert admirer, who caught her with strong, rough hands, setting her gently onto the floor.

"Really, Miss Noelle!" Winifred complained. "Those seams are only tacked. If you aren't more careful, you'll come right out of your gown."

When Zack's green eyes widened with appreciative anticipation, Noelle grumbled, "Thank you so much for that humiliating image. I believe Mr. Dane enjoyed it immensely."

"What's all the commotion?" boomed a voice from the hall, and Russell Braddock stepped into view.

Edward, the butler, was at his side, and now drawled, "It's the very ruffian I was telling you about, sir. I instructed him to wait in the entrance hall."

Noelle turned to face her father. "This is Mr. Zack Dane, and he isn't at all a ruffian. He's simply misinformed. He actually mistook *me* for one of the mail-order brides."

"I can't imagine why," Braddock said with a smile.

Noelle smiled in return. "I'm at a disadvantage in this gown in more ways than one. If you could show Mr. Dane to your study, it would give me a chance to change into something less confusing."

"Or we can just get a preacher in here and take care of business right away," Zack interrupted cheerfully.

"A preacher?" Noelle dissolved into appreciative laughter. "Do you mean a minister? To marry *us?* Really, Father, you'd best find this man a bride without delay! He's uncommonly eager."

Braddock grinned and tapped Zack on the shoulder. "Lieutenant Dane?"

"Yes, sir?"

"As you've undoubtedly realized, I'm Russell Braddock." He pumped his guest's hand enthusiastically. "It's an honor to meet you, Lieutenant. If half of what I've heard about you is true, we all owe you a debt of gratitude for your many acts of heroism."

"Lieutenant?" Noelle studied Zack's rustic fringed outfit, trying to imagine the handsome intruder in a proper uniform. If he were to bathe and stand at attention, she imagined he'd be quite an imposing sight, with his tanned complexion and wavy brown hair. And such twinkling green eyes! His bride would be captivated by those, she suspected.

"You gentlemen—*all* of you—need to give Miss Noelle

some privacy now," Winifred scolded them firmly. "We have hours of work left to do on this gown, and less than a week to do it in."

"A whole week?" Zack winced, then took Noelle's hand in his own. "I don't aim to wait that long, angel. We've got—"

"You've 'got' nothing," Edward interrupted bluntly. "Mr. Braddock? Shall I show *Lieutenant* Dane to your study?"

Braddock chuckled. "Come along now, Zack. Let my daughter have her fitting in peace, while you and I get acquainted."

"With all due respect, sir, it's your daughter I'd like to acquaint myself with."

Braddock chuckled again and took him firmly by the elbow. "You and I need to talk, son. Noelle?"

"Yes, Father?"

"You really do look exquisite. We can hardly blame our guest for noticing."

"Thank you, kind sir." She curtsied mischievously. "Since this gown is costing you a fortune, I'm relieved that you approve." Turning her attention to Zack, she added, "Don't worry, Lieutenant. My father has a talent for finding the right bride for each and every customer."

"You and me are proof of that," he agreed, taking her hand again and kissing it respectfully. "There's something I need to talk to him about, angel. But I won't be long. Don't run off, now." Before Noelle could protest, the cocky visitor had turned and followed Russell Braddock out into the hall.

As soon as the door had closed, Winifred insisted, "Climb right back up there, Miss Noelle. I want to see how much damage this little adventure has done to all my hard work."

"You expect me to stand still after all this excitement? Impossible. Help me out of this gown, and we'll have some lemonade and a nice visit instead."

"The wedding is only a week away."

"Not if Lieutenant Dane has anything to say about it," the young bride teased.

"Miss Noelle!"

"Don't scold. You can't blame me for being flattered. Do you suppose that's how it works where he comes from? A man sees a girl, grabs her off a table, and marries her without giving it another thought?"

Winifred bristled visibly. "He's in Chicago now, isn't he? So he'd better learn some manners. Any other father would have grabbed a shotgun and blown his head off."

"And lose a customer?" Noelle grinned. "Father will enjoy the challenge of finding just the right bride for an uncouth backwoods soldier."

"It shouldn't be very difficult," the dressmaker said with a shrug. "He's handsome, don't you think?"

"And strong," Noelle agreed, remembering the feel of his hands during her tumble from the table. "There must be dozens of brides in Father's files who would love a strong, handsome husband like the lieutenant."

"I'm sure Mr. Prestley is strong, too, Noelle."

"Hmm? Oh!" She laughed with delight. "You needn't worry, Winnie. Adam Prestley is every bit as manly as our dusty guest. And unlike Lieutenant Dane, Adam knows how to treat a woman."

"And he's rich," Winifred began; then her hand flew to her mouth. "I shouldn't have said that. Forgive me."

"It's fine. He *is* rich."

"But I didn't mean to imply—" She grimaced in sincere apology. "Your father is wealthy in his own right—"

"I'm not marrying Adam for his money," Noelle confirmed coolly.

"Of course you aren't! He's such a fine gentleman."

"That fine gentleman will be here in two hours. So let's have that lemonade, shall we? And then I'll have to run upstairs and start dressing for dinner."

"You should wear the navy blue outfit I made for you last month. It looks so lovely with that dark hair of yours."

"That's a wonderful suggestion." Noelle shivered with anticipation at the thought that Adam might soon be staring at her with the same delicious combination of desire and respect Lieutenant Dane had so recently exhibited. Of course, Dane's reaction had been prompted by a wedding gown. She could scarcely wait until Adam saw her that way—in yards of lacy white splendor. She was confident his pale blue eyes would sparkle every bit as wildly as Lieutenant Dane's emerald eyes had done.

Once Winifred had packed up the wedding gown and taken it back to her shop, Noelle tiptoed up to the door of her father's study, anxious to determine whether Lieutenant Dane was still in the house. To her relief, she found her father alone, pouring over the latest letters from anxious grooms and hopeful brides.

"Has the lieutenant gone to a hotel, Father?"

Braddock looked up and smiled fondly. "He's in the third-floor guest suite, actually. I invited him to stay with us for a few days, while I try to find a wife for him who isn't already spoken for."

"He's staying here?" Noelle stared in confusion.

"Why on earth did you arrange that? We hardly know him! What will Adam think?"

"Since when does Adam Prestley tell me whom I can have as a guest in my own home?" Braddock grumbled. "It's bad enough he's stealing my daughter."

"Listen to you," Noelle teased. "No one is good enough for your little girl, is that it?"

Her father grimaced.

"You approve of Adam though, don't you?"

"If he makes you happy," Braddock said with a sigh. "I just don't see the need to rush—"

"To rush? We've been engaged for four months, Father. I should ask Lieutenant Dane to explain it to you. Four months is an eternity by *his* standards."

"That's true." Her father grinned reluctantly. "He would have married you right there in the dining room, if you'd been willing."

"Wasn't it hilarious?"

"Hilarious, yes. But touching, too, in a way. He was so taken with you."

"It was the gown," she explained. "In fact, do you know what we should do? We should ask Winnie to make one just like mine, for Lieutenant Dane's bride to wear. Wouldn't that be romantic?"

"I think it was more than the gown, sweetheart. He says you're the prettiest girl he's ever laid eyes on. He asked me for your hand in marriage. Can you imagine?"

"It's sweet." She settled onto a gray velvet sofa and leafed through a stack of letters on an adjacent table. "Do you have any idea whom you'll match him with? There should be plenty of girls who'd be delighted with such a tall, handsome war hero, even if he is a bit unrefined and impulsive."

Braddock left his desk and crossed the room to join

her on the sofa. "You don't really mind my asking him to stay with us, do you? It will help me get to know him—to know what he needs in a bride."

"It's fine. I wouldn't have objected at all, if it weren't so close to the wedding. And I'm sure Adam will understand." She noted how her father winced again, and bit her lip in confusion. It was no secret that the relationship between Russell Braddock and Adam Prestley was a formal, vaguely uncomfortable one. Still, she thought they'd been making some progress these last few weeks, and it concerned her to sense that perhaps, if her father had his way, the wedding wouldn't just be postponed, it would be canceled.

It's just as you said, she soothed herself quickly. *No man would have been good enough for you in Father's eyes. He sees Adam as too wealthy and sophisticated and old. If you'd chosen someone young and poor and modest, he wouldn't have liked that either. If it were up to him, you wouldn't marry for years yet, and even then, the prospective bridegroom would be found wanting in his eyes.*

"I'm sure you noticed that Adam's been dining here almost every night lately, Father. I've been insisting on it, because I wanted you two to get to know each other better. But if you'd like to have me to yourself this last week, I'm sure he'd understand."

"I'd like that," Russell Braddock admitted. "I still haven't quite gotten used to the idea that you'll be leaving this house soon. It will seem so big and empty without you."

"You make it sound as though I'm moving to some faraway land." Noelle sighed and patted his arm. "You know very well that the Prestley house is less than three miles from here. I'll visit so often, you'll scarcely know I've left."

"Is that a promise?"

"Of course!" Throwing her arms around his neck, she squeezed anxiously. "How can you doubt it? Don't you know I'll miss you just as desperately as you'll miss me? And this house . . ." She felt a sting of tears in her eyes and sighed again. "I'm leaving the girls here, did you know that? That should prove to you that I'll still consider this my home—my second home, but home just the same."

"You're not taking your dolls?"

She felt her cheeks flush under his curious stare. "It's not as though Adam would object, but he's never seen them all at once, and I don't want him to think . . . Well, it just doesn't seem like a married woman should have so many of them. Hopefully, I'll have a daughter soon, and then I can bring them to the nursery." She smiled in frustrated amusement at the expression on her father's face. "Don't you want grandchildren?"

"Of course. Once again, though, I don't see the need to rush into it—"

"And once again, I should ask Lieutenant Dane to explain it to you," she said with a laugh. "It's one of the reasons men get married, isn't it? Because they're ready to settle down and raise a family. And I'm sure Adam's doubly anxious because . . . well, because . . ."

"Because he's thirty-eight years old? Fully twice your age?"

"For heaven's sake, Father! If you disapprove of him so completely, why on earth did you agree to the marriage?"

"There, there," he soothed quickly. "If he makes you

happy, that's all that matters. And you tell me he does, so of course I agreed when he asked me for your hand. Nothing has changed since that evening."

"Adam says that after thirty-eight years of looking for an acceptable bride, I'm the first girl who ever met his standards. Doesn't that mean anything to you? He's been all around the world and has met the finest females from the finest families. And yet he chose *me*. It's romantic, don't you agree?"

"What exactly *are* his standards?"

"Well, I don't really know. He's never put them into words." She smiled mischievously. "You should ask him tonight at dinner. Wouldn't it be fun to ask the lieutenant also? I can imagine they must want very different things in a wife."

"And yet they've both chosen you."

Noelle laughed lightly. "I told you, it was the dress. But Adam has seen women in much finer attire, and still he chose me. I'm surprised that doesn't impress you. It impresses me," she added, more to herself than to her father.

"You're impressed that he considered so many potential brides before choosing you? Yet *you* have chosen to marry the very first man to court you. Don't you ever wonder—" He patted her cheek in apology. "If he makes you happy—"

"That's all that matters." She finished the well-worn sentiment warily. Why hadn't she noticed until now that it was the only nice thing her father could seem to say about Adam? No mention of his charitable pursuits, or his business acumen, or his expansive knowledge, gleaned from years of traveling to the most beautiful cities in the world. And worse, no acknowledgment of Adam's devotion to Noelle!

If Adam were there, she knew exactly what he'd say. What he *always* said to reassure her when she lamented over her father's attitude. He'd remind her that her father had been a matchmaker since before she was born, that he had possibly planned from that very day to use his talent and connections to find her the perfect husband, that she had unwittingly stolen that honor from him by choosing her own husband, without seeking his aid or advice. However, out of love for her, her father had grudgingly abandoned his dream of playing matchmaker for her, knowing in his heart that Adam was a finer, more respectable, wealthier husband than the Happily Ever After Company could ever have found for her.

And Noelle would always respond by admitting that, despite her pride in her father's talent, she had always resisted the idea that he might one day try to usurp her right to choose her own husband. Sometimes, when she'd seen him make a particularly romantic match, she had weakened, but then her natural stubbornness would resurface and she would double her resolve *not* to allow him to play any part in her love life. Still, she had secretly feared he'd find her someone so irresistible that she simply wouldn't be able to refuse, so it had been a relief to find Adam by herself.

It had been so serendipitous—the very first time her father had allowed her to attend a soiree with someone other than himself as her chaperon, Noelle had found the man of her dreams! Adam Prestley—sophisticated, wealthy, confident, and handsome, in a worldly, experienced way that she had found amazingly reassuring. Every unattached female in Chicago—and some attached ones as well!—seemed eager to catch his eye, but he had appeared singularly bored until, by chance, Noelle had stepped onto a veranda for a breath of fresh air. Adam had been there, hiding and smoking a cigar. She had blushed and stammered and apologized, and he had gallantly rescued her by assuring her she was the only girl in Chicago with whom he would like to share a moonlit encounter.

They had danced after that, and the room had buzzed with amazement that so worldly a gentleman had been captivated by so provincial a girl. And a matchmaker's daughter, no less! Given the Prestley family's lofty position in a stratum of society that included royal daughters and heiresses, the fact that Russell Braddock had an unorthodox, albeit solid, enterprise would have seemed to be a disadvantage for his daughter.

"Nonsense," Adam had assured her. "I admire your father's flair for all things dramatic. He capitalized on our Westward expansion brilliantly, and of course, reaped amazing benefits from the gold and silver strikes, all by maintaining a ready supply of the one natural resource the Sierra Nevada Mountains lack. I'm only glad," he had added playfully, "that he kept the jewel in his collection safely here in Chicago for me."

Impressed by the memory, Noelle eyed her father sternly and challenged, "Say something nice about Adam."

"Pardon?"

"Pay him a compliment, please. Something other than the fact that he makes me happy."

"He dresses well."

"Father!"

The twinkle in Braddock's eyes disappeared. "I can sincerely say that, because of his wealth, my only child will never want for material blessings. Adam Prestley will be a consummate provider."

"That's true. And it's important to you, isn't it? You

need never fear that I'm starving, or dressed in rags, or catching my death of cold. Quite the opposite, in fact. I will live in luxury with my devoted husband. Isn't that a father's dream for his only daughter?"

"My dream is for you to be happy. When I say Prestley seems to accomplish that, I don't mean to diminish him. I am honestly hopeful that it's true, and that it will continue to be true throughout your marriage. If so, I will be more grateful to him than you can imagine."

"Well, then . . ." She studied his expression for a moment, then smiled with relief. "You'll see, Father. I'll be deliriously happy, all because of Adam. I only hope I'll make him happy in return. And I suppose the first step is to change out of this dressing gown and into something appropriate for dinner. He'll be here in less than an hour."

"Run along, then." Braddock reached for her and planted a brisk kiss on her cheek. "Take all the time you need. I promise I'll be hospitable if he arrives before you're ready."

She smiled wistfully. "He's very fond of you, did you know that? I think he might be afraid to show it, for fear it wouldn't be welcome yet. But he tells me constantly how much he admires you and the way you built so successful a business. No matter how often I tell him it's all because of your matchmaking talent, he says you must have a shrewd appreciation for opportunity and risk to have come so far, all on your own."

"Yes, I can imagine he'd see it that way."

"Well, he's a banker, and the son of a banker. I suppose they see everything that way," she agreed. "Shall we just say, you exceed his standards for a father-in-law, just as I've been fortunate enough to meet his standards for a bride?" Returning the peck on the cheek, she headed for the doorway, then turned to ask, "Will Lieutenant Dane be dressing for dinner? Perhaps you should offer him something of yours to wear. We wouldn't want him to be embarrassed."

"I don't think Zack would be embarrassed by something so superficial."

"Well, then . . ." She had heard the gentle reprimand in his tone, reminding her that in the Braddock household, one didn't judge others on such terms. And, of course, she knew that. She had only been concerned for the lieutenant, or at least, *mostly* concerned for him. And was it so wrong to want everything to be perfect tonight for the man she loved? Annoyed, although primarily with herself, she muttered, "Perhaps I needn't change, either."

"I would agree, if that dressing gown were a bit less becoming. As it stands, you wouldn't want to entice our susceptible guest any more than you already have, would you?"

His eyes were laughing at her, and she decided to enjoy it. At least it was preferable to the somber expression he'd been wearing during the discussion of Adam. "It's your job to distract him from me, Father, by describing some of the pretty young brides that are just waiting for him in your files. And I'll do my part by wearing something that doesn't in the least resemble a wedding gown." With a fond wave, she turned and scooted out of the study and down the hall toward the narrow back staircase that led directly to the hall outside her bedroom.

She was halfway up the stairs when she collided with their lanky guest, who again steadied her with strong hands, his green eyes sparkling with mischief. "I was hoping we'd get some private time together, Miss Noelle. Seems like this is my lucky day."

"Lieutenant . . ." She flushed under his gaze and backed against the wall, trying not to notice how freshly scrubbed and attractive he was. He had changed into simple brown trousers, a tan shirt, and a loose-fitting vest made of simple gray linen. Yet somehow, he still smelled of buckskin, and the effect was dangerously masculine and unfamiliar. Managing a weak smile, she said, "I was delighted to hear you were going to spend some time with us while Father finds you a bride."

"Shouldn't be too hard," he noted, again with mischief in his eyes.

Noelle ignored the inference. "Have you been in Chicago before?"

"No."

"Is this your first time in a city?"

Zack chuckled. "Did I make that poor an impression?"

"Of course not."

"Good." He took her hand and kissed her fingertips. "Why don't we start over?"

"Lieutenant, please." She pulled her hand away and glared. "Didn't my father tell you about my engagement?"

Zack nodded. "The dress was a hint, too."

"Oh, of course. How silly of me."

He stepped closer, so that she could almost feel his breath on her flushed cheeks. "There's no shame in changing your mind, angel. You couldn't have known—"

"Stop that this instant. For heaven's sake." She tried to take a deep breath as she squirmed along the wall, anxious to gain some distance from the persistent suitor.

"I understand they do things differently where you come from, Lieutenant, but—"

"Don't people fall in love at first sight in Chicago?"

"Gentlemen don't accost young women in narrow passageways in Chicago. Nor do they court engaged women. Please excuse me—"

"Noelle . . ." He backed her flush against the wall. "Just spend five minutes with me and you'll understand—"

"What are you doing?" she gasped. Her heart was pounding so frantically, she thought it might come right through the thin cotton fabric of her dressing gown. "Unhand me this instant! Do you suppose I won't scream?"

"You're the most beautiful girl I've ever laid eyes on," he told her, in a voice so soft and humble it almost relaxed her despite the circumstances. "Don't run away from me, angel. There are things that need saying between us."

She might have agreed to listen, if only to forestall a confrontation, had he not lowered his lips to her neck, as though intending to nuzzle her while pleading his case. Aghast, she wailed, "Edward! Father! *Any*one!"

Zack laughed fondly. "There's no need for that, angel. You're safe with me."

"Would you stop calling me angel? I'm Miss Braddock to you, and even at that, you do not have my permission to address me, ever again. Is that clear?"

"It's clear to me you're confused. On account of that Prestley fella, right?"

"That Prestley fellow? Are you insane? You make him sound like some inconsequential obstacle. He's my *fiancé,* Lieutenant. I'm *marrying* him one week from tomorrow, and—Don't you *dare* shake your head!"

She was no longer cowering against the wall. Instead, she was wagging her finger in his face. "I'm marrying him and that's final. And you'll marry one of Father's brides, assuming she'll have you."

"That's all changed now," he countered stubbornly. "If you'd just listen—"

"Listen to what? To the sound of you breathing on my neck? Do you know what my father would do if he saw you accosting me this way? And 'that Prestley fellow' would tear you limb from limb! Just be thankful neither of them is here to witness this, and *go away.*"

"Miss Noelle?" a guarded voice interrupted from the foot of the staircase. "Did you call out for me?"

"Edward!" She smiled in grateful relief. "Lieutenant Dane lost his way and ended up blocking my path. Could you show him to the study, and let Father know the circumstances of this encounter? In detail?"

"Certainly, miss."

"I'll go with this fella, 'cause you want me to," Zack informed her cheerfully, backing down the stairs without taking his eyes off her. "But it doesn't change how it is between us, so don't go getting any ideas about that. Let's go, Edward." He slapped the butler on the back. "But don't take me to the study. I'd rather pay a visit to the kitchen. I can't remember when I've been so hungry. Angel?" he added innocently. "Do you want me to bring you something sweet?"

She was speechless, despite the driving need to tell him, in no uncertain terms, that she wanted *nothing* from him. Not *ever.* To tell him to stop calling her "angel," and treating her with such ludicrous familiarity. As though he already saw himself as a member of the family! But all she could manage was a shallow, disapproving growl of exasperation before spinning away from him and bolting up the stairs.

"She's like an angel, believe it or not. As sweet and beautiful as a girl can be. I took one look at her—that pretty pink mouth and those silvery eyes, and the way she curves in all the best places, and I was done for. Now, all I gotta do is get her to listen to me with an open heart and all. She wants to. I can tell that, for sure. But she's resisting it with all her might."

When his companion snorted in disgust, Zack chuckled knowingly. "You're saying she has a temper? I reckon that's so. But you've gotta see this from her position, Merc. She was all set to marry this Prestley fella. She didn't even know I was alive. And she couldn't've known how it was gonna be between us, so it figures she'd be a mite confused. She's a fighter, that little angel. I think I like that.

"Her pappy's a decent fella," he added thoughtfully. "Solid as they come. He's got objections to her marrying Prestley. I can see that, even if he didn't come straight out and say it yet. I figure he'll throw some support my way, even if it's just by letting me stay, when me being there makes everyone uncomfortable. I like making *her* uncomfortable," he admitted with a sheepish laugh. "Brings out the she-cat in her."

When Mercury snorted again, Zack laughed aloud. "I guess you just gotta take my word for it, pardner. She's proof that a girl can be half angel, half she-cat. When you see her, you'll understand. I never could've believed it myself, if I hadn't seen her with my own two eyes."

He remembered how that had been—that moment when he'd first laid eyes on Noelle Braddock, in her shimmering bridal gown. The sight had almost blinded him, the way any angel-sighting would do to a mortal man. Then he'd managed to focus, and had seen the amazing details. The luxurious blue-black curls, the silvery eyes that could laugh and scold and inspire at will, the playful pink mouth that seemed to be waiting for Zack to cover it with his own. The mere thought of her made him ache with the need to have her. But not just once, like might be enough where any other girl was concerned. This one was a bride—Zack's bride. To have and to hold forever, and then some. And he had a feeling she was beginning to see that too.

"You *have* to send him to a hotel, Father! I can't abide the sight of him. And I won't be able to sleep one wink tonight, knowing he's under the same roof. He's rude, and crude, and intent on ruining what should be the happiest week of my life! Please, please, *please* send him away."

"I'll admit, he's a little rough around the edges, but—"

"The edges? He's rough through and through! If his behavior is any indication, he's never known a decent woman in his entire life."

"That's a little harsh, don't you think?"

"He accosted me—Oh . . . Hello, Edward." She gave the butler a weary nod. "Did you need something?"

"Pardon the interruption, Miss Noelle, but your fiancé has arrived.

"Oh, dear. Now what shall we do? We don't dare ask Adam to dine with the lieutenant. Who knows what he'll say or do?" She crossed to the servant and pleaded,

"You must make certain Lieutenant Dane doesn't come near Mr. Prestley until I've had time to think."

Edward flushed. "I'll do my best, Miss Noelle, but I don't really know where the lieutenant is."

"Oh, dear." Bustling past Edward, she raced down the hall, bursting into the drawing room just in time to see Adam checking his pocket watch, as he always did when he was annoyed. Still, even with his face twisted into a frown, he was an imposing sight in his exquisite black silk dinner jacket and perfectly tailored trousers.

As always, Noelle felt reassured by the touch of gray in the blond hair of his sideburns and mustache, symbolizing the blend of trustworthiness and stability that had drawn her to him since the very first time they'd met.

"Darling!" She moved to stand before him, hoping he could read the abject apology in her eyes. "Forgive me for neglecting you. Have you been here long?"

"I was beginning to think the house was deserted. But instead"—Adam arched an eyebrow, not toward Noelle but at something behind her—"I see you have another guest as well as myself."

Before she turned toward the doorway, she knew that her nemesis had just walked into the room. Stretching up onto her tiptoes, she whispered into her fiancé's ear, "I apologize in advance for anything he may say. Or do. Or imply."

Turning finally, for the purpose of sending a scathing glance toward Zack, she was annoyed to see that, once again, he was staring at her as though he'd never seen a female before. Furious, she spun back toward Adam and took him by the arm. "Come into the garden with me, darling. I'll explain everything."

"Into the garden? Unchaperoned?" her fiancé teased. "What will your father say?"

"This is all Father's doing in the first place, so he'd best not dare complain," she retorted. "Excuse us, won't you, Lieutenant?"

"Aren't you going to introduce us first, darling?" Adam chuckled, then stepped past Noelle and extended his hand to Zack. "I'm Adam Prestley. Noelle's fiancé."

"Forgive my daughter's breach of etiquette," Russell Braddock interjected, stepping into the room before announcing, "Adam Prestley, this is Lieutenant Zachary Dane. A guest in my home."

Noelle grimaced as the two men shook hands. *A guest in my home*—another reprimand for Noelle. The fact that her father saw *her* as unforgivably rude, without objecting even slightly to *Zack's* atrocious behavior, was beginning to get on her nerves.

Almost immediately, Zack confirmed her worst fears for the evening by announcing, "There's something you should know, Prestley. No sense putting it off—"

"Zack!" Braddock chuckled nervously. "Now is not the time."

"The time for what?" Adam frowned. "Do you have some business with me, Lieutenant?"

Noelle stuck her finger to within inches of Zack's nose and warned, "Don't you *dare* say another word."

Zack grimaced apologetically. "He has a right to know my intentions, Noelle."

"Your intentions?" Adam sounded suddenly fascinated. "Intentions toward what? Or should I say, toward whom?"

"Father! Say something. Or better yet, make Lieutenant Dane be quiet." To Adam, Noelle added weakly,

"Father's guest isn't right in the head. It's as simple as that. Just ignore him, won't you?"

Zack grinned. "It's true, Prestley. I lost my mind the minute I laid eyes on—"

"Father!"

"Let's all just go into the dining room and discuss this calmly," Braddock suggested.

Adam's jaw visibly tightened. "Is there something to discuss?"

"No!" Noelle stomped her foot. "If you want to hit Lieutenant Dane, darling, I'll understand completely."

"I believe I might like to do just that."

"I'd like it, too," Zack admitted.

"There's not going to be any of that," Braddock interrupted. "Noelle, perhaps your first instinct was the correct one. Take Adam to the garden and explain the situation."

"As if I understand it myself?" she grumbled, but she dutifully took Adam by the hand and tugged him into the hall.

Two

Without offering further explanation, Noelle hurried her fiancé toward the lush atrium that served as a focal point for living in the Braddock mansion, with French doors providing access from the parlor as well as from her father's study. As the couple stepped across the threshold into the garden, the fragrance of pure white gardenias soothed her angry mood, and she managed a smile as she patted her distinguished suitor's cheek. "Are you angry with me, darling?"

"Not at all. I'm a little confused, but that always happens when I visit this house."

"Isn't it just ghastly? This barbarian arrives out of nowhere, and the next thing we know, he's claiming to be madly in love with me. All because he saw me trying on my wedding gown."

"I beg your pardon?"

"I was fully dressed," she assured him. "Just having a fitting." The thought of it made her smile in spite of herself. "It was rather charming, in an absurd sort of way. Lieutenant Dane came here with his heart set on marrying one of Father's brides, and there I was, dressed the part from head to toe. It was a logical mistake."

"Does this happen often?" Adam demanded. "I always assumed the business was conducted through the mail."

"It usually is. I've never actually met one of the grooms until after the match was made. The brides come here sometimes, but even that is rare. Lieutenant Dane showed up without warning."

"And your father invited him to dinner? A total stranger? Doesn't that strike you as odd, even for him?"

Noelle grimaced. "I believe they've been corresponding. One of Father's closest friends was the lieutenant's commanding officer. And so, apparently, Father offered to extend every courtesy to him, although I doubt if he expected him to show up on our doorstep without some warning. And the timing couldn't have been worse." With a hesitant smile, she added carefully, "He's not just here for dinner. He's staying in the guest suite until Father finds him a bride. It's absurd, but I'm afraid I have no choice but to endure it. I couldn't bear to quarrel with Father so close to the wedding."

Adam pursed his lips, as though studying the situation, before he said, "I don't like seeing you so upset. Is it too much to ask that this Dane character stay in a hotel? I'd be glad to pay all his expenses, if that would facilitate the arrangement."

"It isn't a question of expense, Adam. Father's simply intent on being a good host. I'm afraid we'll have to suffer his presence for a while. Do you mind awfully?"

"He doesn't bother me," Adam said with a shrug. "But surely your father can see that he makes *you* uncomfortable." He stopped himself and smiled in apology. "We won't let this interloper spoil our dinner, will we? We'll concentrate on each other. And given how lovely you look tonight, that shouldn't be a problem for me."

"You say such sweet things," she said, relieved by his optimistic attitude. "And I agree. With any luck, Father will keep the lieutenant in check, so that you and I can have a lovely visit. I was hoping you and Father could chat, but that will have to wait for another time."

"Actually, this situation may prove to have its advantages."

"Pardon?"

Adam's eyes twinkled. "This is the first time your father has let us out of his sight during one of my visits. With his houseguest to distract him, perhaps you and I will actually be able to spend some time alone tonight *after* dinner, too."

Noelle shook her head. "You know how Father is— either himself or a chaperon at all times. The irony being, he doesn't fret at all when Lieutenant Dane corners me and makes advances—"

"What?"

She flushed and touched his shoulder. "I exaggerated a bit, as usual. I only meant . . . Well, never mind."

"Noelle." He placed one fingertip below her chin, tipping her face up to his own. "If he's been bothering you—"

"It's fine. I'm annoyed, but not bothered. And you're right, darling. We shouldn't be wasting this time alone together." With a shy smile, she rested her hands on his shoulders and moistened her lips. "Would you like to kiss me?"

Adam grinned and lowered his lips to hers, kissing her gently and respectfully. He'd done so dozens of times before, when they'd managed to find a moment alone at a dance or in the park, but this was the first time he'd kissed her in her own home, and she longed to twine her arms around him and make it last forever.

It also made her wish they weren't moving to his mother's house after the wedding. The Braddock residence was such a romantic place, with its vibrant gardens, breathtaking views, and cozy rooms. And all her belongings were here, including her doll collection. And she'd miss her father so much, and the servants who treated her like a princess. It would be different at Adam's house, which was grander, but not nearly as warm and comfortable. And his mother was there, with her imperious stare and snide remarks.

"What are you thinking, darling?" Adam murmured into her hair.

"I was wishing this moment could last forever," she explained with a sigh.

"You're so innocent. So perfectly unspoiled and innocent. It still amazes me, do you know that?"

"What do you mean?"

"When you've seen as much as I've seen . . ." He shook his head and laughed ruefully. "This is hardly a time for philosophy, is it? Shall we just say, I'm delighted to have found you, and leave it at that?"

"I'm pleased you found me, too. Father was just remarking today that you're the first man who ever courted me. The only man who will ever court me. It's such a contrast, you with your endless searching, and me with my . . . well, my . . ."

"Inexperience? Believe me, darling, it's part of your charm. A rather important part, I might add. It's the reason I never complain about your father's overprotectiveness and constant chaperoning. In a very real sense, those odd habits of his have served me well, protecting your innocence for the day you would surrender it to me."

Noelle felt a twinge of annoyance at the remark. Was that how Adam saw it? A surrender? A victory?

Of course he doesn't! she scolded herself silently. *If anyone would see a wedding night that way, it would be a soldier like the lieutenant, not a gentleman like Adam.*

Forcing herself to relax, she enjoyed the feel of her fiancé's arms as they encircled her. Strong, just as the lieutenant's had been. Hadn't she told Winifred that? And the most important thing she'd told the dressmaker was the simple truth—she and Adam were marrying for love. Not money, or convenience, or obligation, or matchmaking. *Especially* not matchmaking.

Adam pulled away hastily at the sound of doors opening, and turned to bow respectfully in his host's direction. "My compliments again on this beautiful garden of yours, Russell. I've been considering some renovations to my own house, and I just might decide to incorporate something like this. To make our Noelle feel more at home."

"It has offered me untold hours of relaxation and enjoyment over the years," Braddock said quietly. "I highly recommend it." To Noelle, he added, "Alice is ready to serve dinner whenever you and your fiancé would like it."

"Right now, then. I'm famished." Noelle cocked her head to the side and asked hopefully, "Will it just be the three of us?"

"Lieutenant Dane is already in the dining room," he replied in a tone so even, she knew Adam could not possibly have heard the rebuke, although to her, it had been a resounding one.

"We'll be right along, then." She waited until her father had disappeared into the house, then instructed

Adam briskly, "We must be civil to the lieutenant. As you've seen, he'll make it difficult, but he's basically harmless. And I'm sure Father will do his best to restrain him, so it may not be as awkward as I'm anticipating, but—"

"Noelle?"

"Yes, darling?"

"I've dined with boors more often than you can imagine. The best way to proceed is to pretend to pay attention to them, without actually doing so. Follow my lead, and dinner should be quite painless."

Conversation was stilted as the meal commenced, but Noelle didn't object. She was simply glad that her father had apparently found a way to muzzle their houseguest. Or perhaps it was Adam's masterful handling of the situation. She had almost forgotten that this was one of her fiancé's strengths—his ability to thrive in any social situation with grace and aplomb. She herself had not yet mastered such intricacies, but hopefully, under his tutelage, she would become one of Chicago's most poised and successful hostesses. Or at least, she might learn to control her temper a bit more successfully than she'd done lately.

"This is the best meal I've had since my mamma died," Zack informed Alice, the Braddocks' cook and housekeeper, when she came to clear away the soup bowls. "If you don't stop spoiling me, I might just decide to move to Chicago for good."

"Didn't Russell say you have your heart set on California?" Adam interjected.

"That's true enough, Mr. Prestley. But a man's gotta

be willing to grab opportunities wherever he finds 'em. Don't you agree?"

"Wholeheartedly. Of course, a man should first learn to distinguish an opportunity from a hopeless quest. Don't *you* agree?" Before Zack could respond, he added magnanimously, "Call me Adam, by the way. Mr. Prestley sounds much too formal for this pleasant little dinner party."

"I appreciate the offer, sir, but I'd rather not."

"Oh?"

"Where I come from, a man respects his elders," Zack explained. "It would be as low as calling Mr. Braddock here Russell. I'd choke on that so quick after meeting him, me respecting him so much and all."

Seething inwardly, Noelle struggled to think of something to say to counter the obnoxious inference, but Adam responded smoothly and directly to the insult by asking, "Are you trying to suggest that I'm too old to marry Noelle?"

"I wouldn't say that." Zack shrugged. "There was a fellow in the town where I grew up, who married a girl thirty years younger than him. I kinda admired that, to tell you the truth. And it came in right handy when he started feeling his age, her being young and strong still, and able to help him get around."

"Did he love her?"

Zack hesitated, then admitted, "Yeah, I reckon he did."

"Well, then, I suppose I 'kind-a' admire him, too."

Noelle laughed with relief. "That sounds like a page out of Father's book. If there's love, the rest will work itself out. Thank you for sharing that inspiring story, Lieutenant."

Her houseguest grinned sheepishly. "If it makes your

eyes shine silver like that, I'll tell stories for the rest of the night."

"Spare us," she began, but her father's eyebrow rebuked her, and so she added sweetly, "You needn't feel the need to entertain us. You are the guest, after all. Father, why don't *you* tell a story?"

"I agree with Adam," Braddock said. "I'd like to hear more about Zack's fascination with California and Nevada. His roots are in Kentucky, and he has impressive connections with Washington." Turning to his young guest, he asked, "Why choose a strange and unknown place to settle down?"

Zack glanced at Noelle, as though concerned with her reaction, then shrugged and answered simply, "There's more opportunity for a fella like me out in those parts than anywhere else in the country right now."

"Opportunity?" Noelle asked.

"Sure. They need men that've had experience with blasting. And someone to ride protection for silver shipments. And I figure they'll be needing more than their share of lawmen—"

"You want to be a policeman?" Noelle interrupted.

Her father chuckled. "I think Zack has something a little less urban in mind. Isn't that so, son? Tom Greer told me General Grant sees you as a U.S. Marshal in one of the western districts. Does that appeal to you?"

Before Zack could reply, Noelle murmured softly, "Do you know General Grant, Lieutenant?"

"Sure. He's one of the finest men I've ever had the pleasure to meet."

"I agree," Adam interposed smoothly. "I met him the last time I was in New York. He may not be as temperate as one would like to see in a presidential candidate, but he seems to command respect in other areas."

Zack's green eyes had darkened noticeably. "I figure, when free men are willing to die for a fella without question, that's all you need to know about him."

"Forgive me," Adam growled. "I didn't mean to wax political."

Russell Braddock turned and explained to his daughter, "Zack was General Grant's bodyguard for a time. Isn't that right, son?"

"No, sir. Not exactly." He sent Noelle an apologetic smile. "I got pulled off my detail once, 'cause Colonel Greer had intercepted a message about some sort of assassination plot against the general. They figured they'd use a sharpshooter to catch a sharpshooter."

"And?" she demanded.

"And it worked. The colonel's plans always worked. He's one of those military geniuses folks like to go on and on about."

Noelle stared in admiration, not only of Zack's accomplishment, but also of his modesty. "What did you mean earlier, when you talked about blasting?"

"Working with explosives."

"Oh, dear. That sounds dangerous."

Her father nodded. "I agree. Have you worked with nitroglycerin?"

"Sure," Zack said with a smile. "It's no different than anything else a man can do. If you take your time with it, and do everything real gentle . . . and real slow . . . and steady and careful, like you've got all the time in the world . . ." He paused as though for emphasis, then murmured, "It almost always turns out just right."

It suddenly seemed unseasonably warm in the dining room, and Noelle wondered why her cheeks were the only ones that were burning. Perhaps the men were more accustomed to such mesmerizing images. But to

her, it was as though Zack's voice had touched her deep
inside. Slow . . . and steady . . . and gentle . . .

"So you're not only a sharpshooter, you also used
explosives during the war?" Adam was observing.
"Sounds like you've killed a lot of men in your career,
Dane."

"That's true enough. And I try to remember every
one of 'em. I figure that's the least I can do."

Humble again, Noelle noted wistfully. Even in the
face of Adam's goading. Not that she blamed her fiancé,
of course. It couldn't be pleasant, listening to the spec-
tacular exploits of his self-appointed rival. She had a
feeling it was *her* duty to find a less annoying topic of
conversation, so she smiled and turned to Adam. "We
keep referring to Colonel Greer. I don't believe I've
mentioned him to you before. His wife was my mother's
dear, dear friend. And Thomas Greer and Father became
close in their own right."

"I see."

She could hear the annoyance in his voice—he might
as well have checked his pocket watch!—but still she
persisted, in hopes of warming his heart with a truly
inspirational story. "The most dreadful thing happened
to Tom Greer during the war. As a colonel, he had un-
pleasant duties, and one of those was to order the execution of a deserter who had compromised the safety
of his men. But you'll never guess what happened after
that."

"You have my undivided attention," Adam drawled.

Noelle winced at the unkind tone, and Zack intervened by informing her, "He doesn't want to hear this,
angel. Let's talk about something else."

She bristled and sent them both reproving glares. "As
I was saying, the deserter's father decided to seek re-

venge on Colonel Greer. But since Tom didn't have a son—just a married daughter—he sought out Tom's grandson, a child of tender years, and kidnapped him. It was his intent to execute the poor child, just as his own boy had been executed, and he almost succeeded, but at the last minute—*Oh!*" She turned to Zack, stunned by the connection she had so belatedly made. "Lieutenant, were *you* the marksman who saved that poor child's life? It didn't even occur to me! Oh, my goodness, how extraordinary. No wonder Father admires you so much."

Zack's eyes had lost all of their sparkle. "It's not something I enjoy remembering, Noelle."

Russell Braddock cleared his throat in warning. "I wanted to mention it to you earlier, sweetheart, so you wouldn't be so harsh with him. But Zack asked me not to."

"She hasn't been harsh." Zack pushed back his chair and stood up with unexpected vehemence. "I had a long ride and a long day. If it's all the same to you, I think I'll turn in." He bowed slightly. "Miss Noelle, it's been an honor. Mr. Braddock. Mr. Prestley. Good night to you all."

Noelle stared after him, even when he had disappeared through the doorway and into the hall. "Father? Did I offend him somehow? If I did, I'm so dreadfully sorry."

"It's fine," Braddock murmured. "Let's give him the respect he's due and not discuss it any further, shall we?"

"But, Father—"

"Noelle!"

She shook her head in disbelief, then turned to Adam. "Have I offended you, too? I know I've been talking too much, but it was only to make everyone comfortable."

"I, for one, enjoyed your story immensely," her fiancé assured her. "It reminds me of a scandal that took place here in Chicago, five or six years ago. Do you remember it, Russell? A young girl was kidnapped, right out of her own bedroom. Our intrepid police force tracked down the culprit and rescued the child, saving the family the anguish of either raising the ransom or losing their precious daughter."

"I remember." Braddock pushed back his chair as noisily and unexpectedly as Zack had done. "If you two don't mind, I'd like to speak with my guest for a moment. Please enjoy the dinner, and I'll join you for dessert."

Noelle stared after him, then turned to Adam and demanded, "Will *you* be leaving next?"

He chuckled fondly. "At the risk of sounding selfish, I couldn't be happier with this turn of events. Do you realize we're actually going to have an intimate dinner alone?"

"That's true." She tried to rally, but failed. "Really, Adam. What could have upset the lieutenant so?"

He shrugged. "We'll probably never know, but I have a theory, if you'd care to hear it."

"Please!"

"Well . . ." He lowered his voice and confided, "I was watching his expression, and he seemed uncomfortable with the details from the start. It occurred to me that if he was in Greer's regiment, he may have been friends with the unfortunate deserter. Or worse, he may have been the man who performed the execution."

"Oh, dear!"

"It stands to reason," Adam continued. "After all,

Dane was the so-called sharpshooter of the group, was he not? Who better to murder a poor, frightened man—a child, more likely—whose only crime was an abhorrence of war?"

Noelle felt her temper flare. "It was hardly murder. You make it sound as though all war heroes are criminals! Just because you never—Oh!" She covered her mouth with her hand and recoiled from his angry eyes. "I didn't mean that, darling. I'm not myself tonight, I'm afraid."

"I had no idea you found me so wanting in military credentials." He stood stiffly, his eyes as cold as ice. "If I were inclined to defend myself—which I am *not*— I would remind you of the thousands of dollars my mother and I raised for the war effort."

Jumping to her feet, Noelle ran to him and threw her arms around his neck. "I don't know what's wrong with me tonight! If you only knew how much I admire you, you'd see this for what it is. Absolute exhaustion and frustration, nothing more."

He smiled reluctantly. "It sounds fairly daunting. How ever do you manage to appear so radiant?"

Noelle exhaled with relief. "It's been the oddest day. But here we are, alone and in each other's arms . . . Oh, dear. I think I hear Father coming."

Adam scowled as he turned toward the sound of footsteps. "Will you do one small favor for me?"

"Anything."

"Please refrain from asking if Dane is feeling better. I can't begin to tell you how much I *don't* care about that. And I hope you don't either."

"Of course I don't," she fibbed, adding more honestly, "You're my first and foremost concern, darling.

The lieutenant is Father's guest, and I'm sure he looked after him, so there's no need to mention it again."

Her fiancé nodded approvingly, then released her just as Braddock reentered the dining room. Thereafter, despite Noelle's concern for their guest's distress, she meticulously avoided the subject of Lieutenant Zachary Dane. The effort made the dinner seem interminable, and although she was ashamed to admit it, she couldn't wait for Adam to leave.

Unfortunately, even when she and her father were finally alone together, no details were forthcoming. "He asked me not to talk to you about it. He'd rather explain it to you himself."

"Don't be silly, Father. I don't want to talk to him about this or anything else. I just want to know if he feels some sort of tragic guilt, because he was friends with the deserter, and can't live with the fact that he was ordered to kill him."

"What makes you think that's what transpired?"

"It's a guess."

"Your guess? Or Adam's?"

She studied him carefully. "Why does that matter?"

"Noelle, come here." Braddock opened his arms and gave her a quick hug. "Didn't I just tell you I gave Zack my word I wouldn't betray his confidence? What makes you think I'd break that word just to satisfy your curiosity?"

"It's more than curiosity," she protested. Then she pulled herself free and complained, "It's very difficult to be your daughter, did you know that? Your standards are unreasonably high."

"And yet you continue to meet them," he replied evenly. When she pretended to pout, he soothed, "You've had an eventful day, sweetheart. Why don't you run on up to bed? Tomorrow, you and Zack can have a long talk, if your curiosity is still bothering you."

"It's not just curiosity," she repeated softly. "He seemed so distressed. At least tell me he's not brooding in his room, Father. I won't be able to sleep otherwise."

Braddock hesitated before suggesting, "Why don't you see for yourself?"

"Visit his room?" she gasped. "Honestly, Father—"

"It's hardly a visit," he corrected with a laugh. "Just a knock on the door, and a sincere wish that he sleep well. You are the hostess here for at least a few days more, aren't you?"

"You're certain he's not upset with me?"

"He adores you," her father reminded her mischievously. "Which brings me to my last instruction. *Don't* go into his room."

She laughed in relief. "Thank you for that, at least. I was beginning to think you'd lost all judgment when it came to our backwoods pest." She planted a soft kiss on his cheek. "Good night, Father. Don't stay up too late."

"I have to find a bride for our guest," he reminded her with a wink.

"In that case, stay up all night." She smiled and headed for the doorway, pausing only to add, "Father?"

"Yes, sweetheart?"

"You approve of Adam, don't you?"

"If he makes you happy—"

"Never mind." She sighed in defeat, but still managed to throw him a kiss before turning to trudge up the two flights of stairs that led to the largest of their guest rooms. Once at Zack's door, she found herself doubting the wisdom of this visit. Wouldn't it encourage his silly attentions? And couldn't the matter wait until morning?

But she couldn't get the image out of her mind. A soldier, devoted to his commander and his duty, forced to aim and fire at a friend. Perhaps even a friend from childhood. It was so tragic, and Noelle couldn't bear the thought that she had unwittingly dredged up the memory under the most awkward of circumstances. She *owed* it to him to apologize.

Taking a deep breath, she raised her knuckles and knocked on the door, rather more loudly than she had intended. Zack pulled open the door almost immediately, an expression of concern on his face that relaxed almost instantly into a deadly smile.

"I had a feeling it was you," he murmured. Then before she could protest, he pulled her into the room, closed the door, and engulfed her in a warm, loving embrace. "I can't stop thinking about you either, angel. I know you're confused—"

"Would you *please* unhand me," she wailed, wrenching free of him and glaring in disgust. "Have you no concept of proper behavior at all?"

Zack grinned. "You're the one who—"

"I did not! I'm a hostess, bidding her guest good night. Unfortunately, my guest is a lunatic."

He stepped back and surveyed her with undisguised appreciation. "You sure look pretty in that dress."

"Well, that's all that matters, isn't it?" she grumbled. "Go and stand over there, by the armoire."

"You mean that big old cupboard?"

"Just go." She waited until he'd ambled across the room before speaking again. "You owe me approximately fifty apologies, Lieutenant. I'm not here to collect any of them. I'm here because I apparently owe you one myself." Lowering her voice, she added wistfully, "I didn't mean to reawaken a painful memory tonight. Can you forgive me?"

"You didn't do anything wrong."

"I think I did." She bit her lip, then asked, "Would you like to tell me about it?"

"No."

"I know men face horrendous choices in wartime. But what you did for that child and for the Greer family is something to be proud of forever. No matter what else happened, a little boy is alive today because of you."

"He's alive," Zack agreed. "But he'll never walk right again. Because of me."

She was almost speechless with confused dismay, but managed to insist, "You may not have gotten there in time to prevent injury, but he's alive—"

"I shot him in the leg."

"Oh, no." Crossing the room, she put her hand on Zack's arm and whispered, "I'm so sorry, Lieutenant. But it couldn't have been avoided—"

"It could've been avoided—*should've* been avoided—if I'd been more careful."

"I don't believe that."

He cocked his head to the side. "You don't?"

"Absolutely not."

"You're wrong, but still . . ." A glimmer of a smile lit his lips. "I like hearing you defend me. I liked it when you defended me to Prestley—"

"I did no such thing!"

"You surely did." He put his hands on her shoulders and confided, "I don't like that fella, sugar. He's got a mean streak in him."

She pulled away and eyed him coolly. "I didn't expect

you to like him. I don't *care* if you like him. It's absurd to discuss whether you like him or not."

"Can we discuss why *you* like him?"

"Absolutely not." With a sigh, she backed away and announced, "I'm going to bed. I suggest you do the same. But if you're not tired, go and talk to my father. He's busy studying his files, to find you a bride."

"I've found one."

"How flattering. Good night, Lieutenant."

"Good night, angel. Sweet dreams."

She had almost reached the door when he caught her by the waist and turned her to face him. "I've gotta give you a kiss, angel. I won't be able to sleep if I don't."

"For heaven's sake—" She tried to wriggle free, but his hands were too strong, and she might have panicked, but the kiss—so gentle and unassuming and brief—was over before she could truly react. It had been less than a brush of his lips across hers, but there had been so much love in it—or what passed for love in his absurdly sweet world—that she almost wished she'd had the presence of mind to savor it before it was finished.

"You're absolutely incorrigible," she lamented weakly. "Don't *ever* do that again."

"Do you know what I think, angel?"

"I don't care!" She bustled to the door and opened it wide, then turned and demanded with a huff, "Fine. Tell me what you think. But be quick about it."

Zack chuckled softly. "I think you're starting to fall in love with me. You sure took your sweet time about it, but I'm not complaining. I suppose that business with Prestley is a mite confusing to you."

"Do you mean my engagement?" She glared. "Yes, I suppose that little detail *has* been keeping me from responding to your obnoxious charms as quickly as you would have liked. Good night, Lieutenant!" With one final scowl, she marched through the door and slammed it so hard, she was certain her father, or at least Edward, would come running.

Apparently, the usual rules in this household don't apply where war heroes are concerned, she complained to herself as she hurried down to her second-story bedroom. *I wish there was a lock on this door to keep that lunatic away. Father certainly won't have the presence of mind to listen for possible assaults on my virtue!*

Then she remembered the gentle, fleeting kiss and sighed in confusion. Her lunatic admirer would never really assault her, she knew. He truly seemed to worship the ground on which she tread. And try as she might to resist, she found herself liking him in return. Not in a romantic sense, of course, but in the sense of admiring him. He had saved Tom Greer's grandson, yet rather than bask in the glory of that heroic act, he tortured himself for having made a mistake along the way. She searched for the word that might describe him, and was surprised when she arrived at "noble."

You can honestly consider that backwoods pest to be noble? she scoffed at herself, but as she settled into bed, surrounded by her dolls, she acknowledged the odd truth of it. Lieutenant Zachary Dane absolutely exuded nobility. Unfortunately, he also exuded some completely exasperating qualities, and she simply didn't have the time or patience to deal with them at a time like this. She had a wedding to plan! She could only hope her father would pore over his files all night, and find a replacement bride for the guest by morning, so that she could get back to the blissful business of preparing herself for the honor of becoming Mrs. Adam Bartholomew Prestley.

For the first time in months, she dreamed of her mother—a beautiful dream, in which Mrs. Tom Greer was visiting, baking a pie and calling Noelle "honey," just as she'd done so often during visits to Chicago. It was a welcome memory, and as Noelle stirred in her bed the next morning, she told herself sleepily that she had Lieutenant Dane to thank for it, and she should be a good hostess and mention it to him the moment she saw him.

Of course, she hadn't expected that moment to arrive before she even climbed out of bed, but it did. In fact, her vision had scarcely come into focus when she realized that the ubiquitous pest was seated in a white wicker rocking chair, not three feet from the side of her bed.

Instinctively yanking her blanket up to her neck to cover the bodice of her pink eyelet nightgown, she gasped in groggy alarm. "Lieutenant!"

"Mornin', angel." His grin was wide, and only slightly tinged with guilt as he leaned forward and asked with casual affection, "How'd you sleep?"

Three

"You sure look pretty in the morning, Noelle. All snuggled up, so peaceful and sweet—"

"Wait!" She sat up and tried to manage a glare, despite the fact that she was still not quite certain she was awake. "How long have you been here?"

"I reckon about an hour. I know I should've been more patient, but I kept wondering if you were really as pretty as I remembered. I just had to sneak in and have myself a peek."

With a groan of frustration, she flopped back onto her pillow and pulled the covers up over her face. She too had wondered, in the wee hours of the night, if her memory of him was accurate, but here he was, even more obnoxious than she'd recalled.

He was also as handsome as she'd recalled, with his smiling, suntanned face, shaggy brown hair, and mischievous green eyes. Fresh scrubbed and unself-conscious, he was Adam Prestley's opposite in almost every sense. No meticulously trimmed mustache or perfectly manicured nails, no hint of tailoring or starch in his loose-fitting clothes; he was simple, uncomplicated, and youthful to a fault.

Thank heavens Adam outgrew such impulsive silliness years ago, she told herself, although she doubted whether her sophisticated fiancé had ever been quite this reckless, or naïve, or indiscreet, even in his youngest, wildest days.

And of course, Zack Dane would *never* outgrow it! He was twenty-six years old, wasn't he? Hardly a boy, despite all indications to the contrary. If twenty-six years and the horrors of war hadn't sobered him, she was fairly certain nothing ever would.

"Are you gonna stay in bed all day, angel?"

"Go away."

"I came here for a reason," Zack assured her. "To finish the story."

"What story?" she asked without emerging from under the covers.

"About Colonel Greer's grandbaby."

"Oh." She peeked her head out, and noticed for the first time that he was holding one of her dolls. "What are you doing with *that?*"

"What? Oh, you mean this here?" He held out the pretty porcelain replica of a princess dressed in lavender satin. Then with a mischievous wink, he pulled up its skirts and quipped, "She's not wearing any drawers. Did you know that? What kind of princess—"

"Father!"

Zack laughed and moved to sit on the side of the bed. "I was just having fun with you, sugar. I promise I'll behave myself now."

"You're sitting on my bed! That's horrible behavior! Don't you know anything?"

"I know all I need to know." He shook his head in amused disbelief. "Dang, you've got a bone-chilling scream. You oughta stop doing that so much. I don't think your pappy takes it seriously anymore. He's heard it too often."

"Apparently so." She took a deep breath and instructed tersely, "Stop staring at my nightie."

"I like it."

"Yes, I know. Please stop staring at it."

"Sure, angel." He raised his laughing gaze to hers. "Whatever you say."

"Stop calling me angel." She grimaced as she added, "Not only is it presumptuous, it doesn't even suit me. Haven't you noticed I *don't* have an angelic temperament? Plus, it's a well-known fact that angels have golden hair."

"It's a well-known fact that angels have pretty mouths and long legs," he teased. "At least, where I come from that's the rumor."

She tried to scowl, but as seemed to happen too often, she found herself enjoying his absurd compliments in spite of herself. "You said you came here to tell me a story."

"To finish a story," he corrected. "About the boy I shot."

"Oh, Zack . . ." She shook her curls in frustration. "I wish you wouldn't put it that way. Even without hearing the rest of the story, I know it was an accident." When he didn't respond, she prodded warily, "Fine. Tell me the rest of it."

He licked his lips, then began. "I have a good eye when it comes to aiming a weapon. Knives, arrows, bullets—they all fly straight for me. It's a talent I've had since I was a boy, and I'm thankful for it. I've tried to put it to good use. I've also tried not to get too full of myself about it. Or to take it for granted."

"Go on."

He smiled and patted her leg through the covers. "A sharpshooter's only as good as his rifle, so I carry the best. And I keep it clean and oiled and working like a fine foreign watch. If the sight's off even by a hair, a sharpshooter becomes a danger to everyone around him."

She grabbed his hand before he could pat her knee again. "Stop that, but go on."

Zack chuckled softly. "That afternoon, when we were tracking the bastard who took Greer's grandbaby, I was packing a pistol along with old Henry, my rifle. We found a shack, where we thought the boy might be. I gave my rifle to one of the other fellas, to hold while I snuck up—with my gun drawn—to listen at the wall. The place was deserted, so we moved on. And the dang fool didn't tell me he'd dropped old Henry on a tree stump."

Noelle gasped. "Something got knocked out of place on Old—on the rifle?"

Zack nodded. "A few minutes later, we saw the kidnapper out in the distance. He'd been waiting for us—waiting for us to witness the boy's murder, so we could carry the details back to Greer. He had the little one all tied up, and was holding him in front of himself, so we couldn't get a clean shot. And he had a pistol to the boy's head. He shouted, 'Tell Greer we're even now!' And I knew I couldn't wait, so I sank right down onto one knee, raised up old Henry, aimed and fired. It tore a hole in that boy's thigh the size of Kentucky."

"But the second bullet killed the kidnapper?"

Zack nodded.

"Well, then . . ." She raised his hand to her lips and kissed it lightly. "You saved him. Don't you see that? He may not be able to walk perfectly, but he can walk, can't he?" When Zack just shrugged, she scolded, "Of course he can. I would have heard about it if the injury had been truly hideous. What did Colonel Greer say to you when he heard what happened?"

"He was decent about it—"

"He was overcome with gratitude and relief," she countered firmly. "I've heard *that* part of the story dozens of times. He sang your praises to Father, and Father sang them to me. The brilliant marksman. Everyone else that was there that day said there wasn't a clear shot to be had, but somehow, *you* managed to save that boy."

"It doesn't seem so bad when you tell it," he whispered, leaning into her and brushing his lips across hers. "I figure that's how everything'll be from now on. Better, 'cause you're there to make it better."

Noelle was so touched by the tribute that she didn't see the glow in his eyes turn into a mischievous twinkle until it was too late. Leaning into her more fully, he covered her mouth with his own in an apparent plan to kiss her with greedy thoroughness.

"What are you doing?" She struggled free and leaped out of the far side of the bed, pointing her finger toward the door with furious insistence. "Get out *now!* If you don't leave this instant, I swear I'll never speak to you again."

"I'll go," he agreed. "I just want to hear you admit it one time first."

"It?"

"How you truly feel about me."

"Fine. I *hate* you."

Zack chuckled, completely undiscouraged. "You're a she-cat, that's for sure. I was telling Merc about that yesterday. He didn't believe it, you being an angel and all. But if he could see you now, he'd agree with me for sure."

Noelle knew she shouldn't encourage him, but

couldn't help asking, in a weak, almost defeated voice, "Merc?"

"Mercury. My horse."

"Of course. Mercury and Old Henry. Did you bring anyone else with you to help ruin my wedding?"

"It's not *Old* Henry. Just Henry."

"But you said—Oh, for heaven's sake, do you honestly suppose I care what your rifle's name is? What kind of person names a rifle in the first place? And *stop* staring at my nightie!"

"You kissed my hand," he told her gleefully. "Where I come from—"

"Be quiet."

"My pappy had a rule, sugar. It went something like this: facts are facts."

"Brilliant."

"There's more. Facts are facts. It never pays to ignore 'em. And if you've got 'em, it never pays to keep 'em to yourself."

"My 'pappy' has a rule, too: *no men in my bedroom!*"

Zack laughed with deep, resonant appreciation. "I like that one. Is this the first time you've broken it?"

She glared in disgust. "You haven't really heard how loud I can screech, but I'm about to give you a demonstration."

"And make that butler fella with the bad heart climb up all those stairs? That's kinda mean, isn't it?"

Ignoring the attempt at humor, she grabbed for her dressing gown, which was neatly folded at the foot of her bed. "If *you* won't leave, I will. Stay as long as you like. Just don't molest any more of my dolls."

He caught her arm as she attempted to sweep past him. "Wait, Noelle. Can we talk serious for a minute?"

"That's entirely up to you."

He nodded solemnly. "All playing aside, there's something I need to say to you. I promise I'll be quick about it."

She hesitated, then sighed. "Fine. Just try to be brief."

His voice took on a low, humble tone. "I have a burning need inside me—a need to make you my wife. To protect you and love you and bring a smile to those pretty lips of yours. It's a new feeling for me, and I like it. If you give it a chance, I think you'll like it, too."

She knew, before he leaned in to her, that he was going to bestow another of his gentle little kisses on her, and she didn't have the heart to reject it. He was so sweet. So simple. So sincerely misguided. Standing still, she waited until his lips had tasted hers; then she stepped back and eyed him with stern indulgence. "That's the last time, Zack. I mean it."

"But you liked it?"

"It was a lovely kiss, but it's wasted on me. I'm in love with Adam Prestley. He's the only man I want to kiss."

"Then why didn't you stop me?"

"I knew it would be quick, and I didn't want to hurt your feelings. That's all."

"I appreciate that." He rested his hands on her hips. "You're a fine girl, do you know that? Prestley's a lucky fella."

"Thank you."

"I never saw a girl with silver eyes before," he continued softly. "I expect it took me by surprise. And with you all dressed up like an angel . . . Well, you can't hardly blame a fella for being thunderstruck."

She blushed at the tenderness of the confession. "It

was just a coincidence, Lieutenant. You were looking
for a bride, and I was dressed like a bride. It's that
simple. Do you see that now?"

"It was like you were floating up there—floating
right down out of heaven and into my arms. With that
pretty little mouth, just aching to be kissed. And I
started aching, too, and I haven't stopped. I don't think
I ever will.

"Something happened in that room, Noelle. Something like magic, except magic isn't real, and this is."
He lowered his mouth to hers for another gentle taste.

She felt as though she were in a trance, brought on
by the romantic tribute, and strengthened by the husky
quality to his soft, rhythmic voice. Without thinking, she
reached up and brushed her fingertips along his cheek-
bone—her own hopeless, innocent tribute—and as she
did so, he backed her against the door and began to
kiss her more deeply, grinding his body gently against
her as though he couldn't get enough of the feel of her.

It sent a jolt of hot confusion radiating from deep
inside her—a primitive echo of the hunger he so clearly
felt. It was meaningless and dangerous, yet for a long
moment she responded to it. Then her senses cleared
and she shoved him away with all her might, wailing,
"Why do you keep *kissing* me?"

His expression was completely unrepentant as he
swung open the door. "You sure know how to warm up
a morning."

"Be quiet!" She stomped her foot in frustrated defi-
ance, but didn't bother shouting for either her father or
the butler. After all her years of feeling safe in her father's house, she was beginning to realize that the
sounds of a damsel in distress simply didn't carry down
the stairwells. Either that, or Russell Braddock *and* Ed-

ward had chosen this week to completely lose their hearing.

Fortunately, Zack left of his own accord, after flashing one last grin and instructing her, "Don't hide up here all day, sugar. Me and Merc wanna take you for a ride along the lake."

Exhausted, she closed the door behind him, then leaned against it, trying to imagine what she should do about the absurd encounters. Zack was simply too bold, and too charming, to be trusted any longer. And of course, it didn't help matters that she had encouraged him—first by kissing his hand and then by stroking his face. A civilized man would have known these gestures were meant to comfort, not to arouse. But Zack either didn't recognize such fine points, or was conveniently choosing to misunderstand them. Either way, she had unwittingly fueled his ardor.

He flattered you, with all that talk of angels and heaven, and you fell right into his trap. What if he tells Father? Or Adam! You won't be able to deny it, and if you try to explain it—well, you'll only succeed in confusing matters further.

But he won't dare tell Father, she reasoned. *He'd have to admit he came into your bedroom uninvited while you were sleeping, and wouldn't leave when you asked nicely. And even though you did kiss him a bit, that's no excuse for the way he took advantage—sticking his tongue in your mouth like some sort of animal, and groping at you the way he did!*

She nodded vigorously. *He won't tell Father, and he won't tell Adam for the same reason—Adam would complain to Father, and Father would take care of it once and for all.*

It would almost be worth it, she realized suddenly.

Her father would throw Zack out of the house, and then she could relax and turn her attentions to where they belonged—the wedding preparations.

Changing quickly into her dark green dressing gown, she bounded down the stairs and up to the doorway of the breakfast room, where she spied her father and Zack sharing the newspaper and reminiscing about Tom Greer over a table laden with croissants and fruit. It was a sight she hadn't been prepared to see, and she watched in wistful silence as they laughed and talked and drank their coffee, like old friends.

Her father looked so happy! She hadn't seen that particular smile—the wide one, full of hope and contentment—in longer than she wanted to admit.

Zachary Dane is the son Father never had, she told herself with reluctant appreciation. *The one who would have made your marriage to Adam more palatable to him.*

It was odd but true, the realization that Russell Braddock needed someone with whom to commiserate over the loss of his daughter's company. It didn't matter that she would visit often. In her heart, she knew it would never be the way it had been for so long. Somehow, until this very moment, she had refused to acknowledge it, but seeing him now, she knew he had been correct to mourn this, at least slightly. And somehow, Zack was making the transition easier for him.

She was reconsidering her plan to send the lieutenant packing when her father caught sight of her and boomed, "Sweetheart! Come and visit with us."

"Lieutenant Dane and I already *had* a little visit this morning," she revealed carefully. "He misbehaved, as usual. Please do something about him, Father."

When Braddock turned inquiring eyes to Zack, the

latter smiled sheepishly. "I can't help it, sir. She makes me forget myself."

"Just the same, I expect you to behave in my house," he scolded. *"Both* of you."

"Me? What did *I* do?" Noelle protested.

"I suspect you haven't been as hospitable as you could be," he countered evenly. "Why don't the two of you start over? Zack, you will remember that my daughter is a respectable young lady who is engaged to Adam Prestley. And Noelle? You will remember that Zack is here by invitation, and that we all owe him a debt of gratitude for his selfless heroism during the war."

"Did you hear that, Lieutenant?" she demanded. "We're starting over. Which means you have to forget all about that silly scene with my wedding gown yesterday."

"I'd sooner tear my heart from my chest than forget about that."

She looked to her father for assistance, but he seemed visibly moved by the dramatic announcement.

"Fine! Then *I'm* not starting over, either."

"That's fair enough," Zack said with a nod.

Exhaling in sharp disgust, she stomped back up to her room, determined to stay there for the rest of the day.

She would ask Edward to send a note to Adam, apologizing for the previous evening's uncomfortable dinner. She even considered offering to dine at the Prestley home that evening, but the thought of spending time with Adam's mother and her snide remarks was simply too unbearable. Of course, her fiancé always protected her—better than she had protected him from Zack, that was certain!

And in less than a week, she was actually going to

start *living* with Adam's mother! It was another fact, like her father's loneliness, that she hadn't quite managed to face squarely yet.

"This was supposed to be a romantic, magical time," she complained to a row of dolls as she arranged them neatly on her bed. "Instead, it's horrid. And it's all the lieutenant's fault. Well, I suppose I can't blame him for mean old Victoria Prestley. And *I'm* the one who's deserting Father, so that's not his fault, either. Still, somehow, it's *all* his doing!"

She was just settling down at her writing desk to pen the note to Adam when she heard a knock on her door. "What nerve!" she told the dolls in disgust. "Watch and learn, girls. I'm going to give this pest a tonguelashing he won't soon forget." Squaring her shoulders, she marched over to the door and threw it open with one grand, imperious tug, more than prepared to berate her presumptuous guest for daring to bother her again so soon.

But it was Russell Braddock, not Zack, who was standing on the other side of the door.

"Oh, Father," she murmured sheepishly. "It's *you.*"

"Who were you expecting?"

"Use your imagination," she advised dryly. "Have you come to scold me again for my lack of manners?" Before he could answer, she added, "I'm sorry I stormed off the way I did, but I knew Zack would ruin breakfast—just like he ruined dinner—so why bother eating?"

Braddock chuckled at the logic. "May I come in?"

"Of course." She stepped aside and smiled sheepishly. "It's been ages since you've been in here. The girls have all missed you. Look!" She reached for a pretty rag doll that was perched on top of the dresser. "Believe it or not, this is the one you gave me right after Mother died. Do you remember how I hugged her so hard, so often, she was all worn out? But Winifred made this pretty new apron to cover the stains on her dress, and put a couple of little stitches in her hand, and now she's good as new."

He took the doll and studied it sadly. "I didn't know how to explain your mother's death to you, or to help you stop crying and asking for her. I was grateful to this little doll for giving you a few moments of comfort in an otherwise dismal year."

"I wish Mother were here now."

"So do I. She'd love helping with the wedding plans."

"And she'd be company for you, so you wouldn't be so lonely."

He seemed surprised by the comment. "I shouldn't have said anything to you yesterday, sweetheart. Can you forgive me? I was just having a sentimental moment."

"I've been having them, too." She hugged him briskly. "We're so fortunate to be so close. We'll always be close, no matter what. I guarantee that."

"I have no doubts." He smiled and patted her cheek. "And of course, as you mentioned yesterday, there will be my grandchildren to keep me company. I'll insist that they visit constantly."

"When they find out how much fun you are, I won't be able to keep them away." She could feel a warning sting of tears in her eyes, and changed the subject hastily. "Did you come to talk about Zack?"

He nodded and sat down on the edge of the bed, still holding the rag doll in his hand. "He's one of the finest young men I've ever had the privilege to meet. I know you see him somewhat differently, and I don't really blame you. With my help, he has managed to put you in an impossible position."

Noelle weakened easily. "He can be charming, Father. And there's no question that he's brave. He saved Colonel Greer's grandson, after all, and I admire that. If it were any other time, I'd find some way to enjoy his visit, but I'm trying to prepare for a wedding."

"Is there so very much to do?" He studied her curiously. "I assumed Alice and Winnie were seeing to most of the details."

"They are. But the most important detail is my composure. I want to be rested and radiant and confident on my wedding day. Not harried and hunted."

He patted her arm in sympathetic amusement. "I may have the solution to your problem as well as Zack's."

"Oh?"

"I'd like you to help me make the match for him."

"Really?" She beamed with delight. For years, her father had discussed the various matches with her, but until this moment, had never asked her to participate in the actual selection.

And he was right that it might be the answer to her problem. All Zack needed was another girl on whom he could lavish his outlandish brand of romantic nonsense, and she would be free to concentrate on Adam.

Her father proffered a folded piece of paper. "I brought his letter for you to study. Try to discern what sort of bride might suit him best."

"I already know what he wants in a girl, Father. Long legs and a pretty mouth—not a pretty smile, mind you, but a pretty mouth. Isn't that silly? And he likes gray eyes. Apparently they don't have those where he comes from."

"He may have to settle for blue," Braddock said with a smile. "Anything else?"

"What did he write in his letter?"

"Let's see. He used the word 'pretty' more than once, but wasn't too specific. He mentioned wanting her to cook—"

"Ooh, remind me to tell him I don't have the faintest idea about all that."

Braddock chuckled. "I believe he's willing to make an exception in your case."

"But still, it's probably the key to changing his mind. Find someone in your files who has extraordinary cooking skills, long legs, and blue-gray eyes."

"Of course, there's no point in finding him a bride if he doesn't know how to court her," Braddock mused. "Would you be willing to give him a little advice along those lines, sweetheart?"

"Me? Wouldn't it be better if you did that? Tell him about your courtship of Mother. I assume you didn't sneak up on her in hallways, or stick your tongue down her throat, or fondle her leg. All of which he has done to me right under your roof, by the way." She smiled impishly. "Why haven't you strangled him by now, Father?"

"He means well. He's just exuberant, which isn't always a bad quality. He just needs to learn to control it. I think you could convince him to try." When Noelle shook her head, he encouraged her briskly. "Just tell him what a girl likes to hear, and what she doesn't like. Tell him what made you fall in love with Adam. Make general suggestions about his demeanor and vocabulary—"

"Civilize him?"

"Exactly."

She was beginning to find the challenge intriguing. "Are you going to instruct him to cooperate with me?"

"Of course. He'll resist the idea of marrying anyone but you. But I imagine he'll be more than willing to learn your standards, if only so that he can try to measure up to them."

"That's not enough. You have to tell him he can't stay unless he does *exactly* what I tell him to do."

Her father smiled knowingly. "If I give you that kind of power, can I trust you not to abuse it?"

"I'll be good. I've actually grown fond of him, in a convoluted sort of way. He can be so sweet. You need to find him a sweet bride, Father. Someone who'll appreciate the tender heart that lurks under that obnoxious exterior."

Braddock cocked his head to the side and studied her. "I take it he explained why he doesn't feel as proud over rescuing Tom's grandson as we would have hoped?"

Noelle sighed. "Do you know whether the boy's injuries were actually crippling?"

"According to Tom, he was scarred, but has no noticeable limp or lingering discomfort."

"Yet Zack tortures himself over it." She pursed her lips as she considered the young lieutenant's dilemma. Finally she said, "We must make certain the bride hears that story right away, so she can soothe him when the memory tries to haunt him."

"It will take a special girl to help ease that particular burden. As gregarious as he is, he's still fairly private. I'm not sure he has anyone he really confides in."

"He has Merc. And Henry."

"I beg your pardon?"

Noelle laughed lightly. "His horse and his rifle. I've

gotten the distinct impression he has actual conversations with them."

"Hmm . . ." Braddock inclined his head toward the row of dolls on her bed. "I can't imagine anyone confiding in their possessions, can you?"

"Shh, you'll hurt their feelings."

He laughed appreciatively. "Will you be coming down to breakfast soon?"

"I want to write Adam a note first, asking him not to come to dinner for a day or two."

"Oh?"

"Don't pretend to be disappointed," she scolded. "Also, there's the possibility he'll reply by inviting me to dine at *his* house. I don't see how I can refuse. Do you?" she added hopefully.

"You can inform them that you'll be dining there nightly in the near future, and that I insist on having your company every single evening until the wedding."

"That sounds reasonable," she said with a grateful smile. "Five more dinners here—or rather, four, since I'll be going to Clara's party on Wednesday night—and then I'll be Noelle Prestley, dining at the Prestley mansion with Adam and his mother."

"I'd almost forgotten about that party." Her father frowned. "Unfortunate timing, to say the least."

"I would gladly have declined the invitation if it didn't mean so much to Adam. And you're not going to be here in any case, isn't that so? Didn't you tell me you have plans of your own? To play cards?"

"I'll cancel my plans if you'll cancel yours," he suggested with a playful wink; then he added quickly, "If it's important to Adam, you should go, of course. We'll ride together—"

"Adam wants to arrive together, so he's sending his

carriage for me." She eyed her strict parent with dour anticipation. "Before you accuse me of unladylike behavior, you should know that Miss Winifred Duschane will be riding with us, both to the party and home again. I shan't be alone with Adam for even one minute, I assure you."

"Oh?"

"Winnie made half of the dresses for that party, and wants to see her handiwork put to good use. She's dear friends with the family's governess, so it's all been arranged. My innocence will be protected at all costs."

"Your innocence is indestructible," he assured her with a smile.

"I only meant—" She caught herself, amused that she had almost revealed the way in which Adam saw her innocence—as something she'd surrender on her wedding night. It was a matter of semantics, nothing more, was it not? And it was only natural that a girl's father would see such things differently than one's intended lover.

And Lieutenant Dane? What would *he* have to say on the subject of her innocence? Something homespun yet suggestive, she decided with a rueful smile.

"We should start the lessons without delay, Father. Give our guest strict instructions; then send him along to me."

"Here? In your room?"

She laughed lightly. "It wouldn't be the first time. That's what I've been trying . . . Oh, never mind. Ask him to meet me in the . . . Well, where?"

"In the atrium," her father suggested. "I'll have the doors from my study wide open. If he misbehaves, simply call out for me and I'll see that he regrets it."

Noelle rolled her eyes. "Believe me, Father, you

won't hear me. I've been calling out for you to rescue me for two days straight—" She broke off in the face of his clear concern, and embraced him reassuringly. "I was teasing you, silly. I'm perfectly safe with Zack. In fact," she added with a sigh, "I think he'd die before he allowed any harm to come to me."

"That's rather remarkable, don't you agree?"

"I'm very fortunate," she agreed. "I already had two such men in my life, and now I've stumbled on a third. The brother I never had, you might say."

Her father took the cue instantly. "There's no reason your fiancé shouldn't come to dinner—"

"And risk bloodshed?" she drawled. "I think we can do without that. With any luck, dinner will provide an opportunity to instruct our barbarian guest on acceptable topics of conversation in mixed company. Go and threaten him now, Father. I'll meet him in the garden in fifteen minutes."

Quelling an unexpected surge of anticipation at the thought of civilizing her handsome guest, she ushered her father out of the bedroom and sat down to pen a quick note to the man she loved.

Zack paused for a moment in the doorway to Russell Braddock's study, impressed by the way his host was poring over a stack of letters. Zack admired dedication in any man, but doubly when that dedication involved a service to others. And what better service could any man perform than to ensure that two persons, who otherwise might have been lonely, would have lives filled with love?

It was because of this man, along with Colonel Greer, that Zack himself could be secure in his future, knowing he'd be sharing it with a pretty, feisty, irresistible angel. It still seemed like a miracle, that a simple letter could lead to so scintillating a love affair.

There had been times when Zack had thought he'd die—from an explosion or gunshot wounds—long before he reached his thirtieth birthday. Instead, he was going to escort Noelle Braddock through a long, amorous, exciting life, and into old age, where they would dote on their grandchildren, and on their great-grandchildren. And, always and forever, on each other.

"You wanted to see me, sir?" he asked finally.

"Zack!" Braddock seemed delighted to see him, almost as though they'd known each other for years. *This fella needed to have a son or two,* Zack realized; then he instructed himself briskly, *That's how you'll repay him for bringing Noelle into your life. Be a good son-in-law to him, and a good husband to his daughter.*

"There's something I'd like to discuss with you," Braddock was saying as he motioned for his guest to sit across the desk from him. "I just had a long talk with Noelle about your future—"

"She agreed we had a future?"

Braddock cleared his throat. "I didn't phrase that well. Let's start again. *Your* future, with the bride I find for you."

"That's Noelle," Zack assured him cheerfully. "I know she doesn't quite see it that way yet, but I was kinda hoping *you* could see it."

"I see that you're very taken with her, and I can't say that I blame you. She's a fine girl—lovely and spirited and good-hearted. But she's engaged to another man."

Zack studied his host knowingly. "I know you can't say it outright, sir, and I respect that. But you'll never convince me you want that Prestley varmint anywhere near Noelle."

"Zack—"

"I know. She's so stubborn, you can't just tell her that outright, for thinking she might just up and run away with him. And it would cause a rift between the two of you. I don't want that to happen any more than you do, sir. She's gotta realize it on her own, that's for sure. And it's beginning to happen, so don't lose hope."

Russell Braddock seemed to be measuring every word as he responded. "I'm not going to lie to you, Zack. If you had met Noelle before this business with Adam became so serious, and if you had somehow managed to make her fall in love with you, I would have been the happiest man on earth. But as it is, I believe she's going to marry Adam. I've made my peace with that, because I would never do anything to jeopardize my relationship with her. And you're absolutely right—if I didn't support this engagement, she would run off with him, and it would be a long and painful road before we could reestablish some sort of trusting relationship. I'd never put her through that."

"I respect that," Zack repeated. "I'm not asking you to do a thing about it, sir, except let me stay here and court her. I'll take care of the rest."

Braddock smiled. "I admire your confidence, son, but I'm not sure you know just how stubborn she can be. And her engagement aside, I think you should know that you aren't exactly the husband she's been envisioning for herself all her life."

"You think she wants an older fella?"

"I don't think she ever thought of it in those terms," Braddock explained carefully. "But I believe she likes the fact that Adam is experienced—"

"Experienced?" Zack winced. Was it possible Noelle thought Prestley would be a better lover than Zack? He'd gotten just the opposite impression when he'd kissed her—almost as though she'd never been kissed at all, or at least, not by someone who knew what he was doing!

Russell Braddock smiled sadly. "She found herself a man who, from all indications, has learned exactly what he wants out of life. A man who is very unlikely to make a mistake. It's a sort of guarantee for her, do you see? I believe it has something to do with the match-making, unfortunately."

Zack cocked his head to the side and studied Braddock sympathetically. "You blame yourself? Why?"

"I suspect that my daughter wanted to make her own choice—as of course, she should. But she was also afraid she might make a mistake. But if a man like Adam Prestley, with all his experience and resources and sophistication, thought their marriage would be a good one, she could rely on that."

Zack nodded slowly. It made a lot of sense. Noelle had spent her whole life watching an older man make excellent love matches, all because he had the knowledge, experience, and objectivity to see what a younger, more impulsive person might miss. But because she was stubborn, she wouldn't let that particular experienced older man make a match for her. Instead, she simply found herself another one!

He grinned fondly. "She's a feisty one, isn't she? Smart, too. Too smart for her own good. She figured she'd show you how it was done, with the help of a fella she thought might be just about as 'experienced' as you."

"I'd appreciate it if you kept this . . . well, this theory, between us. She'd be furious if she knew I saw it this way, and the truth is, I might very well be wrong. She may have fallen deeply in love with him for reasons that have nothing to do with me or my profession. And I think it's safe to say I may be a bit prejudiced against him, if only because he's not the sort of man I've envisioned her with over these many years."

"You pictured her with a fella like me?"

"Not exactly." Braddock chuckled. "But as I said, I would have been delighted with such a choice. For selfish reasons, as well as unselfish ones." Clearing his throat, he announced, "There's no point in belaboring all that. The truth is, she's going to marry Adam. You need to make the best of that, and I'd like to help you. So would Noelle. After all, this episode has given us some valuable information about what you want in a bride. I intend to find you someone like Noelle—"

"I don't want someone 'like' her. I want *her.*"

"I understand." Braddock grinned sympathetically. "But since she's engaged—"

"She'll change her mind." Zack remembered the way she'd caressed his cheek that morning in her bedroom and had to suppress a confident smile. "She's already starting to weaken, sir."

"Just the same, you have to accept the possibility that she might marry Adam. Wait!" He held up his hand to ward off another reassuring interruption. "Try to imagine if the situation were reversed. If *you* were engaged to marry Noelle in six days—"

"I wouldn't wait six days."

Braddock laughed aloud. "That shows me you don't know my daughter as well as you think you do. That girl has her heart set on a formal wedding with all the trimmings, and she always gets her way. You'd wait; believe me."

Zack grinned. Given half a chance, he knew he could convince Noelle to move up the wedding night, or at least, to indulge in some serious prewedding lovemaking, but there was no reason to share such volatile information with the girl's father.

"As I was saying, suppose the situation were reversed, and *you* were her fiancé. And a brash young man arrived out of nowhere and was charmed by the sight of her. A profound case of love at first sight. Would you honestly expect Noelle to listen to him as though he were a viable suitor—"

"He'd be a dead man. That's not a viable suitor."

Braddock eyed him sternly. "You're fortunate Adam didn't choose that particular solution to the problem."

"That's how I know he's a coward," Zack retorted. "If he loved her and had any guts, he would've confronted me, man-to-man, by now. He knows how I feel about her, and he knows I'm staying right here, while he's miles away. I've met his kind before," he added with a scowl. "He expects *her* to be the strong one, and he'll blame her if I make any progress, even though he's the one who left her here alone to deal with me." Remembering too late that he was speaking to Noelle's father, he winced. "I shouldn't have talked that way in front of you, sir."

"You haven't said anything today I haven't said to myself for months." Braddock's smile was a half-hearted one. "If you were Noelle's father, what would you do?"

"Nothing," Zack admitted. "If you tried to interfere, she'd run off, just like we said. I swear, I want to have daughters myself, but I can see now they'll put me in an early grave. I'll end up spending every minute watching 'em, so they don't meet up with the wrong fella—"

"That was my strategy exactly," Braddock confided. "I never let that girl out of my sight, not even for a minute, in any situation where she might meet a man I didn't approve of. I made one mistake—*one!*—and Prestley latched onto her like a leech." He shook his head in defeat. "If her mother had lived, or if I'd had sons, they could have helped me keep an eye on her, but . . ."

"You have *me* now, sir. The next best thing. I'll set it all right. Five days is a long time," he added mischievously. "I'll take every opportunity to sweet-talk her—"

"Speaking of which, she'll be down in a minute or two. To meet you in the atrium."

"Is that so?" Zack grinned in amazement. This was going to be even easier than he'd predicted!

"She wants to start your lessons right away."

"Huh?"

Braddock came around the desk to clap his guest fondly on the shoulder. "In a way, it's an amazing opportunity, Zack. In most courtships, the girl expects the suitor to read her mind, and figure out on his own what she wants him to do—what pleases her, and what annoys her. But Noelle's going to tell you exactly what she likes." Dropping the bantering tone, he advised, "Either you'll marry Noelle, or you'll marry someone very much like her. I've been studying my files to find you just such a girl. In either case, these lessons will be invaluable to you, so my advice is that you pay attention. And behave," he added sharply. "Do exactly what she says, or it'll be over before it starts."

Zack nodded slowly. It made a lot of sense. He could learn some ways to please her—to see that pretty little smile!—and he could teach *her* a few lessons in the process. After all, what she thought she wanted, and what she *really* needed from a man, might be just a little different.

He felt a familiar stab of anticipation at the thought of seeing her again, and flushed to think her father might have noticed, and might have guessed at the depths of his craving for her. But Braddock's attention had been distracted by the sound of doors opening from the parlor into the atrium, and to Zack's delight, Noelle strolled into sight and settled herself gracefully onto a carved marble bench.

He stared, mesmerized anew by her beauty and grace. Then he shook himself briskly, flashed his host a confident smile, and headed outside for his first lesson in being Noelle Braddock's lover.

Four

"You look beautiful, angel. Did you wear that just for me?"

Noelle wanted to fix him with a haughty glare and simply terminate the lesson, but had to admit her choice of so casual a dress might not have been a wise one. The pink checked fabric and modest scooped neckline had seemed an appropriate choice—pretty but not enticing, feminine but not flirtatious. Now she wished she'd worn her high-necked blouse and stiff gray skirt—one of a dozen outfits she'd considered, then discarded, as she prepared for this all-important first lesson. She had wanted to set a particular tone, but should have known Zack would see anything—perhaps even a suit of armor!—as an invitation for mischief.

It had taken her ten minutes just to decide that her thick black hair should be worn in a loose knot between her shoulders, rather than free around her face or tightly drawn into a no-nonsense bun. That had probably been a mistake, too, she lamented nervously. She should have presented a severe, matronly attitude and appearance.

"Perhaps my father didn't explain the purpose of our meeting—"

"Lessons," he interjected cheerfully. "You're gonna

teach me what a girl like you wants a man to do to her."

Do to her? Noelle wanted to jump up and run away, but instead she simply sighed. "You've done quite enough to me already, Lieutenant. You have effectively repulsed me. I assume you don't want to have the same effect on your next potential bride?"

He studied her for a second, then reached down for her hand and kissed it lightly. "It's a pleasure to see you again, Miss Noelle. Nice weather, wouldn't you say?"

She had to suppress a giggle at his exaggerated manner. "I can't remember so warm a day in April, Lieutenant. Would you like to sit with me for a while?" She arched an eyebrow and added quickly, "I'm trusting you to behave yourself."

When she'd gathered her skirts in closely to make room for him on the bench, he settled himself next to her, a hopeful smile on his face. "This garden suits you, sugar. It's almost as pretty as you, and smells almost as nice."

"Are you suggesting that I have an odor?"

"Sure. I can pick up your scent now almost as quick as—"

"Zack!" She stomped her foot in frustration. "That's lesson number one: do not discuss a girl's scent, unless she's clearly wearing perfume, which I am not."

He grinned as though to say he hadn't been referring to that sort of "scent," and she snapped, "You mustn't discuss scent at all, then. Or her legs, or what she might like you to do *to* her. I assure you, if she's a lady, that sort of talk will cause her to end the courtship."

"Why?"

Noelle took a deep breath. "There's more to lesson

number one, so just listen. You're a very handsome
man—"

"Thank you kindly."

She ignored the playful interruption. "You have many
fine qualities, and I'm confident the bride Father finds
for you will be very impressed, not only when she re-
ceives the description of your heroism and ambition, but
also when she first lays eyes on you. Unfortunately, that
will end when you start talking to her."

"You don't like my voice?"

"It's fine," she corrected. "But you use it to say the
wrong things. Some of the things you said to me yesterday were full-fledged insults, although I know you
didn't mean them that way."

Zack frowned. "I'd never insult you, Noelle."

"Do you remember when I came to your room, and
you said you *knew* I'd come? That was a terrible insult.
It implied that I'm the type of girl who'd visit a man's
bedroom—"

"You *did* visit my bedroom."

"I didn't!" She caught her temper and explained, "I
had no intention of entering your room. You *pulled* me
across the threshold. I simply came to the doorway to
bid you good night and to ensure that I hadn't upset
you at dinner."

"I apologize for what I said."

"You do?"

"Sure. What else?"

She smiled in relief. Either he was a very clever actor,
or he was honestly trying to learn! "Do you remember
when you said there was no shame in changing my mind
about my engagement to Adam? The implication was
that I'm the type of girl who would entertain the attentions of one man when I'm engaged to another. It was

terribly insulting, Zack. I know you didn't mean to disparage me, but you did. And of course, when you spoke to Adam the way you did—"

"Let's leave him out of this," Zack suggested. "I don't need lessons in how to talk to another fella. Just to my bride."

She felt her cheeks begin to burn. "You're absolutely right. I apologize. If it means anything, I didn't approve of the way Adam behaved, either."

"He acted like a jackass," Zack agreed. "But even after he insulted me, I tried to be respectful, because of his age and all—"

"Stop that!" she ordered, noticing too late the emerald sparkle in his eyes. "That isn't funny, Zack. In fact, let's make that lesson number two. If you want to please a girl, don't insult the people she loves."

The twinkle left his eyes for a moment, and she knew the reference had confused him. Was he so certain she didn't love Adam? Why? She wanted to ask him, but knew it would further distract them from their purpose, and so she smiled weakly. "We won't talk about Adam anymore. After all, he's irrelevant to your lessons, isn't he?"

"I never met a more irrelevant fella."

"I meant, he's irrelevant, because we're teaching you how to behave with your bride, and she won't know or care about Adam Prestley. So he's irrelevant to *her*."

"Whatever you say, sugar."

Noelle eyed him sternly. "You're not going to call your bride that, are you? I mean, if 'angel' fits her, you could call her that after you're married, but not before. But 'sugar' simply isn't acceptable under any circumstances."

"Why not? You're sweet, and I like to nibble—"

"For heaven's sake!" She jumped up and put her hands on her hips. "You can call her 'angel,' or 'darling,' or 'dear,' or almost anything *but* 'sugar.' Is that clear?"

"Yes, dear." He grinned mischievously. "What about kissing? Can I do that to her?"

"Eventually." She took a deep breath. "I know you're just teasing me, but honestly, Zack. If you ever want a decent girl to allow you to kiss her, you're going to have to learn to talk to her without insulting her. Don't you see that?"

He nodded as he stood to tower over her. "Let's say you're my bride, and we've gotten to where you're gonna let me kiss you. What exactly should I do then?"

"Well, at the beginning . . ." She paused to steady her voice. "I think it's safest if you ask her permission the first few times. Just in case you've misread the situation, the way you've done with me the last few days."

"Fine." He stepped closer. "Suppose I have her permission. What then?"

Noelle felt her cheeks burn anew. "You don't need lessons in kissing, Zack. You do that quite nicely. That wasn't an invitation," she added, sidestepping just before his lips brushed across hers. "But thank you for making my point. You have no idea when a girl has given you permission to kiss her."

"But I can tell when she wants me to do it, permission or not. Come here, Noelle." He rested his hands on her waist and pulled her gently toward himself. "What about the very first kiss? Once she gives me permission and all. Should it be a quick one, or should I take my time with it? Should I just graze her lips, like this here . . ." He brushed his mouth across hers.

"Or should I linger over it a bit, to get her used to the feel of me?"

She couldn't answer, even though she knew he'd take her silence as "permission." She wanted to feel the second kind of kiss—the lingering kind—despite the possible consequences. These were lessons, after all. How could she advise him if she had no idea how a lingering kiss might feel?

He moistened his lips, then leaned down to her, tasting, as he'd done that morning, then tasting again, with the tip of his tongue this time as well as his lips. She felt her own mouth try to mold itself to his, her lips parting slightly, so that his tongue could graze along the soft, moist inside edges. Then he pressed with enough gentle insistence that she gasped, allowing his tongue to enter her mouth to find its mate. Every move was slow, steady, and gentle—the ways of a man who knew how to coax the best out of dangerous weapons and inexperienced women.

Adam had never, *ever* kissed her this way. He had never lingered, but had chosen either a quick brush of their lips or a firm, escalating sort of attack to which she had never known quite how to respond. His tongue had invaded her once or twice during those kisses, but he'd always stopped before she had been able to be either offended or aroused. Those kisses, thus far, had been for *his* enjoyment, and she hadn't begrudged him that. At least, not until now.

Allowing herself to savor Zack's mouth for one last moment, she pulled free and backed away, then gave him what she hoped was an approving yet distant smile. "That was lovely, Zack. As I said, you kiss very nicely. I don't think we need to spend any more time on this topic."

"You liked it? It seemed that way, but I'm never sure with you," he teased.

"It was fine. However, as I said, you'll never be allowed to do that if you don't first master the art of conversation. And of flattering a girl without insulting her."

"I'm gonna try real hard to be careful about all that," he promised. "What about the third kind of kissing?"

She scanned his eyes for the telltale twinkle, but he seemed sincere, and so she sighed to signal her tentative disapproval. "What exactly do you mean by 'the third kind'?"

"Come here."

"No. You're misbehaving, and this time, my father has promised to listen. He may even be watching," she added, hoping to undermine his obnoxious confidence. Then it occurred to her that her father actually *might* have watched them kiss, and she spun toward the doors of the study in dismay, only to see that he was nowhere in sight. His desk was not visible from where she stood, which meant *she* wasn't visible from his vantage point, either, thank goodness.

Zack was chuckling softly. "He can't see us, sugar— excuse me, I mean, Noelle. But if you want to be real careful . . ." He slipped his arm around her waist and pulled her behind a vine-laced trellis.

"For heaven's sake!" Noelle fixed him with a furious glare as she disentangled herself from his grasp. "Did you honestly think I would engage in some sort of mischief with you in broad daylight?"

"What's the light got to do with it?"

She shook her head in disgust. "That just shows how woefully hopeless you are. Don't you even know that there are some things a girl feels more comfortable doing in the dark? For obvious reasons."

"They aren't obvious to me," he said with a laugh. "Are you talking about being naked, 'cause I wasn't gonna undress you right here in the garden, if that's what's got you so all fired up. I was just gonna kiss you some more."

"This lesson is over."

"Wait." He gave her a rueful smile. "I think you just taught me another valuable lesson. Nighttime is better. Isn't that right?"

She hesitated, then nodded. "Actually, that's a good lesson. Nighttime is more romantic, obviously. And there's another reason couples make love at night in a bedroom, not out in the middle of parks or such, don't you think? There's privacy, for one thing."

"That's true enough. Thank you, Noelle. I'll try to remember that one."

"Really?" She was pleased at the sudden change in his attitude, but knew it wouldn't last, so she added quickly, "That's enough for today."

"Can I ask you one more thing?"

"Fine." She exhaled in tentative disapproval. "What is it?"

"Does Prestley know all these rules?"

"Of course." Smiling to ease the possible insult, she explained, "Adam has traveled all over the world, and has met the finest ladies. Royalty, even. He couldn't have survived in that world if he didn't know exactly how to behave."

"Could be, by the time I'm his age, most of the spark'll be gone from me, too. I don't like to think that way, but if that's how you like it—"

"That's enough."

"I should ask your father. He's the same age—"

"Zack!"

He grinned and grabbed her elbow to prevent her retreat. "I was just having fun with you, angel."

"Yes, I know. It's obnoxious."

"What do you think Prestley's been doing for all these years, him not having a wife'n all? Some of the society fellas in Washington had mistresses for all the real lustful sort of fun. They said they had wives for other reasons: raising babies and hostessing parties and such. Do you think that's how Prestley sees it?"

"I beg your pardon?" She stared in disbelief. "Are you suggesting that Adam has a mistress? And that he'll continue to have one after he marries me?"

"I don't know, sugar. Where I come from, a fella figures a wife's enough, but society fellas see it differently, don't they?"

She bit her lip, knowing that Zack was blatantly attempting to plant doubts, yet also acknowledging the glimmer of truth in it. Adam had undoubtedly had beautiful, sophisticated mistresses over the years. And had those "society fellas" actually said such terrible things to Zack? That their wives were for entertaining guests and raising children? Was that how Adam would see Noelle once the novelty of making love to her—the "surrender" of her innocence—had worn off?

"I didn't mean to worry you," Zack murmured. "I was just having fun with you."

"It's fine."

"He'd be a fool to turn to any other girl if he was married to you. And he doesn't seem like a fool. A jackass, maybe, but not a fool."

"I don't want to discuss it." She relaxed enough to give him a rueful smile. "That's all for today."

"I never did get to ask my last question, Noelle." He stepped closer, resting his hands on her hips again. "Is it wrong for a fella to tell a girl how he feels about her?"

He sounded so vulnerable, she didn't have the heart to answer curtly, and so she explained, "It's not that simple, Zack. Sometimes—" She stopped, surprised to hear her father calling to her from the other side of the trellis. Excusing herself quickly, she returned to the main garden area. "Did you need me, Father?"

He arched an eyebrow, as though noting the fact that she and Zack had sought so private a space, then inclined his head toward the parlor. "Adam's waiting for you inside."

"Adam?"

"Your fiancé," Zack prompted helpfully.

"I *know* who he is, for heaven's sake." She turned toward the parlor and could see Adam just inside the door, watching with undisguised interest. Summoning her most confident smile, she excused herself and hurried into the parlor.

As though imitating her father, Adam arched an eyebrow. *"That* was a fascinating scene."

"Was it?" She pecked him on the cheek. "I wasn't expecting you."

"Obviously."

Annoyed despite a twinge of guilt, she challenged, "What is it you're accusing me of?"

"Not a thing, of course. I trust you completely."

"Because I'm naïve and innocent?"

"Pardon?"

"I'm not so naïve I don't know about men like you and their mistresses," she sniffed, pleased that the subject had been changed so easily.

"I beg your pardon?"

"Are you saying you've never had one?"

He pursed his lips, as though considering the appropriate response; then he shrugged his shoulders. "I'm thirty-eight years old, and I've never been married. Suffice it to say, I haven't been a monk. Why do you ask?"

"Do you have one now?"

"No."

"And when we're married?"

He chuckled in relief. "Is that what's bothering you? You'll be pleased to hear that one of the reasons I'm marrying *you* is so I'll never need a mistress again." He took her hands in his own and grinned. "They're much more expensive than a wife, believe me."

"Were you in love with any of them?"

"Noelle . . ." He pulled her to a plush green sofa and urged her to take a seat. Then he knelt before her and presented her with a slender black velvet jewel case he'd pulled from inside his coat. "I've never loved a woman the way I love you. Will you wear this to Clara Moore's party on Wednesday night? As my apology for all the women I spent time with while I was waiting for you to come along?"

She flushed and opened the box, then gasped at its contents, a diamond-laden necklace and matching earrings. "Oh, Adam! I've never seen anything grander."

He rose to sit beside her, then took the string of jewels and fastened it around her neck. "Exquisite," he assured her. "Am I forgiven?"

"You haven't done anything wrong, and I adore this gift. But Father will never—"

"He'll make an exception if you insist," Adam interrupted. "We're to be married in less than a week, are we not? It's time he began to accept my role in your

life, and *this,* my darling, is the role I intend to play
forever. Showering you with jewels, and anything else
your heart desires."

"I can't accept expensive gifts until after we're married. That is my father's rule, and I simply can't defy
it, although I would dearly love to wear these to Clara's
party." With an apologetic smile, she suggested, "Will
you offer it again, on our wedding night? I assure you
I'll find a special way to thank you."

She turned her face up for his kiss, and was pleased
when his lips were as gentle and respectful as Zack's
had been. Determined to kiss him the way she'd kissed
her student, she draped her arms around his neck and
opened her mouth enough to encourage his tongue to
enter. He didn't hesitate, and while she wasn't quite prepared for the taste of stale cigar and whiskey, she forced
herself to ignore all that, and to enjoy the feel of his
arms tightening around her.

Then he released her and marveled, "I'll bring you
jewels every night of our marriage, if that's the way you
intend to thank me."

Noelle flushed. "You won't need to bring me jewels.
I'll kiss you because I love you."

He smiled and touched her cheek. "You're so innocent. I know it bothers you when I say that, but—"

"It doesn't bother me. I just worry over what will
happen when I'm no longer young and innocent and
naïve."

"I'll just divorce you and find another girl."

"Adam!"

He grinned fondly. "For the moment, I love you for
your innocence. I suppose one day, I'll love you for
your wisdom."

Noelle smiled and squeezed his hand. "I like that. Can you imagine it? Me, brimming with wisdom?"

"Actually, no. But I have confidence you will eventually exude it."

"And as for innocence, perhaps that's a quality I'll have forever," she suggested carefully.

"Not if I have anything to say about it."

She flushed under his teasing gaze. "I don't mean untouched. I mean pure."

"Aren't they the same?"

She frowned, and then on impulse tightened her grip on his hand and dragged him to the staircase and up to her room. Her father would be aghast at such conduct, but she suddenly needed proof that Adam's interest in her wasn't based solely on her "innocence" and tender years. Somehow, she was certain his reaction to the doll collection would indicate whether that silly fear had any real foundation.

"Darling, are you sure?"

"Step inside, sir," she insisted. "I want you to see the room I grew up in."

"Well, then . . ." After one last nervous glance about himself, he crossed the threshold and immediately burst into laughter. "I'm surprised you'd allow me to see this. It's the single most absurd sight I've ever seen."

"Pardon?" She glared in warning. "What is absurd about a doll collection?"

He grinned with unrepentant glee. "You aren't planning on bringing these to Mother's house, are you? She'll send you straight off to a lunatic asylum."

"Mother's house?" Noelle frowned. "I've never heard you call it that before."

"Don't try to change the subject. We're discussing your father, not my mother."

"We are?"

"All this . . ." A broad sweep of his arm encompassed the window seat and bed, then moved to the floor-to-ceiling shelves that served as a home for close to two hundred pretty dolls. "I've always known he indulges you, but this! If I needed proof that he wanted to keep you here—his little girl, safe and sound and all his forever—this is it."

"And now you want me to be *your* little girl?"

"I beg your pardon?"

"I'm half your age, Adam! You could easily have had a daughter my age by now if you'd gotten married at the appropriate time."

He stared in disbelief. "I'm beginning to think an asylum might just be in order. What in blazes are you talking about?" Before she could answer, he stepped to within inches of her and growled, "If my age is a source of concern for you, you might have mentioned it sooner."

"Your age isn't the problem. It's mine that concerns me."

"Well, there's not much we can do about that, is there? Unless you'd like to wait five or ten years. Of course, I'll be older by then, too, so I'm not sure you'll find it any more reassuring."

"I know I'm not making any sense—"

"You're making perfect sense. This is about Dane, am I right? It has nothing to do with birthdates or dolls. We never once quarreled before he arrived, and now, it's all we do."

"This has nothing to do with the lieutenant," she declared, but she knew it was a lie. None of this confusion would have surfaced if Zack hadn't given her someone with whom to compare Adam. Zack was young, while

Adam was not; Zack was simple, while Adam was complicated and sophisticated; Zack smelled and tasted as though he'd just bathed in a cool, bubbling brook, while Adam smelled of brandy and cigars and cologne. Zack was the son her father had always wanted, while Adam was the scoundrel her father had always feared would come and steal her away from him. . . .

"The choice is a simple one, Noelle," Adam was informing her curtly. "Do you want to please your father? Or do you want to please yourself?"

"Myself," she insisted weakly.

"Well, I'm the man you chose, am I not? And it was a wise choice by any standard. To be quite frank, Dane is a buffoon who doesn't have the skills or the resources to even consider marrying a beautiful woman like yourself."

"I don't want to talk about Zack. This has nothing to do with him," she repeated stubbornly.

"Why are we quarreling, then? Because I teased you about a roomful of dolls?"

Noelle sighed in agreement. She had feared Adam would admire the dolls, as a symbol of his child bride. Instead, his reaction had forcefully negated that silly notion, yet still she had been offended. Why? Why was it that suddenly the poor man's every word and deed offended her? Was she looking for a reason to break their engagement?

"Forgive me, Adam. I know I'm behaving irrationally. I suppose I'm more upset over Father's reaction to this marriage than I've dared to admit."

"There!" He nodded vigorously. "That's what we should be discussing then, isn't it?"

"What is there to discuss?"

"Darling . . ." He took her into his arms and cra-

dled her against his chest. "I'm not asking you to
choose between myself and your father. I'm just asking
you to be strong, for a few more days. Once we're
married, I predict he'll come to respect me the same
way I respect him. I'll do my best to make certain that
happens. But ultimately it's up to him. You see that,
don't you?"

"Yes, I suppose so." She wrapped her arms around
his chest. "It's all so confusing. But I agree wholeheartedly that we must stop this awful quarreling." Peeking
up at him, she asked cautiously, "When Father's ready
to appreciate our marriage, will you be ready to forgive
him for resisting it? I mean, you don't hate him, do
you?"

"I've told you before, I have the highest regard for
his success in the business world, and I'm grateful to
him for having raised such a wonderful daughter." With
a sly grin, he teased, "Can you say the same about my
mother?"

"I'm sure she can be charming when she wants to
be," Noelle said with a sigh. "She just hasn't wanted
to be charming to *me* yet."

"Then we both have something to look forward to.
Perhaps when we present them with their first grand-
child, they'll abandon their prejudices."

"That's a lovely thought, but I'm afraid your mother
will always see me as 'that matchmaker's daughter.' "

He shrugged. "She has her prejudices, as I said. But
so does your father. I suspect he feels intimidated by
my family's wealth and social status. Not that he should
allow that to bother him. He's done quite well, in his
own way. He has nothing to be ashamed of."

"I should think not," Noelle murmured. "Really,

Adam. Such things as wealth and social success don't matter to my father."

"I'm sure they don't. On the other hand, he knows I can offer those things to you, and so he is understandably jealous."

"But he—" She stopped herself and smiled sheepishly. "We have the rest of our lives to have this particular argument. For now, it's time you met the girls."

"The . . . ? Oh, no." He recoiled in feigned horror. *"All* of them?"

"Every one. I expect you to be charming, Mr. Prestley."

"I can only pray your father discovers I'm in here and throws me out before too long."

"That's quite enough." With a mischievous smile, she reached for a delicate porcelain baby and began the introductions.

"I thought yesterday was special, but danged if today wasn't even better." Zack picked up a brush and began to vigorously groom Mercury's chestnut coat. "She keeps telling me it isn't gonna happen. And her pappy's been warning me, too. But I've never been so sure of anything in my life. I'm gonna marry that girl, Merc. You should see the way she kisses me. It's enough to make a man believe in miracles."

He chuckled as he remembered the scolding she'd given him in the garden. Not because she didn't want to kiss him, but because she was too shy to do it in the daylight. It didn't make sense, but it sure made him feel special. Like it was *him* teaching *her,* not the other way around. Not that he wasn't respecting her lessons, though. He was determined not to call her "sugar" so often—at least until they were married—even though she was as sweet as she could be. And if she needed to meet in the dark, in her bedroom for a while, that was fine, too. He liked it in there, with all her pretty dolls watching them.

Then he frowned, remembering how jealous he'd felt when she'd taken that Prestley fellow upstairs with her. She oughtn't trust him the way she did, but since she'd left the door open, Zack had resisted the urge to burst into the room and rescue her. And Russ Braddock had taken care of the matter in that firm, authoritative way he had—never raising his voice, but letting the engaged couple know he expected them to be downstairs directly. And Prestley had left right after that, without staying for supper, so Zack figured the situation was no worse than it had been before. And hopefully, it was better.

"I think she's starting to see she shouldn't waste all her spunk and sweetness on a pompous jackass like that," he told his horse confidently. "Now all I gotta do is convince her how good it would feel if she'd just relax and let nature take its course between us. She tries not to laugh when I tease her, and not to let me see how excited she gets when I kiss her. But if you could see how she blushes and stammers and gets all warm and nervous, you'd know. That girl wants me to talk her out of marrying that fella, and *into* marrying me."

When Mercury tossed his mane and whinnied, Zack grinned. "It's more complicated than that for people, Merc. I've gotta find just the right words, starting tonight. Like telling her about the pretty babies we could make together. Little girls in pigtails, playing with their dolls. And the boys—big, strong ones, that're good with horses and rifles and women, just like their old man." He laughed in sheepish self-mockery. "I guess it won't matter how many girls I sweet-talked into bed in the old days, if I can't get this one to come around, right? She's the only one who matters now, so I'd better get inside and see if she's gone to bed yet.

"It looks like most of the lights are out, so that's a good sign. Good night, pardner." Slapping his horse on the rear, he gathered up his gear, then headed up toward the house to romance Noelle in the dark, just like she'd asked him so sweetly to do.

It didn't seem possible that the wedding day had arrived, yet there was no mistaking the fact that Noelle was in a bridal gown, walking down the staircase of her father's house toward a roomful of well-dressed guests. None of them seemed to notice her, though, which seemed odd to her under the circumstances. And where was her father? Shouldn't he be standing at the foot of the stairs, waiting to escort her to Adam?

She scanned face after face, but each person was a stranger. Where were her friends and acquaintances? Even the servants were unfamiliar!

Something was terribly wrong, she decided nervously. Her skin was crawling with discomfort, her dress felt heavy, and her shoes were thick and clumsy. Where were her pretty satin slippers? She looked down, and realized with a start that she was wearing a drab, lackluster beige gown, rather than the beautiful creation Winifred had sewn so lovingly. Nothing was right, and her heart began to pound as she searched more frantically for her father.

"Noelle?"

She spun gratefully toward Zack's voice, and was pleased to see her handsome houseguest in full dress uniform. Medals and ribbons decorated his chest, while a gleaming silver sword hung proudly by his side.

She murmured his name, breathless suddenly at the nearness of him.

"Are you awake, sugar?" he asked softly.

"Am I. . . ? Oh! Of course!" She grinned in sheepish relief. "This is a dream." Draping her arms around his neck, she murmured, "Thank you for figuring it out. I was so confused."

"Wake up," he insisted. "I want to talk to you."

"I'm so glad you're here." She raised herself onto tiptoes, despite the stiffness of her shoes, and covered his mouth with her own. On impulse, she urged her tongue between his lips, finding his and playing with it shamelessly. Why not? It was a dream, and they were with strangers, and he tasted so absolutely clean and fresh and naughty!

Through the coarse layers of her skirt, she could feel his manhood as it bulged against her, and she giggled helplessly. "Now I *know* this is a dream."

"Why's that, sugar?"

"Because . . ." She reached down to stroke him with curious, admiring fingers. "Your manliness feels *sooo* big—"

"Noelle! Wake up!"

Startled, she pulled herself out of the dream and opened her eyes to see Zack staring down at her, a mixture of mortification and fascination in his handsome expression.

"Dang, sugar, that was one heck of a dream you were having there," he told her, brushing a lock of hair from her damp cheek as he spoke.

"Zack?"

"I didn't want to wake you, but I figured you'd be mad as a hornet if I let you keep saying those things to me."

"You could hear me?" she whimpered. Then she noticed for the first time that he was snuggled fully against her and she wailed, "What are you *doing* here?"

"Trying to wake you up, so I could talk to you."

"Oh . . ." She grimaced, then wriggled until she was almost sitting. "It was the strangest dream, Zack. I was at my wedding, but all the guests were strangers. They didn't even seem to notice I was there. Father wasn't anywhere, and neither were any of our friends." She sighed as she admitted, "You shouldn't have come to my room, but I'm truly glad you did. It was turning into a nightmare before you got there. I mean, here."

"I wouldn't have missed it," he teased, nuzzling her neck gently. "You kissed me real nice."

"Did I?" She flushed as she remembered the dream kiss. Hopefully, the real one had been less scandalous. "You'd better leave, Zack."

"I've got some good news for you first."

"Really? What is it?"

A mischievous grin spread from his lips to the twinkle in his eyes. "In the dream, you figured you were imagining the size of me, even after you touched it, but—"

"Zachary Dane! *Get out!*"

He jumped from the bed, laughing so hard he almost seemed to double over from the force of it. "You're the wildest little she-cat I ever did meet, do you know that?"

"Go!" She grabbed the nearest doll and hurled it at him, hitting him square in the chest.

"Dang, sugar. Our babies are gonna have perfect aim." With a cheerful wink, he picked up the doll, placed it carefully back on the bed, and headed quickly into the hall.

For the first time in her life, Noelle craved a lock on her bedroom door. Of course, if she'd had one, Zack wouldn't have rescued her from the dream. But could that awful wedding have been any more horrid than this! Not only had she complimented a man's physical endowment, she had actually handled it!

I don't know who's more depraved, you or him, she chastised herself. *Stop thinking about it! Or if you must, think of Adam's.*

But of course, she had never felt Adam's. He was too much of a gentleman. And by the time she did touch it, it would be too late if—

If what? She felt almost hysterical at the traitorous thought. *Stop thinking about it! Go back to sleep.*

A gentle knocking at the door, accompanied by the sound of her father's worried voice, steadied her, and she hurried to admit him. "Father? Is something wrong?"

"I thought I heard someone shouting," he said with an apologetic grimace. "Since I've been so remiss lately, I wanted to check on you. Did I wake you?"

"I had a nightmare," she explained. "I probably called out during it. I'm sorry I woke you."

His smile was soft and loving. "Hop up into bed, now." He waited until she was under her covers, then sat beside her, handing her several of her softest dolls to cuddle. "Do you want to tell me about it?"

She couldn't tell him it was about the wedding. And

she didn't dare mention Zack and his visit. Not when, once again, she had encouraged his bizarre attentions. "It didn't make much sense, Father. Try not to worry. I'm fine now."

"Of course you are." He kissed her cheek lightly. "Sweet dreams, Noelle. If you can't get back to sleep, just knock on my door, and we'll go downstairs and have a game of chess."

"Father?"

"Yes?"

"It's natural, isn't it? To have doubts, even if you know you're in love?"

"Yes, sweetheart," he assured her firmly. "It's perfectly natural. You're making the biggest decision of your life, and you're afraid you'll make a mistake. But if you listen to your heart, I promise you won't go wrong."

"My heart says I should marry Adam."

"Well, then, it's settled. Try not to worry about it any more tonight." Touching her cheek, he added carefully, "Perhaps the lessons with Zack weren't such a good idea, after all."

"They were a terrible idea," she confirmed. "But fortunately, they're almost over. One last lesson tomorrow, and then I'm afraid I'm going to ask him not to speak to me at all until after the wedding."

"Do you want me to ask him to move to a hotel?"

She stared in surprise. "You'd do that?"

"Of course."

"It's not necessary, but thank you." She hugged him and insisted honestly, "I feel so much better. I'm sure my bad dream won't come back."

"Let's hope a beautiful one comes in its place." Her

father pulled the covers up to her chin. "Good night, sweetheart."

"Good night, Father." Resisting an impulse to hop out of bed and prop a chair against the door, she snuggled into her pillow and drifted easily off to sleep.

Five

After a good night's rest, Noelle was able to laugh at herself for the way she'd behaved in her dream with Zack. Wasn't it natural for a bride to be curious about the male anatomy so close to her wedding night? It might have been nicer had she fondled Adam, but wasn't that the way of dreams? It didn't mean anything, or at least, it didn't mean what she was certain Lieutenant Dane thought it meant. And she wasn't about to feel guilty over it. He shouldn't have come to her room, and now, in the clear light of day, she would explain it all to him, and that would be the end of their ill-fated lessons.

She had asked Edward to send him to the atrium to meet her, and this time, she was dressed appropriately, from the stiff no-nonsense gray skirt to the tight bun into which she'd gathered her hair—a style that made her appear stern and unapproachable, both of which she intended to be.

"Good morning, angel. You sure look pretty," a voice teased from behind her, and she turned coolly toward the parlor doors.

"Hello, Lieutenant. Thank you for coming."

"My pleasure. I've been wanting to talk to you—"

"I'll do the talking, if you don't mind." She smoothed

her skirt carefully, then began. "I was very disappointed in you last night, Lieutenant."

"You didn't seem disappointed."

"You know what I mean. It was wrong of you to come to my room."

"You said you were glad I did," he reminded her cheerfully. "You said more than that, too. I woke you up to keep you from saying or doing—"

"I remember!" She took a deep breath. "I appreciate that."

"It was gentlemanlike, don't you think?"

"Yes," she agreed through gritted teeth. "But it was still wrong to come to my room uninvited. That's the point I'm trying to make."

"I thought you invited me," he explained with a shrug. "You said you'd feel more comfortable with me in the dark in a bedroom—"

"I said no such thing! I was talking about you and your bride. Honestly, Zack." She groaned in disgust. "If you ever want a decent girl to marry you, you'd better start paying attention. Everything that happened last night was wrong. Especially—well, you know especially what. I want you to promise me you won't suggest any such thing to the bride Father finds you."

A flicker of concern troubled his emerald eyes; then he managed a wary smile. "You mean, not while I'm courting her, right? Once we're married, we can do what we like, can't we?"

Noelle was about to agree that that was a sensible rule; then she had a wicked impulse and said instead, "Obviously, once you're married, you can make love to her. But there will still be rules, Zack. Surely you know that?"

"What sort of rules?"

She had to struggle to maintain her stern expression. "Don't expect her to remove her nightie, or to otherwise uncover her breasts. And never ask her to touch you in depraved ways—"

"*You* touched me."

"In a *dream*. I was a naughty girl in that dream," she confessed solemnly. "Don't confuse *her* with *me*. I can assure you, Adam Prestley never would. He'd kill himself before he'd ask to see me naked, or suggest that I touch him in objectionable ways. That's what I love about him. He respects me."

"Dang." Zack's eyes were wide with disbelief. "No wonder those society fellas need mistresses." Then he visibly pulled himself together and insisted, "You're wrong about all this, sugar. You'll change your mind once you get used to the idea—"

"Don't be absurd. If you don't believe *me*, ask Father. I'm sure he'll tell you the same thing. He never made those sorts of lustful demands on my mother. There's a difference between that and respectful lovemaking." She gave him her strictest glare. "Do you want to marry a decent woman or not?"

"I was just asking myself the same thing," he muttered under his breath. "I sure hope you're wrong about all this."

She turned away, unable to keep from grinning at the sight of him, humbled and subdued. It was as though he'd lost his best friend, or at least, his best fantasy. She knew she should reassure him, but wasn't this just what he needed? To understand that he had to modify his behavior? Admittedly, not to the extent of her mischievous misinformation, but at least now, he might not be so brash and overconfident when he met his bride.

Father will reassure him, she told herself gleefully.

*But in the meantime, it's what Zack deserves, for the
way he confused you last night. For the suggestions he
made, and the thoughts he made you think. . . .*

If only she had had those thoughts and dreams about
Adam, she wouldn't have experienced even a twinge of
discomfort over them. She knew that such urges and
actions were natural, and that, within the bounds of love
and matrimony, they should be a source of joy and mutual appreciation, rather than shame or embarrassment.
Her father had taken the time, years earlier, to explain
the mechanics of a wedding night to her, and thereafter,
he had flushed and stammered but had dutifully answered a barrage of precocious questions, assuring her
that true love was an infallible guide through such matters.

*Zack has done his best to undermine your faith in
that,* she reminded herself. *That's why he mentions
Adam's age so much. To make you think he might not
have the stamina or virility or interest that a younger
man might have. That's why he mentioned the subject
of mistresses, too—all to make you have doubts about
your wedding night. It's only fair that you've turned the
tables, and given Zack a doubt or two. Father will scold
you for lying, but it will be worth it to teach this pest
a lesson. They say revenge is sweet, and this is the proof
of it, silly as it is.*

Turning back to face him, she smiled and touched
his shoulder. "I'm pleased to see you take all this to
heart, Zack. I honestly want you to be happy, and to
find true love. The key is to remember one cardinal
rule: love without respect is simply lust. And your idea
of lovemaking is *very* disrespectful."

"You're wrong, Noelle. You're the one who should

talk to your father. Whether you marry me or Prestley, these—these notions of yours are dead wrong."

"Father's the one who taught all this to me."

"Huh?"

"Ask him." She bit her lip to suppress a traitorous laugh, then proceeded earnestly. "He'll explain it all very gently and without judgment, the same way he explains it to the brides when they have strange ideas. Some of the poor things weren't raised to be ladies, you know. They think it's fine to be naked and wanton, but Father helps them to see that there's no room for that in a decent marriage. And Father only arranges decent marriages, so you'd best learn the rules, too." She pretended to stifle a yawn. "Winnie will be here soon, to go over the final menu for the wedding with Alice and me. Do you mind if we put off the rest of our lesson until later?"

"There's more?" he demanded. "It's not enough that a man can't have a lick of fun with his own bride?"

"You can kiss her. And have a baby with her. And every night, for the rest of your life, you'll fall asleep in each other's arms. Isn't that beautiful?" She patted his scowling face. "Once you've thought it through, you'll be ashamed you ever had disrespectful thoughts about her."

"I still don't see—" He broke off and shrugged. "Looks like that dressmaker lady's here. You oughta go and meet with her, while I go see how Merc's doing. I'll see you later."

"Think about what you've learned," she repeated cheerfully, and was amused when he scowled again. No attempts to kiss her good-bye, or call her "sugar," or any such mischief. For the moment, at least, she had managed to curb his exuberant attentions. She could only hope that some of the effects would linger, even after her father reassured him.

Or more likely, once he knows the truth, he'll find you and try to have his way with you from pure relief, she warned herself. The thought of Zack teaching *her* a lesson made her tingle, and she had to reprimand herself sternly and repeatedly as she made her way to the parlor for her meeting with Winifred.

She didn't see her guest for the rest of the day, and by dinnertime, she could scarcely walk down a hall without her heart pounding for fear he'd surprise her with a lustful attack. Realizing too late that her little joke had been a dangerous one, she was completely on edge by the time she dashed down the stairs and into the dining room, fully expecting both Zack and her father to tease her mercilessly through the entire meal.

"Where's Zack?" she asked nervously, noticing that only two places had been set.

"He went hunting," her father explained. "Something about too much beef and not enough rabbit. I told him Alice could buy rabbit downtown, but he insisted it wouldn't be the same."

"And so he went hunting?"

Braddock nodded. "There was something on his mind. I just assumed it was about you, since it always is with him."

Noelle shrugged and took a sip of water.

"Did you and he have a lesson today?"

"A short one. Winnie was here most of the day, tending to last-minute arrangements."

"Three short days, and then you'll be Mrs. Adam Prestley." Braddock heaved a weary sigh. "I imagine

Zack's finally trying to come to terms with that. You've been very generous and patient with him, sweetheart. I can't tell you how proud it's made me."

She squirmed and avoided his gaze, determined not to confess despite the twinges of guilt his praise was inflicting. "Winnie brought the rest of my trousseau today, Father. You should see the lovely outfits she designed for me to wear on the ship. I'll show them all to you after dinner."

"I'm looking forward to it."

"I thought she'd bring my wedding gown, too, but she says there are some last-minute details that need attention."

"It's just as well." Her father chuckled. "I'm not sure Zack can survive witnessing another fitting. We'll have to be sure he's hunting again when that time comes."

"Any luck finding him a bride?"

Braddock smiled. "You'd be surprised how few women have your particular combination of attributes. I left some files on my desk for you to look through, though. I thought, with the lessons and all, you might have some new insight that could be valuable."

Noelle bit back a smile of her own. If Zack were there, she had a feeling he'd have only one requirement for his prospective mate: that she have no rules at all. And no clothes either. The poor dear! Why hadn't he turned to her father, as she'd suggested? Why on earth go hunting at a time like this? Was this how backwoods heroes mourned lost fantasies?

She felt a surge of sympathy for him and gave her father a hopeful smile. "You'll wait up for him, won't you, Father? It sounds as though he needs someone to talk to."

Her father beamed. "Again, I couldn't be more proud. It's sweet of you to care so much about our guest."

"If you don't talk to him, he'll come to my room and wake *me* up." She laughed lightly. "It's simple self-preservation."

Braddock chuckled. "Let's hope we've seen the last of that sort of behavior. He may even be willing to look through the files himself by tomorrow. I've set aside a few that claim to be excellent cooks, in hopes that might pique his interest."

"He does love to eat," Noelle agreed.

"And he's anxious to have lots of children, so I've identified cooks who also have child-rearing experience, either by profession or because they came from large families, themselves."

Noelle frowned. "You make it sound as though—" She coughed lightly, then sent him an apologetic smile. "You've gone from finding someone just like me to finding my exact opposite. But I suppose you're right. Those should be the qualities that matter. Not long legs or all that nonsense."

"If I didn't know better, I'd say you were jealous," her father teased.

Noelle grinned sheepishly. For just a moment, it had been true. After three straight days of being adored by Zack, it was humbling to realize that, had they actually married, he might have found her woefully lacking in certain key areas. "It's fortunate that the Prestleys have servants," she quipped. "Can you imagine me trying to raise a family with *my* dismal skills?"

Her father raised a glass of wine and assured her solemnly, "It would be the luckiest family in the world. Anyone can learn to cook and change diapers, Noelle. You have something much more valuable. A heart brimming with love, and a spirit that cannot be repressed. Do you have any idea how proud that makes me feel?"

Her eyes brimmed with tears as she touched her own glass to his. "I'm the daughter you raised me to be, sir. Now let's stop this foolishness and eat our delicious meal before it gets cold."

"Good evening, miss."

Noelle smiled at Alice, a reserved but kindhearted middle-aged woman who had worked as cook and housekeeper for the Braddock family for the last three years. "Good evening. Tonight's dinner was especially delicious."

"Thank you, miss." The woman returned to her scouring.

"Alice?"

"Yes, miss?"

"Was it very difficult to prepare?"

Alice stopped her housework and turned her full attention to Noelle. "Not really. Why do you ask?"

Noelle hesitated before asking, "I suppose rabbit is very difficult?"

That brought a smile to the cook's face. "Don't worry, miss. I won't ruin the lieutenant's meal."

"Of course you won't," she assured the servant hastily. "I was just wondering; how can one ensure the meat will be tender? I suppose you mustn't overcook it; is that the trick? But I suppose you mustn't *undercook* it either, so . . . How does one know?"

"You're asking me to teach you to cook?" Alice beamed with delight. "I'd love to do that, Miss Noelle, although . . . well, I don't imagine you'll ever have the need."

"My mother used to do the cooking around here, Alice. Did you know that?"

"Yes, miss."

"And I used to play in here with her, but unfortunately, I didn't pay much attention. I'd set up the dolls on the preparation table; they were more interesting to me than what Mother was doing. And she probably thought she had years in which to teach me. . . ."

"I've heard what a fine lady she was. Edward tells us you remind him of her."

"He says that?" Noelle flushed with pride. "How sweet. I don't look at all like her, though. I look like my grandmother on Father's side. But Father says I have Mother's smile and her laugh, and I like that." She sighed aloud, then persisted. "So? You'll teach me? You'll need to start at the very beginning, I'm afraid."

"There's a lot to learn," Alice agreed. "And you won't be living here much longer. But I can teach you when you visit." She hesitated, then asked carefully, "Do you suppose Mr. Prestley will approve?"

"Why wouldn't he? It might benefit him one day, don't you suppose?" Noelle suggested playfully. "He and I could be on a long voyage, and the ship might begin to sink, and we'd jump onto a life raft and row to a desert island and be marooned for the rest of our lives—which wouldn't be very long if I didn't know how to cook."

Alice laughed. "Let's hope that never happens."

"It's best to be prepared." Noelle smiled. "Do you know the Prestley cook, Alice? Do you suppose she'd welcome me into the kitchen the way you do?"

"I've met her, and I'm sure she'd welcome you. But the way I hear it—"

Noelle waited for a moment before urging, "Tell me, Alice. Please?"

"Well, *Mrs.* Prestley—the *old* Mrs. Prestley—won't approve. She and her family don't mingle with the staff there. It's different from here, miss. They communicate through the butler, with never a kind word—or rather, never a social word, I meant to say. I know one of the maids real well, and she . . ." Alice flushed. "She tells me it's different there. Formal. You'll have to watch yourself at first, Noelle. See how the mother and sister act, and follow their lead."

Noelle moistened her lips, then asked as casually as she could manage, "What do they say about *Mr.* Prestley?"

"Nothing."

"And what do *you* think of him?"

Alice shrugged. "I don't know him, miss. He hasn't said more than ten words to me in my life."

"That's not true," Noelle protested. "I introduced you to him myself, and we had a long chat."

"He said, 'How do you do.' And then *you* chatted with me. And then he said, 'Nice to have met you.' " Alice had been counting the words on her fingers, and now announced, "Nine."

"And since then, he's never spoken to you?"

"It's not his way," Alice explained, adding carefully, "You made him uncomfortable, bringing him in here at all. He went along with it, to please you, so you shouldn't fault him. At least, not for that. But you should be careful how you act when you go there to live."

"I'll talk to anyone I want!" she declared. "They'd better not criticize me for it, either."

"They won't criticize *you*, miss. At least not directly."

"Oh . . ." Noelle felt her cheeks begin to burn. "You're saying I'll cause trouble for the staff?"

"They have their orders. You won't want to interfere with that." Alice gave her a forced smile. "You'll be too busy to worry about all that. The Prestleys have dinner parties every week, and they're traveling more than they're at home. It will be an exciting life; you'll see."

The conversation was interrupted by a sharp yelp from the corner, and Noelle whirled, then smiled sadly and hurried across the room to kneel before an old retriever, sound asleep on a huge, soft pillow. Ruffling the dog's lustrous red-gold coat, she murmured, "Are you having a nightmare, Copper? Is it about my wedding, like the one I had?" The dog whined softly and opened his eyes; then his tail began to thump the floor with a burst of vigor that belied his fifteen years on earth.

Noelle nuzzled him happily. "I haven't visited you in ages, have I, boy? Can you forgive me? I've been so busy with the wedding plans and with civilizing our guest." Stroking him lovingly, she asked Alice, "How has he been doing these days? Is his limp improving?"

"It's worse by the day, miss. It's gotten so he can't even make it up and down the steps to the yard, to do his business. Edward put a ramp off the service porch, but you can see it still hurts poor old Copper. Of course, these days he hardly eats or drinks anything, so he doesn't need to go out often. Still, it's a pity to watch."

"He hasn't been eating?"

"Your father says it's for the best. It's nature's way of bringing the end before the pain grows too strong."

"Oh, dear." She rubbed the dog's hip gently. "It best that Megan didn't take him West with her when she went. I'm sure they miss one another, but she was right to leave him with us."

"Copper loves it here," Alice assured her. "It's a fine place to live out his days."

The dog had dozed off again, and so Noelle stood and brushed her skirt with her hands, then insisted, "It's time for my first lesson, Alice. What shall it be?"

"Boiling water."

Noelle pretended to glare. "Do you suppose I'm so ignorant I can't even do that?"

"Do you know the difference between boiling and simmering?" Alice asked with a smile. "If you wanted to poach an egg, would you know how to begin?"

"I can make a cup of tea." Noelle laughed. "But an egg is definitely beyond me. I'm as helpless about cooking as the lieutenant is about women."

Alice grinned. "He's been telling us such grand stories about all that. He even had Edward laughing, if you can believe it!" She seemed to notice Noelle's dismay and added hastily, "He mocks himself, miss. Never you. He worships you, as I'm sure you know." She bit her lip in clear distress. "You won't be angry with him, will you? I shouldn't have said anything. He only does it to entertain us while we're working. And usually, his stories have nothing to do with you at all."

"He tells you about the war?"

"No, miss. About growing up. About his brothers, and his parents."

"He has brothers?"

"Had two of them. One died in a hunting accident while the lieutenant was away at the war, and the other was shot in a battle. You didn't know that?"

"I don't know much about him," Noelle mused. "I think I've heard him say his mother isn't alive—"

"His father's gone, too." Alice sighed, then added brightly, "But he'll never be alone, that one. He's made some good friends over the years, from the sound of it. And now he has Mr. Braddock, too. And in a way, he has the rest of us, too. I mean, the servants," she added quickly. "Not you. Even though—" She caught herself again and flushed.

"Even though I'm the one he wants. That's what you were about to say, isn't it?"

The cook hesitated, then reached across to pat her hand. "It'll all be over soon, Noelle. In a few days, you'll be married. We've all been worried about you—the strain of planning the wedding. All the decisions, all the changes. But it'll all be over soon."

"It will be a relief," Noelle agreed. "It's been a strain, just as you said. I suppose that's normal for any bride."

Alice shrugged. "For me and my husband, it was simple. Young, poor, and in love. I suppose that was a blessing. Of course," she added lightly, "he didn't deserve me, as it turns out. They never do, do they?"

"Absolutely not," On impulse, Noelle leaned forward and pecked the cook's cheek. "Good night, Alice. Go home to him now, and we'll start my lessons tomorrow. And, Alice?"

"Yes, miss?"

"Don't tell Lieutenant Dane about the cooking. He'd tease me without mercy if he knew."

Alice's eyes twinkled as she nodded in agreement, and Noelle knew the woman was having fond thoughts of their boisterous guest. Somehow, in three short days, he had managed to endear himself to the staff—even Edward!—while Adam hadn't even bothered to try over ten long months. Not that she blamed Adam for that, of course. It was the way he'd been raised. The way her children would be raised if she wasn't careful.

And of course, she'd be careful. It all just seemed so complicated suddenly. Wasn't anything simple anymore?

Young, poor, and in love . . . She smiled wistfully as she climbed the back staircase to her room. Why did that suddenly sound so right?

Zack let himself into the kitchen through the back door, where he patted Copper and deposited his game before making himself presentable. He had hoped the entire household would be asleep, but the study was brightly lit, which probably meant his well-meaning host was doing some hunting of his own—for a bride for a lonely soldier.

A decent girl who won't be naked with her own husband? Zack grinned in self-mocking amusement. The feisty little Noelle had really worried him with that one, but hunting had cleared his head, and he'd decided it would simply be his honor to convince her that his way of making love was not only decent, but irresistible.

Still, it bothered him that her father had apparently been the source of some odd notions. Undoubtedly, she had just misunderstood him. After all, how easy could it be for a father to talk to his little girl about such things? If that was the case, Zack was hoping he could convince Russell Braddock to have another talk with the misinformed bride, so that Zack's job would be easier.

He watched from the doorway for a moment before clearing his throat and greeting his host.

"Zack!" Russell Braddock jumped to his feet and extended his hand in welcome. "I was beginning to wonder if you'd be back tonight at all."

Zack accepted the handshake firmly. "I hope you

didn't stay up on my account, sir. I just had some thinking to do, and hunting always seems to help."

Braddock smiled. "We all have a lot of thinking to
do, with the wedding so close. I hope your thoughts
weren't too troubled."

"No, sir. My head's real clear now."

"I see."

Zack chuckled fondly. "I still aim to marry her."

Braddock laughed heartily. "I can't say I'm surprised.
You don't seem like a man who'd be discouraged by a
few lessons, even from a taskmistress like my Noelle."

"She's been doing her best to discourage me," Zack
agreed. "But I'm nearly as stubborn as her when I set
my sights on something."

Braddock studied him intently. "Would it help to talk
about it?"

"Actually, sir, it would. Not about whether I'm marrying her or not. Like I said, that's for sure. But these
lessons . . . Well, she's got herself some peculiar notions about men and women, sir—"

"If we're going to talk about my daughter's view of
men and women, don't you think it's a good time to
start calling me Russ?"

"That'd make it easier," Zack admitted.

"Go on."

"Well, Russ . . ." He cleared his throat, then explained warily, "If she had her way, a fella wouldn't do
much of anything, even to his own wife."

Braddock seemed surprised by the observation. "Do
you really want my advice?"

"Yes, sir."

"I think you should follow Noelle's instructions when
it comes to those sorts of matters. I've raised her to be
a lady, but the truth is, she's probably much more—shall

we say, demonstrative and receptive?—than most society ladies. Over the years, she's seen so many happy matches, and has become aware of the needs men have for women, and vice versa. She has a more refreshing and tolerant view of such things than you'll find in most ladies, I assure you. And so, if Noelle says that something is disrespectful or inappropriate, I'd take that suggestion to heart if I were you."

"Is that so?" Zack tried for a neutral tone. "Could be I've just been spending my time with the wrong women."

"That's always possible."

"Refreshing and receptive?"

"Unusually so. The very fact that she's willing to discuss such things with you should tell you that. Most girls of her age who have led protected lives wouldn't be able to put two words together on such matters without blushing or fainting or some such nonsense. Noelle is refreshingly frank when it comes to such discussions."

"That's true. She'll discuss it till the cows come home," Zack agreed. "She just doesn't think she should *do* any of it."

For the first time, Braddock seemed to find the conversation disquieting. "What exactly did you suggest to her?"

"Nothing, sir. I haven't been making suggestions—at least, not the way you mean it."

Braddock laughed fondly. "I'm sure you haven't. It's probably just the contrast with Adam that makes her think you're being forward. I get the distinct impression he hasn't pressured her at all along those lines."

"Makes you wonder," Zack muttered; then he added quickly, "I haven't pressured her, either. Just some teasing is all. I want to marry her first, Russ. You have my word on that."

"I know." He hesitated, then picked up a stack of papers from his desk. "I know the last thing you want right now is to think about another girl, but . . ."

It was Zack's turn to laugh fondly. "There's three whole days left. No need to panic yet. All those letters could do is make me more sure than ever that Noelle's the only girl in the world for me. And I already know that, so if you don't mind, I think I'll just turn in."

"Good night, son. And good luck."

Zack was grinning as he took the steps two at a time up to the guest suite. The Braddocks were a fine family, but they had some mighty peculiar notions about love and marriage. And if Russ Braddock thought his daughter was refreshingly tolerant on the subject of lovemaking, Zack would hate to see his idea of a prude!

It's like you figured before, he advised himself cheerfully. *It'll be your job to set her straight. Can't think of a better way to spend a wedding night, either, so quit your griping and get some rest.*

Resisting a strong, irrational urge to go to her room again, just to see if she needed another dream rescue— or better still, another "depraved" encounter with his "manliness"—he reminded himself to give thanks for what he already had. How many men could sleep under the same roof with an angel, or court one in a fancy garden with her father's blessing? There was no doubt about it—he was the luckiest fellow in the world.

He was also a bone-tired fellow, and so, after a short but heartfelt prayer, he dragged his weary body into bed and was asleep before his head hit the pillow.

Six

By the time Noelle got out of bed the next morning, she had already made herself a solemn vow: to concentrate on Adam Prestley, and ignore Zack Dane's charming but irrelevant distractions. She'd be able to tell if he'd spoken to her father, and would feel guilty if he clearly hadn't, but there simply wasn't time to play any more games or teach any more lessons. Not only was the wedding three days away, there was the matter of Clara's party! Adam had made it clear he wanted to make a stunning entrance, which meant that Noelle had to be both meticulously groomed and absolutely calm—neither of which a girl could hope to be when Zack was around.

The young lieutenant seemed disappointed but not dismayed by her failure to interact with him, and she hoped the new attitude signaled that he was finally abandoning his futile courtship. She wasn't sure what might have finally dissuaded him—the fact that she was openly preparing for a romantic evening with Adam, or the fact that Zack had honestly begun to see her as a frigid bridal prospect. Either way, she was determined to be relieved by the lack of attention.

She was also relieved when her father left the house that evening a full hour before Adam's carriage was scheduled to arrive. The last thing she needed at a time like this was to witness another cool encounter between the two men in her life. Not when she wanted everything to be perfect.

She was wearing her prettiest yellow dancing dress, with yellow roses in her hair—an ensemble almost identical to the one she'd been wearing the night she and Adam had met. Would he notice? Of course he would! Adam Prestley was the most romantic man in the world, was he not?

Still, when Edward announced his arrival, she found herself fidgeting nervously. Adam had made it clear that this evening was vitally important, due to some business venture he was trying to arrange with Clara's uncle. What if he judged the roses too quaint? Or the dress too cheery? What had she been thinking?

His first glance did nothing to reassure her. Instead, she clearly noted disapproval in his soft blue eyes. Then he rallied and crossed to her, declaring her "a vision of loveliness," and apologizing for being late. "I hadn't received the message about Miss Duschane, so we stopped there first, only to learn of her illness," he explained after kissing Noelle's outstretched hand.

"Winifred is ill? Oh, dear!" Noelle's heart began to pound. "Adam, please don't be cross, but Father isn't here, and you know how he feels about these things. Edward!" she added unhappily. "Did Winnie send a message to us?"

"It's all taken care of, Miss Noelle," Edward soothed. "Your father couldn't stay, so he arranged another chaperon for you. He knew how important this evening was."

"Oh, what a relief!" She gave Adam an apologetic smile. "How on earth do you stay so calm and understanding? I've been beside myself all day, wanting everything to be just right. I thought this dress would please you, but if it doesn't—"

"Noelle, darling." Adam was chuckling as he took both her hands in his own. "You're exquisite just as you are. If I seemed less than adoring, it was only because I assumed you'd wear something more dramatic, in honor of your new necklace. It won't go with this at all, but that hardly seems to matter. Diamonds would only distract from your beauty."

Noelle bit her lip, annoyed despite herself at his presumptuous behavior. She had told him she couldn't accept the jewels, not even for this one night. Had he honestly believed she'd defy her father's wishes?

Predictably, he now pulled out his pocket watch and observed, "We will not possibly arrive on time if we don't leave immediately, darling."

Noelle nodded and turned to Edward. "Will you tell Alice we're ready to leave?"

"Alice went home hours ago," Edward reported. "It's the lieutenant who agreed to go along with the two of you tonight. He's probably out there right now, talking to the driver. You know how he is, miss."

Noelle cringed, first from the butler's words, and then from the fury that was slowly, ominously spreading over Adam's face. "Oh, no. Oh, dear . . ."

"Noelle," her fiancé snarled. "I won't stand for it. *Don't* ask it of me."

"I won't," she promised. "Edward, *please?* I'm begging you. Come in Zack's place, please?"

"I would, miss, but your father left strict instructions. Because of my heart," he added carefully.

"Oh, of course." She reached out to pat the servant's arm. "Can you forgive me? In my eyes, you're still so young and strong, just as you were when I was little, and you—"

"Noelle!" Adam's blue eyes blazed with annoyance. "Could you have your sentimental moment tomorrow? There's an obvious solution to this problem—or at least, it's obvious to me."

Noelle took a full step backward and studied him coolly. "You're absolutely right. You could go alone. And Edward and I could have our sentimental moment without annoying you with it. Why didn't I think of that myself?"

Her fiancé's glare didn't soften. "Your father's insistence on a chaperon, even under the most innocent of circumstances—" He caught himself and lowered his voice to an ominous growl. "I give you my word of honor I won't make any dastardly attempts on your virtue. Edward here will be my witness. Isn't that enough?"

Noelle took a deep breath, then sent Edward a reassuring smile before she turned back to Adam. "My father and I drank a toast last night at dinner. Would you like to hear it?" Without waiting for his reply, she told him proudly, "I am the daughter Russell Braddock raised me to be. I don't accept jewels from gentlemen who are not relatives, and I don't ride alone in carriages with such men, no matter how unlikely they are to molest me. I'm sorry if that is a source of inconvenience for you."

"It's a source of endless frustration," he agreed quietly. "But it's also what I love about you. Can you forgive me for implying otherwise?"

She hesitated, but only for a moment, before smiling gently. "It's understandable. This evening is important to you."

"You are important to me," he corrected, taking her hand and kissing it gallantly.

"And so?" She almost cringed again as she dared to ask, "I know he's obnoxious and offensive and a self-declared rival—"

"If the role of a chaperon is to ensure that no romantic mischief transpires, I believe your father has made an inspired choice," Adam observed dryly. "Is it too much to ask that the buffoon stay in the carriage during dinner, or will I be sitting next to him there also?"

"He'll stay outside, or go to the kitchen. If he dares show his face at that party, I'll throttle him with my bare hands."

"And rob me of the pleasure?" Adam crooked his arm and offered it to her. "Your carriage awaits, milady, obnoxious chaperon and all."

Adam took a moment to kiss her gently as they hurried outside to the carriage, and Noelle accepted the gesture gratefully, refusing to acknowledge the nagging doubts that were tugging at corners of her brain, trying to ruin this ill-fated evening. They were less than forty-eight hours away from their wedding day, their nerves were frazzled, and Adam's patience—perhaps even his manhood—was being pushed to the limit by the prospect of spending time with Zack. Determined to set a workable mood, Noelle steeled herself as Adam handed her up into the carriage, where, the driver had informed them, their chaperon had already made himself comfortable.

"Don't you dare say one word," she ordered haughtily as she settled onto the bench across from Zack. "I'm sitting next to Adam and don't you dare object." Her voice faltered to almost a whimper as she added angrily, "I can't believe you brought that ridiculous rifle."

"I don't go anywhere without it." Zack turned his attention to Adam, who had just entered and now sat beside Noelle. "Good evening, sir."

Noelle almost groaned aloud. He was going to make this ride unbearable! What had her father been thinking? "Did my father give you any instructions?" she asked coolly.

"One or two."

"I'm sure he told you to behave yourself, and you'd better, or—"

"It's fine, darling," Adam interrupted. "Just pretend he isn't there."

She took another breath, then turned to her fiancé and smiled gratefully. "However do you put up with me?"

"Petty annoyances fade in the face of your beauty and innocence," he murmured. "I still can't believe I raised my voice to you earlier. Am I forgiven?"

"You yelled at her?" Zack demanded, his green eyes alive with disgust. "Because of *me?* If you have a problem with *me,* Prestley, don't take it out on a helpless female—"

"That's enough!" Noelle stuck her finger to within inches of his face and warned, "One more word out of you and I'll—I'll do something desperate. I *swear* it."

"She will, too," Adam said with a chuckle. "If you think my fiancée is a helpless female, you're sorely mistaken, Mr. Dane." Turning to Noelle, he teased, "As much as I'd love to see you pummel him, darling, I was hoping we could use this time to talk. I have a surprise for you."

Oh, no, Noelle groaned inwardly. *What now?* With a hopeful smile, she insisted, "I've had so many surprises tonight already, Adam. Shouldn't you save one for later?"

He grinned wickedly. "I value my life too much to offer jewels again, if that's what has you so worried. This is something you've hinted at for months, Noelle. I assure you, you'll approve."

"Shall I hold out my hand?"

"Careful, Prestley," Zack warned. "She has rules about that sort of thing."

"Zack!" Noelle blushed frantically and pleaded with Adam, "Ignore him, won't you please?" She was relieved to see that her proper fiancé hadn't caught Zack's scandalous inference. "Surprise me, darling. You have my undivided attention."

Adam smiled slyly. "I spent the morning looking at property. The Jordan house, to be specific."

"Oh, dear," Noelle sighed. "Don't tell me Mr. Jordan is leaving Chicago? Ever since his wife died, I've been so worried about him, all alone in that huge house. I suppose he'll be going to New York with his son—" She stopped herself, suddenly alert. "Why were *you* looking at it?"

"Because you've given me the distinct impression you didn't want to live with my mother, although I can't imagine why."

"Oh, Adam!" She threw her arms around his neck and hugged him happily.

"Here, here," Zack complained.

Ignoring him completely, Noelle embraced Adam again and gushed, "You really are the most considerate, generous, thoughtful man in the entire world."

"I do my best."

She sent Zack a triumphant smile. "Do you see? *This* is how a gentleman treats the woman he loves. Remember it when Father finds you a bride." To Adam, she added softly, "You couldn't have chosen a more wonderful gift for me. For us. Thank you, darling."

"It's not definite yet, but I'm confident I can work out the details so that it's ready for us by the time we return from our honeymoon. Jordan's son has been making some sort of misguided attempt to interfere, but the old man owes so much on the property, I don't see how they'll manage to thwart us."

Noelle bit her lip. "His son doesn't want him to move to New York? How does Mr. Jordan feel about it?"

"He claims he wants to die where his wife died. Have you ever heard of anything so morbid? But it's academic, since he can't afford it. Still, it's a delicate situation—"

"What's delicate about vultures circling a dying man?" Zack interrupted.

Adam sent him a cool, dismissive glance, then patted Noelle's hand. "I can picture you in that Florentine courtyard, darling. A home fit for my princess. I'm glad the gift pleases you."

Noelle stared in wary dismay. "I don't think I could live there, knowing Mr. Jordan had to leave under such sad circumstances. Couldn't your father's bank help him, Adam?"

"It's *my* bank, not my father's," he reminded her quietly. "And we've already lost money trying to help."

"In other words, it's *your* bank that holds the mortgage?" Zack growled, adding for Noelle's benefit, "Don't you see, angel? He's the one kicking the poor fella out into the cold in the first place. Just so you and him can have yourselves a cozy little love nest."

"Damn you, Dane!" Adam stood up enough to pound on the roof of the carriage, shouting to the driver, "Go back to the Braddock house. This ride is over!"

"Adam, please," Noelle begged. "Zack doesn't know what he's talking about—"

"The fact that he's talking at all is an insult to me," Adam seethed as the carriage began to slow. "Another indignity, courtesy of your father."

"You can't blame Father—"

"Can't I? He's been trying to undermine us from the start, only he's too cowardly to do it to my face, so he sends this—this buffoon to do it for him."

Aghast, Noelle sprang for the carriage door, desperate not only for air, but for distance from his harsh words. Without thinking, she jumped to the ground before the vehicle had come to a stop, misjudging the distance so completely that her knees buckled, then crashed against the dull iron blade of a streetcar track. Shrieking with pain, she curled into a ball just as Zack landed beside her and gathered her against his chest.

"Dang it all, angel," he chastised mournfully. "Are you hurt bad?"

"Let her go!" Adam's voice was like a blast from a cannon. "My God, man, you're insufferable! Can't you see you're the cause of this?" Crouching beside them, he demanded, "Darling? Is anything broken?"

"Don't touch me," she warned tearfully. "And you!" She pounded at Zack's arms until he released her. "I hate you both!" Scurrying free, she tried to stand, but her knees gave way and she wailed, "Get away from me!" even as Adam caught her up into his arms.

"Forgive me, darling." He cradled her struggling body against his chest. "Don't fight me anymore. Let me help you back into the carriage—"

"I won't!" She glared through waves of pain. "Not until you promise to help Mr. Jordan keep his house."

"Noelle!"

Turning to Zack, she snarled. "As for *you*, this is *all* your fault. Go back to my father's house, pack your bags, and leave before you ruin everything."

"I'm not leaving you alone with this jackass," Zack protested. "Not with you hurting this way. Yell all you like, but I'm not going anywhere without you."

"Oh, for heaven's sake." She wiped frantically at her face. "I don't know which of you is the more despicable."

"We'll decide that later," Adam soothed. "For now, all that matters is getting you home. Can you stand, darling?"

"I think so." She tried again to put her weight on her legs, and this time, her knees managed to support her. "I'm fine."

"You're not fine," Zack corrected her. "Let one of us put you into the carriage."

"Noelle?" Adam cupped her chin in his hand. "I'll see to it that Jordan stays in his house for as long as he wants."

"You will?" She leaned against his chest and tried not to cry again. "You called my father a coward."

"It was unforgivable," Adam agreed. "In my defense, this buffoon—"

"He isn't a buffoon!" Noelle stopped herself and explained softly, "He's obnoxious and rude, and I despise him with every fiber of my being, but he isn't a buffoon. Don't call him that anymore."

"I won't," Adam promised. "Anything else?"

She shook her head. "My dress is ruined. You'll have

to take me home, and go to the party yourself. All because of *you*," she added in Zack's direction.

"Let's see you walk, angel."

Confused by the concern in his voice, she muttered, "You're impossible," then took a few successful steps. Jutting out her chin defiantly, she insisted, "There, do you see? They're just fine. Purple, I'm sure, but they carry me, so I won't be needing your services. You can ride up top with the driver, or you can walk. Which will it be?"

Zack shrugged and started to climb up the side of the carriage.

"Wait!" She blushed when he turned as though expecting a reprieve. "Your rifle flew under the carriage when you jumped out. You can't just go around leaving firearms on the streets of Chicago," she added weakly.

He gave her a curious stare, then retrieved the rifle and climbed up beside the driver without saying another word.

"I despise him," Adam growled. "Maybe we should elope, darling, if only to get you out of that lunatic asylum you call home."

"And *into* that mausoleum *you* call home?" she demanded under her breath, but she didn't dare start another fight, not with her knees throbbing the way they did. All she wanted was to slip into a hot bath and pretend that all her problems—Mr. Jordan, Zack, Adam's mother—were just figments of her overworked imagination.

She didn't allow Adam to kiss her during the carriage ride home, out of deference to her father, but she did allow her contrite fiancé to carry her up the stairs and settle her into her doll-bedecked bed. Thereafter, he made a halfhearted attempt to insist upon staying with her, but she knew Clara's party was important to him, and so she didn't judge him—or at least, not too harshly—when he finally agreed to go without her.

Once alone, Noelle abandoned her plan to bathe, fearing that she might not be able to get back out of the tub. Instead, she settled for changing out of her torn frock and into a soft, warm flannel nightgown. A distraught and guilt-ridden Edward had left cold packs on her bed-side table for her knees, and had also reluctantly agreed not to send for her father. She only hoped brash young Lieutenant Dane would respect her wishes as well.

He hadn't tried to interfere during the carriage ride home, and had been conspicuously absent thereafter. She could only imagine how much he had longed to be the one to carry her up the stairs. Somehow, she had known deep in her heart that he was feeling every stab of pain, every wave of nausea, every sting of tears that she was feeling. It didn't make sense, and certainly didn't make his love for her any truer than Adam's, but still, it haunted and confused her.

Zack, she chided silently as she pulled a light shawl over herself and settled back into the pillows, *I know you won't stay away for long, but please, just this one night, won't you just fade into the background and let me sort this out for myself?*

"Prestley!" Zack blocked the banker's path toward the carriage and fixed him with a cold stare. "It's time you and me had our talk, man to man."

"Spare me," Adam drawled. "Haven't you caused enough inconvenience for one night?"

"Inconvenience? That's how you see it? She nearly killed herself—"

"Thanks to you and your blundering interference." He hesitated, then assured Zack firmly, "You and I have nothing to say to one another. Step aside."

"That's what I figure *you* should be doing," Zack said. "Stepping aside, before she gets hurt any worse. That girl's too sweet and too innocent to hitch up with a fella like you. I keep asking myself, what does he want from her? I can't quite come up with an answer, but I figure, it's something bad."

"The question is, what does *she* want from *me?*" Adam grinned. "The answer is simple: all the things *you* can't give her. That's what's really bothering you, isn't it?"

Zack studied him intently. "I don't like the way you look at her."

"How exactly do I look at her?"

"With disrespect."

It brought another grin to Adam's face. "If I don't respect her, why am I willing to make her my wife?"

"That's the question," Zack agreed.

The banker met his gaze directly. "I don't owe you any explanation, but I'll give you one anyway, in hopes it'll make you go away."

"Go on."

"I'm a wealthy man, Dane. Wealthy enough to have women from the highest social circles throw themselves at me. Women *you* can't even imagine, let alone touch. They've begun to bore me.

"Noelle, on the other hand, never bores me. She's the perfect combination of youth, innocence, beauty, and—

how can I say this delicately?" His grin took a lascivious turn. "On second thought, I believe you, more than anyone, know exactly what I mean."

"Say it anyway," Zack suggested quietly.

"Let's just say, our little Noelle is alarmingly eager to please. Every man's fantasy, including yours."

Zack hadn't intended to hit the jackass—it wouldn't help his courtship of Noelle, he knew—but his fist was too outraged at the insult to be restrained, and so his knuckles crashed into the leering face, sending the banker sprawling onto the drive.

To his amazement, Adam shook off the blow fairly quickly and once he'd done so, he was leering again, this time as though he'd just won an unqualified victory. "That was your final mistake, Dane. Not even her father will approve of this sort of tactic. You may as well pack up your banjo and your donkey and head out into the sunset."

Standing and dusting himself off, he gave Zack a sympathetic smile. "Give up, man. She'll never choose you. You simply can't offer her the one thing she craves."

"What's that?"

"Respectability. Once she marries me, she'll have immediate and unequalled status in this city and countless others. If she married a backwoods buffoon, her standing in society would plummet. And Noelle cares about all that. Don't ever doubt it. It's the one thing her father, with all his success, hasn't been able to give her."

"You're saying she's not respectable now?"

"I'm saying she wouldn't be if she married you."

Zack shook his head slowly. "I heard what you said, Prestley. You think Russ Braddock and his business— *and* his daughter—aren't respectable."

"You'd like that, wouldn't you? To be able to tell her I said that? But I didn't. At least"—he corrected himself malevolently—"not exactly."

Zack wanted to retort, but wasn't sure exactly what to say. Nothing Adam said made sense. Why would the banker marry a girl he didn't think was respectable? According to his own theory of social standing, marrying a girl like that would bring the Prestley family down a notch, wouldn't it? And what in blazes did he mean by "every man's fantasy"? She was Zack's fantasy, true enough, but from Prestley, it had sounded like an insult, as had "alarmingly eager to please."

"The wedding is in two days," Adam reminded Zack; then he turned and headed for the carriage, adding over his shoulder, "Be gone before then, if you know what's good for you."

"Two days," Zack repeated, his gaze shifting from his adversary to the balcony outside Noelle's bedroom. The room was dimly lit, and he wondered if the angel was crying herself to sleep. Or more likely, making herself another doll—this time, of the style Zack had seen in New Orleans. The kind ladies liked to stick pins into. If so, he had a sinking feeling Noelle would make it look just like him.

"Angel?" Zack poked his head into her room and gave her a hopeful smile. "Can I come in for a minute?"

"No. Go away."

She wasn't surprised when he still ambled into view, eyeing her legs sympathetically. "Feeling any better?"

"I'm fine. Go away."

"What's that? Ice?" He sat on the side of the bed

and discarded the cold packs, then covered both her kneecaps with his huge, warm hands. "It's heat you need for this sort of pain, sugar. How's that feel?"

It felt wonderful as it radiated through her, banishing the ache, at least for a moment. Closing her eyes, she leaned back and greedily savored the relief.

"Why are you letting me touch you?" he demanded. "Do they hurt as bad as all that?"

"Hmm? Oh." She laughed sheepishly, wondering if he was enjoying the sight of her legs, bare up to the knees. If it were any other time, or any other intruder, she'd be mortified, but since Zack had already seen more of her legs in his fantasies than he was seeing now, what was the possible harm? "Are they just as you pictured them?"

He chuckled reluctantly. "Prettiest I've ever seen, real or imaginary." Leaning down, he kissed each bruised joint tenderly, then pulled her nightgown over them, resting his hands on top of the flannel. "You can't marry him, Noelle. He's a heartless fella, if I ever saw one. Dangerous, too."

"Don't be silly. Adam didn't do this. Neither did you, I suppose. I've always been a little reckless when I get angry. So please, try not to make me angry anymore." She opened her eyes and added quietly, "I shouldn't have asked him to let you come along in the carriage. Please don't judge him by anything he said or did. You don't know him at all, Zack."

"I know he was forcing a poor widower out of his house. I know he lets his mama and sister treat you like dirt. I know he should've hit me half a dozen times since Sunday, but he hasn't, because he doesn't want you to see that temper of his. But you caught a glimpse of it tonight, didn't you? The way he talked about your father—"

"Do you blame him for being upset? Father sent you with us just to bother him. It was horridly unfair."

Zack hesitated, then nodded in reluctant agreement.

She bit her lip. "You admit it? You see how unfair he's being? Letting you stay here, just to humiliate Adam?"

"You're wrong about that, Noelle. He likes having someone here to talk to. That's why he's letting me stay around."

It made her heart ache as much as her knees, the thought of her father needing someone, because he was losing her. How would it be for him when she left for London for six weeks? And even when she and Adam returned, they might not see each other as often as she hoped. "Father has friends. The ones he's playing cards with right now, for example."

"He can't talk to them about Prestley."

She bristled for a moment, then had to admit it was true. "If he disapproves so strongly of Adam, why did he give him permission to marry me?"

"He can't say no to you. And I doubt he realizes just how despicable that varmint is. I didn't see it fully myself until tonight."

"You hate him because he's your rival. And in a way, he's Father's rival, too. It's all so unfortunate. Under other circumstances, we all might have gotten along quite well."

"True enough."

She smiled in surprised appreciation. "You admit it?"

"Sure. If you and me were married, and Russ was my father-in-law, and Prestley was our banker, we'd all get along just fine. Until we fell behind in our payments and he kicked us out into the cold, that is."

"Very funny."

"He would've done that to that Jordan fella, you know."

"We know nothing of the kind. You're not going to tell Father about that, are you?"

"Tell Father about what?" Russell Braddock interrupted from the doorway. "What exactly is going on in here?"

Zack jumped off the bed and flushed respectfully, while Noelle giggled in delight. "Finally, you see how the lieutenant behaves when you're not looking."

"She's hurt," Zack explained. "I was comforting her. Look at these," he added, pulling up her nightgown to reveal a pair of reddish purple knees. "She's lucky they aren't broke to bits."

Braddock shook his head, as though unsure of how to reprimand his presumptuous guest; then he stepped between Zack and the bed, eyeing the offending hand pointedly. Zack immediately released the nightgown, and Braddock sat down beside Noelle. "I came as quickly as I could, sweetheart."

"I didn't want them to send for you, but I knew Zack would do it anyway. Believe me, I'm fine."

"What on earth happened? And why am I certain it was my fault, for sending Zack as chaperon?"

"She jumped out of a moving carriage, so you can't take all the blame," Zack explained. "If I hadn't seen it with my own eyes, I wouldn't've believed it."

Braddock patted his daughter's knee. "Unfortunately, I've witnessed several similar episodes, mostly when she was a child. Do you remember, sweetheart? The day you tried to run away by climbing down from the balcony?"

"And broke my arm?" She smiled sheepishly. "Actually, this was more like the time in Adamsville, when I tried to save that doll from a bull pasture."

"Dang." Zack grinned at them both. "Sounds like you've been busy, just keeping her alive for me, Russ. I appreciate it."

"My pleasure." Braddock's smile faded. "You could have been seriously hurt, Noelle. What were you thinking?"

"Everyone was arguing and shouting, and I couldn't think. I needed to be alone, but I miscalculated the distance to the ground and lost my footing. Aside from my dignity, nothing is permanently damaged."

"You were arguing about Anthony Jordan? Is that what I heard when I came in?"

Noelle glanced at Zack, silently pleading with him to allow her to put the unfortunate conversation in its best light. She sighed in relief when he nodded for her to proceed. "It was a misunderstanding, Father. Adam wanted to buy the Jordan house for me—"

"What?" Braddock recovered slightly and murmured, "Anthony and his wife raised their children and several of their grandchildren there. I thought he'd stay there until the end, which I've heard isn't far off."

"Adam's going to see to it that he stays, no matter how much he owes his bank. It was a misunderstanding—"

"He was going to foreclose on the mortgage?" Her father's eyes blazed with annoyance. "That's what you argued about?" He choked on his anger. "I wish I could say I was surprised, Noelle, but this just confirms what

I've heard over and over. Throwing widows and widowers into the street—"

"It's not like that! He was doing it for me, so I wouldn't have to live with his mother. It was all my fault for complaining about her so much."

"The two of you should live *here,*" Braddock interrupted angrily. "But of course, this house isn't extravagant enough for a Prestley."

"We can't live here, because you and Adam would argue and compete," Noelle countered unhappily. "And *I'm* going to be a Prestley soon, Father, as will your grandchildren. Have you forgotten that?"

"Not for a single moment," he assured her sadly. "Sometimes I wish I could."

"You're both too tired to talk about this tonight," Zack intervened nervously. "You'll say things you don't mean, and before long, Noelle'll be jumping out the window. We don't want that, do we?"

Noelle wiped a tear from her cheek and smiled gratefully. "For once, Zack's right. Honestly, Father, I can't bear to quarrel with you about this."

She expected him to echo the sentiment, but instead he shrugged, as though he might have preferred to argue until dawn. "You said you jumped out of the carriage because you needed to be alone, to think. I'd say that's just what you need to do. Think this through, Noelle Elizabeth. Don't make a mistake from sheer stubbornness."

"Father!"

"The other night, you said you had doubts—"

"And *you* said it was natural!" She stared at him in complete dismay. "I can't believe you waited until now—two days before my wedding!—to say all this."

"I shouldn't have waited," he agreed.

"All he's saying is you should think about it," Zack interrupted. "Isn't that right, Russ? If she still chooses Prestley in the end, you'll accept him just fine. Isn't that so?"

Braddock hesitated, then nodded stiffly. "That's exactly right. Once you've thought it through, I'll abide by your decision and never say another word."

It was clear to Noelle that Zack had sent her father a signal—a signal to retreat before Noelle did something crazy. Like elope? Was that it? Had Zack heard and remembered Adam's suggestion that they do just that? Noelle had certainly heard it, and was beginning to see the beauty of it.

How else could she marry Adam? She couldn't very well take her father's arm and parade in front of a roomful of guests, knowing in her heart that Russell Braddock despised the man to whom he was giving her!

Her beautiful wedding was dissolving before her eyes. The flowers, the gown, the little tarts, the champagne . . . It had been slipping away for days, hadn't it? Since the moment Zack had laid eyes on her, giving her father hope that another, finer suitor had entered the fray.

"Could you both just leave? Please?"

"Sure, sugar. Try to get some sleep. And be careful getting up in the morning. Those knees are gonna be stiff."

"I'll be careful."

Her father leaned over and kissed her cheek. "Good night, sweetheart. Forgive me for ruining your evening."

"I appreciate your honesty," she said with a sniff. "I only wish you could have shared it with me sooner."

Her father backed toward the door and exited in silence, and she hoped Zack would do the same, but of course, he did not. Instead, he sidled up to the bed and leaned down to brush his lips across hers. "Sweet dreams, angel. Don't go running off or anything. Understand?"

She grimaced and nodded. "Thank you for finding the right words to say to Father. I've never seen him this way."

"He's hurting, but no worse than you are." Zack brushed a lock of hair from her damp cheek. "I know he told you to think, Noelle, but it seems to me, you need to get some sleep. There'll be plenty of time to think in the morning."

"Plenty of time? With my wedding day only hours away?"

"Sometimes, you can't see a solution till the very last minute, even if it's been right in front of your eyes for days."

"Go away," she groaned, knowing he was referring to himself. It was his usual audacious nonsense, but as so often happened, it made her feel good, at least for the moment. "And Zack?"

"Yeah?"

"Take care of Father?"

"I will, sugar." Brushing her lips with his own again, he bid her, "Sweet dreams, and *don't* run off"; then he disappeared from the room, leaving her to examine, again and again, the events of the day.

Finally, exhaustion drove her to the only possible solution. She would simply leave it to fate. Tomorrow there would be an omen—something so clear and incontrovertible that she would know exactly what to do. Perhaps Winifred would send word that she was too ill to oversee the wedding. Wouldn't that mean Noelle should postpone it? Or elope?

*Elope with a man who throws widows and widowers
out into the street?* She cursed Zack for having charac-
terized it so harshly, but hadn't her father said it, too?
And what else was it he had said? That he'd heard such
things over and over again?

If only there could be an omen that contradicted all
that—an announcement, perhaps, that Adam had decided to contribute his entire fortune to a trust for the
benefit of widows and orphans. Wouldn't that be perfect? But unlikely, she knew. And unfair on her part to
ask. The Prestley family was famous for participation
in charitable enterprises. What right did she have to
judge them? Just because she wanted to be "poor,
young, and in love"? She grimaced, remembering that
even if Adam gave away every penny he owned, it
wouldn't buy back his youth.

*The only omen you really need is to wake up and
find that Zack Dane was just a character in a bizarre
dream!* she informed herself angrily. *He's the cause of
most of these doubts. He's the one who behaves as
though you'll never marry Adam, and now he has Father
believing it, too.*

But Zack wasn't going anywhere, she knew. She'd
have to rely on some other sign to help her through this
dizzying maze of second thoughts.

In her heart, she didn't really believe in omens, but
sheer exhaustion, coupled with hopeless confusion,
made her accept the possibility, if only as a ruse to
allow her to fall blessedly to sleep, despite herself.

Seven

Given her skepticism, Noelle was doubly startled when she opened her eyes the next morning and found not one, but two lovely "omens" on her bedside table. The first was a magnificent bouquet of yellow roses, with a love note from Adam, pledging himself to her. Gushing over her. Begging her forgiveness. And best of all, informing her that Anthony Jordan now owned an irrevocable life estate in his beautiful home.

The second omen was a letter from Winifred Duschane, apologizing for her absence, but assuring Noelle that she was rallying from the fever that had landed her in bed. *The wedding,* the note promised, *will be the most elegant, flawless, romantic event of the decade.*

Just relax and don't worry about anything, Winifred's letter went on to advise. *Your only responsibility is to look radiant and serene, so don't allow anyone or anything to upset you today. You're marrying the most eligible bachelor this city has to offer, and he adores you. What more could any bride want?*

She decided to follow Winifred's directions, although it was difficult to be serene when she slid out of bed only to discover that her knees were so stiff, every attempt to bend them caused a new stab of discomfort.

She knew she should send for Edward to assist her, but that might attract the attention of Zack or her father, neither of whom she was ready to encounter. And so she settled for whimpering, "Ow, ow, ow," on each and every step of the long, magnificent staircase, pausing occasionally, not only to rest, but to marvel at the bustle of activity that confronted her.

More than half the furniture had been moved out of sight, replaced by stacks of chairs that would soon be arranged to somehow accommodate nearly one hundred guests. Unfamiliar maids in crisp uniforms were attacking everything in sight, polishing the chandeliers until they sparkled, and buffing the wood paneling and floors to a brilliant sheen. The house would look even grander, Noelle knew, once the garlands of white gardenias and roses arrived and were threaded through the banister and around the archways. Another omen, she told herself happily. How utterly and completely romantic!

With new resolve, she limped to the study, and was relieved to find her father at his desk. After the way he'd spoken the previous night, she wasn't prepared for the apologetic smile on his face, or the tinge of guilt in his lackluster gaze. On impulse, she threw her arms around his neck and hugged him fiercely, scolding, "Are we finished with all our nonsense? Or are you going to drive me to an elopement?"

Braddock chuckled, but when he spoke, she heard an unfamiliar tearful quality to his voice. "Zack warned me you might do just that. I didn't sleep a wink, and I'm sure he didn't, either. Thank you for staying, sweetheart." He gave her a loving squeeze. "How are your legs?"

"Stiff and purple, which of course serves me right

for such a silly stunt. Do you suppose I've learned my lesson?"

"We can only hope," he said with a smile. "Did you see the roses?"

"Wasn't that sweet of Adam?"

"Yes."

"I was wearing yellow roses in my hair the night he and I met."

"That's very romantic."

She smiled and pinched his cheek. "You're doing quite well. Thank you." Without giving herself time to think, she asked, "What did you mean last night when you said you'd heard other stories about Adam?"

He coughed lightly. "They've always been a complicated family, Noelle. Generous in their charitable pursuits, ruthless in matters of business. I was unfortunate enough to witness his father's handiwork once or twice. He wasn't content to ruin a man. Edmond Prestley had a need to completely break him. And his tactics with women were reputedly similar."

"And in Adam's defense, he and his father never got along," Noelle interjected. "He doesn't talk about him often, but it's clear that he harbors bad memories of him."

"Because Adam disapproved of his father? Or vice versa?"

"Pardon?"

Braddock shrugged. "It was no secret that the two didn't get along. There were rumors—"

Noelle smiled at the hesitation. Her father had always despised rumors, and she knew he was ashamed now to be repeating them. "This is an exception, Father, don't you suppose?" she encouraged gently.

He nodded. "Adam's parents didn't have a good marriage, sweetheart. As a result, the child was forced to take sides."

"And he sided with his mother? And his father resented it?"

"His father saw it as a sign of weakness. Of course, to a man like that, anything short of ruthlessness is a sign of weakness."

"I'm glad he'd dead. It must be such a relief for Adam. And for his mother."

"Adam traveled with her, and acted as her escort, even before his father died. I'm sure it wasn't always a comfortable arrangement for him. A boy wants to earn his father's respect."

"The respect of a cruel and heartless man? Adam was better off without it."

"Was he?"

She took a deep breath, then insisted, "He loves me, Father."

"Yes, I know."

The quiet admission surprised her.

"It's settled, then?" her father asked. "You're marrying him tomorrow?"

"Yes." She wanted to ask if they still had his blessing, but settled for, "Will you be able to do what you need to do? During the ceremony?"

"Yes, Noelle."

"I can just see the newspaper account: the bride limped clumsily down the aisle on the arm of her grim-faced father—"

"You'll be graceful and I'll be charming," he corrected. "I want you to stay off those legs today, though. Let us take care of you. Speaking of which, Edward tells me you never had dinner last night. Aren't you famished?"

She nodded. "Could you ask Alice to fix a tray and bring it to the sitting room? I'd like to spend some time repacking the trunks."

"Let me help you with the stairs—"

"No, thank you. If you want to help, keep Lieutenant Dane away from me for a while. Winnie wants me to be serene, and that's not possible when he's around." When her father seemed troubled by the remark, she assured him, "I'll speak to him, one last time, of course. But at a time of my choosing. I'll be gentle, Father. I promise."

"I'm sure you will." He took a deep breath, then revealed, "I think something's bothering him. I mean, beyond the obvious."

Remembering the playful lies she'd told him about "decent" wedding nights, Noelle winced. "Did he talk to you about it?"

"I believe he wanted to, but couldn't find the words. Which as you know, is not his usual problem."

"That's an understatement," she agreed lightly.

"Believe it or not, his primary concern last night and this morning was ensuring that there was no rift between you and me. There isn't, is there?"

"Absolutely not." She hugged him lovingly, and silently apologized to Zack for failing to fully appreciate him. He could have used his time last night to further poison her father against Adam, but instead had been genuinely eager to help.

And in return, she had been fairly heartless, blaming him for single-handedly ruining this important week, when most of the problems had existed long before he arrived. She owed him an apology, and more importantly, owed it to him to reassure him about his excellent prospects for a lustful, naked bride. Vowing again to speak to him soon, she took her father's arm and allowed him to help her up the stairs to the sitting room.

One way or the other, it would all be over in less than two days. Zack found the notion oddly disquieting. Gone were the bursts of bravado that had assured him he'd win Noelle's heart. There was no room for that sort of thinking now, knowing what he knew about Adam Prestley. It was no longer a question of winning the angel for himself. His only duty now was to save her from the grasp of a soulless varmint.

Why didn't she see the truth about Prestley? That business with the widower—that had been so clear to everyone but her. Why? Because Zack's presence had complicated the whole mess. Every time she had a glimpse into Prestley's true character, she blamed it on Zack—on his campaign to subvert her feelings.

And he'd done that, but only in fun, at least at the start. He'd talked about the fellow's age and all, just to make her wonder. It was the sort of thing any man would say when competing for a girl's affections. But now it had to stop, so Noelle could see the difference between competitive exaggeration and cold, hard facts.

And it can't be just pretend, he warned himself sternly. *She'll see right through that, her being too danged smart for her own good, and all. You gotta let her go—here and now. If you can do that and mean it, maybe she'll be able to see the truth—that she's marrying a coldhearted bastard who doesn't respect her or her father. Doesn't respect anything but wealth and power and whatever it is he thinks he sees when he looks at Noelle.*

Letting her go would be the hardest thing Zack had

ever had to do, but if it saved her from Prestley, it would be worth it. In fact, it would be an honor. He'd be fine as long as he remembered that simple truth.

He knew he should go in search of her right away, before his resolve weakened, but he was a creature of habit, and something was nagging at him that he needed to get out of the way first, so he settled down at the maple preparation table in Alice's kitchen and assembled his equipment before him. Two kinds of oil—one for lubricating, one for polishing. A narrow, tapered brush. A soft rag. And Henry. Quickly and expertly he disassembled the firearm, and as he did so, he remembered how Noelle had drawn his attention to Henry's plight. If she hadn't done that, he would have lost this fine old rifle.

There had been something extra special in her eyes at that moment—something that had touched Zack to his soul. She cared about him, and so she cared about the things that mattered to him. It had been the truest sign he'd ever had that her feelings for him were more than fleeting friendship or simple arousal.

Not that he didn't appreciate arousal. That definitely had its place. But when it came to marrying a girl, a fellow had to know there was more. And the girl had to know it—had to believe it with all her heart.

Unfortunately, Noelle hadn't quite gotten around to recognizing it yet, and now, they'd run out of time.

"Zack?"

He raised his eyes to the doorway and almost groaned aloud. She looked prettier than ever, just to make it all more complicated, and so he reminded himself with brutal insistence that it wasn't complicated at all. He could be selfish, or he could do his duty. It was as simple as that.

"Afternoon, sugar," he murmured. "How're those legs feeling?"

"They're fine. How's Henry?"

Zack grinned sheepishly. "He owes you his life. Don't think he isn't grateful."

When she laughed lightly, he felt a familiar ache, and had to reprimand himself again. This wasn't going to be easy, it seemed.

"Once I put Henry back together, me and Merc'll take him out to the country and make sure he's shooting straight. You should come with us, sugar. The fresh air would do you good, and it would give us a chance to talk."

"We can talk here." She perched on the edge of the table. "The last thing I need is an adventure in the country. Suppose I fell off your horse and hurt myself again?"

Zack grinned. "Merc's a terror, that's for sure, but you'd have me to manage him, so you'd be safe."

"Just the same, I'd rather not take any more chances this close to the wedding."

The sound of conversation had awakened the Braddocks' old dog, who managed to stand and wag his tail hopefully. "Come here, boy." Zack rumpled Copper's thick coat briskly, then retrieved a hard biscuit from the pocket of his buckskin vest. "Here, I've got something for you."

"You two seem to know one another." Noelle beamed as the dog devoured the treat; then she knelt and embraced him fondly. "Hello, darling."

"Lucky dog," Zack murmured, adding cheerfully, "Old Copper here'll vouch for Merc. He likes coming along with me to the carriage stalls for visits."

"That's so far!" she protested. "What were you thinking, Zack? Can't you see how he limps?"

"That's why I carry him. I'll carry you, too, if you'd like."

"As I said, I don't need any more adventures." She eyed him sternly. "I agree that we need to talk. Or rather, I need to talk, and you need to listen."

"Me first," he interrupted.

"If it has anything to do with Adam, keep it to yourself. I won't have my fiancé maligned on the eve of our wedding."

Zack grimaced but persisted. "Do you remember the rule I told you once? The one my pappy was always teaching me?"

"Facts are facts," she drawled. "There's no sense in ignoring them, or something like that, right?"

He grinned, impressed and momentarily distracted. She was so danged feisty! If only Prestley wasn't such a menace. . . .

"You're ignoring the most important fact of all," Noelle assured him quietly. "I love Adam, and he loves me."

"Are you so sure about that?"

"Yes."

"What if I told you—"

"Don't! Not unless you're willing to lose my friendship forever." She blushed and added more gently, "This might be our last conversation before I marry him, Zack. Do you honestly want to spend it quarreling? I was hoping . . ." Her blush deepened to a beautiful crimson. "I thought we might have one last lesson, to prepare you for *your* wedding night. There are a few . . . Well, there are a few details I thought I should clear up. For your bride's sake."

He ached again, this time because he could see a telltale spark in her eyes. A tinge of arousal, sneaking up on her, ready to confuse her. It always happened this way with her. She was so stubborn—so all-fired sure she could resist him—that she never caught the signs until it was too late and she was in his arms. . . .

If he kissed her now, it would be incredible. It might even be the kiss that taught her the truth, once and for all. He wanted that so much he could taste it, but the stakes were too high. What if he was wrong? This was his last chance to win her heart, but it was also his last chance to talk some sense into her. Somehow, he had to find the strength to make the right choice, and he had to make it right away.

You know what you need to do, he ordered himself bluntly. *Let her go, right here and right now. It's the only way she'll ever be able to trust your motives, and see the truth about Prestley. So stop being such a selfish jackass and just end it, before it's too late.*

Noelle watched in fascination as Zack visibly weighed his words before speaking again. She had expected him to seize the opportunity to discuss wedding nights, not only in hopes of clearing up misunderstandings, but also as a chance to flirt and tease. Instead, her remarks had somehow made him uncomfortable, and she chastised herself for the gaffe.

Was she so self-absorbed she couldn't sympathize with *his* plight? The girl he loved—or at least, thought he loved—was going to marry someone else in less than a day. Apparently Zack was beginning to respect that. Wasn't it time she started respecting the awkwardness of his situation in return?

Dropping her gaze from his so that he could take a moment to compose himself, she noted with surprise that, despite his discomfort, his fingers hadn't stopped working on the rifle. It was almost as though he'd done it so often, he could clean and reassemble the parts by touch, perhaps even in total darkness. His hands, it seemed, were so intimately familiar with every ridge and every hollow, he could lubricate and rub and manipulate the various parts into position just by the gentle insistence of his touch. He would touch his bride that way one day, she realized enviously. Gently, expertly, with such smooth, loving insistence to every tiny detail—

"Noelle? Are you listening to me?"

"What?" She looked up, embarrassed by the direction in which her thoughts had drifted. "Excuse me, Zack. Did you say something?"

He was staring at her, his expression dark with exasperation. "You didn't hear a word I said? Dang it all; I'm trying to talk serious here."

"I know. I'm sorry. I was just noticing . . . well, noticing how easily you do that."

"Do what?"

"Never mind." She fought to control the blush she knew was creeping along her cheekbones. "What were you saying?"

He shook his head, as if completely disgusted; then he reached for a vial and drizzled a few drops of oil onto the rifle's wooden stock. To Noelle's amazement, he didn't reach for the nearby rag just yet, but began to patiently massage the oil into the wood with his fingers, coaxing a deep, vibrant glow from its depths.

His hands were so warm, she remembered shyly from the loving moment when he'd placed them onto her poor, bruised knees, sending waves of relief through her, relaxing her and soothing her. He hadn't rubbed her of course, or moved his hands along her, the way he was moving them along the rifle barrel, working excess lubricant into new crevices he encountered on his way. Using the heat from his fingertips to spread a thin, glossy haze every place they touched . . .

"What's wrong with you, sugar?"

"Nothing," she gasped, jolted back by the sharp tone of his voice. "Why do you ask?"

Rather than answer, he grabbed the rag, cleaned his hands, and then leaned up to feel her forehead, frowning as he did so. "Why didn't you tell me you were feeling poorly? Does your father know?"

"I'm fine!" She backed away, confused again at having been so easily distracted. "I thought you wanted to have a serious discussion."

"You're all flushed."

"That's because I'm annoyed," she insisted weakly. "Honestly, Zack. Do you think I have nothing better to do on the day before my wedding than stand here and listen to this?"

"It's gotta be said, Noelle."

"Well, I've heard enough. I have a thousand things to do, and no time left to do them in." Wincing at the flash of hurt in his eyes—couldn't he see she was just babbling to cover her confusion?—she grabbed his hand and squeezed it apologetically. "I didn't mean to snap at you, Zack."

"I don't want to fight, either, Noelle." He studied her wistfully. "You said something earlier, about our friendship being important. That's all I'm asking for now. Friendship. I want you to listen to me, one friend to another. Can you do that?"

"Of course. What is it you want to say?"

"I want you to think about Prestley. About the way

he looks at you. Haven't you ever noticed it, sugar? It's not right—"

"Oh, for heaven's sake!" She stomped her foot in disgust. *"That's* how you want to be friends? By criticizing him, right up until the last minute?"

When Copper whined in protest, Noelle dropped to her knees, heedless of her bruises, and embraced the dog mournfully. "Honestly, Zack, do you see what you're doing? You're upsetting everyone, including the dog, for no reason. Can't you just pretend to accept my marriage? For everyone's sake?"

"No."

She patted Copper and sighed. "Then we need to change the subject. Can I ask you something? Please?"

"Anything."

"You know about animals, don't you?"

"What about 'em?"

"Did you know Copper isn't eating well? Father feels it's nature's way of bringing his life to an end, but I feel just terrible about it. Don't you think we should try to make him eat?" When he didn't answer right away, she smiled hopefully. "I saw how much he loved that biscuit you gave him. Isn't that the sort of thing we should be doing?"

He studied her for a moment, then shrugged. "If he was my dog, I'd fix him up a plate of all his favorite foods—"

"Exactly! You should tell Father that."

"Like I was saying, I'd fix his favorites, and let him eat till he was full up. Then I'd give him a hug, tell him what a great friend he'd been, and put a bullet between his eyes, quick and painless."

"Zack!"

"You asked me, and I told you," he replied simply. "Did you want me to lie to you?"

"No."

His green eyes were clearer and more serious than she could remember having ever seen them. "Sometimes, the right way isn't the easy way, Noelle. Your dog's in pain. He can't do any of the things he loved doing. He doesn't even have his dignity when he tries to relieve himself. I'd put him out of his misery if he was my dog, and if your father asked me to help him out with it, I'd do it today."

She could see he was upset with her, and she really couldn't blame him. She had made his life miserable these last few days, by kissing him when she shouldn't have, and rebuffing him when he dearly wanted her to embrace him, and of course, by filling his head with inaccurate information about the wedding night he'd one day share with his bride. What had she been thinking, being so cruel?

"I'm gonna go check on Merc," he announced quietly. "You oughta get some rest, sugar. We can talk again later."

She watched in mournful confusion as he strode onto the service porch, then disappeared, his moccasined feet making hardly any sound at all. Was this the way they would eventually part? In silence, as she was walking down the aisle or sailing toward London as Mrs. Adam Prestley?

She gave Copper a sympathetic hug, then moved to the table, stroking the butt of the rifle gently with her fingertips. It was still warm from Zack's hands, and still glossy from the oil. Warm and smooth and solid. So much like its owner. With a wistful sigh, she trudged up the back stairs to her room, almost grateful for the twinges of discomfort that shot through her. It was a day for pain, she decided as she flopped onto her bed. How odd, when it should have been a day for joyful celebration.

Sometimes the right way isn't the easy way, Noelle. She knew what Zack had really been implying: that she was taking the easy way, by not breaking things off with Adam and giving her feelings for Zack a chance to grow. Ironically, it was his other advice—that she should put Copper out of his misery—that she really ought to follow. She should simply let Zack go. She was only keeping him here for her father's sake, wasn't she? The handsome lieutenant didn't need to stay in Chicago one minute longer otherwise. Her father had all the information he needed to make the match. Once a bride was selected, that fortunate female could travel later, and meet her groom in California.

The only honorable thing to do was to insist that Zack leave. It seemed cruel, but was it? Hadn't that been his point about Copper?

Zack would ache for a while; then his bride would arrive, and he'd be happy again. Her father would see to that, by choosing a girl with long legs, and a pretty smile, and an appreciation for brash, kindhearted, handsome young war heroes. If the bride had any sense at all, she'd realize quickly that she was the luckiest person on earth to have been matched with such a fine husband.

Then they'd marry, in a simple ceremony, and the groom would take his bride by the hand and lead her off to begin their life together. Noelle couldn't help but tingle with delight as she imagined just how that amazing night would progress thereafter. Zack wouldn't be expecting too much, thanks to Noelle's misinformation, and so, when his bride led him into her room, banished all dolls from the bed, and then actually allowed him to strip away her exquisite wedding gown, his startling emerald eyes would shine with confused gratitude. He would stare, in that lovestruck way he had, as the realization dawned on him that all of her "rules" had vanished into a haze of passion and permission. Then he'd cup her naked breasts in his hands, and warmth would radiate through her as he slowly, methodically explored and caressed her with his fingertips. Then he'd use his mouth, covering her naked body with kisses that wouldn't stop for hours. And then, just when he thought it couldn't be any more wonderful, she'd insist that he remove his trousers, and she'd stroke him, all the while reminding him, in a naughty whisper, how he had impressed her in her dream, and how, in reality, he was even stronger, and harder, and bigger, and more amazing.

"Oh, no," she groaned aloud, pulling herself out of the groggy spell that had been making her insides pulse with need. "No, no, no. Don't picture him with *you!* What are you *doing?*"

Forcing herself to take a deep breath, she tried to picture herself with Adam. That would be just as wonderful, wouldn't it? Hopefully, it would be even *more* wonderful! But when she closed her eyes, it was Zack, touching her, teasing her, making love to her, and she had a feeling that from that moment onward, it would *always* be Zack! Only Zack. No one else.

Do you know what this is? she challenged herself. *It's an omen. You asked for one, didn't you? Now, what are you going to do with it?*

Her favorite doll was propped against a bedpost, as though studying her with amused detachment. It was the doll that had helped her get through the crisis of losing her mother—the only crisis, up until this very moment, that Noelle had ever endured. She needed her mother now, more than she'd ever needed her before, but the doll would have to do, and so she reached for it and asked weakly, "Have I lost my mind completely? I think I want Zack. I mean, I *know* I want him physically, and I think I might want him other ways, too. And"—she lowered her voice to a whisper—"I don't want Adam to make love to me. The thought of it makes me cringe. It's probably just some sort of jitters, and the normal doubts all brides have, but at this moment, if Adam tried to touch me, I just know I'd pull away. And if Zack walked in right now . . . Well, I daren't admit how much my body would welcome him. What should I do?"

The easy way isn't always the right way, Noelle. . . .

"So I've heard," she murmured. "You think I should talk to Adam? I wouldn't know what to say!" She glared into the doll's button eyes. "Don't you dare ask me to talk to Zack. If he knew I was feeling this way, he'd . . . Well, let's just say, we'd do something I'd regret. And if I asked Father, he'd try to be neutral, but he'd be so deliriously happy at the thought of having Zack in the family. . . ."

She could almost see her father's face, and the expression broke her heart. He would be so relieved. Zack would be exuberant. The servants would be pleased. And Noelle would be swept away by the tide of celebration that would fill the house. . . .

And Adam would be humiliated. Not to mention, brokenhearted and betrayed. He had put his trust in her, over all other women in the world. There had been a time when that had seemed so romantic! Why wasn't it enough anymore?

One thing was certain: she couldn't marry him just yet. Not with all these doubts and urges and emotions surging through her. She needed time to think. To explore the attraction she felt toward Zack, to see if it was indeed love. And she needed to explore her feelings for Adam, too. They had seemed like love once, and perhaps, with the wedding postponed, she might rediscover all that. Assuming of course that he would agree to a postponement, and all the accompanying social humiliation and rumors.

"He'll have to make a choice," she decided, hugging the doll to her breast as she spoke. "If he truly loves me, he'll be willing to give me a little more time. And maybe time is all I really need. If he can't endure the embarrassment—if that matters most to him—then we'll break it off completely, and he can circulate any rumor he wishes to save his reputation. He can tell the world I'm flighty and worthless, or that my jump from the carriage gave him doubts about my sanity. Anything he pleases."

She bit her lip, knowing full well that Adam Prestley would never abide a postponement. She admired so many qualities in the man, but knew in her heart that he was weak when it came to appearances. If she gave him an ultimatum, it would be over. Did she dare? After all, she didn't know whether she loved Zack—it could be a simple case of infatuation with his heroism and emerald eyes and warm, dexterous fingertips.

Then you won't marry either of them, she decided with shaky conviction. *You'll be a spinster, which is what you deserve for making such a mess of this. You should have just let Father choose someone for you ages*

*ago. Or you should have eloped with Adam the day he
proposed to you. He suggested it back then too, remember? He probably sensed that you were flighty and naïve
and unreliable. But you had to have a fancy wedding.
And now you have to have Zack. What's next?*

What's next? She sighed aloud, then crossed to her
desk and forced herself to begin:

> *Dearest Adam,*
>   *This is the most difficult letter I've ever had to
> write. . . .*

Eight

She had read and reread the note so many times, every word was burned into her brain, and so, as she paced the parlor from end to end, waiting for Adam to arrive, she recited it in nervous silence:

You are such a wonderful man, and it's an honor that you chose me as your bride. I should be content with that, and not dare ask anything else, but I'm asking nevertheless. I need something from you—your patience, and a few more months before we marry.

Your mother wanted us to wait until June, do you recall? I should have agreed to that. Or perhaps I should have agreed to elope, as you once wanted. I honestly don't know what I should have done, or what I should do now.

I only know I cannot marry you tomorrow. I'm riddled with doubts, but of one thing I'm certain. I don't deserve you, and if you decide that a postponement is not an option, then I will respect that decision and always know in my heart that all that has happened—and will happen—is entirely my own fault.

Come quickly, Adam. The sooner this is resolved,

*the better for both of us. Or if you cannot abide the
sight of me, send a note to that effect, and I will
understand.*

Love,
Noelle

A gentle knocking at the parlor door startled her, and
she steeled herself before calling out, "Come in," in a
tight, unfamiliar voice. When it was Zack rather than
Adam who stepped into view, she silently cheered, then
immediately panicked at the thought the two rivals
might meet.

Hurrying to stand before him, she tried for a casual
tone. "Did you need something, Zack? I'm expecting . . . Well, I'm expecting Adam, actually. He and I
have an appointment. Not that he needs an appointment
to see me." She almost giggled, she was so nervous at
the sight of him. It was the first time they'd been alone
together since she'd begun to admit her feelings for him,
and she felt giddy enough to throw her arms around his
neck and share the wonderful news.

"This will only take a minute," he assured her solemnly. "I came to say good-bye—"

"What?"

"I'm leaving today, Noelle. There's no purpose in me
staying—"

"You can't go! Not *now!*"

"Now?"

"S-so close to the wedding," she stammered. "Father
needs you now. And so do I."

"You do?"

She could feel her cheeks beginning to flame. "I
know it's been awkward, from time to time—"

"It's been awkward till now. Tomorrow, it's gonna be

downright ugly," he growled. "If you're smart, you'll just let me speak my piece, then kiss me on my cheek, and send me on my way."

"I'm asking you to stay."

"Why?" he demanded.

"For my father," she lied. "And for me, too." She stared into his eyes, desperate to tell him of her doubts, but fearful that he might read too much into them. "Please stay, Zack. For me."

"What's got you so upset?" He cocked his head to the side and studied her. "Are your legs hurting more?"

"Please, Zack. I don't have time to complain. Adam could walk in—"

"Dang blast it, Noelle," he complained; then he shook his head in defeat. "I'll stay for your father's sake. Is that what you want me to say?"

"Yes."

"I wouldn't want to do anything to spoil your wedding," he added, his tone now tinged with sarcasm.

"I appreciate that." She tried not to smile at the undisguised jealousy in his eyes. One word from her, or even one look, and she could turn that petulant spark into a flame of confident passion that would engulf them both. It wouldn't be right or prudent, but nevertheless, it was tempting, and she was actually considering it when Edward stepped into the room.

"Miss Noelle?"

She sighed before turning to him. "Yes, Edward?"

"Mr. Prestley is here. Under the circumstances, I thought it best to show him to the atrium."

She gave the butler a grateful smile, wondering if he realized what a total catastrophe he had just prevented. Knowing Edward, he more than likely did.

"You need to go somewhere else, Zack. Just for a

few minutes, so Adam and I can talk." She felt a silly
smile tugging at the corners of her mouth as she added
sheepishly, "I want to talk to you again, too. *After*
Adam."

He seemed to be reading the signs too well, and so
she warned, "It's not what you think."

"What do I think?" he asked softly.

"I honestly have no idea. Please, Zack. You'll ruin
everything if you don't just go to the kitchen and let
Alice feed you for a while."

A disbelieving grin spread over his features, and she
realized she had said too much. In an instant, he would
grab her and do unspeakably heavenly things to her, and
so she backed away while summoning a stern expression. "Edward, please show Lieutenant Dane to the
kitchen."

Zack chuckled, then caught her by the waist and
pulled her against himself, instructing the butler, "Edward, if you're a gentleman, you'll look away," just before his mouth crushed down on Noelle's.

Her mind reeled, but she didn't even consider resisting. Not when every inch of her body was welcoming
him so warmly. She couldn't have molded herself more
completely to him, and as she greedily savored the amorous efforts of his tongue, she only wished his fingers
would begin to stroke and explore as well—

"Miss Noelle! Lieutenant Dane!" Edward's voice was
so sharp and intrusive the couple literally froze in each
other's arms. Then Noelle disentangled herself, while
Zack teased, "Dang, that was nice." Crossing to Edward,
he clapped him across the back. "Good work, pardner.
You can guard my girl any day."

Noelle sank onto the sofa and groaned aloud at the

thought that Adam could have witnessed the insane scene. "Just go, Zack. Please?"

"I'll give you and that varmint ten minutes," he informed her cheerfully as he headed for the hall. "But I want my friend Edward there every minute to protect you. And don't keep me waiting too long, or I'll come find you."

"Ten minutes," she agreed, torn between the prospect of kissing him again and her duty to Adam. Then she smoothed her hair away from her face, took a deep breath, and stood up straight and tall, prepared for the worst. "Please show Mr. Prestley in now, Edward."

She had expected Adam to react with anger, or hurt, or some sort of confident attempt at convincing her she didn't want a postponement at all. But the cold, unfamiliar expression he wore as he stepped into the room told Noelle nothing about the emotions that were plaguing him. And she had to admit that, in an odd sort of way, it frightened her.

But he was still Adam, and so she hurried to stand before him despite her discomfort. "Are you furious with me? I wouldn't blame you if you were. I'm just grateful you came to see me in person, so we can discuss—"

"Is there something to discuss?"

"Well . . ." She coughed in nervous confusion. "Perhaps not. As I said in my note—"

"Don't quote that piece of rubbish to me." Turning to Edward, he growled, "We'd like some privacy, if you don't mind."

She thought of the butler's heart, and quickly moved between the two men before suggesting, "Edward, could you go and fetch my pink shawl for me? I believe I left it on my bed."

"But, Miss Noelle, I told the lieutenant I'd stay."

"Perfect," Adam drawled. "Dane's officially giving the orders now."

"Don't be silly. Edward?" She arched an eyebrow toward the servant. "I'll call you if I need you. Please give us some privacy, as my fiancé requested."

"I'll be right outside," the butler insisted stubbornly.

"I'd be heartbroken if you weren't." She planted a quick, reassuring kiss on his cheek. "Thank you."

When the doors had closed behind the butler, she turned to Adam and informed him quietly, "That was unnecessary."

"A lesson in etiquette? From you? Under the circumstances, I'd say that's the height of irony."

"You're angry—"

"I'm livid," he corrected. "With myself, more than anyone, if you must know the truth. For some misguided reason, I believed true love still had some value in this ridiculous establishment. Obviously, I was wrong. I only wish I hadn't wasted ten months of my life recognizing the obvious."

"This establishment? What on earth does *that* mean?" It was clear that the comment was mildly offensive, but Noelle wasn't angry. Instead, she was fascinated by the odd approach he'd taken. "You make it sound as though it's all my *father's* fault."

"And of course, nothing could be further from the truth? Is that it?"

"Yes, Adam." She shook her head sadly. "If you want to blame someone, blame me. And to some extent, as you've obviously guessed, Zack needs to share in that. But Father is blameless—"

"Your Father is *not* blameless!" Adam roared. "Are you honestly so blind, or naïve, or simply stupid, that you can't see he planned this from the start?"

Noelle stepped backward and caught her breath before warning softly, "Perhaps you should leave."

"I'll leave," he agreed. "After I've said what I came to say. That's fair, isn't it? After all, I had to read that insufferable note of yours, did I not?" His tone grew sarcastic and mocking. "Dearest Adam, perhaps we should have married *sooner,* or perhaps we should marry *later,* but we simply mustn't marry *on our wedding day,* if you don't mind."

She shrank from the blaze of anger in his eyes, but had to acknowledge he was right about that, at least. How foolish she had been to write such things. She hadn't had the strength, or the decency, to write the truth—that she had changed her mind. There was no shame in changing one's mind, at least according to Zack. Would Adam agree?

"It was a dreadful note, and I apologize. I should have been honest, and told you that, well, that I—" She broke off, then tried again. "I thought I loved you. Seeing you here, like this, I can't imagine why, but I honestly believed it at one time. I was confused—"

"By your father!"

"No! By Zack—"

"Are you so blind you can't see they're one and the same?" He grasped her by the shoulders and shook her gently. "My God, Noelle, I thought you were stronger than this. I thought you meant it when you said you wanted to make your own choice, despite your father's occupation. Was I wrong to believe you? Was I so blinded by love I couldn't see the hold he has over you? Did I misjudge you so completely?"

When she simply stared, he continued eagerly. "You see it, don't you, darling? He has subverted us from the start. He wanted to move his business to San Francisco, and couldn't bear to leave you behind. I understand his dilemma, and given half a chance, I might have put his mind to rest about it. I've always intended for us to travel extensively, and we could have visited him—"

"In San Francisco?"

"Of course. We could have visited yearly."

"Why would my father move to San Francisco?"

"To provide brides for wealthy miners, of course." He hesitated for a moment, then moistened his lips and asked carefully, "He never mentioned it to you?"

"Not a word."

Adam was clearly considering how to proceed in light of Noelle's ignorance. "I believe it had something to do with the successful match he made for your cousin there. His fame in that city, and throughout the West, has grown considerably as a result of that particular coup, and he hoped to capitalize on it."

"I never thought of Megan's marriage as a coup."

"His favorite niece entrusted her heart to him and is now living happily ever after. I imagine business would double overnight if word ever got out that he matched his own daughter to a war hero!"

Noelle sank onto the sofa, patting the cushion next to her in stunned invitation. When Adam joined her, she murmured, "I'd say you were insane, only some of what you've said is true. After Megan's wedding, Father went on and on about how much the business had changed. How there were more inquiries—grooms, that is—from California than from all other states and territories combined. But most of the brides still come from the East, so it never occurred to me he might consider moving Happily Ever After. How did *you* know?"

"It was an active rumor in business circles. Of course, once our engagement was announced, he abandoned his plans. Or rather, he *seemed* to abandon them."

"You never mentioned it to me."

"You and he are so close, I actually thought he would have discussed it with you. But apparently he didn't want you to feel responsible for complicating his situation."

"I'm sure that's it," she said with a nod. "Poor Father. Have I unwittingly sabotaged his plans?"

"Apparently so. And apparently, he felt that gave him the right to do a little sabotage of his own."

"Pardon?"

"It's an amazing coincidence, don't you think, that our young war hero just happened to show up on your doorstep a few days prior to our wedding? That he should pursue you, with your father's indulgence, despite the fact that you were already spoken for? That he's just the type of son-in-law your father would love to have? And better still, he intends to settle in that very area! All in all, a convenient 'match' from your father's point of view, wouldn't you say?"

"You're suggesting Father brought Zack here to sabotage our engagement?"

Adam smiled, as though charmed despite his annoyance; then he took her hand in his own and kissed it. "You're painfully naïve, darling. It's one of the things I love about you, but at some point, you need to open your eyes and see your father for what he is."

"And what exactly is that?"

"A matchmaker. In other words, a manipulator—of

people and of their feelings. And he's quite good at it, as I've often admitted."

"He doesn't manipulate people, he *helps* them," she countered stubbornly. "And he would never manipulate *me.*"

"You're determined to ignore all the evidence—"

"There's not one *shred* of evidence!"

"Isn't there? Didn't you tell me yourself that Dane's the first groom who ever came to this house before the match was made?"

"Yes, but that's because . . ." She took a deep breath. "Father has enormous respect for Zack."

"More than he's had for any of the other men he's served?" Adam arched his eyebrow in quiet disbelief. "You can't tell me some of them weren't equally as deserving."

Noelle fidgeted, remembering how, from scores of letters each year, her father had more than once identified a particularly brave, noble, or otherwise deserving groom, and had dedicated himself to finding an equally deserving bride. But always through the mail. Always, until Zack.

Adam was nodding as though reading her thoughts. "The quality that made Dane unique—the reason *he* was invited before the match—was the fact that he was intended for *you.* There's no other explanation, Noelle. That, coupled with the timing, leaves precious little doubt."

His tone grew gentle. "I've been aware of your father's little game for days, but I haven't objected, because I was foolish enough to believe it wouldn't succeed. Do you know why? Because of what you told me the very first night we met. Do you remember?"

"Go on."

"You said you were determined to find your own true love. That it was a frightening prospect, given your father's talent, but that it was also an exhilarating one. And I felt honored to be a part of it. To add my strength and love to your own, so that together we could prove to the world that Noelle Elizabeth Braddock knew her own heart better than anyone else." A wistful, almost self-mocking smile lit his face. "I honestly believed your father's efforts wouldn't succeed, any more than my own mother could succeed with *her* blatant matchmaking attempts."

"Pardon?"

"She's been doing the same thing," he explained. "Arranging chance encounters, which aren't by chance at all, between me and some of the most attractive and respectable women in the city. Extolling their virtues, their lineages, their ability to give me entrance to wider circles of business associates."

Noelle turned her face away, confused at the parallel between mean-spirited Victoria Prestley and kindhearted Russell Braddock.

Adam read her thoughts again. "I love my mother as much as you love your father, darling. And as hard as it may be for you to believe, she loves me, too."

"I'm sure she does," Noelle murmured.

"I can love her without being blind to her faults. And when she tries to undermine our engagement, I inform her clearly that her efforts are both useless and offensive. You might consider doing the same. Or, if you cannot confront your father, at least acknowledge privately, to me, what he's doing. I think you owe me that."

"You're saying he cares more about his own happiness than about mine? That he'd come between me and the man I love, just because he wants me to go with him to San Francisco? You're saying he invited Lieutenant Dane here, and arranged for him to pretend to be—" She felt a surge of hope, and insisted bravely, "You're wrong, Adam. I understand why you believe these things, but if you could have seen Zack's face when he walked into the dining room and saw me there in my wedding gown—"

"That again?" Adam's face contorted with jealousy and hurt. "You dare sing the praises of a man who thinks so little of marriage, he's willing to allow a stranger to select a bride for him?" Taking a deep breath, he added quickly, "I don't mean to disparage your father's occupation, darling. It serves a genuine need, for men who live in areas so remote and underpopulated that there's no hope of finding a bride without a matchmaker.

"But Dane's here in Chicago, and from the sound of it, he's been spending time in New Orleans and all points in between. What's his excuse for taking so dim a view of the institution of marriage? I'm sure he wouldn't allow another man to choose his rifle, or the fuses he employs in his demolition work. But a bride? *That's* another story."

Noelle bit her lip, confused again by the bizarre truth in the indictment. She had seen Zack as the ultimate romantic hero—so dashing and impetuous. Yet he'd thought so little of love, he had been willing to marry a stranger, sight unseen. And when forced to come to Chicago, he had conveniently fallen for the first girl on whom he'd lain eyes. It hadn't been love at first sight at all! It had been a simple solution to the pesky problem of choosing a lifelong mate. Had Noelle not been standing on that table, he would have been lovestruck by someone else—anyone else!—that Russell Braddock had produced for him!

Adam cupped her chin in his hand. "You're a matchmaker's daughter. You were raised to believe your father had some sort of mystical ability." When Noelle nodded, he continued more briskly. "Most people would balk at putting such an important decision in someone else's hands. But for you, it's quite the opposite. You don't trust your own instincts. You don't trust yourself to fall in love naturally. You have some sort of need for him to tell you whom to marry."

His hand dropped to her shoulder, kneading it as he spoke. "Believe it or not, I found it all charming. I thought this bizarre world you grew up in would add a delightful aspect to our relationship. My beautiful little paradox—so innocent and inexperienced, and yet . . ."

"Go on."

He hesitated, then smiled ruefully. "I was a romantic fool. All because you and I chose one another freely. Even the fact that our parents objected seemed romantic. Shades of *Romeo and Juliet,* although I hoped we could avoid the tragic ending."

Her stomach muscles clenched into a knot as she examined the flood of disappointments, one by one. If her father wanted to move the Happily Ever After Company to San Francisco, why hadn't he mentioned it to Noelle? She had assumed his resistance to Adam was personal, but was that only part of it?

And Adam was right about the timing of Zack's visit. The very first groom to ever stay at the Braddock residence prior to the match just happened to be a hero bound for California.

She remembered how stunned she had been when her father had installed a stranger in the guest room during the precious week before her wedding. Given the bustle and distraction of preparations, it would have made sense to put him in a hotel, with promises that he would have the matchmaker's undivided attentions once Noelle and Adam had left for their honeymoon. Unless, of course, Noelle was intended for Zack from the start!

She had been so charmed by the sharpshooter's case of love at first sight, but now had to admit it was probably based on convenience more than anything else. He had probably made up his mind to accept the first girl Russell Braddock offered to him, and there had stood Noelle, ready and waiting, dress and all.

And she herself was the most profound disappointment of all. After bragging that she could choose her own mate in spite of her father's legendary talent, she had easily abandoned her own choice, falling instead into the arms of the first man her father paraded in front of her.

"Forgive me, darling. I know this has been difficult for you, and I've tried to be patient. But your note, combined with that buffoon's unprovoked assault last night—"

"Pardon?"

"He didn't mention it?" Adam winced. "I thought he would have boasted by now, to impress you with his pugilistic skills."

"What happened?"

"Very little, actually. I'm sure he hoped to precipitate a full-blown brawl, but I thought you'd find that sort of thing distasteful."

"Of course I do! Did he hurt you?"

Adam rubbed his jaw ruefully. "He has an excellent left hook, especially when one isn't prepared for it, but I survived. I wanted to throttle him, and if I'd known

I'd already lost you, I would have." He paused, then asked carefully, *"Have* I lost you?"

"No." Her voice sounded weak and unconvincing, so she took a deep breath and explained frankly, "I don't know what to say, Adam. I was confused when I wrote the note, and I'm doubly confused now, but I have to admit that everything you've said this afternoon is true."

"The last thing I wanted to do was hurt you with all this—"

"It's not your fault." She rubbed her eyes, fighting a wave of confused exhaustion. "I need to speak with my father."

"Don't be too angry with him," Adam advised. "Deep inside, he only wants you to be happy. You know that, don't you?"

"Of course. It's sweet of you to defend him."

"I have a prediction, if you'd care to hear it."

Noelle winced. "A prediction?"

Adam smiled. "Whatever misgivings he's had until now, he'll put them aside tomorrow and welcome me into the family without reservation. Weddings have that effect on parents, Noelle. Even my mother is beginning to look forward to the ceremony. My older sister and her husband arrived today, and Mother and Constance have been regaling them with the details ever since. You'd think it was a coronation, the way they've gone on and on."

"And in the midst of all that, my note arrived, asking for a postponement?" Noelle shuddered at the thought. "However do you tolerate me, Adam?"

"I love you with all my heart. It's that simple." He took her hand in his own. "Let me be strong for you, for twenty-four hours. In fact, let me take you home with me tonight. I'll have you back here in plenty of time to dress tomorrow. It will give you a chance to get acquainted with Donna and her husband, Harry. There won't be much time for visiting tomorrow, and then we'll be off for London—"

"I can't come to your house," Noelle protested. Her eyes were beginning to sting with tears. "I've been planning my last night in this house for months. Playing chess with Father, and reminiscing about Mother, and reassuring him—" She brushed a tear from her cheek. "I wanted it to be perfect. I wanted tomorrow to be perfect. Instead, it's all such a m-mess."

"It doesn't have to be. Not if you're strong. Let me help you—"

"No." She took a deep breath, then squared her shoulders with weary resolve. "I'll be strong, Adam. I promise. I owe you that, after all I've put you through."

"You owe it to yourself," he corrected her quietly. "You made a promise to yourself, to resist the temptation to put your future in any hands but your own. Keep *that* promise, Noelle. In the long run, it may be the most important thing you will ever do." He tilted her face up so that he could stare into her eyes. "Are you sure you don't want to come with me?"

"I'm sure."

"And?"

She bowed her head and murmured, "I'll marry you tomorrow."

He exhaled sharply, then lifted her hand to his lips. "Thank you, darling. You won't regret it."

She was relieved that he hadn't chosen to kiss her mouth; then she chided herself, remembering that their wedding night was approaching. What would she do then? Recoil in horror? No, she wouldn't recoil, because she wasn't repulsed by the man, she was simply numb. And if Zack walked in at that moment and took her

into his arms, she knew that her reaction would be the
same. Her senses were deadened, and she could only
hope that a long talk with her father and a good night's
sleep would restore some measure of feeling, so that
she didn't sleepwalk through her wedding night. Not
that that sounded so bad to her at that moment. . . .

"Father?"

"Sweetheart!" He jumped up from his desk and came
around to give her a hug. "Did Adam leave already?
Zack and Edward seemed to think you and he were
quarreling—"

"We weren't."

"Well, that's a relief."

"Is it?"

"Of course."

Noelle gave him another hug, then moved to sit on
the sofa. "If I ask you a question, do you give me your
word you'll answer it honestly?"

"What's wrong?" When she just shrugged, he added
quickly, "Of course I'll tell you the truth. In eighteen
years, I've never lied to you. Why would I start now?"

"Have you ever considered moving Happily Ever After to San Francisco?"

He seemed startled, then nodded slowly. "Chicago
was the perfect location, when the frontier was moving
from the Mississippi westward. Even with the gold and
silver strikes, the exodus might have been temporary,
had San Francisco not been so seductive. But that city
seems to have a magic that turns wanderers into settlers.
Most of the grooms contact me from California now.
And, of course, Megan's there. So the answer is: yes,
I've considered such a move. But of course, it's out of

the question now. I'd never move so far from you, so don't worry on that account."

"It might be for the best," she said quietly. "You and Adam will never get along."

"Noelle!"

"It would have been different, if I had married Zack." Her voice started to tremble, and she had to take a deep breath before she asked, "Did you bring him here in hopes I might choose him over Adam?"

"No, sweetheart—" Braddock raked his fingers through his hair in frustration. "You've asked me to be honest, and so I'll admit that when I read his letter, I wished . . . Well, I wished it had arrived sooner."

He crossed the room to sit beside her. "In the days when Adam was courting you, before he asked for your hand, I devoured every letter, in hopes of finding someone else for you. But once you were engaged, I swear I abandoned all that. Or at least, I thought I had. I didn't realize I was still interfering until last night. Sending Zack along as your chaperon was unforgivable, and it almost cost you your life. When I think of you jumping from that carriage . . ."

Noelle held up her hand to stop him, then sighed aloud. "We're quite a pair, aren't we? Neither of us believed I could make the right choice on my own."

"That's not true. I always wanted you to find your own husband. I know you don't believe that—"

"*I* didn't find Zack."

"That's true." He hesitated before adding, "Don't blame Zack for any of this, Noelle. He came here because Tom Greer told him I could find him a suitable bride. He didn't even know you existed."

"I know that, Father. I don't blame Zack, at least not

for that. But he punched Adam last night. Did you know about that?"

Braddock grimaced. "He didn't mention it. Did Adam say what they argued about?"

"Are you suggesting there might be a good reason for a guest in our home to assault my fiancé?" She dropped the haughty tone and admitted, "I assume he blamed Adam for my injury, which would be grossly unfair. Or, it was some sort of jealous outburst."

"He insulted you, so I hit him," Zack corrected quietly from the doorway. "It's as simple as that." When Noelle started to shake her head, he added bluntly, "I know you think he loves you, but he doesn't. If he did, he wouldn't be able to look at you, and talk about you, the way he does."

"What did he say?" Braddock demanded.

"Father, please." Noelle buried her face in her hands. "Zack, please go away. I know you mean well—"

"I'll go," he agreed. "As soon as you've heard what needs to be said. Prestley's not just selfish and mean-spirited. He's all twisted up inside—"

"That's enough!" She jumped to her feet and glared. "I know this hasn't been easy for you, Zack—"

"I'm not talking about *me*. Or about *us*. I've let loose of all that, for all our sakes. I'll admit," he added softly, "I wanted you so bad I could taste you, but that's done with now. I'll get over it in a year or two and find myself another girl. But your father's never gonna have another daughter, and you're never gonna have another life, so I'm bound and determined to find a way to change your mind about Prestley."

"A year or two?" Noelle struggled to control an unexpected surge of hurt. "So much for protestations of everlasting love."

"Noelle—"

"You needn't worry about my father and me, Lieutenant. I'll always love him and I'll always be his daughter."

Russell Braddock stood up and slipped his arm around his Noelle's shoulders. "I need to hear this, sweetheart. Zack, what exactly did Adam say about my daughter?"

"It wasn't just the words, it was the way he said 'em," Zack explained, adding stubbornly, "He called her 'every man's fantasy.' So I hit him. And if you'd been there, you'd've hit him, too."

Noelle glanced at her father's face and could see that he was having as much trouble as she, seeing the insult in her fiancé's words. "I actually think Adam meant it as a compliment, Zack—"

"Dang blast it, Noelle! Pay attention! I'm standing here, telling you I'm willing to walk away if it'll help you see that varmint for what he is. Even feeling for you the way I do—"

"You'll be fine in a year or two," she reminded him tartly. "In fact, you'll probably be fine in a week. Once Adam and I have left for our honeymoon, Father will find you someone else, and you'll live happily ever after. Isn't that so, Father?"

"We're all upset," Braddock soothed. "And it's almost dinnertime. Why don't we have a nice meal—"

"I'm not hungry," Noelle interrupted, adding more gently, "I'm exhausted, Father. Do you mind if I take a nap while you and Zack eat? I'll be back downstairs later." She embraced him and explained, "I've been hoping we could spend this last night together reminiscing about Mother. We could have cocoa, and tell stories. How does that sound?"

"Wonderful," he admitted.

"And we need to talk about Copper."

"The dog?"

"I can't bear to see him suffer anymore," she began; then to her amazement, an unexpected sob welled up in her throat, as though all the heartache and confusion of the day had combined in this one, mournful predicament. Turning to Zack, she pleaded, "Could you explain it to him? I thought I could, but I just can't."

"I'll take care of it. Go and have your nap."

"Thank you." Turning to her father, she hugged him fiercely, then sped past Zack without another word.

Zack watched with wistful longing as she disappeared down the hall to the back staircase. Then he murmured to his host, "I can't hardly stand seeing her that way."

"I know what you mean."

"I've tried my best to talk to her—to prove it's more than jealousy that's got my back up—but she won't listen."

Braddock rubbed his eyes, as though he was as exhausted by all the consternation as his daughter. "I'd do anything to save her from this, son. And I know you would, too. But I think it's something she needs to work through on her own."

"Because she doesn't trust our advice," Zack agreed. "She thinks you set out to sabotage her engagement, and she *knows* I did my best to bust it up. But she knows things about Prestley, too. That business with the Jordan fella, and the way he talks about you. So why does she trust *him?*"

"She doesn't."

"Huh?"

Braddock patted Zack's shoulder. "As I said, it's painful to watch her go through this without help. But I no

longer doubt she'll make the right decision." With a
weary smile he reminded his guest, "I've studied these
things my whole life, and I can see when a match is
falling apart. Noelle's engagement to Adam is in sham-
bles. She's just not ready to admit it yet. I don't envy
her the next twenty-four hours, but the best thing we
can do for her is let her work it out on her own."

"There's no time—"

"There's plenty of time," Braddock assured him.
"We've reversed positions on that particular issue, I see.
But you were right all along. You and she were meant
to be, and deep inside Noelle knows it now, too."

Zack winced. "You don't want to see the truth. Neither do I. But facts are facts, Russ."

Braddock nodded. "Fact number one: my daughter
was raised to marry for love, not from obligation. Fact
number two: you and she were meant to be. Together,
those two facts will prevent her from marrying Adam."

Zack shook his head. "She's so danged stubborn—"

"And we wouldn't change that, even if we could.
So . . ." Braddock's eyes began to twinkle. "Tell me
about this fight you had with my ex-future son-in-law.
And *don't* leave out any details."

Nine

Winifred arrived the next morning before Noelle's feet touched her bedroom floor, and from that moment onward, the hours were a blur of frantic preparation as the bride was bathed, coiffed, manicured, and otherwise pampered and scolded into a vision of absolute loveliness.

"What were you thinking, bolting out of a carriage that way? You might have broken your neck! After all the hours I've spent planning this wedding and designing your gowns!"

"It was selfish of me," Noelle drawled. "I promise I'll wait until after the wedding before I kill myself."

"Young brides." Winifred sniffed. "They never appreciate how fortunate they are. Here you are, hours away from becoming Mrs. Adam Prestley, and all you can do is snap and sniffle. Be grateful that a fine man like him wants to marry you."

"You make it sound as though . . . Oh, never mind."

Winifred eyed her knowingly. "I've planned dozens of weddings, and it's always the same. Spoiled brides, convinced they're making a colossal mistake."

Noelle turned her full attention to the dressmaker. "What sort of mistake?"

"That he's the wrong man, of course. All brides have

these moments, Noelle. Suddenly, every other man in their life—including suitors they rejected without a second glance—seem preferable. I should prepare a handbook, so young brides know what to expect. Or better still, a handbook for their families, so they aren't shocked when the tears and tantrums start. There!" She flashed the bride a satisfied smile. "What do you think?"

Noelle studied her new manicure with honest admiration. "You're so talented, Winnie. Can you cook, too?"

"Of course."

"I can't do anything."

"Well then, be glad you're marrying a wealthy man, and stop frowning so much. Do you want to have wrinkles before you're twenty?"

Noelle shrugged. "Why should I care? By then, Adam will be bored with me, don't you think?"

Winifred laughed. "From the sound of it, it's you who's bored with him."

"I'm numb to him. And to all other men, as well."

The dressmaker laughed heartily. "I haven't heard that complaint before. Repulsed by the bridegroom, or attracted to the bridegroom's closest friend—those are the two most frequent. But numb?" She hugged Noelle and insisted, "Of all the brides I've ever assisted, you're my favorite. Do you know that?"

"Do you always say that?"

"Yes, but in your case, it's true. It's like dressing a princess—a temperamental one, with a wild imagination and a wonderful heart."

"I don't want to be a princess. I want to be madly, hopelessly in love with a man who's madly in love with me. Is that too much to ask?"

Winifred pursed her lips. "A week ago you were insisting that you and Adam were just such a couple."

"Was I?" Noelle sighed. "In love, perhaps. But madly? Hopelessly? No, Winnie. For a few moments, I thought maybe I could have that with—Well, with someone else. But maybe it's just not possible. At least, not for me."

"Are we talking about the dusty lieutenant with the big green eyes?" The dressmaker scowled. "I couldn't believe my ears when I heard he was still here. I'm surprised Adam allowed it."

Noelle bristled. "Adam Prestley doesn't determine who can and cannot visit my father's house. And the truth is, Lieutenant Dane is good company for Father. He's staying through the ceremony, as a favor to our family, and I'm grateful to him for it."

Winifred studied Noelle suspiciously. "You haven't done anything—well, let's just say, irreversible—with the young lieutenant, have you?"

"Honestly!" Noelle tried to glare, but found herself laughing instead. "What a thing to say."

The dressmaker grinned. "As I said, I hear many things from brides, and that particular confession is not as rare as you might hope. Did you have some fun with him, at least? He may be uncouth and uncivilized, but he's a strapping specimen. And he was so completely smitten with you."

"It was the gown."

Winifred seemed about to argue, then smiled instead. "It's just as well. I may have had doubts about you and Adam at the beginning, but those faded quickly."

"You had doubts about him?"

"I thought he was too old for you," she admitted. "And so stuffy! Always looking at his watch or tapping his foot, as though the rest of us are inconvenient pests. But apparently *you* please him. Everyone says he seems happier since he met you."

"They do?"

Winifred nodded again. "We all thought he'd never marry, but here you are—the most unlikely candidate imaginable."

Noelle cocked her head to the side and studied her intently. "Why am I such an unlikely match for Adam?"

"Well, you're not exactly—" Winifred stopped herself and smiled apologetically. "You're perfect, of course. But you're also somewhat unconventional. And softhearted, almost to a fault. Hardly the qualities a man like Adam Prestley seeks out in a wife. On the other hand, he couldn't ask for a more beautiful bride."

Noelle bit her lip before asking, "When the other brides tell you these things—their doubts and their fears—do you ever talk to them afterwards, to see if, or rather, *when* they know it wasn't a mistake, after all?"

"I don't need them to tell me. I can see it on their faces, after the kiss." The dressmaker's eyes began to sparkle. *"That's* the moment, Noelle. If you're not happy then, you'll never be happy with him. If you have even a *twinge* of doubt at that moment, I'll see it in your face and I'll send the young lieutenant to rescue you and carry you off on his horse."

"What a thing to say!" Noelle grinned at the romantic image. "You'd do that, in front of all those society snobs? Can you imagine what it would do to your business?"

"As though any of the Prestleys' friends hire me now?" Winifred sniffed. "It's a thankless business at best, Noelle. But I tolerate it, just for the privilege of witnessing that one moment, when I see love shining in the couple's eyes. It makes me proud to be a part of uniting them forever."

"I never knew you were such a romantic." Noelle exhaled loudly, trying to imagine the moment when Adam would kiss her after the ceremony. Would Winifred get her wish then, and see love shining in Noelle's eyes? Her father would be watching, too, as would Zack. What would they see? What would Adam see?

Would Adam even care? He knew about her feelings for Zack, and knew further that she had been having serious doubts, but still he had gone forward, confident that all would be well. Why? Because Noelle was "every man's fantasy"—whatever *that* meant.

"Noelle?" Winifred patted the bride's cheek. "Do you want to know a secret?"

"Yes."

"I've assisted at more than twenty weddings, and I've made dresses for twice that many brides. I've always attended the ceremony, and I have never, ever been disappointed. It will happen just as I told you it would. I give you my solemn word." With a sly smile, the dressmaker grabbed a pink velvet bathrobe from a hook on the bedroom door. "Put this on and go have a peek. Maybe that's all you need."

"A peek?"

"At the decorations. While you're gone, I'll get the gown ready. It's almost time, you know. The guests will be arriving in less than an hour. But go down the back stairs," she cautioned. "It wouldn't do for Adam to see you."

"Do you think he's here?"

"No, but he and his family will be the first to arrive, don't you suppose?"

The bride hesitated, but only for a moment, then

slipped the robe over her petticoats and cinched it tightly. Maybe Winifred was right. Maybe a glimpse of the kitchen filled with delicacies, and a whiff of the perfume from hundreds upon hundreds of white roses, would remind her how she'd dreamed of this day.

Scooting down the narrow, wood-paneled staircase, she listened hopefully to the excited chatter below. Alice and one of the maids who had been hired for the occasion sounded almost hysterical as they rattled off lists, one to the other, clearly fearing they'd forgotten something vital. If only they knew that the missing ingredient from this particular wedding was confidence!

"Miss Noelle!" The cook rushed over and gave her a hearty embrace. "I was afraid I wouldn't get a chance to wish you the best, one last time. Look at your hair! It's lovely. You'll make such a beautiful bride."

Noelle patted the woman's back, touched and amused by the gushing that had come so unexpectedly. "Thank you, Alice. Everything smells so delicious. You mustn't forget your promise to teach me to cook when I return from London."

When Alice had composed herself, Noelle turned to the maid, who couldn't have been a day over fifteen. "You're Rachel, aren't you? Thank you so much for all your hard work. And please thank your sister for me, too, if I don't have the chance."

"It's our pleasure, Miss Noelle." The girl blushed with pride. "It's grander than anything I ever hoped to see—especially all the flowers."

"Are the garlands all arranged? I wanted to take a peek, but . . ." She grimaced slightly. "Do you know if Mr. Prestley and his family have arrived?"

"Not yet. Mr. Braddock said they won't likely come until the last minute."

"Do you know where my father is?"

"He's getting dressed, miss. Did you want me to tell him you're looking for him?"

Noelle resisted an impulse to agree. She would see her father soon enough, after all—waiting for her at the bottom of the magnificent front staircase. In the meantime, she was content with her memory of their visit the night before. It had been so perfect, as they exchanged stories—some tearful, some hilarious—of the days when Noelle's mother had been alive. No mention of Adam or Zack—those had been the rules, and each had scrupulously followed them.

"I'll just have a quick look around; then I need to get dressed, myself." She hugged Alice again, then on impulse hugged little Rachel, too. "You'll have a pretty wedding yourself one day. Just marry for love, and it will be the grandest thing you'll ever, ever see."

Brushing hastily at a tear, she turned to give Copper a hug, but he wasn't in his bed. "Where's the dog?"

"Out in the yard, with the lieutenant."

"Oh, no!" Noelle gasped at the gruesome image that had flashed before her eyes; then she sprinted for the service porch, down the steps, and onto the lawn, heedless of the deliverymen and waiters who had chosen that location to have a smoke or go over last-minute instructions.

"Noelle? What're you doing out here?"

She spun toward the voice from the shadows, only to see that Copper, his coat gleaming from a recent grooming, had apparently been having one last visit with Zack's horse, a huge chestnut with a silver-white blaze across his face. "When I heard you and Copper were out here, I was afraid you might be . . . be . . ."

"An hour before your wedding?" Zack pulled her into

a soothing hug. "I know you think I'm uncivilized, but I surely know better than that."

Bursting into tears, she buried her face against his linen vest and insisted, "It's natural for me to be nervous. All brides are this way."

"That's right, sugar. It's natural as can be. Get it all out now, or you'll have red eyes for the guests."

She pulled free of him and summoned a grateful smile. "You're the last person I expected to talk to today, but I'm so very, very glad you're here."

"I said I'd stay, and I will. Till after it's over. Then Merc and me are heading out. Some of your pappy's friends are gonna stay late and play cards, so don't go worrying about him."

"You don't need to run off! You should stay one more night."

"I'm not in a partying frame of mind."

"I know." She stroked his cheek fondly. "Promise me you won't wait a year or two to find another girl, Zack. You'll make such a wonderful husband and father."

"That wouldn't be fair to the girl, me feeling the way I do about you," he said with a shrug. "But there's a promise I'd like you to make to me, if you're willing. It's not what you think," he added sheepishly.

She flushed and nodded. "If it's reasonable, I'll agree. What is it?"

He cleared his throat. "If the time comes—tomorrow, or next week, or ten years from now—"

"Oh, Zack." Tears spilled down her cheeks anew. "Please don't say that. If I marry Adam, it'll be forever."

He started to protest, then stopped himself and eyed her quizzically. *"If* you marry him?"

"I meant, *when* I marry him. Did I say—" She tried to scowl. "I don't want to argue, Zack."

"Who's arguing? I'm just listening."

"And hearing what you want to hear?" She took a deep breath, then shrugged off the confusion. "If you're leaving right after the ceremony, what will become of Copper?"

"I'll take care of him before I go. Alice is gonna fix him some tasty treats; then me and Merc'll take him over by the lake. It won't disturb the party."

"I didn't mean . . ." She sighed, then noticed he was staring at her coiffure. "What do you think?" she asked, patting the sophisticated pile of curls.

"Fancy. I like it. I guess I was just picturing it different—the way it curled all pretty around your face that day in the dining room. But I reckon this is how it's done hereabouts."

"Noelle!" Winifred shouted from the doorway. "Have you lost your mind? The guests are starting to arrive!"

"Oh, dear." She touched Zack's cheek again. "I suppose we should say good-bye now? Just in case?"

"Just in case?" He studied her hopefully. "In case you go through with it?"

"That's not what I meant!" She caught her temper and scolded, "The guests are arriving, and Father's upstairs dressing. Do you honestly believe I'd change my mind at the last moment, in front of dozens of strangers, after all the planning and expense that have gone into this?"

"Don't get all riled up, sugar. If you wanna say good-bye, just in case, it's fine by me. Come here." Without waiting for her to cooperate, he set his hands on her hips and drew her against him, lowering his lips to hers and brushing them gently, once and then again.

She knew by now what he'd do next, and to her shame, she welcomed it. The lingering, loving interplay of their mouths and tongues, each tasting the fresh, innocent sweetness of the other—

"Noelle!"

She spun toward Winifred and called out unhappily, "I'll be there in a minute!" Then she turned back to Zack and admitted, "I'm glad we did that. It was wrong, but it's the way I want to remember you. Good-bye!" Before he could answer, she gathered up the long velvet skirt of her robe and raced onto the porch, past Winifred's puzzled frown, and up the staircase to the safety of her room.

She would have thrown herself across the bed and allowed Zack's last kiss to thrill her for a few long, guilty moments before she dressed, had Victoria Prestley not been standing in the middle of the room, her pale blue eyes cold with disapproval and disdain.

"Oh! Mrs. Prestley!" The bride struggled to appear composed. "I didn't know you were here."

"Obviously."

Noelle winced, then took a moment to study her future mother-in-law. She had clearly been a beautiful woman once, and even now, her skin was like alabaster, with tiny lines so evenly distributed that they seemed to accentuate her delicacy rather than to signal any measure of decline. She wore pearls and diamonds, along with a severe pale blue gown that echoed the color of her eyes.

"You look lovely," Noelle told her quietly. "Your dress is absolutely exquisite."

"Shouldn't *you* be dressed by now?"

Noelle began to answer, then smiled gratefully when Winifred stepped into the room. The dressmaker was as startled by Mrs. Prestley's presence as Noelle had been, but she recovered quickly and smiled. "How nice to see you again, Mrs. Prestley. Especially on such a happy occasion."

"Have we met?"

Winifred nodded. "Several times. I'm Winifred Duschane." Turning to Noelle, she murmured, "Could I see you in the hall for just a moment?"

Noelle had no doubt but that Winifred intended to scold her, so she shook her head. "I need to dress immediately."

Winifred turned to Adam's mother. "Noelle and I thought you and your daughters might like to use the sitting room down the hall for last-minute preparations. We readied it for you, if you'd like me to show you—"

"The butler explained the arrangement, and my daughters are there, in fact. I wanted a chance to speak with Noelle before the ceremony."

"I'm pleased we had this chance, too," Noelle assured her. "And you're welcome to stay, as long as you don't mind watching Winnie put me in my gown."

"I'll stay. Please, go about dressing while we talk."

"Noelle?" Winifred gave the bride a tight, no-nonsense smile. "If I could have just one minute first?"

"There isn't time," Noelle interrupted; then she turned back to Adam's mother. "Wait until you see what a beautiful gown Winnie has created."

"If it's half as unusual as your doll collection, I'll be very impressed, dear."

Noelle winced at the hint of mockery in the woman's tone. Never in her wildest imaginings had she thought Victoria Prestley would actually visit this room. She certainly would have put the dolls away—

But why? Why shouldn't her mother-in-law have a

glimpse into her daughter-in-law's personality? What had Winifred called it? Unconventional? Was that suddenly something of which to be ashamed?

With a burst of confidence, she smiled and explained, "I love each and every one of these dolls. Some are gifts from Father's customers, from all around the world. And some were my mother's. This porcelain baby was my grandmother's, if you can believe it. One day, your granddaughter will play with these. Can you imagine how much fun she'll have?"

Mrs. Prestley stared at her as though she'd lost her mind; then she arched a knowing eyebrow. "Are you nervous, dear?"

Noelle winced again. "Aren't all brides nervous?" When her guest didn't respond, she added carefully, "Is Adam?"

"No." The dowager hesitated, then admitted, "That's what I wanted to talk to you about. He's quite beside himself with love for you, Noelle. I've never seen him so pleased with himself in his life. And as his mother . . . well, I love seeing him so happy."

Resisting an impulse to exchange furtive glances of pure amazement with Winifred, Noelle smiled gracefully. "It's something we have in common—a sincere desire for Adam's happiness."

Mrs. Prestley nodded. "He tells me I've been less than cordial to you in the past. I intend to make an effort to change that."

"Thank you."

"It will require your cooperation, of course, but if you honestly want him to be happy, that shouldn't be a problem."

"I agree."

"Noelle?" Winifred pretended to rest a hand lightly

on the bride's shoulder, while actually digging her nails into the skin with unmistakable insistence. "Now that you and your mother-in-law have had your talk, you and I *must* speak also. *In the hall.*"

"There's no time for sentimental nonsense," Mrs. Prestley complained. "Noelle needs to dress immediately. The guests are undoubtedly taking their seats at this very moment."

Almost as though to underscore the remark, the gentle strains of violins were replaced by a burst of organ music, and Noelle grimaced. That was the official signal. Ten more minutes, and then it would be time for her to descend the staircase. "Really, Winnie, I wish we had time—"

"Never mind all that." The dressmaker gathered up the endless layers of satin that made up the skirt of the wedding gown. "Fifteen years, and I've never had a bride miss her cue. We'll find a minute at the top of the stairs. Mind your hair, now. There'll be no time for last-minute repairs."

Noelle slipped out of her robe and wriggled carefully into the gown, then stood still, with her back to the mirror, while Winifred's skillful fingers fastened thirty-nine tiny pearl buttons, all the while adjusting the lacy bodice so that Noelle's pale, firm breasts were lifted and showcased. And all Noelle could think about was the way Zack had stared at her that afternoon in the dining room, mesmerized by each and every part of her, but especially greedy whenever his gaze scanned the low, square-cut neckline.

She couldn't wait any longer, and so she pulled away from Winifred's busy hands and turned to the mirror, then gasped in delight at the artless beauty of the gown, its pure white elegance so stunningly offset by the delicate silver threads that had been painstakingly pulled through the fabric.

"Didn't I tell you?" Winifred murmured. "You're a princess. Or should I say, an angel?"

Noelle wanted to reprimand her for the clear reference to Zack, but she had to admit it was true. There was something ethereal and heavenly about the total effect, and she could only imagine how the gown had appeared to Zack as he stood at the foot of the table and looked up at it with his huge, sparkling green eyes. Then her slipper had caught in her hem, and he had caught her—

"My slippers!" she wailed softly. "I can't remember where I put them."

"Goodness, Noelle!" Winifred's eyes had widened with distress. "If you'd kept your thoughts where they should be—"

"Don't scold me, please? Just look for them. In the sitting room, I think. I was trying them on with the pink dancing gown—"

"Don't panic." Winifred sent Mrs. Prestley a reassuring glance. "Isn't this the way of it? Something always seems to go awry at the last minute, but it always works out in the end."

"It's what comes of socializing when one should be performing one's duties." The dowager sniffed. "Go and find the slippers, please."

Shrugging off the rudeness, Winifred bustled out of the room without another word.

"Please don't speak to Winifred that way anymore," Noelle murmured. "She's my friend. And even if she weren't, I was raised to treat everyone—even servants—with courtesy and respect."

"I see." The pale blue eyes were cold with disdain.

"Perhaps we simply define 'courtesy' differently." She turned toward the door, which had opened again, and smiled in exaggerated relief at the sight of her two daughters. "Darlings! You look exquisite. And doesn't our little Noelle look pretty, too?"

Adam's younger sister, Constance, grinned. "It's a beautiful gown, Noelle. And your hair looks *ever* so much better than usual." Pulling her companion into view, she continued. "Noelle Braddock, this is my sister Donna Harrington."

"We met over Christmas," Noelle reminded them with a smile. "It's nice to see you again, Donna. You both look lovely."

"It's always the same when I come to Chicago," Donna confided. "So many new faces, they all blur together. And speaking of faces"—she grinned impishly—"I don't believe I've ever seen quite so many dolls in one place, outside of a toy shop. I was sure my brother was exaggerating, but here they are. It's really rather disconcerting."

"Noelle loves each and every one of them," Victoria Prestley informed them.

"So we heard. Adam says you even named them all!"

Noelle studied Constance intently. "Why wouldn't I?"

"Pardon? Oh . . ." The sister giggled nervously. "Did it sound like a criticism? Please don't tell Adam. We've sworn to be on our best behavior with you."

"I see."

"You should be flattered, Noelle," Donna chastised her lightly. "Adam spent two full hours last night instructing us. And another hour with my husband, Harry, raving about you. I should add that Harry was so impressed, I was almost jealous."

Noelle sighed, acknowledging that in her own way

this awful woman was right. Noelle should be flattered that Adam cared enough to bring his whole clan into line, despite their obvious disapproval. And the fact that he had told them about the doll collection seemed flattering, too, in a sense. At least he wasn't ashamed of it, or her. Not that he should be, of course, but these three women were making her feel as though *they* thought he should be.

"What was it Adam told Harry?" Constance was prodding. "That Noelle was every man's dream come true?"

Noelle forced herself to relax despite a twinge of foreboding. "It's sweet of Adam to exaggerate."

"According to Harry, it's true." Donna was visibly fighting a fit of giggles. "He and I had the most awful row last night because of it."

"Oh?"

The sister's blue eyes were twinkling mischievously. "How can a banker's daughter hope to compete with you? It's really quite unfair. The very thing that should drive decent gentlemen away is the thing Adam can't resist. And apparently, neither can Harry."

"Donna, don't," Constance warned under her breath. "Adam will be furious."

"Why?" The older sister turned to Noelle and smiled. "She knows I'm just teasing. And it's not as though she doesn't know how her father makes his living. That's part of the allure, isn't it? The fact that she *knew* about it while she was growing up. I mean . . ." She eyed Noelle curiously. "You know what your father does, don't you?"

"He's a matchmaker."

"Exactly!" She gave Constance a victorious smile. "Didn't I tell you?"

Noelle eyed the sisters impatiently. "That still doesn't explain why you think Father's business attracted Adam to me. I mean, he's always admired Father's business instinct, but . . ."

Donna shrugged. "It's all part of the fantasy. Wait! That's what he said—every man's *fantasy,* not every man's dream come true. I got that wrong, I think. He said fantasy, not dream, didn't he, Constance?"

"So I hear," Constance murmured.

Noelle frowned. "Are you saying Adam fantasizes about matchmaking?"

"Of course not, silly. He says—and Harry agrees, the rogue—that every man dreams of walking into a brothel and finding a virgin waiting for him in one of the bedrooms—"

"Donna Harrington!" Victoria Prestley's blue eyes flamed with reproach. "I will not tolerate that sort of talk. Noelle doesn't know any better, but you girls should be ashamed."

"I didn't say anything," Constance complained. "And if you want to blame someone, blame your darling Adam. He's the one who told the story in the first place."

Noelle had been staring at them in stunned disbelief, and now whispered, "A brothel? What on earth?"

"He doesn't mean this house," Constance assured her gently. "He knows the girls aren't here. He just means your father's business. Out there somewhere," she added, gesturing toward the window. When Noelle stared again, she added defensively, "He told me himself he's never seen whores or criminals or any sort of wretch at all here, so—"

"Constance Prestley!" Mrs. Prestley stepped to within inches of her daughter and seemed about to slap her;

then she exhaled loudly. "Why don't we leave Noelle to find her shoes in peace? I'm sure everyone's wondering where we are—"

"Wait!" Noelle glared at them through a haze of anger bordering on hatred. "Are you telling me that Adam Prestley actually used the word 'brothel'—or 'whore'!—in connection with my father's matchmaking business?"

Donna started to speak, but her mother silenced her with a glance, then turned to Noelle. "What did your father expect? That he could raise a daughter in the shadow of so provocative a business and not have her associated with its seamier side? You should be grateful my son finds it all so maddeningly enticing. You're a very fortunate girl—"

"Be quiet! Be quiet and get out of my room! All of you!" Before they could react, Noelle added sharply, "On second thought, stay. *I'm* leaving."

While they watched in stunned silence, she gathered up the skirts of her luminous gown and hurried into the hall in her stockinged feet, then paused for a deep, mind-clearing breath.

Every man's fantasy. A virgin in a brothel . . .
It added a delightful aspect to our relationship . . .
My beautiful little paradox . . .
I'm marrying you so that I never need a mistress again. They're much more expensive than a wife. . . .

Her heart was ricocheting in her chest, and she thought for a moment that she was going to cry; then she remembered the look in Donna Harrington's eyes. Taunting her. Daring her to reconsider her marriage to Adam now, with guests assembled and organ music filling the air. She thought she was humiliating Noelle with impunity. Or perhaps she thought she was saving her brother. Or worst of all, she thought it was all true, and thought Noelle was actually relieved at the opportunity of escaping from a brothel into a social stratum that did not usually admit prostitutes or their associates!

Enraged anew, she stormed down the staircase, ignoring the gasps of the few guests who had not yet taken their seats. Her father was nowhere in sight, but it didn't matter. There was only one person in the world she wanted to see at that moment, and she spied him easily, in his elegant black silk, chatting with the judge as he waited for his precocious fantasy to begin.

He didn't notice her until she was halfway down the aisle, when the murmur of the astonished guests alerted him. And then she was within inches of him, demanding sharply, "Did you tell your sister I was raised in a brothel?"

To her surprise, he barely seemed to hear the question. Instead, he grasped her by the shoulders and whispered hoarsely, "My God, Noelle, you're so beautiful. I always knew it, but—My God, *look* at you."

"Answer me!" She wrenched free and glared. "Did you say my father runs a brothel?"

"No, darling," he insisted solemnly. "I said no such thing. If anything, I said you were the most protected and sheltered girl I've ever had the honor to meet. I swear to you, darling—"

"Did you say I was every man's fantasy?"

Adam hesitated; then his tone grew confident. "So, Dane told you about our conversation? And put it in its worst light? I thought we agreed—"

"This has nothing to do with Zack. You said it to your brother-in-law." She choked back her anger and then accused, "It's been this from the start. The famous paradox. The virgin in the brothel. Zack told me you were all twisted up inside, and now I know—"

"Darling, please." He grabbed her again and shook her gently. "You're making a scene over nothing. A compliment, in fact. If you knew how I worship you—"

"I know *why* you worship me, and it makes me sick to my stomach."

"Noelle! I've put up with more than any man—"

"Be quiet!" She stared at him in disgust. "To think I almost married you out of a sense of loyalty. Out of respect for the way you felt about me. *There's* your paradox, sir. Enjoy it." Lowering her voice, she added contemptuously, "I hope you choke on it."

"Miss Braddock?"

She turned toward the unfamiliar voice and flushed. She had barely noticed the judge, much less the beautiful sprays of perfect white roses that surrounded them. Slowly, her gaze began to travel over the throng of guests—some strangers, some strangely familiar. And the room, she noted quietly, was absolutely exquisite. Just as she'd always hoped it would one day be, from the time she'd played with her bride dolls on the landing, to the day Adam had asked for her hand in marriage.

"Miss Braddock?" the judge repeated.

"Yes?"

"Am I safe in assuming there's not going to be a wedding today?"

"It's a misunderstanding—" Adam began, but Noelle silenced him with a murderous glare, then turned to scan the crowd once more until her eyes found what they'd been seeking.

"Lieutenant Dane?"

He was at her side in an instant. "Let's go, sugar. Me and Merc'll take you for a ride around the lake, and in no time, this'll just be another bad dream."

Noelle cocked her head to the side and studied him for a long moment, then asked quietly, "Do you still want to marry me?"

His green eyes blazed with instant commitment. "I surely do."

"Well, then . . ." She turned to the judge and smiled sweetly. "It looks like we're going to have a wedding today, after all."

Ten

Zack stood straight and tall at his bride's side, hoping she couldn't sense the commotion raging within him at that moment. She needed him to be strong—that was clear enough—but he felt like a schoolboy who'd just caught his first frog. Proud and excited and not quite sure what to do next. But happy? He'd only felt such pure, unadulterated joy once before in his life, when he'd stepped into a stranger's dining room and found out what a woman could do to a man's insides. And now she was doing it again, but this time, it was not only her idea, it was legal!

He repeated the vows without really hearing them—he would have said anything that judge-fellow asked him to say, if it meant ending up with Noelle in his arms. And she was taking vows, too, with a voice so pure and clear he half suspected it was a dream. Her pappy had said this would happen, and Zack had wanted it so bad, he'd tried to will it to happen. But never had he honestly believed that a girl like this would take a man like him to be her wedded husband. It was enough to make a fellow believe in miracles.

"And so, by the power vested in me by the state of Illinois, I'm honored to pronounce you man and wife." With a broad grin on his face, the judge nudged Zack and explained, "You may kiss your bride now, Lieutenant Dane."

Zack turned to Noelle, certain that this was the moment where she'd say it had all been for show. A way to torture Prestley. And Zack would go along with that, because of the other vow he'd made—to keep her out of that varmint's clutches. If it all ended here, he would have to be content, because he'd done what he'd set out to do, and his sassy little angel was safe.

"Don't you want to kiss me, Lieutenant?" she teased, her silver eyes shining with anticipation. "Or at least, finish the one Winnie interrupted?"

"Dang." He slid one hand around to the base of her spine, while the other moved to cradle the back of her head. "I love you, Noelle," he murmured, one instant before his body took over completely and he crushed his mouth down to hers.

He didn't know what to expect, and didn't really care. His love for her was so strong—such a driving, relentless force—that he savored any chance, however brief, however wrong, to hold her in his arms. The last thing he expected was for her to kiss him as she'd kissed him during her nightmare, but she seemed to remember exactly how that went. And as her arms tightened around his neck, her tongue sought out his, and for a long, luxurious moment, their bodies melded into one hot, perfect tribute to the passion they'd been denying for too long.

And Zack wanted to be inside her. Not from any sense of lust, but from a hopeless need to be closer still. And she wanted it too—he was sure of that now—so he gathered her up off her feet and into his arms without actually disengaging his mouth from hers, then turned away from the judge, hoping to stride down the aisle unimpeded.

"Going somewhere?" Russell Braddock asked cheerfully, blocking his path while the entire audience tittered with delight.

"Dang . . ."

"I decided not to marry the varmint," Noelle explained, a throaty giggle in her otherwise solemn voice.

"So I see." Her father turned to Zack and announced mischievously, "The two of you are welcome to stay, of course. But under the circumstances, if you'd like to spend a night or two at the inn on the outskirts of town, about ten miles south of here, I'd understand."

Zack looked to Noelle, and was thrilled when she nodded. Not that he would have objected to taking her to her room. It was closer, and he really didn't mind letting the dolls watch. But this first time, he liked the thought of having her all to himself. "I'll take good care of her, sir," he promised.

Ready again to carry her off, he was annoyed when Noelle's dressmaker grabbed him by the arm and piled a pair of silver shoes into the bride's lap. "A lady never goes out in bare feet, Noelle Braddock. I mean, Noelle Dane."

Noelle seemed inordinately touched by the gesture. "Are you disappointed, Winnie? After all your successful weddings—"

"This is the most successful of all," Winifred declared, wiping her eyes with a lace handkerchief. "I was so afraid you'd marry that—that pretentious snob. *That's* what I wanted to tell you in the hall. That kiss out in the yard convinced me, and for the first time, I actually witnessed it *before* the wedding!"

Noelle patted the woman's cheek, then clutched her

slippers against herself and asked Zack slyly, "Are you going to keep Mercury waiting forever?"

He grinned and assured her, "No, ma'am," silently vowing to ignore anyone, regardless of their importance, who tried to get in his way from then on out. Then it occurred to him that he might just make an excuse for Prestley. Giving *him* another crack in the jaw would almost be worth the delay! But when Zack turned his head to see where the bastard was, he couldn't find him.

Off somewhere, licking his wounds, he told himself in silent satisfaction. *If he's got the sense the Good Lord gave a turnip, he'll stay away from us for good.*

He strode down the hall, into the kitchen, and then, with a wink toward a wide-eyed Alice, carried Noelle onto the porch and out into the yard, where he spied Mercury, all packed up and ready to go. Zack had taken the time to saddle and outfit him, in the belief that it would be so hurtful to watch Noelle hitch herself to Prestley, he wouldn't be able to hang around that house one minute thereafter.

He would have liked nothing better than to swing her up onto Mercury's back, then jump up after her. She would respond to the romantic drama, he knew, but he couldn't trust the horse to behave himself. Mercury didn't allow anyone but Zack to ride him, and it wasn't worth risking Noelle's pretty bones just for the sake of flair, so he set her onto the top step and instructed, "Don't run off," then sprinted for the horse, jumped into the saddle, and rode over to her, scooping her up onto his lap in an easy, and hopefully romantic movement.

"Oh, Zack." She sighed with exaggerated delight.

"How will I ever thank you for this? It's so perfect. So utterly and completely perfect."

He wanted to assure her he'd find some way for her to thank him, but was too choked up to actually respond, so he tapped his heels against Mercury instead, urging, "Let's go, pardner." The horse burst forward, and Noelle wrapped her arms more tightly around Zack's neck, laughing happily in that way she had that nearly drove him to distraction.

He wanted to tell her he loved her again, but if she didn't know it by now, he figured she'd never know it. And she seemed content somehow, just to cuddle against him, heedless of the strangers on the sidewalks who stared in amazed delight at the sight of a bride being carried off on horseback.

Ten miles south, and then she's really yours, he told himself with a measure of awe. It didn't even matter anymore that she wasn't going to let him undress her. None of her rules mattered, at least, not for the moment. Tonight, they'd do it any way she wanted, and maybe by tomorrow night, she'd want more. No matter what she said or did, he wasn't going to get frustrated or impatient. She was his wife—Mrs. Zachary Dane—and that was plenty for now.

In what seemed like mere minutes, the city was behind them, and while the inn wasn't yet in sight, Zack knew it had to be close. Noelle appeared to read his thoughts, and she tugged on his vest as she asked, "Can we stop for just a minute? Please, Zack? We need to talk about—about what's going to happen now."

He grinned down at her, remembering her father's words. She was refreshingly candid when it came to this kind of talk, and it might just put her in the mood quicker, so how could he object? Plus, he couldn't deny her anything, could he? So he pulled gently on Mercury's reins and insisted, "Wait up, pardner. Mrs. Zachary Dane's got something to say."

When the horse had slowed to a walk, Zack covered his bride's mouth with his own, and was surprised when she responded easily. So much for talking! His heart began to pound as she continued to allow his liberties; then his hand crept up to her breast, fondling it eagerly, and she scolded, "I said 'talk,' not 'manhandle,' " as she brushed him away firmly.

"Whatever you say, sugar." He pulled up beside a low stone wall and set her atop it; then he jumped down to the ground and studied her from head to toe. "Just like the first time I saw you."

"It's romantic," she agreed lightly; then she pulled her silver slippers onto her feet, stepped down from the wall, and wandered a few yards away before turning to face him.

"Something on your mind, sugar?"

"Go and stand over there, by that big tree."

He chuckled, knowing she could see in his eyes how much he wanted to "manhandle" her again. She was right to send him a safe distance away, as long as she didn't expect him to stay away too long, so he cheerfully complied with her instruction, then motioned for her to speak.

"I loved the wedding," she began simply. "It was just like I always dreamed it would be. I love this gown, and the flowers, and the smile Father gave us when we left. And I think you're the most wonderful man in the world." Her eyes began to shine. "I can't remember when I've felt this relaxed and happy, Zack, and I think I owe it all to you. If you hadn't come along, I might have married Adam. And even if I hadn't, the wedding would have been a disaster. The guests would have been so disappointed, and Father wouldn't have known what to say or do to make it better. But instead, it was gloriously romantic. Thank you."

"My pleasure." He tried not to grin too broadly, but it was tough, seeing her bursting with happiness the way she was doing. He'd seen her tease and smile and laugh before, of course. But until now, he'd never seen her this way—so buoyant and free, as though an anvil had been resting on top of her spirit, keeping her from floating like an angel should.

That was why she was thanking him, he realized humbly. For some reason, she was giving him all the credit for freeing her from her confusion, and even though he knew he didn't quite deserve it, he couldn't resist going along with it, at least until the wedding night was over.

"I especially liked the kiss," she added mischievously. "That was the third kind, wasn't it?"

"Huh?" He wracked his brain to understand the reference, then just decided to go along again. "I liked it, too, sugar. Enough to do it again, here and now, if you're willing."

"I am." She held up a hand and added quickly, "After this, though, we need to behave ourselves. Just for a little while, until we're sure. After that . . ." She blushed to a beautiful crimson and admitted, "I'll never again ask you to stop."

Zack considered the words for a moment before asking, warily, "Until we're sure about what?"

"Sure about each other, of course." She smiled and took a few steps toward him. "I know you think *you're* sure, and that's so flattering and sweet, but marriage is a big decision, Zack. I almost made a mistake once.

I'm not about to do it twice. But if you want to court me," she added shyly, "I can't think of anything I'd love more."

"It's a little late for courting, don't you think?"

"Late? Do you mean, because of the ceremony?" She bit her lip, scanning his face anxiously. "Honestly, Zack, you can't really think I'd marry a man I only met last week."

"I figure you already did just that." He grinned sympathetically. "Don't go telling me it was just for show, either. I'm the fella you kissed, remember? I figure"— he stepped close enough to feel the heat from her body—"we're just about as married as two folks can be, except for one little detail. And it's gonna be a pleasure taking care of that."

"That's enough," she reprimanded firmly. "Here I thought you were being gallant, rescuing me from an embarrassing situation. I should have known better." She set her hands on her hips and continued coolly. "Do you want to court me, or not? And please don't tell me it's not necessary, because it is. Adam courted me for six months before we got engaged, and the engagement lasted four months more. Ten full months, yet I still didn't know him at all. Do you see my point? It takes time, and it takes effort."

"I knew it from the first minute—"

"Don't say that any more," she warned. "Under the circumstances, I've decided it's insulting."

"Insulting?" He stared in amazement. Didn't women love that sort of romantic talk? Love at first sight, and all that? And in this case, it was *true,* which made it even better!

She sighed and walked away from him, as though

gathering her thoughts; then she turned and asked casually, "Can I ask you a personal question, Zack?"

He folded his arms across his chest and studied the situation. One minute they were lovebirds, the next they were arguing, now it appeared she wanted to have a chat. "Go ahead," he answered finally. "I don't keep secrets—personal or otherwise—from my wedded wife."

"It's about your rifle."

"Henry?"

"That's right. Did the army supply it to you?"

"Not likely." Zack had to smile at the simplicity of such a suggestion. "You don't get a fine firearm like Henry from the army. They issued me a Spencer, and I used it for a while. But for long-distance shooting, it wasn't accurate enough."

"Tell me how you got Henry."

"Well, let's see. I studied up on it a bit, and asked around. Tried a few models—more than a few, I reckon—before I decided what I needed. Then it was just a question of trying 'em out, rifle by rifle, until I found just the right one. The right weight, the right balance—the right fit, I guess you'd say. Don't you worry about Henry," he added with a reassuring smile. "He's just about the finest weapon a man could have, short of his fists. Between him and me, you're as safe as a girl can be, from here on out."

"Sounds like you put a lot of thought into selecting him."

"A man'd be a fool not to."

"Silly me. Here I thought you walked into a gun shop, saw him up on a shelf, and just knew you wanted him by your side for the rest of your life."

"Huh? Oh . . ." He winced as her point hit home. "I see where you're going with that, sugar, but—"

"I don't even see why you had to go to the gun shop at all," she continued coolly. "Seems to me, a letter to the gunsmith would have done the job just as well. After all"—she paused to glare—"it's just a rifle."

"Dang it all, Noelle—"

"I don't want to discuss it. If I'm not as important to you as a silly rifle, why did you marry me? And if I'm important, I'm worth spending some time with before we make any hasty decisions."

Zack felt his jaw tighten but said nothing. There was nothing to say, was there? She was dead-set on frustrating him, and there really wasn't anything he could do about it for the moment. She was safe from Prestley, and she was happy. In fact, he'd never seen her this alive. So he had to rein himself in for a while, but not for six months! He'd never survive that, and he had to believe she wouldn't, either.

Noelle flashed him a hopeful smile. "We can go to the inn tonight, just as Father suggested. I'd be too embarrassed to go home just yet, knowing how much people are talking as it is. And . . ." Her silver eyes began to sparkle with poorly disguised anticipation. "This particular inn has the most romantic fireplace, Zack. We can sit in front of it and talk, and kiss a little when no one is looking. I'll do my best to make it enjoyable, within reason. And then we'll have a delicious dinner, with champagne perhaps, and something scrumptious for dessert." She paused for a deep breath, then added weakly, "Of course, when it's time to go to bed, we'll have separate rooms. Is that clear?"

Zack turned away, unwilling to allow her to see the sly grin he simply couldn't repress. If ever a girl was ready to give herself to a fellow, it was this girl, and he'd give thanks every night for the rest of his life that she'd chosen him to be the fellow. The fireplace, the kissing, the champagne, the dessert—she could barely speak of them without growing aroused, and he knew for certain she wouldn't survive this night with her prim-and-proper misconceptions intact.

Composing himself, he turned to face her, intending to agree to her every demand, but she had backed away to the low stone wall, her hands on her hips in reproach. "I can see you need some time alone, Lieutenant. Maybe after a nice long walk to the inn, you'll see I'm right. And if not"—her eyes twinkled mischievously— "at least you'll be too tired to misbehave."

"Noelle!" he warned, but she had already grabbed Mercury's reins as she jumped onto the wall, and in an instant, she was expertly mounting the huge chestnut beast, still gleeful at her own audacity. "Don't keep me waiting too long!"

He sprinted toward her, growling, "Mercury, stand your ground!" But before he could seize the reins, Noelle had touched the horse with the heels of her silver slippers, urging breathlessly, "Let's go, boy!" and the confused animal reared up, whinnying loudly, his eyes on Zack as though pleading for clearer instructions.

Noelle shrieked Zack's name as her seemingly weightless body catapulted backward and high into the air, while Zack thundered, "No!" in a mindless attempt to prevent her from impacting with the deadly stone wall. By some miracle, her head cleared the obstacle by inches, and she crashed to the ground with a sickening thud.

"Noelle . . ." He rushed to her, gathering her into his arms and frantically brushing back the tangle of blue-black locks that had loosened from their combs and spilled down around her face. "Talk to me, angel. Open your eyes."

She visibly struggled for a breath, and he realized that the wind had been knocked out of her lungs, so he cradled her gently, murmuring and reassuring while she steadied herself. Finally, she managed to inhale deeply, but rather than benefit her, it made her insides seize into a fit of nausea, and she rolled free of Zack, vomiting onto the ground.

"That's fine, angel." He pulled her back against himself. "Don't worry about anything, just take another breath. Noelle?"

She opened her eyes, but to his dismay, the beautiful silver irises were barely visible, and he panicked. He'd seen men this way—their eyes rolled up into their foreheads, foaming at the mouth, after being hit by a cannonball or caught under the wheels of a speeding wagon. Death had never been far away in those cases—

"Noelle!" He shook her gently, and almost cheered when she responded, her tone groggy and confused.

"Wh-what? Wh-what happened?"

"You near to killed yourself again," he informed her, his voice breaking with relief. "Dang it all, sugar. I thought I'd lost you this time, for sure."

"What?" She rubbed her eyes; then her hand moved to the back of her neck and she winced.

"Your neck hurts? How about your head? Don't try to move, angel. Just let me hold you."

"My stomach . . ."

"It's still sore? Do you want to try to bring up some more?"

"I don't know." She bit her lip, then added unhappily, "I don't know *anything*. What happened? Where am I?"

"Merc threw you," he explained. "I should've warned you about him, sugar. He doesn't trust anyone but me. But he's as sorry as he can be, and so am I. Can you ever forgive us?"

"Us?"

"Me and Merc."

She moistened her lips, then looked up at him with eyes so vacant he knew she was about to pass out again. But before she lost consciousness, she rallied, as though struggling with all her might to say something to him.

"What is it, sugar?" he urged gently. "Do you want some water?"

She nodded gratefully.

"I'll be quick," he promised, adding in a feeble attempt to amuse her, "Don't run off now."

"I won't. I promise."

Her voice was so solemn, so forlorn, he almost couldn't leave her, even for the few seconds it would take to get the canteen from Mercury's saddlebag. Brushing his lips across her forehead, he murmured, "I love you, Noelle. Don't fret about anything. You'll be fine again in an hour or two—Noelle?" He watched in dismay as her eyes rolled back up into her head again.

He couldn't wake her again, even when he splashed water on her forehead and lips, and so he bundled her up and loaded her onto Mercury's strong back, cussing and threatening the steed soundly all the while. Then he jumped up behind his bride, and within seconds the three were hurtling back toward Chicago.

Each time she tried to rouse herself, countless stabs of pain shooting from her head and down her neck into her shoulders, convinced her otherwise, and so she slept, or at least tried to sleep, despite the dizzying images and unfamiliar voices that assaulted her.

"Who are you?" she wanted to scream at them, but she didn't dare. Not when they might ask that same question in return. What would she say then?

She would say she was "Noelle." Not because she knew it for a fact, but because the man with the gentle voice had called her that. He had seemed to know her, and more importantly, seemed to care about her. Or at the very least, he felt responsible for her condition, because his friend Merc had thrown something at her.

It must have been a brick, she decided ruefully, rubbing the back of her neck with both hands as she prepared to finally awaken. For the first time, her efforts were not greeted by a wave of nausea, and she decided to take that as a sign that her situation was improving.

When she opened her eyes, she was further encouraged. The room wasn't spinning, although she was apparently seeing double, or perhaps even triple. How else could one account for the impossible number of pretty dolls staring down at her from countless shelves? Then she spied an exquisite wedding gown, fashioned from endless yards of silvery white satin and lace, and she smiled with relief. Finally, something she recognized! She *knew* this was hers. In fact, she was certain she'd been wearing it when the stranger had rescued her. Her earliest memory, other than his voice, was her fear that she would soil the gorgeous creation with vomit. But there it was—absolutely perfect, and indisputably hers.

So, you have two facts now, she informed herself with shaky confidence. *Your name is Noelle, and you're someone's bride. Which means someone loves you, and you love him. Unless you were running away from him when the brick hit you, of course.* She grimaced and acknowledged that she actually had *no* facts.

And she needed some quickly, so she scanned the room for more clues, then sighed in frustration. It was a child's room, which meant she was someone's guest. Someone else to whom she needed to be grateful. If only the stranger with the reassuring voice had brought her to a hotel! Then she noticed a piece of paper on the bedstand, and reached for it, squinting slightly to focus on the haphazard penmanship.

Oh, dear. She took a deep breath and tried to convince herself that the letter didn't make sense—that it was as confusing and untrustworthy as all the other thoughts and dreams she'd been having since the brick hit her. Almost on cue, the shooting pains intensified, and she leaned back into the pillows, closing her eyes and trying to make sense of the words she'd just read.

Lieutenant Zachary Dane—a soldier, then. Ordering a bride through the mail, from a man named Braddock. And coincidentally, she—"Noelle"—had been wearing a wedding gown. Did that mean her full name was Noelle Dane?

You're jumping to conclusions, she scolded herself. *Just go and find someone and ask them. Tell them the truth—that you can't quite remember who you are. Find out who else is in this house. Perhaps the little girl whose room this is will answer your questions, or if not, perhaps someone will be willing to send for a doctor or constable or minister to advise you.*

Bracing herself for a disorienting round of pain, she slid out of the bed and noticed for the first time that she was wearing a soft pink nightgown. A modest one, which she hoped meant she had been undressed by a person of decent inclination. There was a large mirror over the dresser, and she squinted at her reflection, noting through bleary eyes that she had pretty hair, at least. But Lieutenant Dane hadn't asked for a pretty-haired bride; he had requested a cheerful, healthy one—a description she didn't fit at all, at least for the moment.

Unsteady, she grasped the edges of the bed, and then the bedstand, as she made her way to the door, which she opened just a crack, intent upon gathering further clues before exposing her vulnerability to whomever lurked in the hall. There was no one there, and she leaned against the doorjamb, relieved but unwilling to venture further until she was certain she wouldn't collapse.

As she mustered her strength, she heard voices moving toward her. Two females, or perhaps three, were chatting casually somewhere in the distance. Noelle exhaled sharply, and realized for the first time that she had been terrified that strange males of every size and temperament might be the sole occupants of the house. Straightening in preparation for walking toward the conversation, she frowned slightly as the words became clearer.

"Poor Miss Noelle—"

"She's Mrs. Dane now, for all the good it'll do either of them if she doesn't recover."

"Don't talk that way! Of course she'll recover. It's been no time at all—hours, only—since the accident. And the doctor will be here soon, and he'll set it all to rights. He and Mr. Braddock have been friends for years, you know."

"Poor Mr. Braddock," the older voice mourned. "This match has taken its toll on him, hasn't it?"

Noelle frowned. Mr. Braddock? The matchmaker from the letter? What did *that* mean? Could her husband have returned her to the matchmaker, because of her damaged condition? Was her marriage over before it began? She knew she should be relieved—marriage to a stranger, after all, should be a dreadful prospect—but she had been hoping the man with the soothing voice was Lieutenant Zachary Dane, and hoping further that somehow, by some miracle, the love in his tone had been something real, like the dress, to which she could cling in the midst of this confusion.

"If only *I'd* known Mr. Braddock years ago," the younger of the women's voices was sighing. "To think he might have been able to find me a husband like Lieutenant Dane, instead of the shiftless man I found for myself."

"The world would be a better place if Mr. Braddock made all the matches," the older one agreed. "But not if it meant all the weddings would be here. Even with the extra help, it'll be midnight before we have the place back in order."

"Here, let me help you with that. . . ." The voices faded away as the women went about their housekeeping.

Confused, but also comforted, Noelle stumbled back to bed. Apparently, she had been married in this house. For some reason, the matchmaker had allowed her to marry the lieutenant from the letter here, earlier this same day. It was logical, then, that her husband would bring her back to this place, to seek advice and assistance after "the accident." Perhaps he wasn't rejecting her, after all.

Snuggling under the starched white linens and lacy coverlet, she wondered if perhaps she shouldn't sleep again, just for a bit. She was in safe hands, apparently, and a doctor had been summoned. Either her memory would return before she next awakened, or it would not. In either case, she needed to be rested before she conducted any further investigation.

She had barely closed her eyes when the door creaked on its hinges, and she turned her head on the pillow, hoping that one of the housekeepers had come to check on her. Instead, she saw a well-dressed, middle-aged gentleman with kind eyes and an extremely cautious smile on his face.

"Noelle? Are you awake?"

"Yes. Come in, please." She pulled the coverlet up to her neck before sitting. "Are you the doctor?"

"No." He studied her for a moment. "You don't recognize me at all?"

She bit her lip, then guessed, "Are you the matchmaker?"

His look of complete amazement brought a genuine smile to her lips, and she explained, "I don't remember you yet, but I know enough to be grateful to you."

He hesitated, then sat on the edge of her bed and took her hand. "Grateful?"

"You're Russell Braddock. Lieutenant Dane asked you to find him a bride, and you found *me*. And as if that weren't enough, you provided us with a lovely wedding. I've been poking around a bit. I hope you don't mind. It just felt so odd, knowing nothing at all."

"I can imagine."

"I read Lieutenant Dane's letter." She motioned toward the piece of paper, which she had returned to its original position on the bedstand. "And I overheard some of your servants talking. That's how I knew you held the wedding here. It was remarkably generous of you."

"It was my pleasure," he assured her softly. "You remember nothing at all?"

"I'm afraid not. But it doesn't bother me nearly as much as it should, so please don't be distressed." She paused to acknowledge the truth of what she'd just said. How strange that she wasn't in a panic, or withdrawn into a corner! Either she was a brave person, which didn't feel likely, or she hadn't much cared for her old memories. Or perhaps she was still in shock from the accident. That seemed the most logical of the explanations, and so she squeezed her host's hand and said, "I'll have another nap, and then you'll see—I'll remember everything."

"I'm sure you will," he agreed. "How do you feel?"

"Just awful. My head, my neck, my shoulders—I don't want poor Mr. Merc to feel too badly, but he really should be more careful."

Russell Braddock chuckled. "Merc is a horse, Noelle. Mercury, to be precise."

"How on earth did he throw a—" She caught herself and laughed ruefully. "He didn't throw a brick, then?"

"He threw a bride," Braddock explained with a grin. "And if Zack hadn't needed him to transport you back here, it would have been the last thing he ever threw."

She tensed slightly, then dared to ask, "Is that how it went, then? The wedding was over, and we were on our way to somewhere else? And I was injured, so he brought me back here? Is he—Did he stay?"

"Of course. He's been at your bedside most of the time since then, but we finally convinced him to have a meal. Shall I call him—"

"No!" She grimaced in apology and explained, "I'm sure this is all very difficult for him. Shouldn't we wait until after my nap? I'm sure I'll recognize him then, and . . . Well . . ."

"Yes?"

She could see that he was receptive, and so she asked carefully, "I don't suppose I've known him for very long, have I? So it's not as though there's much for me to remember."

Braddock hesitated before saying, "You've known him for just over a week."

"A week?" She hoped he hadn't heard the shock in her voice. After all, it wasn't Braddock's fault she and the lieutenant had chosen so odd a course for their lives. He was simply the matchmaker. "I suppose in your business a short courtship is not unusual?"

"It varies." He seemed about to say more, then politely changed the subject. "The doctor will be here momentarily, Noelle. Why don't you try to rest until then? You're safe here—"

"I know that." She gave him a confident smile. "It's one of the few things I do know. And in a way, I suppose I'm fortunate. I don't remember why I was unhappy in the past. I only know that because of you, I have a wonderful future ahead of me."

"That's right," he murmured. "Your future is completely secure now. Go to sleep, and when you wake up, everything will make more sense."

"This way, Doc. And thanks for coming. We've been worried sick, her sleeping so much and all."

"She fell from a horse?"

"*My* horse," Zack admitted as he led the physician up the stairs. "I should've warned her about him, but everything happened so fast. He threw her ten feet at least."

"And you say she's been sleeping a lot?"

"Pretty near all the time since it happened. At first, she was waking up, but you could see her head wasn't clear. She vomited once, and her eyes kept rolling clear back in her head—"

"That's not unusual," the doctor interrupted reassuringly. "You've kept her comfortable and quiet. That's the important thing with these head injuries."

Head injuries? Zack felt a chill run down his spine. It sounded so official. What if her skull was cracked, or worse? What if she could never see straight again? All because of Zack! After he'd bragged about how safe she was with him and Henry—

"You shouldn't worry so much." The doctor smiled. "Is this the room?"

Zack nodded and was about to tap lightly on Noelle's door when Russell Braddock opened it from the other side and stepped into the hall to join them.

"This is Doc Long," Zack explained. "Jason Long, this is Russell Braddock. Noelle's father."

"I was expecting Ben Jackson," Braddock murmured.

"He's handling a crisis, and asked if I could come. I hope you don't mind—"

"I've heard only the best about you, Dr. Long," Braddock assured him. "Thank you for coming."

"How's your daughter? Any change?"

"She woke up briefly." Braddock turned to Zack. "She was calm and coherent. But she doesn't remember anything."

"Then she isn't mad at me? Or Merc?" Zack exhaled in relief. "I'll tell her all the details when she's better, but for now, I'm kinda glad she doesn't remember it."

"She doesn't remember *anything*," Braddock repeated. "Not me, not her room, not this house—not anything."

Zack stared in disbelief. "She said that? That she didn't remember *you?*"

"Yes. In fact, she thanked me politely for my hospitality."

"Dang."

Braddock nodded. "She knows she's a bride—from the way she was dressed. And for some reason, she has your letter in there, asking me to find you a wife. She put two and two together and managed to get something other than four. But I must say, she seems content with her version of the truth. For the moment, she only knows that she is Noelle Dane, bride of Lieutenant Zachary Dane. And she knows my name is Braddock, but doesn't know this is her home, or I'm her father."

"None of this is unusual," Dr. Long assured them. "And it's fortunate she isn't upset over it. I imagine she's still in shock."

Braddock cleared his throat. "I'd appreciate it if you'd just play along with her, Doctor. At least until we know more about her condition. As I said, she seems content. I don't want to see her upset."

"I don't know about that," Zack protested. "Wouldn't it make her feel safer, knowing she was with her father? In her own bed?"

"I think the additional information might confuse her. And the whole truth—that unfortunate business with Adam, and the bizarre nature of the wedding ceremony—would unduly upset her. She's calm and relaxed for the moment. If that changes, we can tell her the rest. Do you agree, Doctor?"

The physician shrugged. "With any luck, she'll have

her memory back the next time she wakes up. These things are usually fleeting, sir. Let me have a look at her, and then we'll talk again."

Zack shook his head, uncomfortable with the idea of deceiving Noelle, but didn't interfere. Instead, he followed the others into her room and watched as the doctor moved to her bedside and whispered. "Noelle?"

She stirred, and when she opened her eyes, she seemed momentarily alarmed. Then her gaze shifted away from the doctor, and toward Zack and her father. Smiling uncertainly, she asked, "Have I been asleep long?"

"Only for a few minutes," Braddock assured her. "This is Dr. Long, Noelle. He wants to take a look at that lump on your head."

"Hello, Doctor."

"Good evening, Mrs. Dane."

Zack felt his heart ache at the sound of his bride's new title. Mrs. Dane. He could only imagine how frightening it must be for her, to learn that she was married to a stranger. He wanted to go to her and reassure her, but her father took his arm and urged him gently back through the doorway, calling out as he did so, "Zack and I will be right outside if you need us, sweetheart."

"You don't mind being alone with the doc, do you, Noelle?" Zack asked quickly.

"Not as long as you're nearby."

"Always," he promised; then he cleared his throat, embarrassed to have sounded so doleful, and hurried out of the room.

Noelle craned her neck, hoping to catch one last glimpse of the tall, handsome stranger before he disappeared into the hall. He had seemed so honestly concerned for her condition. So anxious to reassure her, while so clearly needing reassurance of his own that he hadn't just made the biggest mistake of his life. He had asked Mr. Braddock to find him a healthy bride and instead, after less than a day, his bride was bedridden and muddleheaded. It was hardly an auspicious start.

Zack—such a darling name, and with a face to match. Those big green eyes, and the soulful voice . . . He deserved a better wedding night than this.

She sighed again, then remembered the doctor and murmured, "Everyone's being so kind. And so patient."

The physician sat on the side of the bed and pulled back her eyelids, one at a time. "Mr. Braddock tells me you're having a little trouble remembering things. Is that getting any better?"

"I'm afraid not." She smiled uncertainly. "How long do you suppose it will be?"

"It's hard to say. Show me where your head hurts."

She leaned up and gathered her hair out of the way. "Here, in the back. And over here, all along the top. And down my neck, and my shoulders, too. And there's a sort of throbbing behind my eyes. But none of it is nearly so bad as it was."

"And are you dizzy?"

"Yes. Especially when I try to walk."

"Then don't try. The last thing we need is for you to fall again. Do you have any other injuries?"

"Nothing, other than a little soreness all over."

"I can imagine. Are you nauseated at all?"

"A little."

He lifted her eyelids again. "You probably won't be hungry for the rest of the day, but if you are, I'd like you to take clear broth only. And if you're thirsty, take small sips of tea. Do you take it with lemon?"

"I don't know."

He flushed apologetically. "Of course you don't. Forgive me." For the first time, she saw a tinge of uncertainty in his eyes as he inquired carefully, "Are there any questions you'd like me to answer before I leave?"

"Will you be back?"

"Yes. I'll visit you tomorrow morning. Until then, the more rest you get, the better."

"Will my memory come back all at once, or just in bits?"

"That's difficult to predict."

"Will it be soon?"

"My guess is, the amnesia will clear by morning. Just relax and let your husband take care of you. There's nothing to be alarmed about. This is a fairly common phenomenon after a blow as sharp as the one you took."

Relieved, she closed her eyes and leaned back into the pillow. "I'm not at all alarmed. Just ever so slightly embarrassed."

"Nonsense. You've nothing to be embarrassed about. Most girls would be crying or frightened to death, but you—you're remarkable, Mrs. Dane. Your husband's fortunate to have such a brave wife."

"I'm certain he's not feeling at all fortunate at the moment," she lamented. Then she opened her eyes again and asked hopefully, "I know you want me to rest, but couldn't I speak with my—with Lieutenant Dane first? For just a few minutes?"

"Certainly." He gave her one last encouraging smile, then rose to his feet. "I'll send him right in. And I'll see you tomorrow before noon. Have a good night, Mrs. Dane."

Eleven

"Hey, sugar." The tall, handsome stranger sat on the edge of her bed and smiled warmly. "How're you feeling?"

Hoping he couldn't sense the tremor of excitement that ran through her every time she heard his voice, she returned his smile shyly. "A little better, thank you."

"I hear you don't remember much."

"I remember your voice. And how you helped me after the accident."

"I thought I'd lost you." He paused to clear his throat. "If anything had happened to you, I never would've forgiven myself, or that danged fool of a horse."

"You mustn't worry. I intend to recover fully. And you mustn't blame your horse. After all, he barely knows me. I like his name," she added sincerely. "Mercury—it sounds fast. And temperamental."

"That's Merc, all right. *Too* temperamental. But I swear, sugar, he knows he's done something real wrong. All the pride's gone out of his eyes. I'm not making excuses—"

"I'm sure he regrets the incident," she teased. "And at least he didn't ruin my dress. *That* would have been unforgivable. As it is, I apparently have a very hard head, so no real damage was done."

He smiled reluctantly. "Does it scare you, not remembering things?"

"No. Isn't that odd? I'm a little afraid of my old memories, in fact."

"Why?"

Noelle shrugged. "I suppose because I forgot them so easily, almost as if I was *looking* for a way to forget them. But not the ones about you," she added quickly. "Just the other ones."

Zack hesitated, then reached out to cup her chin in his hands. "There's nothing to be afraid of, sugar. Not in your past and not in your future. I promise you that. Just rest and get better, so we can get on with it."

"I'll do my best." She blushed as she insisted, "I don't remember what I used to call you. Do you have a preference?"

"At first, you called me Lieutenant. But lately, it's been Zack. I like it both ways."

"So do I."

She could see that he was struggling with something, and hoped it was the same emotion that was stirring inside her. Not love yet, of course. But curiosity, along with a bit of amazement that they had developed so sweet a rapport so quickly. In one short week, he had clearly grown fond of her. And she had been drawn to him—to his voice and his eyes and his warm, strong arms—instantly. Either Mr. Braddock was a genius, or Noelle and Zack were amazingly fortunate. Or she was imagining it all because of her hazy, dizzy state. In any case, she felt fortunate, despite her injury, and could only pray her husband felt the same way.

"The doc wants you to sleep. He thinks you might wake up remembering everything."

"That would be a relief." She smiled apologetically.

"I really am sorry to put you through this, Lieutenant. I know it hasn't turned out the way you expected—"

"It's fine, angel. Once you're feeling better, I'll have everything I want in this world. I figure that makes me a pretty lucky fella."

Noelle's heart swelled with delight, hearing how closely his sentiments matched her own. If those words had been spoken under other circumstances, they would have been unmistakably romantic. Was it possible there had actually been *that* sort of spark between them?

She wanted to ask him how it had been, the first time they met. Had they known, at first sight, that this match was an inspired one? Of course, Zack had had an entire week to evaluate Noelle, so perhaps it hadn't been so immediate on his part. And given the fact that he had used a matchmaker, it could be he was simply relieved that she wasn't a total disappointment.

But for herself, she had no doubt about that first meeting. Her heart must have soared, first with relief, then with a giddy sort of astonishment that her prospective groom was so charming and attractive. Why on earth had he felt the need to use a matchmaker?

And why had Noelle used one? What was there in her past that had made her turn to strangers for a future? The silent questions sobered her, and she began to knead her aching neck, suddenly exhausted.

"Is that where you're hurt?" Zack slid his hand behind her neck, and in an instant, a soothing burst of heat radiated through her.

She felt her cheeks flush, not only with gratitude, but also with a healthy dose of arousal. "That feels wonderful. Your hand is so warm."

His green eyes twinkled mischievously. "I'm glad you like it, Mrs. Dane."

Noelle's heart began to pound, and she wondered if he was considering kissing her. It seemed outrageous for her to welcome such intimate gestures from a virtual stranger, but they *were* man and wife, and in lieu of a traditional wedding night, this seemed somehow appropriate.

He seemed to be reading her thoughts, and leaned in to her, brushing his lips across her forehead. "Time to sleep now, sugar. When you wake up, we'll have ourselves a nice long visit. How does that sound?"

"It sounds wonderful," she admitted breathlessly.

"Do you want me to stay with you?"

"Just for a while, if you don't mind."

"There's nowhere else I want to be."

"Well, then . . ." She gave him one last shy smile, then succumbed to another wave of exhaustion and snuggled under her covers, pleased that, for the first time since the accident, she had something definite about which she could dream.

Zack stood outside the open door to Russell Braddock's study and listened for a moment as the doctor reassured the worried father. "She'll doze off, then wake up, again and again, over the next few days. That's to be expected with this sort of injury, so don't be alarmed."

"She had a similar injury when she was ten years old, but without the memory loss. She couldn't keep any food down—Oh, Zack!" Braddock motioned for his son-in-law to join them. "Is she sleeping?"

Zack nodded and ambled over to the sofa, glad for a chance to sit and relax after the tumultuous events of the day. "Her neck hurts her something fierce, Doc. But she's all tuckered out, so I expect she'll sleep awhile."

"Dr. Long was just telling me what we should expect over the next day or two."

"The important thing is to watch her when she first starts eating solid food. Small meals of tea and toast, I'd say, and keep her awake for at least an hour afterwards."

"You'll be back tomorrow?"

The doctor nodded. "I'll come every day until she's fully recovered."

Zack cleared his throat, then asked, "What about her memory? Is it possible it'll be gone for good?"

"Possible, but highly unlikely. I'm frankly surprised the amnesia has lasted this long."

"Does it worry you?"

Dr. Long hesitated, then admitted, "Russell here was just telling me some of the—well, the unusual circumstances surrounding today's nuptials. Before I forget"— he interrupted himself—"congratulations, Lieutenant. You've found yourself a remarkable bride. Not only is she beautiful and charming, but she's amazingly resilient."

"She's a fine girl," Zack agreed. "You were saying something about the unusual circumstances? You agree with Russ then? That she's forgetting it on purpose—"

"Not in the sense of having any control over it. I'm sure she's trying to remember things. But her mind is protecting her—or at least, I find the theory intriguing. She was probably on the edge of exhaustion, even before the accident. I've treated more than one young bride in such a state—that's how important it is to them that the wedding day be perfect in every way. And this one . . . Well, I suspect Noelle never intended for it to be so unusual."

Braddock had been nodding vigorously. "In her heart, she knew she didn't want to marry Adam Prestley, but the self-reproach and confusion she must have gone through in those last twenty-four hours—my heart breaks for her every time I think of it. And even though the wedding was the most romantic one I've ever witnessed, it was also the most bizarre. After all, half of the guests were Adam's friends and family. And Noelle must know—or would know, if not for the amnesia— that tongues will be wagging for weeks over the way the ceremony proceeded."

Zack shook his head, annoyed that anyone would dare mock Noelle when it had so clearly been Prestley's shortcomings that had caused the scene. But he also knew this was just the sort of thing gossips would love to dissect and misinterpret.

"Even aside from the wedding, I believe the strain on Noelle has been enormous over these past few weeks, perhaps even for longer," Braddock was lamenting. "She's been wrestling with indecision and confusion—her understandable need to believe Adam was a good choice, even when her heart was telling her otherwise."

"She said it herself," Zack admitted quietly. "Right before Merc threw her, she was telling me how she hadn't felt so free in months. And even if she hadn't said it, all you had to do was look at the expression on her face. She was purely happy and relieved. And dead set on not making another mistake."

Braddock grinned sympathetically. "Can you blame her? Her feelings for you were the most confusing part of that final week. Now, thanks to the amnesia, it's all very simple. I for one am grateful she's found a way to relax—to avoid responsibility and decisions for a while."

The doctor stood and shook Zack's hand. "Give it a day or two, Lieutenant. I suspect it will work itself out without any interference by us. If you decide you must be completely honest with her, my only advice is to proceed with caution. Don't tell her too much too quickly. I'd hate to see her agitated or distressed."

"I don't want that, either. But I've never been much for lying, especially to someone I care about."

"Don't think of it as lying," Long advised. "You're protecting her from distressful facts until she's stronger. But not forever. I agree with you about that. If this condition persists, Noelle is entitled to hear the whole truth, no matter how upsetting it may be."

Turning to Braddock, he offered his hand with a smile. "I'll be back late in the morning. Send for me if you need me sooner. And watch her closely in the meantime."

"We appreciate your dedication, Doctor."

"Yeah, Doc," Zack echoed. "Thanks for coming."

"I'll show myself out. Good evening, gentlemen."

Zack waited until the physician's footsteps had faded away, then turned to his father-in-law and smiled wryly. "One week with me, and she's almost killed herself twice. Are you sure you still approve of the match?"

"More than ever," Braddock assured him. "I meant what I said earlier, Zack. It was the most romantic wedding I've ever attended. I don't think I'll ever forget the sight of her in her stockinged feet, storming up to Adam and giving him that tongue-lashing. And then, when she kissed you—" His voice caught in his throat. "I've dreamed of that moment for her, ever since she was a newborn girl smiling up at me from her mother's arms. Over the years, I've vacillated, from wanting to arrange it myself, just to be sure, to wanting her to find someone all on her own, so that there'd never be any doubt in anyone's mind about whether the love was true. Somehow, you're the best of both possibilities, and I couldn't be happier."

Zack grinned ruefully. "Before she hit her head, she said she wants me to court her. For six months."

Braddock burst into laughter. "I can almost guarantee you she won't hold you to it."

"I figure she won't," Zack agreed.

"In a way," the father added carefully, "you're courting her now, wouldn't you say?"

"Huh?"

"Did you kiss her good night?"

Zack winced. "I kissed her forehead. I'd never take advantage—"

"Exactly. While you're waiting for her memory to return, you have the perfect opportunity to make a good impression on her. It was all so confusing, with Adam in the way. But now she'll respond to you the way she would have if she'd been free to fall in love, that first day in the dining room."

"That's true," Zack murmured, intrigued by the thought. She *had* seemed receptive, welcoming his attention in a way she'd never done during her engagement. Of course, the poor girl also thought she had no choice but to be receptive, given that she was married to him. She was probably just relieved he hadn't crawled into the bed next to her.

"Just be yourself," Braddock was advising. "She was falling in love with you this week, despite the fact that she tried with all her might to resist. Now that she's not resisting, it should go very smoothly. By the time she's well enough to travel, you'll be able to take her with you to San Francisco and start a new life together without any more delay."

Zack cocked his head and studied Noelle's father. "And you'll move your business out there?"

"Unless you have an objection to living in the same city as your father-in-law."

He grinned. "If all this works out that way, it'll be an amazement. Almost like you planned it that way from the start." He hesitated, then had to ask, "You didn't, did you?"

"No. Or at least, not consciously. I almost wish I *could* take credit for it," he admitted, half to himself. "But the truth is, once she told me she intended to marry Adam, I gave up hope—" He caught himself and smiled wistfully. "Even at my worst, I never wanted more than a good husband for Noelle. It didn't occur to me that I might end up with a son for myself. I hope you know how much that means to me."

Zack crossed the room and grasped Braddock's hand in his own. "I'm honored, sir. I'll try to be worthy of it, and of Noelle." *Just don't ask me to keep secrets from her much longer. . . .*

The sun was bright and high in the sky by the time Noelle opened her eyes again, and to her dismay she found that she was alone. Not that she had expected her husband to sit in a chair all night, of course, but somehow, his absence was disturbing. She still couldn't remember anything from before the accident, but the new memories, especially the warm, romantic moment with her husband just before she dozed off, were precious, and she suddenly suspected they were in jeopardy.

What if he and Mr. Braddock decided to reconsider their bargain in light of her infirmity? Her husband was clearly an honorable man, but he had asked for a healthy bride, not a bedridden one. Even if he found Noelle somewhat attractive and endearing, he had to be sensible. And Mr. Braddock was also an honorable man, with a reputation to protect. Wouldn't he be anxious as well to see that Lieutenant Dane was a satisfied customer?

A knock at the door startled her, and she quickly smoothed her hair before calling out breathlessly, "Come in!" When it was Russell Braddock rather than her husband, she sighed in disappointment, but managed to insist, "Come in, Mr. Braddock. It's so nice to see you again."

He winced slightly, and she imagined he was disappointed to see that she was still in bed at so late an hour, and still so obviously useless. But he rallied quickly and moved to sit near her, taking her hand in his own. "How are you feeling, sweetheart?"

"Much, much better," she assured him. "Strong and healthy."

"And hungry?"

"Ravenous," she lied.

"And you still remember nothing?"

"Does it matter? I left that life behind for a reason, Mr. Braddock. Don't you suppose that, in some ways, this accident was a blessing in disguise?"

"That's how you see it?"

"Yes, I truly do."

"Well, then . . ."

She studied him anxiously. "How much do you know about my past?"

"Pardon?"

"Did I write you a letter? Like the one my husband wrote? I suppose I should read it," she added, although inwardly she recoiled from the thought. *Be brave,* she chastised herself. *Your husband has probably read it.*

"There isn't always a letter," Braddock explained. "In your case, there wasn't. I didn't need a letter to tell me you were a perfect match for Lieutenant Dane."

She smiled in relief. "He's such a wonderful man. So gentle and respectful. I don't know how to thank you—"

"Thank me by resting and relaxing."

"I will. Once I've gotten dressed, I'll join you downstairs—"

"That's out of the question," Braddock interrupted briskly. "Dr. Long wants you to stay off your feet for another day at least. I'll bring you a tray of food—tea and toast, if that's agreeable."

"Do you mind if I ask. . . ?" Noelle took a deep breath. "I assume this is your little girl's room? I don't want to inconvenience her—"

"It's not a question of that. My daughter is a grown woman, and she lives with her husband."

"But you've kept it this way for her? That's sweet." Noelle eyed him with hesitant curiosity. "Did you find her husband for her?"

"The credit for that goes to Cupid."

She laughed in delight. "But you approve?"

"Wholeheartedly. But I must admit, I'm not yet accustomed to the notion that there's another man in her life. She and I were very close." He smiled apologetically. "I'd rather not talk about her anymore, if you don't mind."

Touched that a father could be so lonely for his

daughter, Noelle reached over and patted him on the arm. "Consider the subject closed. I'd rather talk about my husband, to tell you the truth. Do you know much about him, other than what he wrote in his letter?"

"He's a war hero, several times over. He's honest and reliable, and he has a good heart. And he was smitten with you from the moment you first met."

Noelle moistened her lips, enthralled by the statement, and anxious to believe it was true. "I feel the same way about him. I mean, that he seems honest and good-hearted. And he has the most wonderful voice. When I was hurt, the world was spinning, so I focused on that voice, and knew everything would be better soon." She hesitated, then asked carefully, "Did the doctor say anything about my traveling? I mean, would my husband and I be able to travel soon, even if my memory doesn't come back?"

"Is that what you'd like?"

"Well, I feel safe and welcome here, but it's somewhat anticlimactic. We rode away on his horse, off to start our new life, and here we are, back again."

Braddock chuckled. "Actually, you were going to spend a few nights at a nearby inn, then return here in any event. All of your clothes are here, packed and ready for when you and Zack set sail for California."

"What a relief," she said with a sigh. "Perhaps I haven't thwarted his plans so very much after all. Except of course, for the nights at the inn." She knew she was blushing, and was pleased when Braddock chuckled once again.

"Lieutenant Dane is impulsive by nature, but I can assure you he is infinitely patient where you are concerned. Just rest and recuperate, and don't worry about keeping him waiting. He's only known you a week, after all. Most men are required to engage in a much longer and more rigorous courtship than that."

"Most men are allowed to select their own brides," she reminded him. "The convenience of ordering one through the mail should be that one doesn't need to follow the usual rules of courtship. And I'm fully recovered in any case, except for my memory, which may never come back—"

"Don't say that," Braddock murmured. "Concentrate on regaining your strength, so that you'll be ready for the memories—pleasant or otherwise—when they return."

"I'll have new memories by then," Noelle predicted. "That's where my strength will lie."

"I agree. But a good meal can't hurt, so why don't I just go and fetch that toast?" He smiled slyly. "Shall I ask Zack to bring it to you?"

"You really are a matchmaker, aren't you?" she teased happily. "Yes, please ask him to bring it. And thank you again, Mr. Braddock. For everything."

Her stomach wasn't really quite ready for a meal, but she was determined to prove to Zack that she was the healthy, cheerful bride he had ordered, and so she took small bites and chewed them carefully, aware that he was scrutinizing every motion for some sign that she was going to choke or worse. They were both relieved when the butler finally took away the tray.

Thereafter, she was torn between proving she was fully recovered and admitting that her neck was aching, in hopes he might again put his big, warm hand on her. Finally, she settled for insisting upon going downstairs, suspecting accurately that he would never allow her to walk so far. Still, when he scooped her up into his arms and carried her, she found herself feeling faint with delight, and giggled at the thought that he might misunderstand and send for the doctor again.

When Dr. Long did arrive, he seemed pleased with her progress, albeit surprised that she still had no recollection of her life before the accident. She could see the concern in her husband's eyes, and wanted to reassure him—to explain that she didn't even want those old memories, for fear something in them was horribly sad or shameful. She liked the way she saw herself—as a young bride, full of innocence and hope. Certainly, if she'd felt that way in her old life, she never would have placed her future in the hands of a matchmaker. Why on earth would she want to recapture the loneliness or despair that had led her to so hopeless a course?

Her new life was already a special one, with Zack hovering over her, handsome and attentive. The servants at the Braddock household hovered, too, along with the matchmaker and the doctor, who visited twice a day those first two days. She wanted to be appreciative, but longed to be alone with her husband. She even tried to suggest, in a ladylike way, that he might be more comfortable if he actually slept with her rather than in the guest room, but he pretended not to hear her, and she had a feeling the doctor had given him some sort of annoying instructions along those lines.

Not that she was ready to face a true wedding night yet, but some time alone, and some kisses other than fleeting ones, would have been welcome. The only real kiss came from a loveable old dog named Copper, who behaved as though he'd known her all his life when Zack brought him to her for a visit. The dog was dying, or so Zack explained, and so she took pains to fuss over

it in case it was its last day. Later that afternoon, while
Noelle was visiting with Braddock in his study, a gunshot rang out, and the matchmaker explained sadly, but
with evident appreciation, that Zack had just made certain the poor animal wouldn't suffer anymore.

By the third day, Noelle no longer had to pretend that
she was hungry, or that her dizziness had passed. Although she tired easily, and her head still throbbed, she
was feeling stronger and more normal by the hour, and
was convinced that she was well enough to travel.

But her husband seemed aghast at the suggestion, and
so she tried her best to soothe him. "I discussed it with
the doctor, and he didn't think there were any real concerns of a physical nature, as long as I continue to rest.
And what else would I do on the long voyage to San
Francisco? It seems ideal, Zack."

"No concerns of a *physical* nature," Zack repeated.
"That means he has other concerns. The same ones I
have. You need to stay here until you get your memory
back."

"You should talk to Mr. Braddock about it. I think
he agrees with me, that it's silly to wait for something
that might never happen, and won't make a difference
even if it does."

"He said that?" Zack scowled.

"Not exactly, but I'm sure he's anxious for this match
to become more—" She flushed and added lamely, "We
can't stay here forever, Zack. It's a lovely home, but it's
not *our* home. And I'm anxious to see San Francisco.
Aren't you?"

"A few more days or weeks shouldn't matter."

"But somehow, they do." She stopped herself and

murmured, "If you have reservations, that's different. I don't want to be a burden to you. But that's still no reason for *you* to stay. You could go on ahead without me, and when I'm better, I could follow."

"I'm not going anywhere without you. Either we both stay, or we both go."

"And you prefer that we stay?"

"I think it's best, for your sake."

She noted the determined set to his jaw, but decided to persist, in hopes of finding some way to convince him to be alone with her. "I'm not comfortable here, Zack. Don't ask me why. Mr. Braddock has done everything he could to make me feel at home, but it just doesn't feel right. Please try to understand."

He studied her warily. "I just don't want you to wake up one morning and find yourself in the middle of nowhere, away from everything you know and trust—"

"As long as I wake up with you, I'll be just fine."

"Dang . . ."

"Does that mean we're going to San Francisco?"

"It means I'll think about it." He gave her a sheepish grin. "If you weren't so danged pretty, I'd be able to argue with you better."

"If you think I'm so pretty," she teased, "why don't you kiss me?"

"Huh?"

"Here, on my lips." She tapped her mouth, then leaned toward him hopefully. "Haven't you ever wondered how I taste?"

His green eyes twinkled as he cupped her face in his hand, then brushed his lips across hers. "You taste sweet, sugar."

"So do you. Don't you want to be alone with me, Zack?"

"Sure. But we've got the rest of our lives for that. Right now, I want you to be healthy—"

"I *am* healthy," she protested; then she cautioned herself just as sharply. He wanted a healthy, *cheerful* bride, not a temperamental shrew. What would he think if she started making demands the very first week of their marriage? "We'll do whatever you decide, Zack. I just wanted you to know that, if you're ready to leave, I am, too."

"I'm gonna have a talk with your—with Russ. This is more complicated than it seems, Noelle."

She tried not to wince, wondering what sort of complications there could be. It was a mail-order marriage, after all. What could be simpler? Of course, there was probably some kind of payment involved, and money always complicated things. Perhaps Zack still owed Braddock the last installment on the contract. There could even be final papers to sign!

What if Zack didn't want to finalize it all until he knew she was fully recovered? And here she was, nagging him and complaining, and pressuring him to kiss her when he was trying to be a gentleman about the whole arrangement. "Go and talk to Mr. Braddock," she agreed softly. "Whatever the two of you decide will be fine with me."

"Are you mad at me, sugar?"

"Never," she said solemnly. "I'm just a little tired. Which I suppose proves that you're right. I'm not quite myself yet, after all."

"Get some sleep, then." He brushed his lips across hers again, then tucked her into her bed. "I'll come back for you at dinnertime. Don't you go taking those stairs on your own. The last thing we need is another accident."

She flushed and nodded, then closed her eyes until she heard him leave the room. The poor man was being such a saint about all this, given that he'd paid for something much less complicated. A simple transaction, not a series of accidents, tantrums, and medical conditions. She vowed that from that moment onward, she would be the healthy, cheerful bride he'd ordered. He called her "angel," and "sugar," but she knew the truth—she was neither angelic nor sweet. But she could learn to be, for this man, and she was going to start right away.

"I can't believe you agree with her! You'd let her go thousands of miles away, knowing she's hurt, and knowing she could get her memory back at any minute and need to talk to you?"

"She has you now."

"There are times when a girl needs her father," Zack grumbled. "And I reckon one of 'em is when some fella kidnaps her and pretends to be her husband."

Braddock chuckled. "I'm a coconspirator in both crimes, remember."

"Even if she was healthy, which she isn't, this house is the best place for her. There are hundreds of things here that might bring back her memory. Remember what Doc Long said? A familiar sound, or smell, or object— the dolls alone should have done it by now," he added, his voice hoarse with frustration.

"I agree. Doesn't that tell you something? She doesn't *want* to remember. And I'm beginning to agree with her instincts on the subject."

"Huh?"

"Think about it, son. Once her memory returns, her thoughts will be on Adam."

"Him?" Zack shook his head. "You think she still has feelings for that varmint?"

"No, but she almost married him. She'll brood about it, and worry it to death. She won't be able to hear a word you say, no matter how eloquently you plead your case. But she'll hear the rumors and the gossip, and believe me, they'll be vicious."

"With all due respect, sir, you're not making any sense. It sounds like you *never* want her to get her memory back."

"Nothing could be further from the truth." Braddock's gentle eyes flashed in warning. "I'd love nothing more than to march up those stairs and embrace her as my daughter. All I need to do is tell her the truth, and I'll be able to hear her call me 'Father' again. You can't begin to imagine how much I miss that."

The matchmaker shook his head, then continued. "Even if we decided to tell her the truth, do you really know what that is? For example, if she asks us how she feels about you, what would we say?"

"I'm not exactly sure," Zack admitted. "She loves me. I'm almost sure of it. But I wouldn't feel right, telling her so." He nodded slowly. "I see your point. Maybe telling her the truth isn't as easy as it sounds."

"And it would unduly upset her," Braddock persisted. "Why cause her such distress, when she can be happy while she recuperates on board a huge sailing ship, being courted by a man who loves and respects her? She put it so charmingly herself—that the new memories will give her strength, so that she can deal with the old ones when they finally reappear."

"That makes sense," Zack agreed carefully.

"You tried to win her heart last week, but couldn't, because of her engagement. If she stays here, and her memory returns, other emotions—embarrassment and self-reproach, to name a few—will get in the way. But you can take her away from all that. You've been given a rather remarkable opportunity."

"To take advantage of her injury? Her ignorance? She thinks it's her duty—as my bride—to let me take liberties with her," he informed the father bluntly. "Liberties she'd never allow if she wasn't hurt."

"I trust you, Zack, even if you don't trust yourself," Braddock assured him with a fond chuckle. "You'd never take advantage of my daughter. It's simply not in your nature. But you'll care for her, and charm her, and court her, and by the time her memory returns, she'll be your wife in every way possible. And you're legally married, which is convenient from a practical point of view, don't you think?"

Zack eyed the man in pure frustration. Was he listening to what he was saying? It sounded dead wrong, deceitful, and manipulative, not to mention foolhardy. But he had to admit, some of the matchmaker's arguments contained a grain of truth. Not because Noelle needed protection from gossips who weren't worth one hair on her head, but maybe she did need more time before dealing with the uncomfortable truths about that bastard Prestley.

And Noelle had made it clear that, for her own reasons, she didn't want to remember things yet. That was something Zack was willing to respect. And in that sense, this house was indeed a liability, holding as it did just about every memory she'd formed since the day she was born.

She could rest and grow stronger on the ship, with nothing and no one that might stimulate unwelcome memories. Just breathtakingly unfamiliar seascapes, bracing winds, and beautiful sunsets.

"If I do this," he growled finally, "I give you my word, I won't compromise her."

"Unless she agrees to it."

Zack felt his patience snap. "Even then, if her memory isn't back, how can I be sure she's agreeing? If she and I—If something happened between us, and then she got her memory back and wished she'd saved herself for another man, another wedding night, I'd never forgive myself. And," he added, half to himself, "she'd make me wish I'd never been born."

"If I didn't know better, I'd say you're afraid of my daughter."

"It's true," he admitted sheepishly. "I've never been so scared of anyone in my life. When she gets riled up—" He grinned in defeat. "Her honor will be safe with me, Russ. I'll be taking my life in my hands just looking at her, much less touching." He shook his head, the grin fading as he predicted softly, "She's gonna be so danged mad."

Twelve

Noelle Dane stood on a fourth-floor balcony of the Jupiter Hotel in Virginia City, Nevada, and allowed a gust of cool mountain air to rifle through her loose black curls. Below her, the crowded street bustled with activity, but her eyes were focused eastward, on the golden Sierra Nevada mountains, home of the Comstock Lode and a source of endless fascination for her bridegroom. He was up there somewhere at that very moment, just "having a look around," and exercising his powerful horse, who had been subjected to seven long weeks of confinement in ship holds, cattle cars, and livery stables.

Zack had grown almost as restless as Mercury, Noelle knew. She'd seen him pacing the long deck of their steamship day after day, anxious for dry land and adventure. This certainly seemed to be the place to find it, although he had promised her he wouldn't handle any explosives, track any wild animals, or pursue any criminals anytime soon.

She smiled at the thought of him—so brash and daring, except when it came to his bride, whom he treated with overwhelming care and respect. It had been two months since her "accident," and her symptoms, other than amnesia, had diminished greatly, yet Zack behaved as though she were still an invalid. If he had his way, she suspected she'd still be ensconced in Russell Braddock's daughter's bed, guarded by hundreds of pretty-faced dolls.

She remembered Braddock's sentimental send-off fondly. His entire household had turned out to say good-bye to the newlyweds, with several of the servants, including the old butler, weeping openly. The cook had even stuffed half a dozen handwritten recipes into Noelle's hands, claiming that they were "the lieutenant's favorites," and might be useful in California. It had been such a thoughtful gesture. But it was Russell Braddock himself who had truly touched Noelle's heart, with his hesitant, last-minute suggestion that perhaps she wasn't ready to leave, after all, and should reconsider.

Noelle had comforted him, reminding him that he too would be traveling to San Francisco in a month or so, to visit his niece and to evaluate the feasibility of moving his mail-order bride business to the new city. In the meantime, Zack had promised to keep the matchmaker informed of Noelle's progress, and she knew he had sent at least two telegrams in that regard.

"Zack is like a son to him," she reminded herself with a sigh. "Which means, over the years, perhaps Mr. Braddock will start to see *you* as a daughter. Wouldn't that be lovely?" It all seemed so comforting, as though Noelle herself would have a warm, loving family around her, despite the fact that she suspected she was an orphan, or worse, an outcast.

"Don't think about all that," she ordered herself as she did whenever such thoughts tried to haunt her. "Think about some way to make Zack kiss you before you go mad with romantic starvation."

She almost giggled aloud at the silliness of her predicament. Her sweet, attentive husband had dedicated himself to finding a cure for his wife's amnesia, when she needed something quite different from him. As her strength had grown, so had her desire to spend time in his arms, but he didn't seem to share her need, or at least, he didn't succumb to it. Instead, he greeted her with respectful kisses, rubbed her neck whenever she asked, and took her arm when they walked together. Beyond that, he kept his distance, despite her subtle attempts to seduce him. He didn't even sleep in the bed with her! His habit of stretching out on the floor at night had been somewhat understandable on the ship and other cramped quarters, but the hotel bed was a spacious one, and Noelle didn't intend to allow either of them to spend another lonely night.

"You can hardly complain about lack of male attention, Noelle Dane," she teased herself. "Are you forgetting the seven doctors who have examined you? You could scarcely pass through a city without Zack hunting down each and every expert, and he'll probably find one here, too, before long."

It had occurred to her more than once that the kindest thing she could do for Zack, not to mention for herself, was pretend that her memory had returned. After all, he knew so little about her, she could invent almost any tale of her childhood, and he couldn't be certain it wasn't true. And as for the details of the week between their first meeting and the accident, she could claim that those were still a bit hazy.

He'd be so relieved! And if only she'd had the presence of mind to tell that benevolent lie before they left Chicago, Russell Braddock could have relaxed too. And the journey to San Francisco could have been much, *much* more romantic.

And your marriage would have been based on a lie,
she reminded herself sternly. *You would have been
plagued with guilt, and if Zack ever found out, he'd
never trust you again. You know how noble and honest
he is, Noelle Dane. It's one of the reasons you've come
to love him so much, so don't you dare do anything to
jeopardize it!*

A familiar voice called "Noelle!" from the street below, and a shiver of delight coursed through her. There
he was, tall and confident and cheerful, tying Mercury
to a post without taking his emerald eyes off his bride.
Smiling shyly, she raised her hand in greeting, wondering if he knew how easily his handsome grin made her
insides melt.

When he stomped onto the wooden sidewalk and disappeared from view, she leaned over the rail, eager to
catch one last glimpse, to sustain her until he'd sprinted
up the four flights of stairs to their room. A disconcerting sound—of wood beginning to splinter—warned her
to back away, which she did quickly. Then she grimaced
and moved up to the railing again, jiggling it carefully
with her hand.

"Your marriage can't survive another accident," she
chided herself aloud. "Be more careful."

She stepped back into the room just as Zack burst
through the door, a broad smile on his face. "Hey, sugar.
Did you miss me?"

"Of course." She went to him, moistening her lips in
preparation for the predictable brush of his lips across
hers. If only she had the nerve to wrap her arms around
his neck and demand more! But she knew it would
make him uncomfortable, and so she restrained herself
as always.

"The railing on the balcony is loose, Zack."

"Dang." From the way he shook his head, she knew he, too, was thinking of the havoc another accident might wreak. "Don't step foot out there again till I have a chance to fix it."

"I won't."

His green eyes began to twinkle. "I've got some good news."

"Oh?"

"I met a doctor—"

She groaned. "Another one?"

"A better one." He took her by the hands and urged her to sit on the edge of the bed. "He's new to these parts, just like us. And he's young, and real smart. He says he saw us in the dining room last night and had a feeling something was wrong. I figure if he could see that, it was a good sign."

"He could probably see that you were in pain from sleeping on the floor. Why don't we have him examine *you?*" she teased halfheartedly. "I already know what he's going to say about me—that I'm perfectly healthy, and the amnesia will pass when it passes. Nothing we can do will change that."

"Everyone thought you'd be better long before now, but you're not." Sitting down beside her, Zack slipped his arm around her shoulders and murmured, "Do it for me and Merc, so we won't feel so danged guilty about all this."

"I'm perfectly healthy," she repeated with a sigh. "But I'll see this one last doctor, for Mercury's sake. After that," she dared to add, "there's something I want from *you.*"

"All you've gotta do is ask."

"I want you to start sleeping in the bed with me."

She smiled hopefully. "There's plenty of room, and we'd both sleep more soundly if you were comfortable."

"That floor's more comfortable than it looks," he assured her. "I've spent most of my life sleeping on hard, cold ground. Compared to that—"

"Never mind." She winced at the impatience in her voice, and reminded herself dutifully that he had ordered a cheerful bride, not a shrew. What right did she have to complain, when he was trying so hard to be a gentleman?

And it wasn't as though he wasn't romantic. He brought her flowers and sweet treats almost every day, and insisted that they watch the sunset together every night before he kissed her cheek and tucked her into bed.

He just wants to be certain you're completely recovered before he makes any demands on you, she scolded herself. *And perhaps this new doctor will be able to convince him of that, so . . .*

With an apologetic smile, she suggested, "Let's go find the new doctor, shall we?"

"He'll be here in a minute." Zack's tone was tinged with remorse. "I didn't think you'd object, and I was anxious, so I invited him up. I'm real sorry, sugar."

"It's fine."

He flushed, then murmured in a soft, warm voice that made Noelle's breath catch in her throat, "Maybe I *will* join you in this big old bed tonight, just to see if it's as comfortable as you claim."

"I'd like that."

When his green eyes began to twinkle, she felt a familiar stab of excitement, along with renewed hope that he was as tempted as she to reach a new and more intimate stage in their relationship. She even considered suggesting that they not wait until bedtime to explore

this enticing prospect, but a knock at the door reminded
her that they were expecting a guest, and so she settled
for one of their quick, innocent kisses, then hurried to
the mirror to check her appearance while Zack ambled
to the door.

The man who stepped into the room and shook Zack's
outstretched hand was young, just as Zack had described
him. To Noelle's surprise, he was also attractive, with
startling blue eyes and a roguish smile, quite unlike any
of the other physicians she'd seen since leaving Chicago.
It almost made her hesitate to allow the examination,
but she knew that reaction was ridiculous. Zack would
be there, and this man was a professional, so she summoned a cordial, yet hopefully distant smile and murmured, "Thank you for coming, Doctor."

"My pleasure." He took her hand, kissing it with a
playful flourish. "Philip Davenport, at your service."

"He knows all about amnesia, Noelle," Zack explained with undisguised enthusiasm. "Tell my wife
what you told me, Doc."

"Why don't we have a look at that head first?" Davenport suggested, motioning for Noelle to sit on the bed.

She shot him a reproachful look, then sat instead on
a straightback chair. "I hit my head here," she explained,
tapping the back of her skull. "But the headaches were
here, in the front. And it was my neck that was the
most uncomfortable. It throbbed for weeks, but it's fine
now, except for an occasional twinge."

"You hit it here in the back," Davenport repeated,
digging his fingers expertly into her scalp. "But most
of the pain was in the front. Did the other doctors explain why?"

"No."

"Think of it this way: Your brain is loose inside your

skull. When the back of your skull impacted the ground, the force sent your brain in the other direction. It crashed against the front of your skull, here. I imagine there were blinding lights and nausea? And blurred vision for a week or two?"

Noelle nodded, reluctantly impressed that he was taking the time to explain the phenomenon to them.

"Let's have a look in those pretty gray eyes." He knelt in front of her and studied each eye in turn, then put his hands on either side of her neck and explored carefully. "Any pain?"

"No, not at all."

"And your back?" He slid his hand behind her, then ran his knuckles straight down her spine. "How does that feel?"

Her cheeks had warmed at the unfamiliar thoroughness of the examination, but she forced herself to respond evenly. "My back is fine, Doctor."

"Stand up now, Mrs. Dane."

She bit her lip, but cooperated, hoping Zack was alert to any nonsense.

"Now, stand on one foot, please."

"I beg your pardon?"

"He's testing your balance, sugar," Zack explained.

"That's correct." Davenport watched as Noelle complied with his instruction. "Fine, now close your eyes. Good. Bring your hands out here. . . ." He stretched her arms out to her sides. "Use one finger now, and touch the tip of your nose. First with one hand. Good. Now the other. Excellent. Open your eyes."

She wanted to be annoyed at the boyish grin he flashed directly into her face, but had to admit that this was the most interesting examination she had yet experienced. Moving away, so that she was closer to Zack, she asked, "What about my memory? The other doctors told us it would be back in a matter of days, but it's been weeks, and I don't remember a single thing."

Davenport pursed his lips, as though intrigued by the statement. "Do you dream, Mrs. Dane?"

"Yes, of course."

"What do you dream about?"

She flushed again. "About my husband, I think. I don't really remember, but I know . . ." She took a breath, then explained shyly, "I feel safe in my dreams. That's how I know my husband is in them."

"Quite a tribute," Davenport murmured. "I asked your husband earlier if there was any trauma in your past, other than the accident. He says there was not."

She glanced at Zack, wondering if perhaps, for this doctor, they shouldn't be a bit more honest about their marriage. They had agreed, from the start, not to mention the mail-order nature of their arrangement, and so the physicians had naturally assumed that, during a normal courtship, Zack had learned most of the important details of Noelle's past and could report them accurately.

"Your fall was more than enough to cause your condition, even if your life up to that moment was completely blissful," Davenport continued. "I only asked about your past because amnesia can also be associated by terror or tragedy."

"She's had her share of disappointments, but not terror or tragedy," Zack interrupted.

"Fine, then. We can assume this is a physical case, rather than an emotional one." He hesitated, then observed, "It's odd that you chose to travel at a time like this. Do you have family in Nevada, Mrs. Dane?"

"I'm her family now," Zack explained. "They've entrusted her to me completely."

Noelle bit her lip, surprised and touched by the statement. "As you can see, I'm very fortunate, Doctor."

"That's abundantly clear," Davenport agreed.

But Zack was shaking his head. "There must be something we can do, Doc. Don't you have any ideas?"

The doctor's eyes began to twinkle. "Aside from another blow to the head, which I wouldn't recommend, I believe time and patience are the only proven treatment."

"Some of the other doctors said a familiar voice, or fragrance, or song, might do it," Noelle said quietly. "Do you agree with that?"

"It's been known to happen. But in your case, it seems unlikely. You've spent two full months with your own husband since the accident, hearing his voice, feeling his touch, et cetera. If *he* hasn't triggered your memory, I doubt if anything else will."

"You're saying she should've remembered by now?" Zack demanded.

"No. I'm saying a familiar voice or fragrance isn't the answer. Time, my friend," he added sympathetically. "That's the answer."

"Or a hit on the head," Noelle reminded them. "Really, Zack, if you're this impatient, perhaps I should go out onto the balcony and lean against that loose rail."

Zack chuckled. "It's too bad a hit on *my* head won't do it. You look like you'd be willing to oblige me, right about now."

She smiled and touched his cheek. "I just don't like seeing you worry this way. Doctor, please explain to my husband that I'm perfectly healthy."

"I know she's healthy, Doc," Zack interrupted. "But amnesia isn't normal. There must be something we can do."

Noelle was about to rescue Davenport when he surprised her by nodding. "You should drink peppermint tea, Mrs. Dane. And when you bathe, the water should be as warm as you can bear it. Also, wear loose clothing as often as possible."

"Why?"

The doctor shrugged. "All of these things will stimulate the flow of blood to your brain. That might just speed up your recovery."

"What else?" Zack demanded eagerly.

"You could rub your wife's neck and shoulders."

"We've already tried that."

"Of course you have." The doctor grinned. "I'd almost forgotten you were newlyweds. Let's just say then, massage of *any* sort will help increase the flow of blood."

Noelle blushed, wondering if Zack had lost his mind, discussing such intimate matters with a stranger. Couldn't he see that Davenport was teasing them?

On the other hand, Noelle had to admit that anything that encouraged Zack to touch her was a blessing, even if it did embarrass her a bit.

It suddenly occurred to her that Zack might be willing to massage her as soon as they were alone, and so she announced briskly, "We don't want to take any more of your time, Doctor. Thank you so much for your advice. We'll do everything you suggested."

"Yeah, Doc. Thanks. You're brilliant," Zack enthused.

The doctor bowed toward Noelle. "It's been my pleasure, believe me."

She eyed him sternly, hoping she had imagined the hint of flirtation in his voice. Apparently this was Davenport's way, and she suspected it didn't mean anything, but still, it was presumptuous. And if Zack ever started noticing it, it could be downright dangerous!

Crossing the room, she opened the door and gestured meaningfully. "Good-bye, Doctor. Thank you again for coming."

Unrepentant, he grinned and took her hand, kissing it lightly. "The two of you must agree to dine with me one night soon."

Before Noelle could politely decline, Zack had accepted the invitation and sent Davenport on his way; then he closed the door to study his bride. "That was interesting, wasn't it?"

"He was flirting with me right under your nose."

Zack grinned. "He couldn't help himself, sugar. You're too danged pretty for your own good." Reaching for her, he pulled her to within inches of himself. "I can't help myself, either."

"Zack . . ." She turned her face up to his, and was thrilled when he covered her mouth with his own, kissing her with a hungry insistence she had barely glimpsed in earlier encounters. Wrapping her arms around his neck, she allowed his tongue to play with hers, breathless with anticipation over what he'd do next. It was so unexpected, as though his decision to sleep with her had opened the floodgates of his passion at long last!

Then she remembered the doctor's instructions and pulled free enough to glare. "I suppose you were just trying to stimulate the blood flow to my head?"

"How'd I do?"

She moistened her lips, seduced despite her annoyance. "I'm not sure. Maybe you should try again."

"Yeah." He slipped his hand behind her head and

lowered his mouth to hers, kissing her deeply while his free hand massaged her waist. "You feel so good."

"So do you," she assured him weakly.

Backing her toward the bed, he lowered her onto the coverlet, then stretched out beside her and pulled her against himself, nuzzling her neck and nipping at her earlobe, while his huge hands massaged her waist and neck. Then one hand slid to the small of her back, urging her against him as he began to kiss her again.

"How're you doing?" he asked finally, his voice hoarse with arousal.

She gathered her wits and managed to report, "I'm sure this is good for me. I've never felt so stimulated. And I'm sure my brain has never had so much blood in it."

He chuckled ruefully. "It's purely the opposite for me."

"Pardon?"

"The blood's left my brain for greener pastures."

"Where? Oh!" She stifled a laugh, realizing that *his* blood had indeed been enlisted in a more passionate function. Without thinking, she slid her hand down his torso, anxious to investigate for herself, but he caught it in his own before she had managed to caress him.

"Hold on, sugar." He flashed her a rueful smile, drawing her hand up to his lips and kissing her fingertips lightly. "You're so danged sassy sometimes."

"I imagine some men *like* sassy women."

"All men like 'em. But some men misunderstand 'em. I'm not that sort of fella."

"What does *that* mean?" she demanded, frustrated by the sudden change of mood.

He propped his head up with his elbow. "It means I

respect you too much to take advantage of your condition."

"My condition?" She shook her head, amused despite herself. "All new brides have this condition, Lieutenant. As my husband, it's your duty to cure it."

She expected him to laugh, but his smile was shaky at best. "There's plenty of time for that, Noelle."

"But—"

"You oughta try and get some rest before supper. I'll go find some of that peppermint tea the doc recommended."

"You should nap with me," she complained softly. "I don't want tea; I want you."

"I want you, too. But for now, you need tea and rest." He rolled off the bed and stood straight and tall. "I'll sleep with you tonight, just like I promised."

"Don't bother." She slid off the other side of the bed and began to undress with her back to him. "You'd better run away, Lieutenant. You wouldn't want to see me naked, would you?"

"Dang it all, Noelle—"

She held her breath, praying he would come to her and throw her onto the bed again, but instead she heard the sound of the door as he took his leave of her without so much as a good-bye.

"So much for being a cheerful bride," she muttered to herself. "Why on earth did you send him away?"

But she knew why, and for the moment, couldn't really blame herself for the outburst. Couldn't he see how much she wanted to make love with him? And they were married, weren't they? Did he honestly see her as such an invalid? Didn't he long for more?

Of course he did! That had been flatteringly evident, and even now, through her annoyance, she could remember the hard, insistent feel of him against her. If only he hadn't stopped!

Discarding her clothes, she climbed into the bed and buried her face in the pillow, reminding herself, as she did so often these days, that Zack had his reasons for proceeding cautiously with her. He was convinced that she was still injured, and nothing Noelle or the doctors could say would change his mind. He didn't intend to take advantage of her "condition" until her memory came back, so rather than berate him or feel sorry for herself, she decided to turn her full attention to accomplishing that task.

A light shudder ran through her, and she realized how hard she had tried, over the last six weeks, *not* to remember her past. She was convinced it held something shocking, just as Dr. Davenport and the others had suggested. Zack wouldn't know, since she wouldn't have dared share it with him. She probably hadn't told Russell Braddock, either, for fear he wouldn't match her with a decent, upstanding groom. She might be from a long line of thieves, or be a criminal herself! What if she was a killer? Did she want to remember *that?*

You aren't any such thing, she chastised herself quickly. *It could be something tragic, like losing your entire family in some painful disaster, that made you turn to a matchmaker. You're probably a poor but decent orphan, and Zack would never turn his back on you because of any such tragedy in your past.*

You mustn't be a coward anymore. Think how happy he'll be—how amorous he'll be!—when you tell him you've finally remembered everything. Concentrate, Noelle. The only reason you haven't remembered before now is that you've been resisting it. Relax and try to remember your childhood.

On impulse, she jumped out of bed and located her traveling bag, digging to the bottom until she found a worn but pretty doll. Russell Braddock had insisted she take it with her, explaining, "My daughter would want you to have someone to whom you can confide your most secret hopes and fears." Noelle had seen tears in his eyes when he'd said that, and had wanted to comfort him, but given his reluctance to talk about his own past or his relationship with his daughter, she had simply promised to cherish the doll forever.

Snuggling back under the covers, she asked it, "What do you think about all this? Shall I be patient forever?" With a grimace, she accused playfully, "I know what you're thinking. *You* want me to remember, too. But why? I intentionally abandoned that life, and I'm happy with Zack. He and I will have a lovely future. But you're correct, of course. It will be a celibate one, with no lovemaking and no babies, until the amnesia is gone, so . . ." She hugged the doll close and concentrated with all her might.

To her surprise, her head began to ache for the first time in days, and so she reluctantly abandoned the effort, choosing instead to cuddle the little doll close as she drifted into sleep, in hopes she would be in a more agreeable mood by the time her husband returned.

Zack wasn't usually a drinking man, but he needed something to settle himself down after the burst of frustration and exhilaration his encounter with Noelle had engendered, and so he headed straight for a nearby saloon. Rebuffing the advances of a pair of lively bar girls, he ordered himself a whiskey, then leaned on the bar and groaned under his breath.

Noelle's body had felt *so* good against his, and her responses had been so heated. So encouraging. So seductively irresistible. And he had almost given in to her, after two full months of resisting that pretty pink mouth and those silvery eyes—two months of behaving himself, not just out of respect for her injury, but because he wasn't willing to jeopardize their future for a few wild, passionate nights.

Now she was angry and confused, and he didn't blame her. From her point of view it was simple: they had chosen freely to marry each other, and each of them wanted to consummate that marriage, so how could it be wrong? But Zack knew better. Sure, she had freely married him, but she had made it clear to him that she wouldn't consider consummating the marriage until she'd had her "courtship," and nursed the wounds Presley had inflicted. When her memory came back, all of that would return, too, along with her dang-blasted rules.

If only he had been honest with her from the start! His every instinct had told him to do just that, but he had allowed her father, and his own weaknesses, to convince him otherwise. Now, after weeks of romancing and deceiving her, he didn't dare just blurt out the truth, at least not without Russell Braddock and his niece Megan present to help explain the benevolence of their ridiculous scheme.

Braddock would be in San Francisco in a month or so—a long, celibate, torturous month. If Zack wanted to find an interim solution, his only option was to help Noelle remember her past by herself, and he was grateful to the new doctor for having the knowledge and interest to try to help them.

Of course, Davenport's "interest" had been focused,

at least in part, on Noelle's womanly charms. Still, by the end of the examination, Zack had sensed the doctor had become professionally intrigued, despite his flirtatious conduct.

Hot baths, peppermint tea, and massages. Zack grinned ruefully. The rubbing was going to be dangerous, given the ease with which they aroused each other. But he had to admit, he liked having an excuse to indulge himself despite his vow to behave. And how angry could she be, given that his motives were at least partially honorable?

She'll be mad as a hornet, he answered himself frankly. *But it's not like you haven't touched her before. Just don't touch anything you didn't touch while she was engaged to Prestley—and don't break any of her danged rules—and she won't be able to stay mad for too long.*

"Lieutenant Dane?"

Zack turned toward the voice and was surprised to see Davenport lounging against the bar a few yards away. "Hey, Doc. I didn't see you there."

"You were preoccupied. With thoughts of pretty Noelle, I assume?"

Zack eyed the physician coolly. "Do you always flirt with your female patients?"

"In the case of Mrs. Dane, it was completely self-defeating." Davenport chuckled.

"How's that?"

"Every time I complimented her, she became more amorous toward *you.*"

"Yeah." Zack couldn't help but grin. "I kinda noticed that, myself."

"You're a very fortunate man, Lieutenant."

"Call me Zack." He shook the doctor's hand vigorously. "I appreciate the advice you gave us this afternoon."

"It's a fascinating case." He pursed his lips. "Have you known Mrs. Dane for very long?" When Zack didn't respond right away, the doctor added hastily, "The reason I'm asking is to determine how much of her past you know firsthand, and how much you simply heard about during the courtship."

Zack shrugged. "I know everything I need to know about her. She's been well-loved and protected every minute of her life."

"I didn't mean to imply otherwise."

"You're still looking for something in her past to explain the amnesia?" Zack hesitated, then decided to be blunt. "You mentioned tragedy or horror. What if there was something else? Embarrassment or disappointment. Or confusion. Would that be enough to cause this?"

"Has she been profoundly embarrassed or disappointed recently? The wedding night, perhaps?" The doctor blanched. "I'm not suggesting *you* disappointed her, believe me. But embarrassment, or even shock, isn't all that uncommon, depending on a girl's upbringing. Was she—"

"It's got nothing to do with the wedding night," Zack growled. "I was just asking about embarrassment in general."

Davenport's eyes began to twinkle. "If embarrassment were enough to cause amnesia, we'd have an epidemic on our hands. But I suppose disappointment or confusion on a profound level could trigger it. If you'd provide specifics—"

"There aren't any. It was just a question." Zack shook his head. "I'm not making much sense, am I?"

"You're concerned about the woman you love, and

so you're exploring every alternative. That makes perfect sense."

He nodded gratefully. "Is there a chance she'll never remember?"

"A slight one, I suppose." The doctor studied Zack carefully. "Would that be so terrible?"

"Yeah, it would." He took a deep breath, then explained. "I figure I won't know she's fully healed until then."

"She's fine, Zack. Unless the headaches and nausea come back—" Davenport interrupted himself with a broad smile. "Of course, if she starts having nausea, our first suspect will be pregnancy." His smile broadened at the shocked expression the suggestion had elicited from Zack. "I can't say I blame you for wanting to have her all to yourself for a while longer, but it *is* a natural consequence of marriage, so you'd best be prepared."

Zack shook his head, then downed his whiskey in one swallow. If he had needed more incentive to keep his hands off Noelle, the doctor had just provided it. It would be bad enough for her to recover her memory and find that she'd lost her virginity to Zack. But a baby? She'd truly strangle him! And she'd be within her rights to do just that.

"Do you have any more questions, Zack?"

"Actually, I do," he admitted. "When Noelle's old memories come back, will she remember these new ones, too?"

"Almost certainly." When Zack grimaced, the doctor added firmly, "It's to your advantage, isn't it? She'll remember your love and devotion. And she'll remember this romantic honeymoon."

"Yeah, I reckon she'll remember everything, and

that's the way it should be," he muttered, trying not to think about how angry she was going to be.

"Will you and she settle in Virginia City?"

Zack shrugged. "I figure we'll stay for a few weeks, then head back to San Francisco to visit friends. After that . . ." He shook his head. "It depends on Noelle. I can be happy anywhere, as long as I'm with her."

"From what I've seen, she feels the same way."

"Yeah. Kinda makes you wonder what I'm doing *here*, doesn't it?" Zack threw a couple of coins on the bar. "Have a drink on me, Doc. I gotta get home to my bride."

"Noelle?"

"Hmm?" She shifted toward his voice. "Zack?"

"Wake up, sugar." He resisted the urge to slide under the covers with her, and tried for a cheery tone instead. "I'm starved. Drink this tea I brought for you; then we'll go downstairs and have ourselves some big, juicy steaks."

She opened her eyes and gave him a shy, hopeful smile. "Does this mean you forgive me for sending you away? I'm so sorry, Zack. I promise I won't be moody anymore."

"Moody?" He chuckled, remembering her past outbursts. "You're an angel for sure these days. And I'm trying my best to deserve it. When your memory comes back, you'll understand more, I promise."

"I've been trying to remember my childhood." She struggled to a sitting position, then pulled a worn little doll into view. "Do you see? Mr. Braddock gave her to me, to keep me company. And she agrees with you, that I should try to get my memory back, so I did my best."

"That's fine, sugar," he murmured, trying to focus on the doll despite the allure of his bride's high, firm breasts, straining against the bodice of her lacy chemise.

"But it made my head hurt." Noelle sighed. "So I decided to sleep, instead."

"Huh?" The announcement jolted him out of his amorous reverie. "Your head was hurting?"

"Just because I was tired. I'll try again later."

"I don't want you trying to remember if it hurts," he protested. "We should tell the doc about that. Maybe you shouldn't drink the tea—"

"That's silly," she said with a smile. "The tea will help me remember naturally. That's the best way, don't you think?" She stroked his cheek. "You were gone for more than an hour."

"I had a drink with the doc. And I fed Merc. Then I talked to the desk clerk about that railing. They're gonna fix it tomorrow, so stay away from it till then."

"I will." She reached for the teacup Zack had placed on the nightstand and took a tentative sip. "Mmm, delicious. Thank you, Zack. I only hope it works, so we can be—" She blushed but persisted. "I want us to be married in every way."

Zack took the drink from her and set it back on the nightstand, then cupped her blushing face in his hand. "I know you're wondering why I don't make love to you, Noelle. It's not all because you're hurt. Even if you didn't have amnesia, I kinda like the notion of courting you before we consummate this marriage. Like it would've been if we'd met at a party or dance, instead of in Chicago. Does that make sense to you?"

"It's sweet." She sighed and snuggled close to him. "I like that notion, too. It's what we've been doing for eight lovely weeks. But isn't it time for our courtship to . . . well, to become more intimate? We're married, after all."

"And you still have amnesia. I don't want you to make important decisions—"

"I made *this* decision before I hit my head."

Zack smiled at the hint of petulance, so reminiscent of her outburst near the inn, and decided to be as honest as he could with her. "On our wedding day, you told me you wanted me to court you before we consummated this danged thing."

Her beautiful silver eyes widened with delight. "And you agreed? That was so sweet of you."

"You asked for six months."

She stared for a moment, then laughed sympathetically. "You agreed to *that?*"

He tried not to smile. "Not exactly."

She laughed again. "I don't blame you. I was wrong to ask such a thing." Her eyes warmed as she draped her arms around his neck. "I can guarantee you I would have changed my mind after a week or two of kissing you."

"Yeah, that's what I figured, too." He lowered his mouth to hers and kissed her, lightly at first, then with insistence, until their bodies began to entwine. "Dang, Noelle . . ."

"Don't stop," she pleaded.

"I've gotta." He pulled away gently. "You can't truly know your own mind until you have your memory back."

"Zack!"

"I know. We can't wait forever. But—"

"We can't wait six months!"

"I know that, too, sugar," he agreed with a chuckle. "But we can wait just a mite longer, can't we?" He took a deep breath, then dared to suggest, "Let's say, one month?"

"One?"

She was clearly intrigued, so he persisted firmly. "That's not too long, is it?"

"I don't know. . . ."

"Sure you do. It's fine." He smiled reassuringly. "In the meantime, I'm gonna sleep with you, just like we're doing now. We'll kiss and snuggle, and see if your memory returns naturally. But one way or the other, in one month's time, we'll be doing everything you want. I promise."

"One way or the other," she agreed as her fingers moved to unbutton his shirt. "This fabric is so rough, Zack. If we're going to snuggle . . ."

He grinned and stripped the garment off obligingly. Then he joined her under the blanket and pulled her against his bare chest, savoring the feel of her nipples through the thin, delicate fabric of her undergarment.

"Your trousers are rough, too."

He laughed as he nuzzled her neck. "If your memory came back right now, you'd kill me on the spot, just for *thinking* about taking off my britches." Rolling onto her, he allowed her to feel, for just a moment, the full extent of his arousal. He even pulsed against her, half expecting her to push him away in alarm or disgust. Instead, her grip around his neck tightened, so he pulled back and insisted lamely, "Have some more tea, sugar."

Her silver eyes glittered with impish delight. "I'll do anything you ask, Lieutenant. You've just convinced me you're worth another month's wait."

"Dang," he murmured, wondering what he'd done to deserve so sassy and receptive a lady. And wondering

further what Noelle Braddock would say if she could
hear the way Noelle *Dane* was talking.

His thoughts went back to the moment, two months
earlier, when she had had a nightmare that turned into
an erotic encounter. She had stroked his manhood with
just such admiration that night, only to announce, the
following day, that he must never expect such conduct,
outside of a dream, from any true lady.

With mischievous appreciation, he told his bride,
"You're like a girl from a dream, do you know that?"
Then he remembered Adam Prestley's insult—that he
expected Noelle to be a "fantasy"—and blanched.
"That's not what I want from you, though. I just want
you to be yourself—a decent, kindhearted girl who loves
me. Don't ever think I'm asking for more."

When she cocked her head to the side and studied
him blankly, he chided himself for making things so
complicated. Summoning a reassuring smile, he rolled
out of the bed, then extended his hand to her. "Come
and have some supper, angel. I'll tell you all about the
talk I had with your new doctor, and then we'll sleep
together, just like you wanted. How's that?"

"Perfect." With a mischievous smile, she scooted
away from him, toward the opposite side of the bed.
"Close your eyes now, Lieutenant. It wouldn't do for
you to see me in my undergarments, would it? At least,
not for one more month."

He chuckled and turned away, knowing that she was
mocking him, but knowing further that it was true. After
all, one of Noelle Braddock's most solemn rules was
that her husband shouldn't expect a naked—or presum-
ably, near-naked—bride. Under other circumstances, he
intended to take issue with that, but for the moment,

he was glad to hear that Noelle Dane had the same inclination, even if hers was infinitely more negotiable.

Noelle Dane stared with lusty admiration at her husband's strong, muscled back, aroused by the knowledge that they would be making love that very night. He had *said* one more month, and she had agreed, but they had originally agreed on *six,* and that figure had gone by the wayside the moment his naked skin had met her welcoming breasts. She had a feeling the timetable could be discarded altogether if she wore a provocative dress to dinner, made just the right conversation, and then stripped down to bare, warm skin when they next met in bed.

She had respected his restraint when she thought it was due to concern for her injury, but now she knew the truth—that she herself had insisted on a post-wedding "courtship," most likely in response to Zack's expectation that they would consummate the marriage on the wedding night. And being a gentleman, he had agreed, although he had yearned and planned to convince her otherwise, and would clearly have succeeded, had she not hit her head.

Tonight, I'll free you from your vow, for my own selfish reasons, she told him with silent delight. *One way or the other, I'll become Mrs. Zachary Dane in every sense, and even if it shocks you, I have a feeling you'll thank me profusely in the morning. It's time, Zack. We've both been patient long enough.*

In spite of her excitement, her heart ached, just a little, for the Noelle who had existed before the accident—the Noelle who had abandoned her past and allowed a stranger to make her choices for her. That poor girl had needed six months—either to heal, or to learn. Either way, there must have been some fear behind the requested reprieve—innocent fear, because she'd been a virgin who for some reason lacked confidence in her ability to love or be loved, or true fear, because she'd been treated badly in another man's bed. Noelle didn't want to know which it was, because it really didn't matter anymore. She was Mrs. Zachary Dane now, and Mrs. Zachary Dane simply wasn't afraid of anything.

Thirteen

In addition to the tailored traveling outfits Noelle had brought with her on her journey, her trunk had contained several stunning dresses, apparently designed to be worn at fancy parties in San Francisco. The patrons of the Jupiter Hotel dining room would stare at such attire, she suspected, but as she tugged the low-cut bodice of a navy blue satin gown into place, she reminded herself that only one person's reaction would matter. Zack had seen her in such finery only once—or at least, she only *knew* of one time. Her beautiful wedding gown had been flattering and provocative, and he had wanted to make love to her because of it, but for reasons she didn't care to fathom, she had suggested they wait. This gown would signal to him that his wait was over.

Dabbing her cleavage and shoulders with perfume—a heady fragrance reminiscent of pure white gardenias—she sifted her fingers through her dark curls one last time, then smiled hopefully at her reflection in the huge mirror that sat atop the hotel dresser. The woman who smiled back at her was a married woman in love—strong, confident, and attractive. Again, Zack would know what it all meant without any further prompting, although she intended to prompt him in any case, just so that he would be suitably amorous by the time they returned to their room.

She had asked him to go ahead, to arrange a table by the huge stone fireplace that dominated the Jupiter's richly paneled dining room. It was a magnificent room, and could have been a wonderful setting for a tryst, had the Virginia City patrons not been so rowdy a bunch. One was more likely to find the tables filled with dusty miners than with couples sharing a romantic moment, but the Jupiter catered to all, provided they had the money to buy the huge, overpriced steak dinners and decadent chocolate desserts.

Taking one last deep breath, Noelle pinched her cheeks to a rosy hue, then stooped to don the butter-soft black leather boots Zack had bought for her upon their arrival the previous day. The lightweight shoes barely covered her ankles, but were better protection than anything she'd brought with her. Given Zack's habit of suggesting a stroll in the moonlight after dinner, she didn't dare wear anything flimsy. She had no intention of slipping on the uneven Virginia City sidewalks and injuring herself again.

Remember what the doctor said, she teased herself as she descended the four flights of stairs that would take her to the lobby. *If you fall, be sure at least to hit your head. The only true guarantee that Zack will make love to you tonight is if your memory has returned. But this dress . . .* She rustled the skirts happily, thinking that with any luck, the effect would be almost as arousing to her husband as a full recovery.

She nodded toward the desk clerk, and would have swept past the sixteen-year-old boy had he not rushed to stand before her, his eyes wide with youthful admiration. "You look beautiful tonight, Mrs. Dane. Would you like me to locate your husband for you?"

"That won't be necessary, but thank you." She started to walk toward the dining room, with her admirer still on her heels.

"We'll fix that loose railing tomorrow, just like we promised, ma'am."

"Thank you." She tried not to smile at the boy's desperate attempts to find reasons to speak with her.

"I'll do it myself, as soon as I'm off duty."

"That's sweet of you." She patted his arm, touched by the attention, but unwilling to allow him to spoil her entrance. "I'll see you tomorrow, then?"

He nodded and backed reluctantly away. "If you need anything—"

"I'll know just whom to ask," she assured him. Waiting patiently until he was safely behind his counter again, she adjusted the short, puffy sleeves of the dress one last time. Then she stepped through the doorway, hoping that Zack would be watching for her and would be beguiled by what he saw.

Unfortunately, his back was to her, as he stood by the fireplace engaged in conversation with Philip Davenport. It wasn't the entrance she had planned, but still, she had to smile at the sight of his tall, lanky body and rich, wavy brown hair—a dashing specimen, even from the back.

At least someone *is aroused,* she teased herself. *Now if only you can return the favor.*

The hush that had fallen over the room seemed lost on Zack, but Davenport had taken notice, and it was he who flashed her an approving grin and motioned for her to join them. Gathering up her skirts, she began to thread her way through the crowded tables, trying to appear casual despite the gawking faces of the miners, some of whom stared as though they hadn't seen a woman in months.

Then Zack turned toward her, his emerald eyes smiling in welcome, then widening with amazement as his jaw visibly dropped. Relieved and gleeful, Noelle maintained her casual air as she approached them, nodding toward the doctor, then gracing her husband with an innocent smile.

Zack seemed about to speak, but didn't quite manage it, so she turned to Davenport and extended her hand. "It's nice to see you again, Doctor."

"Call me Philip." He kissed her fingers respectfully. "Your husband and I were just discussing your condition."

"It's his favorite topic of conversation."

"So I've noticed. I was assuring him that you're perfectly healthy, although I'll admit, I didn't realize exactly how radiant you could be until this moment."

"What a sweet thing to say."

"I was about to suggest that the two of you join me for dinner—"

"Find your own girl, Doc," Zack interrupted, his voice close to a growl. "This one's spoken for."

Noelle bit back a laugh. "Perhaps another night, Doctor? This is a special occasion for my husband and myself."

Davenport chuckled. "It's special for all of us." Flashing Zack a grin to show that he was just jesting, he insisted, "I'll send a bottle of the hotel's finest champagne to your table, as my contribution to the occasion. Enjoy yourselves."

When he had bowed and left them alone, Noelle flashed her husband a playful smile. "I'm glad you sent him away. I've been looking forward to being alone with you."

Zack's gaze traveled over her appreciatively. "I kinda like the idea myself." Then he reached for her and pulled her against himself, lowering his mouth for a quick but incendiary kiss.

Heedless of the other diners, Noelle reveled in the burst of attention. Then she stroked his face and teased, "Shouldn't we have dinner first?"

Zack groaned, his hands still resting on her hips. "You sure make it hard for a fella to keep his word."

"Good."

"Sit on down here and we'll have ourselves a little talk." He pulled back her chair for her, and they settled at a small table lit only by the dancing flames from the fireplace. "You sure look pretty, sugar."

"Thank you."

"Kinda makes me wish I'd worn something more formal."

She reached across the table and fingered the top button on his simple tan linen vest. "I love the way you look in this. It reminds me of our lovely honeymoon on the steamship. It was almost perfect, wasn't it?"

Zack nodded carefully.

"Of course, for a honeymoon to be perfect—"

"Noelle?"

"Yes?"

He was visibly trying not to smile. "I thought we had ourselves a deal."

"I've been thinking about that. Oh . . ." She turned her face up to beam at the waitress, who had just brought their champagne in a silver ice bucket. "Thank you. And please thank the doctor for us again."

"Sure, ma'am. Do you know what you want to eat?"

Noelle glanced toward her husband. "I'm famished, but I think I'll let you decide how best to deal with that."

He arched an eyebrow in mock rebuke, then told the waitress, "Those steaks you served us last night were good. Unless you can recommend something better—"

"There's nothing better within fifty miles," she advised cheerfully. "When trout's available, that's good, too, but no one seems to have time to fish anymore. All anyone wants to do is dig."

"Sounds like we're having steak, then." Zack waited until the woman had left, then observed dryly, "It's strange how a fella can ignore a stream bursting with trout, just to dig in the dirt."

"They want to be rich."

"That's what I'm saying," he explained. "Living up here, with the sweet smell of pine in the air, and food enough to raise a strong, healthy family—if they'd stop to think about it for a minute, they'd see they're *already* rich. But the way I hear it, they'll likely up and leave this spot if they hear about another strike somewhere else."

Noelle cocked her head, intrigued by the statement. Until now, he had claimed they were just "scouting around," and would probably settle in San Francisco eventually. "You and Mercury must have liked what you saw up there on Mount Davidson."

"The whole area's beautiful." Zack reached for the champagne bottle and filled each glass with sparkling gold bubbles. "I hear it can be kinda rough here in winter, but if you plan for it right, I reckon even then—" He stopped himself and assured her hastily, "It's not like I'm making decisions without you, sugar. Me and Merc are gonna take you around for a look soon, too.

I figure we oughta use this month for scouting as much as we can—"

"This month?" she teased. "What if I told you I have other plans for this particular month?"

"I sorta guessed that." His grin was sheepish. "But the way I see it, we shouldn't be making any important decisions for a while. Russ Braddock'll be in San Francisco in a month. That seems like time enough—"

"Pardon?" Noelle stared in confusion. "I'm looking forward to seeing Mr. Braddock again, too. And I know he helped us make the most important decision of our lives. But—" She stopped herself, distressed that their romantic dinner had been placed in jeopardy so easily.

Zack reached across the table to pat her hand. "You gotta admit, sugar, that fella knows a perfect match when he sees one."

She hesitated, then forced herself to relax. Surely she had misunderstood. He couldn't possibly have been suggesting they needed Braddock's advice on when to consummate their marriage!

Lifting her glass, she proposed softly, "Shall we drink to Russell Braddock, then? For bringing us together?"

"To Russ Braddock," Zack echoed, taking a sip, then grimacing at the taste. "Never did like this stuff much."

"I wonder if I did."

"Huh?"

Noelle set down her glass and turned to stare into the flames that were dancing in the fireplace. "I wonder if I liked champagne before I hit my head. I like it now, but I don't suppose that means much."

Zack reached across the table for her hand. "I liked it better when you were flirting with me. Now you seem sad. Did I say something?"

"No."

"Does your head hurt?"

"For heaven's sake!" She glared in disgust. "Didn't you hear what the doctor said?"

"Settle down, sugar. I didn't mean anything by it—"

"Do you know why he sent the champagne to our table and told us to enjoy ourselves? Because he thought you'd seduce me and carry me off to our room and make love to me all night long. *He* apparently feels I'm ready for that. But if you and Mr. Braddock don't agree, I suppose you know best." Rising haughtily to her feet, she announced, "I'd best get back to my sickbed now before I exhaust myself. Enjoy your steak, and when you're ready to go to bed, too, *feel free to sleep on the floor!*"

"Noelle!"

She jumped back to evade his grasp, then gathered up her skirts and stormed toward the doorway, ignoring the chuckles of the other diners. When Zack caught up with her and grabbed her elbow, she spun on him with a look that made him unhand her instantly; then she turned away again and bolted up the stairs.

He's not making any important decisions until he confers with Mr. Braddock, she taunted herself mercilessly. *For all you know, he promised him he wouldn't take your virginity until he had his express permission! It's probably part of the contract! Perhaps he hasn't even paid for that particular privilege yet!*

Humiliated, she burst into their room and immediately began to strip off the enticing gown, knowing now that her husband couldn't possibly be "enticed" by it without first consulting with their matchmaker. Zack hadn't chosen one month of forbearance at random. He was actually coordinating the consummation of their marriage with Braddock's arrival in San Francisco!

Who does Russell Braddock think he is, extracting a promise like that from my husband? she fumed as she paced the length of the room. *Who is he to decide when I lose my virginity? That's my decision! It's not as though I'm unconscious or delirious, after all. I'm perfectly capable of making up my own mind, amnesia or not. What gives anyone the right to interfere with my love life?*

For all he knows, I lost my virginity years ago! she added in disgust. *How dare he presume to protect my honor from my own husband. And how dare Zack agree to such a ridiculous arrangement!*

As furious as she was with the two men, she was even more angry with herself. *You've known all along they were keeping secrets from you, Noelle Dane, so don't pretend otherwise. A professional matchmaker doesn't select a bride for a war hero unless he has thoroughly investigated her past, if only to be certain she doesn't have a dozen children or a criminal history! You could see it in their eyes—they've been sheltering you from truths about your past since the first minute you regained consciousness. And you allowed it, because quite frankly, you didn't want to hear those truths any more than they wanted to tell them. They had to make secret agreements. Mr. Braddock is a businessman with a reputation to protect. What would the newspapers say if they found out he sent virgins with amnesia into marriages with strangers?*

Every secret arrangement Zack and Braddock made was designed in part to protect you, Noelle Dane! You should have returned the favor by telling them a nice reassuring lie—that the amnesia was gone—and everything would have been just fine! Then she took a deep breath and urged herself boldly, *Do it now! Tell him you*

*remember distinctly that you lost your virginity years
ago! Then at least he won't feel the need to wait any
longer on* that *account.*

The ridiculous plan brought a reluctant smile to her
face. So many odd twists to this unusual marriage—using
a matchmaker, marrying a stranger, losing her memory—and
the pièce de résistance, convincing her
bridegroom she *hadn't* saved herself for him!

Wrapping a blanket around herself, she ventured out
onto the balcony, still toying with the idea of putting
Zack's concerns to rest by pretending to recover. *It's
silly,* she scolded herself finally. *He'd never believe you.
He'd ask you about other facts—verifiable ones, like
what you were wearing when he met you—and you'd
have to confess. And then he'd see you as a lunatic and
a liar for the rest of your marriage.*

Overhead, the beautiful mountain sky taunted her with
thoughts of the romantic walk she'd planned to take with
Zack, so she hurried back into the room. Reminding
herself that there was only one rational solution to her
dilemma, she took a deep breath and tried again to remember.
Only this time, she didn't reach for details of
a forgotten childhood. She thought of men—short ones
with golden hair, stern-faced ones with blue eyes. Anyone
but Zack. *Imagine them kissing you,* she directed
herself firmly. *Or raising their voices to you, or dancing
with you—*

A familiar stab of pain made her recoil from the effort,
and she stumbled to the bed, burying her face in
a pillow and vowing *not* to remember *anything*—not the
past, nor the argument with Zack, nor the humiliating
arrangement with Russell Braddock—for the rest of the
night. In the morning, she would simply give Zack an
ultimatum: either he loved her and wanted to be her

husband immediately, or he was willing to let her go, in which case she'd board a stage, return to San Francisco alone, and . . .

And what? she challenged herself sympathetically. *Even if you hit your head a thousand times, you could never forget a man like him, so go to sleep. It's going to be a long, lonely month, whether he sleeps on the floor or not, so you'd best rest up for it.*

Summoning his courage, Zack leaned down to give his slumbering bride's cheek a kiss. "Hey, sugar? Are you asleep?"

"Don't you dare get into this bed, Zachary Dane."

He smiled to realize that she hadn't been asleep, at all. She'd been lying in wait for him. "I brought you some food."

"I'm not hungry."

"I know you're mad—"

"Then be quiet and let me sleep."

"I want to talk to you."

"There's nothing to talk about. And even if there were, I can't stand the sound of your voice."

He chuckled nervously. "I don't blame you for that, Noelle. But there are things you should know—"

"Oh really? And you're going to tell me a few of them? But you'll keep the other ones from me until some other time? No, thank you."

"It's not like that this time," he assured her sincerely, remembering the decision he'd made as he paced the wooden sidewalks of Virginia City. "I'm gonna tell you everything, straight out—"

"Don't bother." She sat up in the bed and glared at him. "We talk when *you* want to talk. We kiss when *you* want to kiss. We do what *you* want to do—or rather, what your agreements and contracts *allow* you to do. That ends tonight. From this moment forward, I do what *I* want to do. And right now, I want to sleep. If you want to talk, I'm sure Merc would love the company."

"You want me to go sleep in the livery stable?"

"Yes, please."

"I like it when you're this way," he cajoled. "Just like a little firecracker. It shows me you really are feeling better."

"That just shows how wrong you are," she said with a haughty sniff. "I haven't felt this horrible since the accident."

"Huh?" He felt a familiar rush of concern. "Should I get the doc?" When she sent a pillow crashing toward his face, he grinned in relief, then pulled off his boots and vest and climbed under the covers with her. "I'm just as sorry as I can be, sugar. Don't be mad at me anymore." Lowering his voice, he added seductively, "You looked so pretty tonight, Noelle. I was proud to be your husband."

"Except of course you're *not* my husband yet."

"Noelle—"

"If you intend to do something about that tonight, fine. You can stay. Otherwise, go away. In either case, I don't want to talk anymore."

"Maybe you're right," Zack murmured. "We've been talking too much tonight, when all I've wanted to do since I saw you in that pretty dress was kiss you." Slipping his hand around her waist, he pulled her gently toward himself, then began to nuzzle her ear apologetically. "I love you, Noelle."

"Do you?" She slipped her arms around his neck. "I need to ask you something, Zack."

"Sure, sugar. Anything."

She licked her lips, as though afraid of what she was about to hear. Then her gaze locked with his, and he saw that something—confidence or desperation—was driving her to hear it nonetheless.

"You don't have to be afraid to ask me," he encouraged softly. "There's nothing I won't tell you. And nothing in your past so terrible, you and me can't face it together."

She smiled and stroked his face. "It's not *my* past I'm worried about, it's yours."

"Huh?"

"Why did you order a bride through the mail? You're so handsome and charming and irresistible. You could have had any girl you wanted. Why did you trust Mr. Braddock more than yourself?" Before he could answer, she added weakly, "If someone broke your heart once, and you'll never recover—"

"I never gave my heart to any girl but you," he promised. "But you're right about one thing. I didn't trust myself to make a good decision."

"Why not?"

Zack shrugged. "I figured when the time came, I'd choose a girl for all the wrong reasons—because she had a pretty smile or smelled good or had long legs. I figured Russ Braddock didn't care about all that. He'd choose someone who could be a good wife. A good mother to my children."

Tilting her face until she was gazing into his eyes, he continued. "I was wrong not to trust myself, 'cause when the time came, I chose just the right girl. I didn't need a matchmaker to tell me you were the bride for me. I knew it the minute I laid eyes on you."

"Oh, Zack," she whispered. "What a perfect thing to say. Are you really that sure?"

"Didn't I just say it?" he murmured, pulling her against himself and petting her back gently. "I love you so much, it scares me to death."

"I'm sorry I lost my temper."

"I'm not." He chuckled fondly. "I like it when you get all feisty like that. Sets my blood rushing to all sorts of interesting places."

"I couldn't help but notice." Noelle laughed ruefully, then began to grind her pelvis against him gently. "It's the real reason I've decided to forgive you so easily."

Zack allowed himself to enjoy the tantalizing motion, and even dared to pump against her a time or two, his imagination reeling with thoughts of what he couldn't allow himself to do to her. Even when she groaned and tightened her grip on his neck, he couldn't bear to stop. Not quite yet. Not when she felt so good against him.

Then her hand slid down his torso, and she stroked him as she'd tried to do that afternoon, and for a guilty moment he allowed that, too; then he reluctantly gripped her wrist and tugged it back up, kissing her fingertips in grateful apology.

"I want to touch you," she protested, her voice groggy with arousal.

"I know you do. And I'd like it just fine. But you told me once it's something a fella should never ask a lady to do—"

"You didn't *ask* me; I volunteered." She sighed in frustration. "I'm your wife."

"These are *your* rules, Noelle. You made them plain to me before the accident. I should have told you all about 'em, right from the start. About the six months, and this, and not being naked, and—"

"Pardon?"

"You told me a fella should never expect a lady—even if they've been married for years—to get naked—"

"Never?" She eyed him warily. "Are you sure I wasn't just being—well, coy?"

"Real sure," Zack confirmed. "You believed with all your heart that a lady won't do certain things. And when your memory comes back, you're gonna believe it again. And you're gonna be powerfully disappointed in yourself, and powerfully mad at me, if you did things that make you feel ashamed. I don't want to be any part of that."

She sandwiched his face between her hands. "We can't know why I felt that way before, but it's silly to think it'll come back, even if I do get my memory back. I want you, Zack. I want to touch you, and I want you to touch me. That's not going to change. It gets stronger every day, every night, every time you kiss me. I give you my word, I'll never be angry with you, or myself, for consummating our love for each other every way we can."

"I want to believe that," he whispered, his voice cracking with desire. "But there's something else, sugar—"

"There's *nothing* else. Just you and me and this love we feel for each other. Nothing else matters to me. Whatever was said and done in the past—"

"I've lied to you, Noelle."

"And I've lied to you," she assured him breathlessly.

"Huh?"

"Don't you see? I'm almost sure it was all a lie, Zack—my pretending with you, to be such an innocent 'lady'—I probably lied about all that so you wouldn't suspect the truth about me. I'm beginning to think I'm not even a virgin, and I pray that doesn't matter to you, but—"

"Hold up!" He stared in alarm. "I don't know why you're talking this way, but if I'd been truthful with you from the start, you wouldn't be having such doubts—"

"For heaven's sake!" Her eyes flashed a silvery warning. "Hasn't any of this ever occurred to you? Think about what you told me on the ship—what your father used to say. Facts are facts, and there are a few facts we know for sure, amnesia or no amnesia."

He shook his head, completely confused. "What facts?"

"You met me for the first time this year in Chicago. That's a fact, isn't it?"

Zack nodded warily.

"And when you met me, you were certain I was a virgin. Either from the way I acted, or the things I told you, or things Mr. Braddock told you—"

"Noelle!"

"But Mr. Braddock can't know, and you can't know. If I didn't have amnesia, *I'd* know. And the men would know, of course—the ones I gave myself to, I mean—"

"Noelle!" Zack forced himself to take a deep breath. "We're having ourselves the wrong conversation here."

"I know it's hard for you to hear this," she said with a sigh. "But it doesn't really matter, does it? I mean . . ." Her voice grew shaky. "You'd still love me, wouldn't you? Even if I weren't a virgin?"

"Noelle—" When she shrank from him, as though wounded by his failure to immediately agree, he grasped her by the shoulders and muttered, "I'd love you, even if you weren't a virgin. But I know for a fact—"

"How?" Almost immediately, her face turned a sickly white. "Did you and Mr. Braddock have me *examined?*

Is that how it's done? I suppose that's all part of his famous guarantee—"

"He'd never do that! And neither would I. You're talking crazy now—"

"Then you can't know for a fact. And unless I get my memory back, there are only two ways we can find out. Either we can make love . . ." Her pause was clearly meant as an opportunity for Zack to agree, and when he didn't, she chided sharply, "The only other way is to have Dr. Davenport take a look."

Zack felt as though his insides were being drawn through a sieve. "Dang blast it, Noelle—"

"It's all settled." Her eyes were bright with renewed warning. "If Dr. Davenport says I'm a virgin, we'll wait a month, just like we said. But if I'm not, there's no reason to wait, is there?" Her tone grew haughty. "There's no point in discussing it until we know for certain, so I suggest we both just get some sleep."

Frustrated, he rolled her onto her back and pinned her shoulders against the pillow. "You're gonna listen to me now—"

"No!" She covered her ears with her hands. "Please, Zack? Don't say anything that might make me remember. It hurts too much. My poor head can't take any more today."

He released her shoulders and watched in helpless dismay as she turned and buried her face into the pillow. She had mentioned her head hurting earlier, but he hadn't realized until now how intense the pain must have been, and he cursed himself for having reawakened it with his selfish need to tell her the truth after all these weeks.

Almost as though she sensed his distress, she assured

him weakly, "It's not your fault. I know you want to talk—"

"I just want to hold you," he corrected. "We don't need to talk at all. Just let me hold you while you fall asleep."

"I'd like that." She turned to snuggle against his chest. "I wanted this to be such a special night."

Zack petted her hair remorsefully. "I'm sorry, sugar. I know I ruined everything."

"You're just trying to do what's right. But that doesn't mean you should make my decisions for me, does it? You don't have that right, and neither does Mr. Braddock."

"Whatever you say, sugar."

"And I can't make *your* decisions either. So if you don't want to make love to a virgin who has amnesia, I suppose I should respect that until you're ready." Snuggling closer, she murmured, "I'm sorry if I gave you a scare."

"I just love you so danged much."

"I know." She kissed his mouth lightly. "Tell me the truth, Zack. Won't you be relieved, just a little, if the doctor says I'm not a virgin?"

"Stop saying that," he begged. "You're not going to talk to the doc about this and that's final."

He wanted to tell her he'd make love to her, right then and there, just to close the subject and prove himself to her all at one time, but he didn't dare. He still believed she couldn't give her consent to marriage much less to losing her virginity and possibly conceiving a little Dane baby, unless she knew the full truth. He would gladly tell her, right this very moment, and endure her wrath for as many days and weeks as nec essary, if he didn't think he'd cause her excruciating pain in the process.

Her silence began to concern him and he prodded cautiously, "Noelle?"

"Even if *you* aren't curious, it's something *I* need to know. For myself." Her silver eyes scanned his face anxiously. "It won't be easy for me, either, you know. I don't like the idea of him looking at me . . . well, down there. But it's really the only way. Unless . . ." She flushed but held his gaze. "I've just been assuming *you* wouldn't be willing to . . . well, to take a look yourself, would you?"

He almost laughed, the situation had grown so hopelessly bizarre. "It's not something a fella can see, sugar. And even if it was, I wouldn't let any fella—not even a doctor, and especially not that rascal Davenport—look at my wife that way."

She studied him suspiciously. "How do *you* know whether or not a fellow can see it?"

"Just take my word for it," he said, his cheeks warming unexpectedly. "Go to sleep, Noelle."

She seemed charmed by his embarrassment. "You've looked at girls that way?" With a sly smile, she added, "I think we can safely assume they didn't meet *my* standards of ladylike behavior."

"Go to sleep."

"So? You're saying the doctor would need to . . . What? Touch me? I'd hate that, Zack."

"And he'd lose a hand, so let's not talk about it anymore." When she wriggled away and sat up, propping the pillow behind her back, he groaned. "Are you mad again?"

"No, I'm just thinking. Go to sleep, Zack."

He could see that she was thinking just a little too

intently, and reminded himself of her reckless nature. A girl who'd throw herself out of a carriage or onto the back of a half-wild horse might just be headstrong enough to march up to a doctor and—

"I'll do it," he announced suddenly.

"Hmm?"

"I'll do it for you on one condition."

"Do what?"

"Noelle," he growled. "I'll do it, but you've gotta give me your word this time. You've gotta swear—on our love, and our future—that if you're a virgin, you won't ask me to take that from you until I'm convinced you know what you're doing."

Noelle arched an eyebrow, as though beginning to understand for the very first time. "That's where Mr. Braddock will come in? Somehow, he can help me convince you I'm truly consenting?"

He nodded warily.

"Well, then . . ." She licked her lips, her eyes beginning to sparkle. "You'll do it right now? Tonight?"

"Yeah. I'll be as quick as I can be—"

"Wait!" She grimaced apologetically. "Will it hurt? I mean, you've touched girls before that way, haven't you?"

He nodded.

"Have you touched a virgin that way?"

"Once or twice, a long time ago. I wasn't looking for proof or anything," he added defensively. "Just having some fun."

"Oh." She moistened her lips. "Was it fun for her too?"

"Seemed that way at the time," he admitted. "The trick is . . ." His words caught in his throat. "Let's just get it over with."

"Is that what you said to her?" Noelle teased.

"Huh?"

"You're blushing again! It's so sweet." Wrapping her arms around his neck she suggested impishly, "Just pretend I'm her. What was her name?"

"I can't even remember my *own* name right now," he complained weakly.

When Noelle collapsed in helpless laughter against his chest, Zack found himself grinning in return. "I'm counting on you to remember *why* I did this, sugar. And how you threatened to let another fella do it if I wouldn't. I don't want you biting my head off about it when the amnesia goes away."

"I'll remember," she promised. Then she eyed him sternly. "If I'm not a virgin, you'll tell me, won't you? I'd never forgive you if you lied about *that*. I have a right to know—"

"I won't lie to you," he promised, his heart beginning to pound with anticipation. It was foolish, of course. He'd just get himself all worked up without any real chance of being satisfied. But the thought of touching her the way she was asking him to touch her was an intoxicating one, blinding him to any other consequences or concerns. *Be careful, pardner,* he warned himself one final time; then with another, shakier grin, he took her into his arms.

Fourteen

Noelle's mind was reeling as Zack urged her onto her back, then dared to slip his hand under her petticoat. His skin felt rough and hot against hers, and she realized that if she didn't stop him, he was actually going to insinuate his fingers between her thighs and touch her! "Wait!" she pleaded, her tone unexpectedly husky. "You're going too fast for me."

He didn't withdraw his hand, but did move it a safer distance from its intended target. Stroking along the side of her hip, he cajoled, "We'll take as long as you like, sugar. Just let me know when you're ready."

"You said there was a trick."

"Yeah." He nuzzled her ear for a moment, his breath ragged and warm, and then he explained. "It's easier if you're real wet. Do you know what I mean by that?"

"Yes," she gasped. "It was that way this afternoon when you kissed me so much—"

He chuckled softly. "That's mighty encouraging. Do you want me to kiss you that way again?"

"Mmm . . ." She wrapped her arms around his neck. "Kiss my mouth, and kiss my throat, and then . . ." She could scarcely breathe as she dared to suggest, "Kiss my breasts, Zack. Please?"

"Dang." His mouth crushed down to hers and as i

did, his hand moved from her hip to her buttocks, forcing her to arch against his swollen manhood as he gently, rhythmically pumped. "I'm not gonna touch you till you're ready, sugar," he promised as his hungry mouth moved to her neck. "Don't be afraid to open those legs up a mite. It'll feel better if you put 'em around me."

She wanted to protest that he was moving too quickly again; then his free hand was caressing her breasts through the lacy fabric of her camisole. Before she could react, his dexterous fingers had opened the lacing, and then he was cupping one full breast in his palm, his green eyes fixed on the nipple with greedy appreciation. As Noelle watched in mesmerized delight, he tasted the rosy tip, first with his tongue, then ever so gently with his teeth, pulling it into a peak of pleasure that sent shockwaves through her body.

She heard herself moan his name with such utter adoration that she almost expected him to laugh, but he didn't. Instead, he took the opportunity to coax her again, this time by running his hand around to her thighs and stroking insistently, until he had managed to work his way between them. "I'm not going to do anything yet," he assured her, his voice soft and gravelly. "I just want to see if you're getting wet."

"I am," she assured him weakly. "You don't need to see for yourself yet."

"Come on, sugar. Just open up a little now." His hand urged her thighs to cooperate. "That's right . . . Just a little . . ." The tip of one finger grazed the soft, moist skin of her outer folds, and she would have wrenched away, had he not anticipated her reaction and pinned her gently in place. "Do you want to stop, Noelle?"

"No. Just don't . . . don't do any more yet."

"You know what I think?" he murmured, lowering

his mouth to nip playfully at her other breast. "I think you're liking this more than you thought you would."

"I knew I'd like it," she countered shyly. "I just never thought you'd really do it."

"Wrap those pretty legs of yours around me now."

"No."

Zack chuckled and moved his hand back to her buttocks. "I've got an idea, sugar. A real good one."

"What is it?"

"I'm gonna take that look you suggested earlier."

"That look? Oh!" She flushed under his innocent gaze. "You said there wasn't anything to see."

"I never said *that*," he corrected with a chuckle. "I said I didn't think I'd be able to see your pretty little maidenhood, but the truth is, I never looked for one before. Maybe I'll see it, after all; then I won't need to do it with my fingers. And even if it doesn't work, it'll give you more time to get used to the notion of me being down there."

"I like it when you touch me, even down there." She sighed. "I'm just not ready."

"This'll get you nice and ready. You trust me, don't you, sugar?"

Confused but almost desperate to get back to their lovemaking, she nodded. "Keep your hands away from it, though. You promise?"

"I promise I'll keep both my hands on your pretty little bottom. You like it when I do that, don't you? All you need to do is put your legs around my neck, like you do with your arms when you're hugging me. That sounds good, doesn't it?"

With a nervous smile, she nodded again, and then watched as he disappeared under the covers. In an instant, he was nuzzling his face between her thighs, while his palms slid up to her derriere, tilting it up for a better view. Without giving herself a chance to think about what she was doing, she draped her legs over his shoulders, then waited in embarrassed delight for his verdict.

His rough hands began to caress her buttocks, while his lips grazed along the inside of each thigh, nipping and kissing the pale, soft skin. Noelle squirmed, enjoying the sensations but confused by the delay. Of course, he probably couldn't see anything, she reasoned nervously. It was dark under the blankets, and she was about to suggest he might need more light when to her shock, he planted a reverent kiss right in the middle of the moist, sensitive folds between her legs. Paralyzed, she tried frantically to remember exactly what he had promised, but it didn't seem to matter, because his lips were tugging and sucking, and then his rough tongue was being drawn along the throbbing edges, in clear preparation for exploring within.

"What are you doing?" she wailed softly. "Zack? Oh, Zack . . ." Her loins were beginning to pulse with excitement, and when she protested again, she knew it sounded more like encouragement. "You promised, Zack."

His only response was to suck and lick with even greater relish, drawing such delicious tremors from her that she had no choice but to arch against him, desperate for more. But he seemed to be lessening his efforts, not intensifying them, until he was simply nipping at her again, and so she laced her fingers in his thick hair and boldly urged him to plunder her.

Disentangling himself from her, he reappeared, a proud grin on his face. "I figured you'd like that."

"Why did you stop?" Wrapping both her legs around his right thigh, she pulsed unhappily against him. His manhood was hard and long, and even through the thick fabric of his trousers, she could feel that it was throbbing for her as much as she for Zack. But the waves of pleasure that he had awakened in her were quickly being replaced by an agonizing emptiness, and she could think of nothing but the need to build again, this time without stopping until her body had had its fill.

"Are you ready for my fingers now, sugar?"

"What?" She stared at him, wondering how he could keep his mind on his mission, when their bodies had moved on to more scandalous and splendid pursuits. It was his sense of honor, she realized in complete frustration. His body ached for her, and they were man and wife, and her consent was free and unqualified, yet he was still willing to deny himself. And to deny her!

With a playful grin, he slipped his hand between her legs, stroking her folds for only a moment before one fingertip entered her. "I think you're wet enough, sugar."

"Wait!" She pushed at his chest, then wriggled out from under him. "Something's happening to me, Zack."

"I know, sugar. It's nice, isn't it?"

"Zack!" Straddling him, she caught his face between her hands and announced breathlessly, "I need to talk to you."

"Now?" He regained his composure and nodded for her to continue. "Are you saying you want to stop?"

"I don't *ever* want to stop. And thanks to Dr. Davenport," she announced reverently, "we'll never need to stop again."

"Huh?"

"He's a genius, just like you said." She didn't have to pretend to be excited—her voice was still husky and filled with wonderment at the sensations he had evoked from her. "He told us I'd remember if we could just get my blood flowing to my brain—just stimulate it more—and now you've done that! Don't you see? You've done it, Zack—"

"Done what?" His mind seemed to be struggling with disbelief. "Are you saying you're starting to remember?"

"It's hazy," she qualified carefully. "But I remember sooo much. My mother—you would have loved her, Zack. She was so sweet and kind—and so very, very beautiful. She loved me so much." When he nodded, as though entranced, she continued eagerly. "And I can remember my favorite doll, and the children I played with, and . . ." She leaned her cheek down to his chest and murmured truthfully, "I remember seeing you and hearing your voice and knowing deep inside, that you would be my lover one day. It's like you said earlier, Zack. I was afraid of making the wrong choice, just like you were. But by some miracle, we ended up together."

"I can't believe my ears," he croaked, rolling her onto her back and hovering over her anxiously. "You remember everything? Are you mad at me? I know I shouldn't've kept it all from you—"

"I'm glad you did! You protected me, until I was ready. But now . . ." She grasped his face between her hands again and insisted desperately, "I'm ready, Zack. Please don't make me wait one more minute."

"Dang." He licked his lips hopefully. "Your head—"

"I feel wonderful," she told him honestly. "So alive—completely alive, and completely in love." Moving her fingers to his chest, she began to unfasten his shirt. "Are you going to keep me waiting forever?"

"No, ma'am." His green eyes began to sparkle with roguish anticipation, and he stripped off his shirt, revealing a bronzed chest layered with smooth, hard muscles.

"Mmm . . ." Noelle slipped out of her camisole and enjoyed the way his eyes widened with desire as they surveyed her full, alert breasts. Then she wrapped her arms around his neck, reveling in the feel of his skin against hers. "Kiss me, Zack."

His mouth covered hers, hot and eager, enjoying her lips for only a moment before plundering her thoroughly. Noelle gasped for breath as their tongues sparred, and then she gasped again, this time because his fingers had found a fevered nipple and were coaxing spasms of delight from it.

"Zack," she groaned, running her own hand down his torso, enjoying the feel of his dense muscles through hot skin. Then she continued downward, until her fingers had worked their way under the waistband of his trousers.

"Wait a minute, sugar."

"Zack!" she wailed. "I told you—"

"I know." He started unfastening the placket of his pants. "Just let me get these britches off, and then you can do whatever you want."

"Oh . . ." She flushed as he stripped off the garment and threw it to the floor.

Then he stretched over her again, grasped her hand firmly in his own, and placed it onto his hard shaft. "Is this what you want, Noelle?"

She stroked it with tentative adoration, stunned by the velvety smoothness over rock-hard desire. The thought that he might soon penetrate her with it both frightened and thrilled her. It reminded her of how much his tongue had pleased her, and in an instant, her insides were pulsing with arousal just as wildly as they'd done when his mouth had been on her.

"Zack," she pleaded.

His hand moved between her thighs, playing gently with the soaked, swollen folds. Then he began to work his manhood into position, first gently between her legs, then closer and closer, until the tip was insinuating itself into her. She held her breath, uncertain of what to expect; then Zack's free hand began to fondle her breasts again, and she arched in delight, against both his hand and his shaft.

"I love you, Noelle," he proclaimed in a voice laced with reverence and passion; then he began to thrust into her, with careful, exploratory strokes that made her hold her breath again. Despite the flood of slick, honeyed liquid that lubricated the pathway, she could feel a slight burn, from the sheer size of him as he penetrated deeper. When a single bold thrust caused a searing blend of discomfort and certainty, she knew without caring that indeed she had been untouched until this very moment, and she moaned his name happily into his ear.

"I know, sugar." His voice cracked and he added lovingly, "I'm gonna take you now, unless—"

"Take me," she agreed, burying her fingers into his thick hair and pulling his face to hers for a quick kiss. "I want this, Zack. As much as you do."

He chuckled and thrust again, and to Noelle's delight, the burning was gone, replaced completely by a new sort of heat that radiated from every nerve that had the pleasure to be stroked by his masterful shaft. Pumping rhythmically, he nuzzled at her neck and shoulders, his breath growing increasingly hot and ragged. Noelle's pelvis responded by tilting and thrusting in a desperate attempt at furthering his every lustful impulse. Then he paused for a long moment, and she heard herself wail his name in confused protest.

"You feel so good, sugar," he explained hoarsely.

It made no sense to Noelle, and she gyrated against him, intent on encouraging him to move again. To her surprise, it felt almost as satisfying as his thrusts, and so she grinned mischievously and began to wriggle and pulse with slow, methodical self-indulgence.

Zack laughed and cradled her buttocks in his huge hands. "We're gonna have ourselves some fun now, sugar," he promised, and as his mouth covered hers, he began to thrust wildly, with strokes so sure and deep that Noelle's loins convulsed in shocked appreciation. Wave after wave of pleasure assaulted her, and between each wave came another, sharper spasm, as she tightened around him in a mindless attempt to imprison him forever.

And just as her own fervor peaked, he began to climax, too, with groans of appreciation so heartfelt and lusty, so fraught with satisfaction, that Noelle almost laughed out loud. For all that she had wanted this moment, her husband had apparently craved it in ways she couldn't even begin to understand. It made his months of forbearance all the more noble, and made this moment all the more perfect.

"Dang," she teased him as she snuggled her face into his chest. "You were willing to wait six months for that? I guess you really do love me."

A low, rumbling chuckle vibrated against her ear. "I reckon I do." His hands began to wander appreciatively over her back and buttocks. "I swear, Noelle, I'm gonna find some way to be deserving of this."

"Mmm." She stroked his arm, loving the feel of his muscles against her small hand. "Whether we deserve it or not, we've found each other. With Mr. Braddock's help, of course. I imagine you'll be sending him another telegram first thing in the morning? He'll be so relieved."

Zack chuckled again. "You're still calling him Mr. Braddock?"

Noelle coughed lightly. "How silly of me. I meant— Russell. Russ . . ." She coughed again, then turned her face up to his and explained sweetly, "I suppose that's one of those details that'll be hazy for a while."

When he stared back at her as though she'd grown another head, she soothed, "It's understandable, Zack. I mean, he's a very sweet man, but it's not as though—"

"Noelle!" he growled, sitting up and grasping her by the shoulders. "I can't believe—"

"Can't believe I lied to you?" she countered cheerfully. "It's not as though you never lied to *me*, is it? And you have to admit," she teased, "this was a wonderful lie, for a wonderful cause."

"Dang blast it!" He jumped out of the bed and glared. "I should've known. I *would've* known, if I hadn't let you get me so riled up!"

Noelle allowed her eyes to travel playfully over his lean, naked form. "As I said, it was for a good cause."

His green eyes flashed; then he turned away from her, retrieved his trousers from the floor, and donned them quickly. Turning back, he seemed about to scold her further, but he was either speechless, or simply furious at the mischievous smile on her face, and so he turned away again, striding across the room and out onto the balcony.

Noelle laughed lightly, confident that his distress would fade quickly. He had trusted her, and she had betrayed that trust by lying to him. He had every right to be shocked and wary, but in a moment or two he'd begin to remember the rest—the flood of pleasure and relief his poor body had experienced, thanks to Noelle's harmless deception. They had lied—each to the other—but now that the marriage was consummated, they could put all of those lies behind themselves in favor of a future filled with scintillating lovemaking and renewed trust.

That's all he needs to hear, she decided. *That this was the one and only lie you'll ever tell him. That you did it partially out of love for him, and you'll never do it again. And he'll make the same promise to you. After all, he felt guilty for keeping secrets from you all these months. It'll be a relief to start fresh, and you can spend the rest of your life proving to him that this was an aberration.*

When he didn't return after five full minutes, she slipped out of the bed and located her modest white nightgown. There was a more beautiful outfit in her trunk—a sleeveless gown made of shimmering white lace and gauze, with an elegant robe to match—and she was tempted to wear that instead. After all, those sinfully romantic garments had obviously been designed for her wedding night. And wasn't that what this was?

Save them for another time, she counseled herself as she opted for her usual attire. *With any luck, you'll be naked again within minutes.*

Pulling a blanket around herself, she stepped out into the moonlight and smiled at the sight of Zack standing with his back to her, staring up at the brilliant night sky. So many silver-white stars. She could almost hear what he was thinking: that the miners were fools to hunt in the ground, when all they had to do was lie on their backs and look upward for a true treasure trove.

"Zack?" She tapped his shoulder, and when he turned to face her, she smiled hopefully. "Aren't you ever going to come back to bed?"

He shrugged, then began to shake his head slowly, as though still speechless over her seduction.

"Are you angry?"

"I can't believe you did that."

"You did it, too," she teased.

His jaw tensed visibly. "Go on back to bed, Noelle. I need some time to think."

"Can't you think in bed with me?"

"Apparently not."

She winced at the unfamiliar tone, more reminiscent of a haughty aristocrat than a homespun hero. "You've lied to me, too, over the last two months," she reminded him defensively.

"I know. I take full responsibility for everything that's happened, including tonight."

She felt her patience snap. "You can't take responsibility for *my* lie! Or for my decision to give myself to you, even though"—she paused in dramatic warning—"I'm beginning to agree with you. It was a terrible mistake."

He caught her by the arm as she tried to storm back to the bedroom. "Wait a minute, sugar." Pulling her against his bare chest, he assured her mournfully, "I'm a danged fool for sure. Here you give me the most precious gift a girl can give a man, and all I do is complain. Can you forgive me?"

She sighed in relief. "I'm sorry I lied to you, Zack."

"It's fine," he insisted, as much to himself as to her. "When the time comes, it'll be fine. I promise."

"Of course it will," she soothed. "It already is. There isn't a memory in the world—in my past or anyone else's—that can compete with what happened between us tonight. And"—she smiled impishly—"it was fun, wasn't it?"

"It surely was," he admitted, brushing his lips across her forehead, as he'd done so often in the early days after her accident. "I know I'm acting like a danged fool, but"—his green eyes blazed with confusion—"before this, I could always make things right with you, if I needed to. Now we've gone and done this, and there's no going back." Cupping her chin in his hand, he explained, "I wanted to keep things simple until you got better. But that doesn't mean I didn't ache for you, sugar, 'cause I did. I still do. I always will."

"That's so sweet." She looped her arms around his neck and gave him a mischievous smile. "What's done is done, and there's no going back, just like you said. So . . ."

"I was just thinking that same thing," he admitted. Then with one last sheepish shrug, he swept her up into his arms, nuzzled lustily at her neck until she screamed with laughter, and carried her off to their bed.

The blushing bride was radiant after her first night in her lover's arms, awakening early with memories of his touch seared into her brain. He was nowhere in sight, but that didn't alarm her. She even imagined playfully that he'd gone to tell Mercury the news—that they were married now for better or for worse, and so far, it had been better than either of them could have dared wish.

Once Zack had decided that the damage was done, he had proven himself more than willing to enjoy himself with a gentle sort of hedonism that had made

Noelle tremble with delight. Between bouts of lovemaking he had fed her bites of steak and sips of champagne, but even then he had trailed kisses over her naked form, murmuring tales of what he intended to do to her next.

In some ways, he had seemed almost possessed, she remembered fondly. Like a dying man being granted his last wish. At the time, she hadn't given it any thought, but now, as the sun began to rise over Virginia City, she suspected that he might still be concerned that her consent, while lusty and frequent, had not been completely well informed.

You're too honorable for your own good, Zachary Dane, she chastised him with a sigh. *Don't you see the truth? That our marriage was vulnerable for only one reason: the fact that we hadn't consummated it. Now it's invincible. Nothing anyone can say or do can change that.*

There was a commotion in the street, and she frowned as she scrambled for her nightgown, then peered through the balcony doors. The rambunctious miners were usually quiet in the morning, either because they were sleeping through a drunken stupor or simply nursing their headaches in painful silence. Those who were too diligent or ambitious to indulge in such revelry didn't usually stay in town at all, but rather in camps closer to the mountains. Zack had told her that some men were so protective of their claim, they hid in the woods for weeks on end rather than betray the location of their labors.

But this morning, something had gotten them "all riled up," as Zack would say. Had someone made a rich strike? Or perhaps a miner had been shot during some argument over a disputed claim. Her curiosity piqued, Noelle hastily dressed in her boots and a modest gray dress, anxious to investigate, and even more anxious to locate her wandering lover, whom she now suspected was somewhere in the throng below, unable to resist all the excitement.

He probably thinks you'll sleep till noon, after the way he exhausted you last night, she teased herself cheerfully as she headed down the stairs. A shiver of anticipation ran through her as she imagined how he'd react—how they both would react!—when they saw each other again. Would he sweep her into his arms again? Would she allow such outrageous conduct in front of a street filled with rowdy strangers?

Absolutely.

The young desk clerk who had admired her so much the prior evening was standing in the doorway, staring out into the street. Approaching him confidently, she tapped his shoulder and asked, "Has something happened?"

When he turned, the weary expression on his face became a wary smile. "You should go back upstairs, Mrs. Dane. You don't want to see this. The lieutenant'll explain it all to you soon, I'm sure."

"The lieutenant? Do you mean my husband? Is he out there?" She tried to push past him. "Why don't I want to see it? What is it?"

"Two men have been killed. And a third one's almost dead. Doc Davenport—Oh, here he comes. He'll explain it to you, only please don't try to see the bodies. It almost made me lose my breakfast."

Noelle bit her lip as Philip Davenport approached, leading a group of men who were carrying a motionless form. "Doctor?"

"Noelle!" He turned to the men and growled, "Bring him to my room. I'll be there in a minute." Then he took Noelle by the arm and led her quickly toward the dining room. "I'm glad you're here. There's something you should know."

She stared in disbelief. "Oh, my God! Are you saying—"

"No, no," he assured her hastily. "I'm handling this so stupidly. Zack's fine, of course. Three miners were attacked last night by some sort of wild animal. Zack's looking at the wounds on the dead men. . . ." He winced and added lamely, "He's going to track the animal, Noelle. Apparently, he's rather good at such things, although I don't imagine I have to tell you that. I'm sure you've heard stories—"

"Zack's going to hunt the animal?" She took a deep breath and then nodded in reluctant assent. She had married a brave, noble champion, so this sort of thing was to be expected. And he would be careful, knowing that her heart was his to protect. "You'd better get upstairs and care for the survivor," she admonished Davenport. "Do you need some help?"

He nodded gratefully. "Could you ask the staff to send up the usual? They'll know what I mean. And ask them to send coffee, too. Have you eaten, Noelle?"

"No, but don't worry about me. Oh!" She jumped to her feet as she glimpsed her husband stride into the lobby and toward the staircase. "There's Zack! Give me a moment with him, and then I'll be at your service."

"Wait, Noelle." Davenport clutched at her arm. "Before you talk to Zack, there's something you should know."

She eyed the doctor impatiently. "I don't want him to leave without saying good-bye."

"He insists on going alone, even though the sheriff and some others offered to assist him. I did my best to talk him out of it, but he wouldn't listen. I know he's a good tracker, but—"

"He's going alone?" She scowled. "We'll just see about that. Go and tend to your patient. I'll join you as soon as I've talked some sense into my husband."

Rushing away before Davenport could detain her further, she took the stairs as quickly as she was able, then burst into their room in time to see Zack making a last-minute inspection of his rifle. "Zack!"

"Hey, sugar." He pulled her into a hearty embrace. "I was just gonna come looking for you."

"I was talking to the doctor. He told me about those poor men and that dreadful animal."

"It's probably just a little ole polecat, but I gotta move quick, while the trail's still warm." He studied her anxiously. "You understand why I need to do this, don't you?"

"Of course. But I don't understand why you want to go alone. Some of the other men must have experience—"

"I hunt alone. I can't concentrate if there are other folks around. That's just how it is with me."

"Well, that's going to have to change," she informed him dryly. "You're a married man now, Lieutenant Dane. You can't take those kinds of risks anymore." Stroking his tensed jaw with her fingertips, she cooed, "You have responsibilities now, especially after last night."

"I remember," he grumbled.

"I was referring to *pleasant* responsibilities. Or at least, you seemed to enjoy them last night."

He took a deep breath, then gave her a reassuring smile. "My mind's halfway up that hill, sugar. If you want sweet-talking, you'll have to wait till I get back."

"That's why I want you back in one piece," she said with a sigh. "Let a few others go with you—"

"I can't." He tipped her chin so that she was looking straight into his troubled green eyes, then explained solemnly, "I shot a boy once, Noelle. It was an accident, but it's haunted me something fierce, and ever since then, I shoot best when I know I'm the only fella around."

"Oh, Zack . . ."

"I gotta go." He kissed her apologetically, then started for the doorway. "Don't worry, angel. This is what I do best."

"Zack!" She grabbed his arm and pleaded, "Be careful, won't you? It killed two men—"

"Those fellas never had a chance. They were sound asleep when that critter attacked them. But me and old Henry . . ." He lifted the rifle before her eyes and smiled grimly. "We're gonna teach him a lesson. Stay here and don't worry—"

"I told Philip I'd help him with the wounded man."

Zack seemed to consider the notion before nodding. "Don't let his injuries worry you. Remember, he wasn't prepared for the attack. I'm wide-awake, and I've got Merc and Henry to help me. And I gotta go right now, so . . ." He brushed his lips across hers again, then strode out of the room without a backward glance.

"Sometimes I feel like I don't know him at all, Philip. I love him, but I don't know him." She patted the unconscious miner's head with a cool, damp rag. "He smiles and teases and protects me, and never tells me about *his* past, but I'm beginning to realize it might have been horrible. All the horrors of war—and if you could have seen his face when he told me about that boy he shot! I'm his *wife*. He should have told me about that weeks ago."

"Perhaps he did," Davenport said as he carefully finished the last of a hundred stitches he'd painstakingly sewn throughout the morning.

"What? Oh, yes . . . I see what you mean."

"I was teasing you, Noelle." The physician set down his needle, checked his unconscious patient's temperature with his hand, then took Noelle by the arm and led her to a table laden with coffee and muffins. "Eat something now, and stop worrying about Zack. If ever a man had a reason to be careful, it's him."

"You're sweet. Do you think he'll be back before dark?"

Davenport shrugged. "He told me it could take days, so try to relax. Maybe you should go and rest—"

"I'm fine. I want to keep busy. In fact, you're the one who should rest. Or better still, go and have a real meal in the dining room. I'll keep watch over Mr. Patterson for a while." With a weary smile, she added, "You saved his life, you know. In your own way, you're as much a hero as Zack."

"And I'm much better looking," he agreed cheerfully. "You ought to consider leaving him for me."

"That's enough."

Davenport grinned. "I'll have the dining room send up something more substantial—*anything* but beef!— and after that, if you're still determined to resist me, I'll let you sit with Patterson for a few hours while I attend to one of my other patients."

"I'd be happy to. Take as long as you need."

"You seem so comfortable with all this. Was your father a doctor by any chance?"

"I don't know," she murmured.

"Pardon?"

Noelle flushed. "I don't know very much about my family."

"I understand that you don't remember, but surely Zack . . ." Davenport studied her intently. "I thought it was just my imagination, but it's true, isn't it? Between the two of you, you know almost nothing about your past. How does he explain that to you?"

"My husband doesn't owe me any explanations," Noelle chided. "He's taken care of me since the moment we met—"

"And when was that?"

"Never mind."

"He implied that he knows your family—"

"I don't want to discuss it anymore, Philip." She shook her head and tried for a gentler tone. "I'm not really sure how much Zack knows about my past. I've instructed him not to talk about it, because I have reason to believe it wasn't pleasant."

"That's absurd! If he knows—"

"He knows very little, and I've asked him to keep it to himself."

"Embarrassment and confusion," Davenport muttered.

"Hmm?"

"That's what he said you were hiding from. Embarrassment, confusion, and disappointment."

"Zack said that? How odd."

"I agree." The doctor scowled. "You're a spirited woman who can watch a man sew gaping wounds without flinching, but you cower from your own past? That makes no sense."

"My head hurts when I try to remember."

"A small price to pay for knowledge," he countered.

"That's a fine thing for a doctor to say!" She dropped the bantering tone. "In any case, I won't be hiding from my past much longer. I believe my husband intends to tell me all the awful details soon. He agrees with you—that I need to know everything, although I can't imagine why. I'm deliriously happy with things just as they are. I have a wonderful husband, a wonderful future, and an adequate doctor. What more could a woman want?"

Davenport chuckled. "Your wonderful husband and your adequate doctor will help you confront the old ghosts. I can't imagine they're anything too terrible, or I'm sure Zack would have told *me* about them, if only so I could treat you properly." With feigned annoyance, he added, "No wonder I couldn't cure you. And here I considered you my favorite patient."

"Shh . . . If Mr. Patterson hears, he'll be jealous."

The doctor studied her with obvious fondness. "You aren't really afraid of your past, are you, Noelle?"

"No. I don't think I ever really was," she mused. "Just having a holiday from it, I suppose."

"And now the holiday is over. That's the reason Zack was so hell-bent on sending his telegram this morning?"

"Telegram?"

"He didn't want to leave until he knew it was taken care of."

"Oh." She grimaced, annoyed that he might have reported the consummation to Braddock. "My husband is noble to a fault, I'm afraid."

"I agree."

The door opened and a waitress wheeled a cart into view. The aroma of grilled steak filled the air, and Noelle sent Davenport a sympathetic smile before walking to the window and staring wordlessly into the distance, trying not to let the telegram bother her. It was

Zack's way, and there was nothing she could do about it. Why allow it to mar their newfound love?

I shot a boy once, sugar. It was an accident, but it's haunted me something fierce. . . .

More than the telegram, she knew it was these words that were truly weighing on her. Zack was "haunted" by this memory, but hadn't shared it with his bride, or at least, not since the accident. What other secrets was he keeping from her? He hadn't wanted to consummate the marriage until the amnesia was gone. Perhaps he hadn't wanted to confide his innermost secrets to her until then, either.

I wanted to keep things simple. . . .

"Enough of that," she murmured under her breath. "It's time you both stopped keeping this so simple. You're married now, and it's not just your futures and your bodies that are entwined. Somehow your pasts are, too, or at least, they should be."

"Noelle? Did you say something?"

She shook herself and turned toward Davenport, hoping her smile was at least somewhat carefree. "I said I'm starving. Let's eat."

By the time night began to fall, Noelle was completely exhausted. Not only had Patterson grown delirious, requiring constant attention on her part, but a pair of twin babies had chosen that very afternoon to come howling, feet first, into Virginia City. Davenport had handled every crisis masterfully, but even he had lost some of his usual zest by the time additional help arrived in the person of a bighearted bar girl.

Noelle had been suspicious at first, given the obvious acquaintanceship between the newcomer and the doctor, but she had learned how dedicated Davenport could be, and so, when he delivered her to the doorway of her room and insisted she get some sleep, she contented herself with arching an eyebrow in stern warning.

"I'll behave," he responded glumly. "I'm too tired to do anything else."

"Do you promise to send for me if Mr. Patterson takes a turn for the worse?"

"One would think you're the doctor," he grumbled; then he smiled wickedly. "Perhaps you are. Perhaps that's the secret you're trying not to remember."

Noelle groaned and ordered him away. He had been merciless since he'd learned that Zack was keeping things from her with her blessing, and she could only imagine what he'd say if he knew the rest! What would a man like Philip Davenport think of mail-order marriages between total strangers?

When the doctor had departed, Noelle stared at the bed, knowing she needed sleep, but knowing also that she wouldn't be able to rest until Zack was there with her again. And she was sure the bed would smell of him, and of their lovemaking, even though it was clear that the hotel staff had changed the linens.

How mortifying, she lamented. *One minute you don't know if you're a virgin or not, and the next day the whole town knows!*

The bloodstains on her gray dress were further reminders of her odd predicament, and so she stripped it off quickly. Once again, she thought of donning the lustrous white nightgown that waited so patiently in her trunk for a night of romance, but even if Zack returned during the night, he'd be too tired to do anything but kiss her cheek, mumble, "You sure look pretty," and collapse in a heap. And if Patterson's condition wors ened, Davenport might need her on a moment's notice, so she settled for a soft, pale blue dress that Zack had admired during dinners onboard the steamship.

If only you were here, she told him mournfully. *I can't bear the thought of you out there, all alone. What if that animal attacks you while you sleep?*

She had been too busy during the day to worry much about his safety, and even now, she knew he was an expert shot, a talented hunter, and most of all, a man with reasons to come home safely. Still, she couldn't help but remember the gaping wounds the unknown predator's fangs and claws had inflicted on Patterson.

"Think about something else," she counseled herself shakily. "Write a letter to Mr. Braddock. No! Better still, write a telegram of your own, assuring him that you and Zack are the finest match he ever made, and he needn't worry about you anymore."

Inspired, she settled down at the desk, and noticed that Zack had written his message there, too. His heavy-handed penmanship had left so deep an imprint on the remaining stationary, Noelle could easily make out most of the words.

Intrigued, she used the pen to carefully enhance the indentations, then cocked her head to the side, confused by what she saw. It wasn't directed to Russell Braddock at all, but to his niece, Megan Steele. Zack had written t as a letter first, with another, more abbreviated version right below that, as though he'd needed to think his words through carefully before converting them to telegraph form.

Dear Mrs. Steele,
   Your uncle said he'd write you a letter to explain this situation. I surely hope he did, because I need

your help. Noelle is healthy, so don't worry on that account. But there's no improvement in her condition. I've done my best, but this was a mistake from the start, and now I'm worried that it's gone too far. The whole arrangement never did set well with me, but I went along with it of my own free will, so I'm not blaming anyone but myself. I only hope it's not too late to make things right.

This can't wait for your uncle. I'm bringing Noelle to San Francisco this week. If you're willing to help me explain it all to her, I'll be grateful till my dying day.

Humbly yours,
Zack Dane

Below that, the telegram text read:

Hope your uncle explained situation—need help—bringing Noelle to SF in one week. Grateful. Z.D.

"A mistake from the start?" Noelle bit her lip in dismay. Did he really feel that way? Why?

I'm worried that it's gone too far. . . .

Hadn't he said something similar after their lovemaking? *Before this, I could always make things right with you if I needed to. Now we've gone and done this, and there's no going back. . . .*

"Why would we want to?" she chastised her absent husband nervously. "All of that foolishness is behind us now. What business is it of the Braddocks, unless you owe them money, which I suggest you pay right away. We've gotten our bargain, haven't we? Unless it's that foolishness about a 'healthy bride,' and if it is, I'll strangle you with my bare hands!"

She tried to smile, but couldn't. Something was wrong—more wrong than she had suspected when she'd thought it was simply a matter of her virginity or her consent, in Zack's eyes *or* in Braddock's. She had been so certain they were looking out for *her* interests, it hadn't even occurred to her that it was Zack who might not be ready to "consent."

"You're jumping to conclusions," she scolded herself aloud. "Have you forgotten last night? The man couldn't take his hands—or his mouth!—off you! And he told you he loved you so many times. . . ."

He loved her—she couldn't doubt that. And he was aroused by her—that was laughably apparent. So what could it be? And what did Braddock have to do with it?

Then it hit her, so hard she actually had to grab the edge of the desk to keep the room from spinning. Braddock had *everything* to do with it! Zack had put his trust in the matchmaker because he didn't trust himself to make the right decision. He'd been afraid he'd choose a girl for all the wrong reasons—her smile, her scent, her legs. Qualities that made for scintillating lovemaking—the kind Zack enjoyed with Noelle. Her "pretty laugh," her "silver eyes"—how many times had he praised those to her? They aroused him, just as he'd feared they would do. But Braddock would be immune to such distractions, and would select a good wife—a good mother for Zack's children. Not a girl with amnesia. . . .

A knock at the door made her jump out of her chair, and she had to take a deep breath before even imagining who it could be. Zack? He wouldn't knock. He'd burst in and take her into his arms. Or perhaps he wouldn't. She simply didn't know anymore.

It's the doctor, she scolded herself. *Poor Mr. Patterson is probably bleeding to death while you stand here like a silly goose.* Forcing herself to forget about the telegram, she hurried to the door and threw it wide open, only to find herself face-to-face with a complete stranger.

She could almost hear Zack chastise her from afar— *Dang it all, Noelle!*—but she shook off the warning impatiently. After all, this newcomer was clearly a gentleman, from his blond hair, so elegantly tinged with gray, to his pale blue eyes—eyes that were widening as though the sight of her somehow flabbergasted him.

"Sir?" she asked softly. "Can I help you? Did the doctor send you for me?"

He continued to stare for another long moment; then to her shock, he grasped her by the shoulders and backed her into the room, exclaiming, "My God, Noelle! I can't believe I finally found you!"

His eyes blazed with such confusion and passion, she thought he might be about to assault her. Instead, he pulled her into a tender embrace and murmured in a voice so fraught with love it sent a chill of uncertainty down her spine, "Don't worry, darling. I'm here now, and I'll never let you out of my sight again."

Fifteen

Wriggling free of the stranger's grasp, Noelle eyed him with wary dismay. It was so clear that he knew her, but how could that be? They were thousands of miles from anywhere she'd ever been, or so she thought. Yet here he was, staring at her as though he'd known her all her life.

Praying fervently that he wasn't her father, or uncle, or worse, she insisted in as strong a voice as she could summon, "Leave my room this instant, sir."

"Noelle," he whispered. "Why are you treating me this way?" Before she could stop him, he reached for the door and slammed it shut, then moved toward her again, as though planning to embrace her anew.

"One more step and I'll scream," she warned as she backed away.

"I deserve better than this," he protested. "I've come all this way—that alone entitles me to some small courtesy, you must admit."

"I admit only that you're frightening me to death," she told him unhappily. "I have amnesia, sir. If I knew you once, I apologize, but you really must leave—"

"Wait!" He stepped closer and asked hoarsely, "Amnesia?"

When Noelle nodded warily, he surprised her again,

this time by waving his arms in the air and striding across the room to stand by the balcony doors. "Amnesia! My God. It's the only palatable explanation! That idiot Long and his so-called ethical obligations! *This* is how he protects his patients? Letting them run off with buffoons?"

She knew this was her chance to escape, but strangely, she no longer wanted to do so. This man was so sincerely outraged and so clearly wounded. By her? She had to know, and so she asked carefully, "You spoke with Dr. Long?"

"For all the good it did me."

"That means you were in Chicago." She cocked her head to the side and studied him. "Why did you come to Virginia City?"

"Believe it or not," he drawled, "I'm here to rescue you."

"To *rescue* me? From *Zack?*" She composed herself and asked carefully, "What is your name?"

"Adam Prestley. Does that sound at all familiar, darling?"

"No," she admitted.

He stepped close to her again. "I can only imagine what you've been through, darling. What he's done to you, and the lies he's told you. But it's all over now. Let me take you home—"

"No!" She backed away a safe distance. "Your name is Adam Prestley, and you knew me in Chicago. And you don't get along with my husband—"

"Don't call him that!"

She shrank from his angry glare. "You'd better leave."

"Forgive me, darling." He smiled apologetically. "This must be incredibly confusing for you, especially if Dane had the gall to tell you he was your husband. It isn't true, Noelle. I swear to you it's not."

A sickening knot began to form in her stomach. "Don't be ridiculous—"

"I am never that," he assured her. "If you'll sit with me for a few minutes, I'll explain it all to you."

"No."

He patted the seat of the satin-covered sofa that adjoined the balcony. "I won't bite. You sense that somehow, don't you? You may have amnesia, but some feelings are so strong, they transcend all other conditions. Tell me the truth, darling. I seem familiar to you, don't I?"

She shook her head, wondering how to make this strange man understand that he was nothing to her. At one time, he had apparently been an important figure in her life—that was evident from his tone, his gaze, and most chillingly, from his use of the term "darling."

And there was something more—an odd light in his eyes when he looked at her, as though he were imagining himself with her in ways that were at once sublime and base. Was *that* how it had been with them? Not full intimacy, of course, but some sort of romantic episode? It seemed impossible! This man was too old, too overbearing, and much too unsettling to ever inspire trust, much less passion, in a girl.

Small wonder you didn't want to remember your past, she told herself uneasily. *Something is terribly wrong here, Noelle. You should have let Zack tell you about it last night.*

But it was too late for that now, so she squared her shoulders and announced briskly, "It's obvious that you've come a long way because of some genuine affection you once felt for me. I appreciate that, so I'm willing to go to the hotel dining room with you. We can talk there for as long as you like."

"Chaperons again? Have we come so far, only to end up back at that?" He crossed to her and asked quietly, "Tell me about the amnesia. What do the doctors believe caused it?"

"I fell off Zack's horse and hit my head."

"I see. That was clumsy of him."

Noelle flushed. "He wasn't on the horse at the time."

"Oh?"

"I was teasing him," she explained halfheartedly. "I jumped on the horse's back without realizing that it wasn't fully tame. The poor animal reacted instinctively and threw me."

"You remember that? Or is that Dane's version of the event?"

Noelle frowned in warning. "What are you implying, sir?"

"Are you prepared to listen with an open mind?"

"No." She grimaced and added defensively, "Zack told me that's what happened, and he would never"—the words caught in her throat, and by the time she was able to insist—"he'd never lie to me," she knew Adam had heard the rampant doubt in her voice.

But rather than pounce on her weakness, he seemed anxious to reassure her. "You've been through so much, darling. I have no intention of hurting you further. I you don't want to hear the truth—"

"I want to hear it," she corrected softly. "There wa a time when I was afraid of it, but that time is gone Now, I need to know everything. If Zack were here, I' ask *him* to tell me, but he isn't. So please, proceed."

"Will you sit with me?"

"Can I trust you?"

He bowed reverently. "I would give my life for you. I've come thousands of miles just to find you again. Yes," he added simply, "you can trust me, Noelle. I may be the only person in the world you *can* trust right now."

"Fine." She sat on the sofa, and was relieved when he left a respectable distance between them. "I'm ready to hear your 'version' of the truth."

He took a deep breath. "You and I were engaged, Noelle. We would have been happily married, and honeymooning in Europe, if that insufferable bastard had just stayed out of our lives."

"Oh, dear." She forced herself to be polite, despite her certainty that she never could have found this man attractive. But it was conceivable that she had agreed to marry him out of gratitude or desperation or ignorance. And at the last minute, she had changed her mind and turned to the Happily Ever After Company for another, more romantic solution. And Mr. Braddock had worked a miracle—at least, until the accident.

With a wistful smile, she murmured, "You and I were engaged, but before we could be married, I fell in love with Zack?"

"Love? What does a barbarian like him know about love? He was more than happy to marry a stranger. He ordered one through the mail no less, as though love were something one could find in a catalog. And then, by some disgusting twist of fate, he mistook you for her and abducted you."

"He *mistook* me for her?" Noelle's jaw dropped open in disbelief. "You're saying I wasn't a mail-order bride?"

"Good God, no!" He laughed harshly. "Do they not have mirrors in Virginia City, darling? Don't you know how breathtakingly beautiful you are? And you're the sweetest girl I've ever had the privilege to know. Do you suppose you needed to settle for a buffoon like Dane?"

Noelle took a deep breath. "You said he abducted me. I know for a fact I was wearing a wedding dress—"

"Because he abducted you from *our* wedding," Adam explained. "He grabbed you and threw you on the back of his damned horse and ran off with you. And I've been searching for you ever since. Why do you think he brought you to this godforsaken place? To hide you, so no one could tell you the truth. And to imprison you, so that you'd be at his mercy if your memory ever returned."

"I don't believe you," she said quietly. "Either this is all a lie, or you're intentionally twisting the truth." She turned her face away from him and tried to imagine what that enigmatic "truth" might be. Zack had tried to keep it from her, for fear it would "embarrass" her. And he had postponed the consummation of the marriage because of it, for fear she had never truly given her consent to the arrangement.

"Tell me," she demanded suddenly. "Tell me the whole truth, or leave right now and never come near me again."

He seemed about to protest; then an apologetic smile spread over his face. "I didn't come here to lie to you darling. I came to win you back. Forgive me for twisting the facts, as you say, but the amnesia is such an unexpected phenomenon, and I suppose I thought I could capitalize on it."

"You cannot."

"I see that now." He inhaled sharply. "The truth, in all its vainglorious splendor, is that you and I had quarrel on our wedding day. A rather public one, I might add. Believe me, the tongues are still wagging, and I'll admit, I was humiliated. But when the embarrassment faded, I found I still adored you. And I believe the same would have been true for you, had you not had so convenient an 'accident.' "

"Don't say it like that," she ordered. "You make it sound as though Zack hurt me on purpose."

"Fine. He's a prince," Adam drawled. "In any case, our wedding had begun, and there you were, so ravishing it took my breath away. And then I said something monumentally stupid, and offended you, and you ordered me to step aside."

"What?"

He grimaced self-consciously. "You had quite a temper before your little mishap, darling. You wanted to punish me—swiftly and with the most heinous weapon at your disposal—and so you called for the buffoon to step up and take my place. And of course, he did. He was obsessed with you, Noelle. You told him countless times to find someone else, but he persisted, in hopes of finding an opportunity to best me. And damned if I didn't give it to him."

She covered her eyes with her hands, fighting an overpowering urge to shriek. It was so bizarre, she almost had to believe it was true! And it fit with the other facts, however meager, that she had. The embarrassment, the virginity, the consent, the lies, and most strikingly, the guilt Zack felt over what had happened between them.

"Noelle? I know this is painful for you. Won't you let me help? I can take you far away from this place, and in a month, this will seem like a bad dream."

"It already does," she murmured. "I appreciate the

offer, sir. But I need to stay and face Zack with all this. And you need to leave," she added gently. "Whatever there was between us—"

"Whatever we had before, we can have again," he corrected solemnly. "That's what separates true love from other, baser emotions. You and I were meant to be together, darling. If you give me half a chance, I'll prove that to you all over again." Taking her hands into his own, he promised confidently, "I'll shower you with jewels and attention—"

Pulling free, Noelle shook her head. "That can never happen, Mr. Prestley. I may not know how I felt about Zack when I married him, but I can assure you, I'm completely and utterly in love with him now."

He cupped her chin in his hand. "I don't know how much you've been told about your upbringing, darling, but the truth is, your instincts are tainted when it comes to love and romance. I've always known that, but still I was willing to marry you. To teach you the difference between true love and Dane's sort of rutting pleasure—"

"Wait!" She jumped to her feet and eyed him with disgust. "Is this what we quarreled about at the wedding? Your insulting attitude toward my instincts and upbringing?" Before he could answer, she gestured harshly toward the door. "I'm sorry you came all this way just to learn another lesson—"

"Noelle!" He grabbed her by the arm and glared. "The only lesson I'm learning is that I never should have considered marrying you once, let alone twice. You deserve a life more suited to your tastes. Naughty romance and sinful self-indulgence, but always with that innocent patina you wear so beautifully."

"Let me go!" She wrenched at her arm, but his grip was like iron, and as he drew her hard against himself his free hand clapped over her mouth. Still, she tried to scream, and then, as he wrestled her to the sofa, she was gasping just for air. Desperate, she twisted and wriggled, then drove her knee upward, aiming for his crotch, but hitting him squarely in the stomach instead.

"Damn you, Noelle," he snarled. "I swear I'll teach *you* a lesson now. If love doesn't impress you, I'll try something more to your liking."

Terrified, she sank her teeth into his hand, and he pulled it away from her mouth with a yelp of pain. Yanking herself free of him, she tried to run for the door, but he caught her by the waist and wrestled her against the balcony doors, slathering her face and neck with kisses that reeked of whiskey and tobacco.

"Stop," she pleaded, her voice now choked with sobs. "If you don't—if you don't—"

"Your husband will kill me?" His laugh was ugly but confident. "I'll make you forget all about him, believe me. I've learned things in Europe that make girls like you drool. Or are you drooling already?" he suggested, pawing at her skirt with one hand while the other held her firmly in place.

"No!" She wrenched backward against the doors with all her might, and they sprung open, sending both her and Adam sprawling onto the balcony floor. A twisted grin lit his face, and she suddenly knew he intended to take her right there. Terrified, she sent her knee against him again, then rolled free of him and jumped to her feet.

"Damn you to hell!" He caught her by the skirt as she tried to run for the bedroom; then he, too, was standing, forcing her against the balcony rail as he stared down at her with absolute loathing. "There's only one thing I want from you now, you stupid little whore, and I'll have it if it's the last thing I do."

She shrieked at the top of her lungs, desperate not only for help, but for some way to blot out the sounds—of his voice as he continued to taunt her, of his ragged breath on her neck, of her own sobs, and of her pounding heart. Then she heard another sound—a splintering one—as they struggled against the overtaxed railing, and in her frenzy, she welcomed it. They would plunge to their deaths now, and it wouldn't matter. All that mattered was to silence him. To stop his hands from groping with such maniacal fascination . . .

And then a truer sound split the night—a single sharp discharge from a well-oiled Henry Repeating Rifle. The bullet passed so close to Noelle's ear she was sure she felt the vibration, but it was Adam's face that had been the sharpshooter's target, and it was only Adam who was hit. Wriggling free, Noelle shoved his body off of hers and against the rail, which broke completely under his weight. Then, as she watched in numb relief, the lifeless corpse plummeted to the street, landing within a whisper of a buckskin-clad hunter astride a magnificent chestnut horse.

Too shaky to manage a smile, she raised her hand in grateful greeting, then turned and stumbled back into the room. He would be there in less than a minute, she knew, and she was so desperate to see him—to thank him, to feel his arms around her, to pretend all was well—that she scarcely knew how she'd endure the wait. Then he burst through the door and crossed to her in three long, masterful strides.

Pulling her into a protective embrace, he crooned "It's all over now, sugar. I'm here now, and no one's ever gonna lay a hand on you again. I swear it."

"Did you get the polecat?"

"Huh?" He cradled her face in his hands and murmured, "Turns out, it was a mountain lion with the disposition of a polecat. And yeah, we got him."

"We? Oh . . ." She snuggled against him and savored thoughts of the powerful trio—Zack, Henry, and Merc. Her heroes.

"Come and lie down, sugar," Zack was urging. "You've had yourself a powerful scare."

"Which one?" she asked unhappily. "The one where he almost killed me, or the one where I found out I almost *married* him?"

"He told you about that?"

She nodded and buried her face against his chest. "He told me everything, Zack. I think he was honest with me."

"Honest? Him?" Zack snorted. "A fella like that wouldn't know the truth if it hit him square in the face. He was an abomination, Noelle. I knew all along he was twisted up inside, but I swear I never thought he'd come after you this way. I'll never leave you alone again; you have my word on that." He hesitated, then asked cautiously, "What did he tell you?"

"He said I only married you to punish him. He said I wasn't a mail-order bride at all." She waited for a moment, then turned her face up to his and flushed at the pain in his eyes. "We don't need to talk about it right now, Zack—"

"I reckon maybe we do," he countered gently. "The doc said he'd keep the sheriff busy till I had a chance to check on you, so we have some time."

A tremble of foreboding infiltrated her voice. "I can't believe I almost married him. You should have seen the way he looked at me."

"I know. I always hated that. So did your father. But you never seemed to notice it before." Clearing his throat, he explained, "He had it in his head that you were the perfect female. Innocent, because you were constantly pampered and chaperoned. But worldly, too, because of your father's business."

"And"—she raised her eyes to his—"what exactly *is* my father's business?"

"He's a matchmaker." When Noelle stared in confusion, he confirmed, "Russ Braddock is your father, Noelle, and he loves you more than any man ever loved a daughter. Whatever else you think, and however mad you get—"

"Mr. Braddock?" She shook her head as she slowly backed away from him. It didn't make any sense! Was he trying to protect her again, by telling such a reassuring yet impossible lie? "Tell me the truth, Zack. I promise I won't be angry or traumatized. There's no need to pamper me anymore."

"It's the truth, Noelle. He wanted to put as much distance between you and Prestley as possible, and now I see how right he was about that. But we shouldn't've lied—"

"Stop!" Her mind was reeling again. "He wanted to separate me from Adam Prestley? Because I loved him?"

"No, sugar. By the time your wedding day came, you knew you didn't love him, after all."

"But before that, I thought I did?"

Zack nodded. "We figured it was because you didn't trust your heart to do the picking, so you let an older man do it for you. Only not your own father, 'cause you're too danged stubborn for that."

She almost smiled, but there was one more question

and for reasons she couldn't quite grasp, she feared the answer to that one most of all. "Before the accident, did I ever tell you I loved *you?*"

"No, but deep inside—"

"Did I marry you just to humiliate Adam Prestley in front of our wedding guests?"

Zack was quiet for a moment. "There's only one person in the whole danged world who knows the answer to that one, Noelle. But I can tell you what I saw in your eyes when that judge said I could kiss my bride. There was a light there so pure and beautiful, it could only have come straight from your heart." He paused as though momentarily speechless at the memory, then continued. "After the wedding, when we were finally alone together, you said we could kiss and cuddle, but nothing more, till we were sure. You didn't want to make another mistake."

"That's why you wanted to wait six months?"

"I didn't *want* to wait even a minute. But I respect you, so I was willing."

"You were willing to wait six months," she repeated softly. "Can I ask you to give me just a few more minutes? I need some time alone, to think."

"Sure, sugar. I'll go talk to the sheriff."

"Zack?"

"Yeah?"

"Mr. Braddock is really my father?"

A rueful smile lit his face. "That's why he's on his way here right now, more anxious than a fella can be to hear you call him 'Father' again." Stepping closer, he added in a husky whisper, "There's one more thing you need to believe, Noelle."

"What's that?"

"I fell in love with you the minute I laid eyes on

you, and it's grown stronger each and every day. I figure it'll be that way till the day I die."

"Thank you," she murmured.

Zack winced at the gentle dismissal, then turned and disappeared into the hall without another word.

She wanted to call out to him—to beg him to come back—but knew that she needed to be alone with the torrent of confusing information the evening had yielded. There were simply too many questions, and not nearly enough rational answers to go around.

What had she seen in Adam Prestley? Was Zack correct that she hadn't trusted either herself or her father enough to choose a husband for her, and so instead she had entrusted that decision to a twisted stranger? Was it pure stubbornness that had driven her to act so foolishly, or was it something more? And if Zack hadn't come along, would she have married Adam Prestley, or would her father—or her own heart—have found some other way to stop her?

Her pulse raced as other, more intriguing puzzles sprang to mind. Had she loved Zack, just a little, right from the start? If not, how had she resisted him? Had she simply denied her true feelings, again from pure stubbornness? Amnesia or not, she knew it was within her character to do so. And if that was the truth—if she had loved Zack even then—then the wedding must have been so romantic! It must have been the sort of blissful perfection of which every young bride dreams. There in the beautiful Braddock home, surrounded by servants who had apparently adored her and pampered her for years. And the dolls! Was it possible all those precious little sweethearts were really hers?

Inspired, she ran to the dresser and pulled out the little rag doll Braddock—or more precisely, *her father–*

had sent along to act as confidante in his absence. With a hopeful smile, she said softly, "I have a feeling you and I have been through a lot together. Can you help me one more time?"

Almost instantly, she was flooded with memories, although not because her amnesia had cleared. These were memories from the last two months—enough happiness and love and hope to last a lifetime, all because of Zack. She could see his handsome face—his emerald eyes, shining with love for her—and she hugged the doll close, knowing that it didn't matter whether she'd known it from the start, or simply learned it in his arms as he'd escorted her into a new life filled with adventure and passion. Even if she couldn't really remember their wedding, she knew now that it had been the most romantic event of her life, if only because Zack had been there, loving her and wanting her as his bride.

"And my father was there, proud and happy to see me with such a wonderful husband. I know I should be angry with him for deceiving me this way, but he so clearly did it out of love, I suppose I'll just have to forgive him." She gave the doll another squeeze. "The wedding was so beautiful, especially my dress. If only I'd brought it with me." She locked eyes with the toy and squealed with inspired delight. "Of course! It's perfect! You're a brilliant little dollie, and I love you almost as much as I love him. Now sit right here on the dresser and watch while I do what I should have done the first moment I laid eyes on Lieutenant Zachary Dane."

Moving quickly, for fear he'd return before she was ready for him, Noelle stripped off her simple dress and replaced it with the shimmering sleeveless silk nightgown that had stayed packed away in patient anticipation of her wedding night. She could feel it hug her curves, and could imagine how Zack's hot hands would feel through the thin, cool fabric. The she donned the matching robe, a lustrous creation of white gauze and silver thread, edged and belted by shimmering bands of pure white silk.

Brushing her ebony curls until they gleamed, she fastened them high on her head with silver combs, then remembered the slippers that had been tucked into a corner of her trunk, and slipped them onto her feet. The effect, she was certain, was glorious, but she couldn't quite confirm it, since the dresser mirror allowed her to see herself only from the waist up. With a mischievous smile toward the doll, Noelle pulled the desk until it was right in front of the mirror, then brought the chair over as well, climbing up until she could clearly see herself from head to toe.

Delighted with the effect of the radiant garment, she turned toward the door and scolded her absent husband cheerfully, "I said a few minutes. It's been much longer than that! Are you going to keep me waiting for six months, after all?"

When the doorknob began to turn at that very moment, she panicked and began to gather up her skirts quickly, anxious to climb down before he stepped into view. But there was no time, and she didn't dare risk another fall, so she summoned what she hoped was an angelic smile, hoping he'd be too busy admiring her in her finery to scold her for taking chances with her safety by standing on so precarious a perch.

Then he stepped into view, a handsome, emerald-eyed hero clad in buckskin, with the warmest smile and truest heart a man could have, and Noelle's brain began to throb with confused admiration and longing. It was so romantic. So perfect. So eerily familiar!

She wanted to ask Zack if it seemed familiar to him, too, but her throat was too dry to speak. Then, before either of them could understand what was happening, the room began to spin and she toppled into his waiting arms.

Epilogue

"Noelle . . . Sugar . . . Talk to me. Can you hear my voice?"

She stirred, disoriented for just a moment, then realized she was in bed, with a handsome man hovering over her, his emerald eyes blazing with love. "Zack?"

"Dang." He exhaled sharply. "You had me worried there for a minute. What were you thinking, climbing up there like that? What if I hadn't been there to catch you when you fell?"

"You're always there when I need you," Noelle corrected with a sigh. Then she bit her lip and asked shyly, "Did it remind you of anything?"

"Yeah," he admitted. "It was like we were back in your pappy's dining room again, and I was seeing you for the first time. The prettiest angel in the world."

"It reminded me of that, too," she confessed. "The first time I saw a brash, dusty, green-eyed soldier, and knew that if I wasn't careful, I might just lose my heart to him."

"Yeah?" He smiled; then his eyes widened. "You *remember* that?"

She nodded, then wrapped her arms around his neck. "I remember everything. How hard I tried to resist you and how hard you tried to seduce me." She knew he eyes were shining as she added softly, "It's all been so gloriously romantic, Zack. Every moment of every day since we met. Promise me it will always be like this."

"I promise," he murmured; then he asked warily, "You aren't mad about me breaking all those rules with you?"

"The rules? Oh, dear." Noelle struggled for a second before dissolving against him in a musical burst of laughter. "Oh, Zack, it's so hilarious! I made up all those rules just to torture you. And the irony is, they ended up torturing *me,* instead! All those weeks when you wouldn't make love to me, or touch me, or let me touch you, and all that time—"

"You made 'em up?" He scowled in disbelief. "You don't believe *any* of 'em?"

"Of course not," she assured him. "I was just 'having fun with you,' as you would say."

"Dang." Zack's eyes narrowed ominously. "I should've known better than to try to oblige city folk. I should've just followed my instincts from the minute I first saw you up on that big ole table."

"Oh? What exactly should you have done?"

"Pulled you right down and made you mine on the spot."

"In front of Winnie and Edward?" Noelle taunted. "In front of my own father?"

"I reckon they would've seen the wisdom in it and just given us our privacy."

She smiled mischievously. "You've had two opportunities, Lieutenant, and each time, you've just stood there and gawked. But because I adore you, I'm going to give you one last chance." Wriggling away from him, she sprang across the room, then used the chair to hop back into position on the desk, where she fluffed the skirt of her beautiful gown, curtsied, and gave him an encouraging smile. "Are you going to keep me waiting forever, Lieutenant Dane?"

"Dang." He stared up at her for a moment, as though truly mesmerized again. Then, with a wicked grin, he strode right up to her, pulled her down into his arms, and proved to her in his own special way that their love had always been meant to be.

If you liked MEANT TO BE, be sure to look for Kate Donovan's next release in the "Happily Ever After Co." series coming from Zebra in May 2002.

Because of an unhappy childhood, Maggie Gleason is determined never to marry. Still, she loves children, so she contacts Russel Braddock with a novel request: Could he use his contacts to find her a position as a schoolteacher?

The matchmaker places Maggie in an idyllic little town, where her plans for celibate self-denial are threatened when she meets fellow boarder Alex Coburn—an arrogant bounty hunter with piercing blue eyes.

Alex is involved in a deadly game of cat and mouse with a bloodthirsty murderer and can't afford to be distracted by the pretty new schoolteacher. Still, sparks fly between them night after night, and despite their desperate attempts to resist one another, a torrid and dangerous affair—one that threatens to either destroy or save them both—erupts.

ABOUT THE AUTHOR

Kate Donovan was born in Ohio and grew up there and in Rhode Island, then moved to Northern California to attend college at Berkeley and law school at King Hall on the UC Davis campus. Today she divides her time equally among her many loves—a great husband, charming son, and delightful daughter; her love stories; and a career as an attorney in Sacramento, California. This is her eighth book. You can email Kate at Katedonovan@hotmail.com.

COMING IN JULY FROM
ZEBRA BALLAD ROMANCES

Experience the Romances of
Rosanne Bittner

The Queen of
Romance
Cassie Edwards